D0211279

Salt and Sugar

REBECCA CARVALHO

ISBN-13: 978-1-335-45433-1

Recycling programs
for this product may
not exist in your area.

Salt and Sugar

Copyright © 2022 by Rebecca Carvalho

All rights reserved. No part of this book may be used or reproduced in any manner
whatsoever without written permission except in the case of brief quotations
embodied in critical articles and reviews.

This is a work of fiction. Names, characters, places and incidents are either the
product of the author's imagination or are used fictitiously. Any resemblance to
actual persons, living or dead, businesses, companies, events or locales is entirely
coincidental.

For questions and comments about the quality of this book, please contact us
at CustomerService@Harlequin.com.

Inkyard Press
22 Adelaide St. West, 41st Floor
Toronto, Ontario M5H 4E3, Canada
www.InkyardPress.com

Printed in U.S.A.

For anyone wondering if they should follow a dream.

For my mom, who first encouraged me to pursue mine.

And for Michael, who never let me give it up.

1

FRIDAY, APRIL 22

Trust neither thin-bottomed frying pans nor Molinas, Grandma Julieta Ramires always said.

I watch the growing darkness stretch over my family's bakery. Our sign, Salt, written in Great-grandma Elisa's own handwriting, disappears in the twilight, this strange limbo hour before streetlights illuminate the Olinda hills.

I can't make myself go inside. Not yet. The bakery is quiet, as if lulled by the heavy breeze blowing from the ocean. And so I wait another minute. And another. I wait for the moment Salt will suddenly—I don't know—yawn.

"Wake up," I urge it under my breath.

But Salt doesn't startle awake just because I'm staring. And while Salt fades, the Molinas' bakery glows in comparison. They call it Sugar, but don't be fooled by the name. It's the sort of toxic sweetness you find in certain poisons.

While all the other neighbors have closed their shops in mourning, the Molinas kept Sugar's doors wide open like an insult. The happy twinkle of the lights on their facade makes my stomach churn.

It's not like I was expecting Seu Romário Molina, who was Grandma's lifelong enemy, to send a flower wreath to the cemetery, but how *dare* they be this showy tonight? I feel like marching across the street to scream at them, but the headlights of Salt's fusquinha shining down the street stop me. Mom's getting home, and she must be worried about me. I took off from the cemetery without letting her know.

Mom gets out of the sunshine-yellow car, the same color as Salt's facade, but instead of taking the side door that leads up to our apartment, she hurries straight for the bakery's entrance without noticing me.

When Grandma was hospitalized one month ago, Mom had to close doors, so it's like Salt's been waiting for Grandma to come back home. But how can we reopen without her? There's no Salt without Grandma.

Mom hesitates to unlock the door.

The wind picks up, ruffling her hair and bringing down a slanted drizzle. The fluttering flags my neighbors have already fastened to celebrate St. John's Day in two months, multicolored like a rainbow, snap from strings above our heads.

I didn't realize I took a tentative step forward until Mom looks at me. And I see the hurt in her eyes.

I open my mouth to speak, but I don't know what to say.

Without a word, Mom turns the key and steps into Salt, immediately finding her apron just by reaching into the semidarkness hiding the wall pegs. Muscle memory. Only then Mom switches the lights on. And the bakery reveals itself.

I take my first step into Salt, too. My first time in the bakery without Grandma.

And seeing all the things that have already changed without Grandma's care *hurts*. Everything seems so dull. The wooden surfaces lack a coating of the lustrous peroba oil Grandma loved to use, which gave the bakery a subtle woodsy smell. The silence, absent of Grandma's chatter with neighbors, is heavy. Even all the ingredients to Grandma's magic are gone, the glass jars that should have been filled with various flours—tapioca, wheat, corn, rice—sitting empty. Same as the display below the main counter.

My heart does a painful somersault, but I hold back tears. I don't want Mom to see.

She goes to stand in front of Great-grandma Elisa's fubá cake recipe like she's answering a summons. We keep the sheet of paper with the ingredients and instructions folded and protected behind a glass box on the wall like it's Salt's own beating heart.

My legs feel heavier than normal, but I go stand next to Mom.

I don't know what to say or do to comfort her.

She closes her eyes. Is she praying? So I close mine, too, and in my mind's eye, I try to revive Salt.

I picture the customers pressing their faces to the display window outside to look at quibes, pastéis, and codfish bolinhos. I listen for our old stereo alternating between static crackling and forró songs swelling with melancholy accordions. I search for the tangy scent of ground beef simmering in a clay pot ready to turn into coxinha filling. And all I find is…nothing. Just this sense of unfamiliarity within my own home that is dizzying, painful, and so, so lonely.

"We're reopening tonight," Mom announces. "Your grandmother worked every day, until she couldn't anymore."

She's still facing the recipe.

"I think you should rest," I say.

I've dreamed and dreamed of the day we'd reopen. But Mom hasn't slept in ages, and the dark circles under her eyes have deepened this past month.

"I looked for you everywhere," she says, finally addressing my disappearing act earlier. "At the ceremony."

Her voice is a little hoarse and it holds so much disappointment, guilt shoots through my chest like a knife.

I should apologize, and I *want* to apologize, but how do I tell her that it hurt more than anything to see Grandma in that coffin? That I hardly recognized the person I loved—*love*—the most? My brain kept telling me, yes, it's her. She's nestled in a bed of sunflowers, so that's her. These are her favorite flowers, so that's her. But my heart kept shouting, *That's not Grandma. That can't be Grandma.* And before I knew it, I'd already left. I just turned around. I crossed the cemetery gates and kept going, hopping on the first bus home.

How do I tell her that?

I can't.

So there's just…silence between us.

Mom doesn't ask again. She turns and heads into the kitchen, leaving me alone in the bakery.

I want to run upstairs and lock myself in my bedroom. I should change into black clothes. I went to the cemetery straight from school and there wasn't time to change out of my uniform. The red-and-white-striped shirt and sweatpants feel wrong. Too happy.

But, if I'm honest, if I go, I'm not coming back downstairs. I've done enough running away for today.

Instead, I pick up the stools off the counter and put them down on the floor to distract myself. When I'm done preparing Salt for customers, Mom's cooking in full force.

The first smells of caramelized onions fried with garlic and ground cumin travel to me. They'd have been heavenly any other day. But, tonight, they only bring more heartache.

The bells above Salt's door jingle, startling me. I turn to see neighbors poking their heads in. Just for a moment, I can imagine that the smell of Grandma's cooking is what brought them inside. Any minute now, Grandma will come out of the kitchen and greet them, and this whole day—the whole year—would have been just a freaking nightmare.

But the neighbors wear sorrowful faces and offer condolences. As hard as I try, I never know what to say back. I feel pulled in all directions, my nerves stretched thin, until Mom steps out of the kitchen and rescues me.

"Go sit down. Dinner will be ready soon," she whispers to me. She's tied her hair into a tight bun—her "ready for work" style.

Mom shakes hands, offers hugs, and says encouraging words. It's painful to see the way people are mesmerized by her, like they're searching for Grandma's eyes when they look at hers, checking to see if they are the same shade of brown.

Grandma's closest friends are beginning to arrive, too. Dona Clara. Seu Floriano. They burst into tears at the sight of Salt's open doors, and Mom promptly comforts them.

I worry this is too much for her. But I'm paralyzed. I don't know how to be there for anyone when I feel adrift myself.

The gathering at Salt becomes a wake, with people sharing stories and happy memories, like when Grandma climbed up a tree to dislodge a kite and got stuck up there herself. Some just listen solemnly, taking slow sips of café com leite, because, sometimes, when it's too hard to talk, it's easier to just eat and drink.

After a while, plates of buttered couscous covered in beef jerky, caramelized onions, and fried chunks of squeaky coalho cheese get passed around. Mom brings me a plate, too.

"Eat," she tells me, before slipping back into the kitchen. But despite the deliciously savory smell, my throat is tied in too many knots to eat.

The bells above our door chime again. I look over my shoulder to see Dona Selma making her way inside. Grandma's best friend, who is like a grandmother to me and a second mother to Mom. Seeing her now in these black clothes instead of her usual bright, festive colors makes everything seem more…real.

When Dona Selma spots me, I must look as lost as I feel, because she comes straight over, pushing past people trying to speak with her. She pulls me into a tight hug. *I'll never hug Grandma again*. The pain is like a shock through my ribs.

"Lari, I need you to remember one thing," she says in my ear. "You are loved. And you aren't alone. You aren't alone. Do you know this?"

Her dark brown eyes scan my face. I try to smile to show her she doesn't need to worry, even though I know Dona Selma doesn't expect me to act brave. But then she tears up, and it makes it harder to keep my own from bubbling up.

She gives me another hug. When she steps back, she looks around the room with concerned eyes like she's searching for someone.

"I think Mom is in the kitchen," I say, assuming Dona Selma is looking for her.

"I need you and Alice to take better care of yourselves." Even the way she says Mom's name reminds me of Grandma. The same accent. Ah-lee-see. "Why is Salt open tonight?"

"Mom wanted to."

Dona Selma finally spots Mom in the crowd.

"I'll go check in on her," she says, giving my shoulder a comforting squeeze before leaving.

Isabel, who's Dona Clara's assistant at the market, approaches me.

"I think there's something burning," she says.

Isabel has a habit of letting the cooking oil to deep-fry pastéis burn, so she's become a bit of a walking smoke detector.

I wrinkle my nose at the faint burnt smell in the air.

Across the room, Mom is still talking with Dona Selma. I should go tell her about the food burning, but I don't want to interrupt that conversation. I know Mom needs Dona Selma's words as much as I needed that hug a moment ago.

"Was your mom frying eggs?" Isabel asks, antsy. "You better hurry up."

"Me?"

I get a jolt of fear. Mom never lets me cook.

"Yes, *you*. You don't want the kitchen to burn down, do you?"

I've already disappointed Mom at the funeral today, and I can't just sit around when there's food burning. But the moment I cross the threshold into the kitchen, my heart beats even faster.

Walking into Salt was hard. But walking into Salt's *kitchen* knowing I won't find Grandma behind the counter is even more painful. The red brick walls feel like they're closing in.

There's a frying pan on the stove, the contents—scrambled eggs with tomatoes and cilantro?—already sticking to the pan with an angry hiss. Smoke swirls up, leaving the area near the stove hazy.

I try to open the foggy glass window in the back, but it's stuck. I turn around frantically looking for a spoon to salvage Mom's cooking, but there are so many types. Wooden, metal, plastic spoons of all sizes. Which one am I supposed to use? I can feel my pulse in my ears.

I grab the nearest one. A metal spoon. And I start scraping at the bottom of the pan as best I can, but I'm not sure I'm doing this right.

The warmth of the stove seeps through my clothes. The smells are all around me like a net—oregano, black pepper, and cheese coming from another frying pan, and the savory smell of sweet potatoes boiling in a pot behind.

This is nerve-racking.

Deliciously nerve-racking.

Usually, my anxiety is fully aware of every way I could mess up Mom's cooking. But this time, I'm filled with excited butterflies.

The sizzling grows louder. Like a volcanic eruption. The other frying pan is beginning to smoke, too. The hot bubbles in the boiling pot filled with potatoes burst too close to my hand. Dangerous, I know. And yet I let my eyes fall closed, my ears picking up on the full symphony of cooking sounds all around me.

The metal spoon is getting hotter in my hand. Heat travels into my bloodstream. Fast. It feels electrified, like it's forming a connection, and suddenly—

I'm not so alone anymore.

There's a warm feeling in the pit of my stomach, and I understand that the women in my life, past and present, are here with me.

Grandma isn't truly gone. Not while Salt stands.

There's a sudden pop, and my eyes shoot open.

Sizzling oil splashes at my wrist and stinging pain replaces my musing. I jump back in surprise and accidentally hit the pan's handle. It all seems to happen in slow motion. I watch as the frying pan with the eggs goes flying off the stove, food splattering everywhere.

Mom's screech pierces the air.

2

You'd think a girl like me would have had the best cooking training, right? But, like we say around here, casa de ferreiro, espeto de pau. *The shoemaker's children always go barefoot.* Or, in my case, the baker's child can't bake…or cook…at all.

When I was a toddler, I used to wander into the kitchen to explore on my own. I was drawn to this magical world where Grandma seemed the happiest. While everyone slept, I would climb up a chair and perch on the counter, my legs tucked underneath me. An hour later, Grandma would wake up to find bed-haired, entranced baby-me busily scooping sugar or manioc farinha out of the bowl and pouring it on a spot by my side. Despite the mess, she'd never get mad.

Grandma would pick me up every time and whisper:

"You and I have a secret, minha pequena."

In second grade, I got into gathering flowers and leaves so I could crush them with the mortar and pestle I'd taken from the kitchen. I'd add water and pretend I was making the most lavish soup, trying my best to emulate Grandma's cooking. It was the best game I'd ever invented, until a bunch of kids saw me.

"What's that nasty thing?" they asked me.

"It's soup," I said. "And it's not nasty."

Pedro Molina, Seu Romário's grandson, looked at my flower mixture like he was the biggest authority in soups. Even though he was my age, he was already helping in his family's kitchen. He pushed a hand through his curly bangs, clearly flaunting the bandage wrapped around his finger.

"What happened to you?" one of his friends asked.

"I was cutting slices of guava paste with my grandfather to make bolo de rolo," he said with a pleased grin. "It didn't even hurt."

All the neighborhood kids looked at Pedro in awe.

But I had seen Pedro after the injury and knew the truth. "I heard you crying earlier," I contradicted accusingly.

The other kids began whispering behind him, and Pedro seethed.

All knobby knees and elbows, he took one step toward me, wrinkled his nose at my cooking, and said, "If this is soup, then let me see you drink it."

I held the mixture up to my mouth. The sweet smell of decaying leaves and chlorophyll turned my stomach. The color was a dangerous reddish brown. I *had* to drink it. Pedro had challenged me in front of everyone.

I was ready to take the first gulp—

But I chickened out.

"Is this the kind of disgusting food that your family serves at Salt?" he mocked me.

Everywhere I went, his friends made sure I heard variations of the same accusation. I even caught them warning each other not to come to Salt, because of how terrible my soup looked. Things were getting out of control and I had to do something to defend Salt's reputation.

My list of failed cooking attempts only stacked up, though:

I brought Mom's leftover soup to school, but accidentally dumped too much salt in it. That's why people call me Salty to this day.

I brought lollipops I'd secretly made with a recipe I found online, but they were so hard they chipped my classmate's tooth.

I then tried boiling water on the stove at Salt to make *real* soup, but I accidentally burned Grandma's hand when she found me. She let out a cry of pain that scared me so much I wanted her to go see a doctor, but she said it was nothing.

Mom learned then that I'd been sneaking into Salt's kitchen. That it had been my fault Grandma was hurt. She grounded me and made me promise I'd never again cook behind her back. And she didn't have to ask. I finally realized cooking wasn't for me, that every time I stepped into the kitchen, something really wrong happened.

Like I was cursed.

When people are born with a gift for cooking, that special ability to turn meals into magical experiences, we say they were born with fairy hands. The women in my family all have it. But, when my turn came, I guess the fairy was on vacation at Fernando de Noronha Island, because I got the exact opposite.

I got an impish thumb for disaster.

3

FRIDAY, APRIL 22

Mom cradles my wrist under cold water, but my skin is still turning an angry shade of red where hot oil splashed on me.

"It doesn't hurt that bad," I lie, but Mom still looks shaken.

"What business did you have poking at a frying pan with a metal spoon?" she shouts, reaching to fish a wooden spoon out of a drawer. "That's what you should have used!"

Our neighbors crane their necks from behind the counter, and I feel like I'm in second grade again, causing trouble in Salt's kitchen. My face gets hot with embarrassment.

"I'm sorry," I say in a low voice.

Mom looks like I just committed a crime. I might as well have. I am the daughter, granddaughter, and great-granddaughter of famous bakers, and yet I can't even figure out how to fry an egg without setting it off like a grenade all over the kitchen floor. *What a disaster.*

She lets out a heavy sigh. "Go upstairs."

"Let me at least help you clean," I say, reaching for a mop.

"You've done enough already." She takes the mop from me. "Go."

I drag my feet toward the stairs, avoiding eye contact with anyone who witnessed Mom scolding me. I'm halfway to my room when I hear honking outside. I turn around, crouching down on the step to see who's pulling up in front of Salt.

Mom goes to peer into the street from behind our empty window display. Dona Selma joins her and I catch the look they exchange.

Mom's thin lips have gone pale, her eyes wide and shining like there's a storm brewing behind them. She looks almost unrecognizable.

I race down the stairs two steps at a time.

"What's wrong?" I ask.

Dona Selma puts a hand on Mom's shoulder, but that doesn't stop her from darting outside. And that's when I see a big white van clumsily maneuvering down our narrow street to try to park in front of Salt.

"You should go to your room, love. Don't worry," Dona Selma says to me before heading out after Mom.

Don't worry? Well, now *I am worried.*

There's no way I'm leaving Mom to deal with this alone. I step outside.

An accordion-heavy song, the type that's popular this time of the year, blasts from the van. The driver, a guy probably in his early twenties, is distracted, drumming his fingers on the steering wheel, mumbling along to the lyrics.

Mom knocks on his window, which he quickly rolls down to speak with her.

"Too much traffic getting here, senhora," he says. "I've come to pick up the catering order for the wedding."

I would have known if we'd rented a catering van. And it's not like we have a gig lined up with everything going on.

Mom's about to say something, but then Sugar's door opens from directly across the street, and Dona Eulalia Molina—Seu Romário's only daughter and Pedro's mom—rushes out.

Dona Eulalia waves her arms at the driver, a white apron fastened around her waist.

"I hope this isn't another of their pranks," Mom says to the driver like a warning. She's in no mood to be messed with tonight.

And I begin to understand the situation. The reason why Mom is so on edge.

She thinks the Molinas are up to something.

That family loves coming up with ridiculous ways to attack us. Some are mild and uncreative, like sending fake customers to come berate our dishes in front of real paying customers. Other times it can get *bad*.

Is it possible they sent this van here, today of all days, as a way to show off?! No wonder Mom is having a hard time containing her anger. Now *my* blood is boiling, too.

The driver just stares at Mom, waiting for instructions, totally oblivious to the fact that Dona Eulalia is trying to get his attention from her side of the street.

"You got the wrong bakery," Mom says, sharply.

The driver glances from our sign to Sugar's. He finally notices Dona Eulalia.

"Too many bakeries on this street," he says as an apology and Mom raises an eyebrow at him.

The Molinas' entourage of bakers streams through Sugar's doors with trays brimming with lavender-colored surpresas de uva, brigadeiros, and bem-casados under protective plastic films, which they load into the back of the van.

And then they bring out a full tray of empadinhas! Even from my spot across the street, I see the dough flaky and golden like Grandma's recipe.

The thing is, everyone knows that only Salt makes empadinhas on our street. That's the deal our families made generations ago, when our great-grandmothers drew the battle lines:

Ramires only prepare savory foods.

Molinas only prepare sweets.

Sugar crossed the line baking empadinhas, and they know it. Those shameless, dishonest, garbage snakes!

"They're doing this on purpose," Mom says, gritting her teeth.

"Alice, ignore them," Dona Selma urges. "Come back inside."

But Mom's frozen to the spot, watching the catering procession across the street.

Dona Clara and Seu Floriano step out of Salt to join us, both looking indignant.

"Tell me this isn't for the wedding Julieta got fired from!" Dona Clara brandishes her cane at the van.

Salt had been booked to cater a small wedding reception, but the Molinas spread rumors in the neighborhood that we had a rat infestation in our kitchen. The rumors got to the client, who then fired us. It broke Grandma's heart, and shortly after that, she went to the hospital.

Sugar *is* showing off. Excitement is plastered on their faces like they just saw the Brazilian soccer team score seven to one against Germany. Only they're the ones who scored. This catering gig was supposed to be ours! They stole it from us!

"They're a villainous lot capable of anything," Mom says, rushing past us like an arrow back into Salt, Grandma's friends on her heels.

I *hate* the Molinas.

I can't hold back my tears anymore. They roll down my cheeks hot with anger. Instead of returning to Salt, I march across the street toward the group of junior bakers bringing out the catering trays.

How dare you sabotage my family? I'll say to them. *How dare you spread lies and steal our client? How dare you rub your treacherous victory in now, knowing we're in mourning? How dare you laugh tonight?*

"How dare——!"

I don't get any other words out because just then my foot strikes something unmoving and one second, I'm vertical. And then——

I'm not.

"Watch out!" Dona Eulalia shouts, and I realize soon enough that it's not for my sake.

I spread my arms to catch myself just as someone carrying a giant three-tier wedding cake steps out of Sugar. The cake is so tall I can't even see the person carrying it, just a mountain of white glaze. My hands sink into it, reaching the golden brown inside. I topple forward, taking the cake and the person carrying it down with me in one big, sugary crash.

4

FRIDAY, APRIL 22

There must have been a bride and groom topper on the wedding cake, because I spot the decapitated groom's head rolling to the curb. Grandma would have pointed out this could be a bad omen for the marriage.

Well, I guess it's a sign alright. A sign that I'm in serious trouble.

My face is covered in icing, and my hair sticks to my cheeks with sugar. There's screaming all around me. And one of the strangled cries is coming from underneath me. I look down through the smeared lenses of my glasses to find a pair of eyes staring right back.

Wait… I know these eyes. Big, round, light brown. *Molina* eyes.

I can't believe I just crashed into the bully of my childhood. My rival at school and in the neighborhood. The seventeen-year-old baker prodigy who is Seu Romário's grandson. *Pedro Molina.*

The smell of sugar in the air is so heavy that the speech I

had ready for his family dies on the tip of my tongue. I didn't even know he was in town. No one has seen him in about two weeks, gone who knows where.

He looks like he can't believe what happened, and just as our eyes lock, his expression hardens with ice.

"Get off me." His voice is equally cold.

I scramble to push myself away from him, but there's too much icing on the sidewalk. My feet slip and I come crashing down again against Pedro's chest, our faces so close that I smell the dizzying, sweet scent of frosting in his hair. His eyes widen.

Hands grab me by the armpits to hoist me up, and Mom's high-pitched shouting echoes in the background. "Don't touch my daughter! DON'T. TOUCH. HER!"

"Your girl ruined the cake!" Dona Eulalia barks at Mom.

"It was an accident," I try to explain, but no one's listening to me.

Mom comes running from Salt like a hurricane ready to destroy anyone—*anything*—near me. When she pulls me away from the chaos, there's a raw fire in her eyes like I've never seen before. I'm stunned. She's never looked more like Grandma than she does now.

"Are you hurt?" Her fretful eyes look me up and down.

"I'm—I'm fine," I stammer. Covered in cake, I'm sure I don't look convincing.

Mom starts steering me across the street, and I realize that the customers who were at Salt and Sugar have already stepped out to watch the scene unfold.

"Your daughter destroyed the cake on purpose!" Dona Eulalia shouts after Mom. We turn as she strides toward us.

"Aren't you going to do something about this?" She unfastens her apron and throws it dramatically at Mom's feet, but it lands on the rain-washed cobblestones.

Dogs begin barking from inside houses up and down the street.

"I swear I didn't do this on purpose," I try again, looking from Mom to Dona Eulalia. "I didn't even see the cake until the last second."

"It was a three-tiered cake!" Dona Eulalia snarls, raindrops glistening like dew on her hair.

"If my daughter says it was an accident, it was an accident. Ponto final," Mom says.

In the background, I see some bakers dig up Pedro from underneath the pile of cake. He has his back to me when he gets on his feet, and the moment he steadies himself on the slippery sidewalk, he marches straight into Sugar.

Mom tries to take me home again, but Dona Eulalia doesn't look like she'll let us walk away from her so easily. This woman is always in the mood for arguing in the middle of the street. It's like she sees the whole neighborhood as her stage.

"Back off!" Mom snaps. "I swear if you come near my daughter—"

"What a low blow, Alice!" she accuses Mom. "You're ruining someone's wedding! What am I going to tell the bride?" Her angry eyes find me like a homing missile. "You came straight for the cake!"

A chorus of "yes, she did!" echoes from the other Sugar bakers.

"Lari Ramires would never!" Grandma's friends shout back.

Mom's face turns a deep shade of red. "Your family started

that awful rumor that Salt had rats, just so you could steal the client from us!"

Dona Selma approaches us, her expression strained with worry.

"This isn't the time for this. Please, Alice, come back into Salt."

But Mom and Dona Eulalia start yelling at each other again. Decades of anger ricochet back and forth between the bakeries, the buildings stuck in a staring contest, backed up by two crowds of neighbors. One for Salt. One for Sugar.

"What is going on here?" a voice says, and the neighborhood—heck, the entire *city*—quiets.

Mom grabs my hand, her fingers cold against mine.

Seu Romário walks up the street toward us. He looks from the destroyed cake on the sidewalk to the icing covering me from head to toe.

"It's just a little bit of cake that fell from the tray. Everything is under control," Dona Eulalia lies, but Seu Romário isn't even looking at her.

He's in his late seventies, and his health is no longer what it was, but his presence is still commanding.

"Do we have any birthday cakes left?" he asks a junior baker, while the others lower their heads like most of my classmates do when they're afraid of getting picked to answer a question at the whiteboard.

The junior baker visibly trembles.

"No, Chef," she says.

"What do we have left from this morning?"

"We have a Souza Leão cake, a marble cake, and a passion fruit cake. They're all small, unfortunately."

Seu Romário frowns. "Any frosting left?"

"Some ganache, Chef."

"Use it as frosting on the marble cake. Add a few strawberries on top. Then take all the small cakes we have left to tonight's wedding. Grab an assortment of guava and doce de leite bolos de rolo, too, that we were going to put on display tomorrow. It's not the same as a wedding cake, but it can't be helped. Apologize to the bride. If she's unsatisfied with the cake assortment, tell her we'll give her a refund."

At the sound of the word *refund*, Dona Eulalia jumps in.

"But, Father, a *refund*?! I didn't want to upset you, but you need to know the truth. *They* should be covering the damage! They destroyed the cake on purpose!" She points a finger at Mom.

The junior bakers look from Dona Eulalia to Seu Romário.

"You didn't hear me well enough?" he snaps at his staff, his voice like thunder. "Do what I said. Get the cakes and the rest of the trays loaded into the van. *Now*."

"Yes, Chef."

"I'm sorry, Chef."

"Right away, Chef."

They all scurry back inside Sugar, nearly tripping over each other.

At Salt, it's always just been Mom and Grandma in the kitchen, while the Molinas have a big rotating batch of junior bakers, like they're building an army of their own. And a traitor's money is the reason why their business has always been a little bigger than ours.

It's a story I've known since I was little.

Great-grandma Elisa Ramires was a promising cook at an

inn. The job was her only opportunity to raise Grandma on her own, so she made herself famous with a buttery, delicately savory fubá cake recipe. Dona Elizabete Molina had been at the inn longer than Great-grandma, and she was also famous for her own recipe. Milk pudding. It was said to be so smooth it slid on your tongue.

The two were often at odds. They each wanted to prove to the neighborhood who was the best cook in town, and the opportunity came about with a cooking contest.

The night before the contest, Great-grandma and Dona Elizabete were busy preparing their entry dishes and tending to the many guests at the inn. It was a busy night, with many tourists in town for Carnival.

Nerves frazzled, shoulder to shoulder, and vying for space in the small kitchen, the story goes that the cooks accidentally tripped each other and sent their cake and pudding flying off the trays.

Miraculously, the layers stacked up. Dona Elizabete's milk pudding landed atop Great-grandma's fubá cake. Maybe Dona Elizabete held the tray at the right angle until the last second and the pudding had enough surface tension to just slide off the right way without breaking. Maybe Great-grandma's cake was firm enough to hold the delicate layer of pudding atop. Whatever the case, they tried this new, accidental two-layered cake and realized that their recipes complemented each other beautifully. When they passed samples around to the guests, their reaction was proof that they'd produced perfection.

No one remembers if they still entered the contest. Because from that moment on, the only thing everyone could talk about was their new recipe, the one they called "Salt and Sugar." One layer fubá cake, one layer milk pudding.

Great-grandma Elisa and Dona Elizabete planned on opening a bakery together, which they would name after their new, legendary recipe. But then Dona Elizabete betrayed Great-grandma by selling the recipe to a cake factory, and Sugar was born. A bakery that Dona Elizabete opened right across the street from the inn with the money the factory paid her.

A *lot* of money. The price for her betrayal.

The inn passed down to my great-grandmother when the innkeeper died, and she turned it into a bakery she called Salt. My home.

And here Mom and I are now, a few generations down the line, but still feuding with the Molinas.

You see, in my neighborhood, where people rarely move out of their family homes, time stands still and old wounds don't close. Perhaps it's best they don't—these wounds are a reminder of who I can and cannot trust.

Mom tries to pull me back to Salt and I'm shaking as I take the first step, my legs still frozen.

"Alice," Seu Romário calls out behind us. "If you have a minute, I'd like to speak with you."

I glance at Mom, waiting to hear her say no. She can't walk into Sugar. The Molinas will throw her into a pot and serve her for dinner.

But, despite the anger in her eyes, she looks at Seu Romário and nods in agreement.

"Mom?"

Dona Eulalia looks just as surprised as I feel. "Father, no.

This isn't a good idea. These people, they've already caused a huge scene. I don't want them to upset you."

He ignores her, still looking straight at Mom. "Alice, please, this way."

I pull on Mom's arm to stop her.

"Let's hear what he has to say," she says, like a challenge.

In her grief, I'm afraid Mom wants an opportunity to blow everything up between our families, once and for all.

5

I've lived my whole life across the street from the Molinas, but this is the first time I set foot in Sugar.

The theme inside is very gaudy. Twinkling lights shaped like icicles hanging from the ceiling. Red walls, just like the facade, the shade of Santa Claus's clothes. Glass shelves and counters polished until they sparkle, not one sign of fingerprints or kids' fogged breaths.

There's a translucent wall in the back with display slots. Most are empty by now, but an assortment of bolos de rolo, Seu Romário's famous cakes, takes the main spot at the center. The special lighting shows off the traditionally super thin spiral layers—*twenty* layers in this roll cake, he claims—filled with guava and sprinkled with sugar granules that glisten like a dusting of crystals.

The shelves to the right and left are packed with jujubas, bright candies, condensed milk puddings, cookies, broas, and sweet buns, filling the air with a strong, sweet perfume, the type you can actually taste. It's like being inside a candy factory.

Some of the Salt and Sugar customers that watched the cake disaster outside rush in after us at the pretense of getting the pastéis de nata samples a junior baker is offering at the counter. When the baker sees us walking into Sugar, she freezes, a hand still stretched out with the tray.

My stomach is in knots.

When the crowd parts a little, I spot Dona Elizabete Molina's famous milk pudding recipe locked in a glass box on the wall. My jaw drops. I guess I wasn't expecting hers to look so much like my great-grandmother's recipe back at Salt.

If our families' feud were an object, Dona Elizabete's recipe would be the other half of it. Not a polar opposite. But a soul mate.

"Please, follow me," Seu Romário says, guiding us around the counter, and I get a jolt of adrenaline. Because there's nothing more sacred than the world behind the main counter of a bakery. It's the place where science turns into magic. What would Grandma say if she saw us now?

Dona Eulalia rushes past us to Seu Romário's side.

"Father, wait. I don't want you talking alone with them," she says in a low voice. "We should be a part of this conversation, too."

Seu Romário frowns. *"We?"*

"Pedro and I," she explains, and he looks surprised when she mentions Pedro. She adds quickly, "Yes, he's home. He arrived this afternoon."

"Pedro!" Seu Romário calls. His voice sends a tremor down the whole bakery's foundation.

"Father, watch your blood pressure," Dona Eulalia begs.

Pedro steps out of Sugar's kitchen, wiping cake off his face with a dish rag.

"Grandpa," he says in greeting, lowering his eyes in submissive respect.

I spot his blue backpack, the one he brings to school, on the kitchen floor behind him, fat with his laundry, the zipper burst open at the seams. It's like he tried taking his whole wardrobe with him, wherever he went.

Seu Romário gives him a long look, and Pedro's eyes remain trained on his cake-smeared shoes.

"So you're back," the man says, and maybe it's my imagination, but there's a hint of "I told you so" in his tone.

"Yes, yes," Dona Eulalia butts in. "And he's not going anywhere, right, Peu?"

Peu? I stifle a laugh at his nickname.

Pedro glares at me.

He opens his mouth to say something to his grandfather, but the man turns around without giving him a chance, and I catch the hurt look Pedro launches at his back.

"Go be with your grandfather," his mother mouths to him, and after some hesitation, Pedro gives in.

Something must have happened between them. I wonder if it's the reason why Pedro left suddenly.

Dona Eulalia enters Seu Romário's office right behind Pedro, not even looking back to see if we'll follow.

The room is narrow like Grandma's office in Salt, not much bigger than a broom closet. It smells like cologne. Strong. Suffocating. Filing cabinets stand against each side of the desk.

And wherever there's wall space hang framed awards for excellence in pastry baking from when Seu Romário was younger.

Seu Romário sits at his desk. His bloodshot eyes droop like he hasn't been sleeping well lately. Dona Eulalia stands to his right, and Pedro flanks his grandfather on the left. There's only one empty chair in front of the desk, so I motion to Mom to sit.

And an awkward silence falls upon us.

Seu Romário shifts in his chair as if trying to find a more comfortable position. And then he *smiles*.

My throat goes immediately dry, because I don't think I've ever seen the man smile. At least not like this, and definitely not at us. The smile reaches his eyes and makes them all misty.

"Has anyone ever said you look a lot like your father, Larissa?" he says.

I see Mom's hands tighten on the arms of her chair, knuckles going white.

Dad died before I was born, so I never got to see him in person. But I've seen photos.

"Sure..." I say to Seu Romário.

"Gabriel also had a similar, how can I put it, *predisposition* for clumsiness."

I feel myself blush. I don't know if he's insulting Dad or me. Or maybe both of us.

When Dad was a little older than me, he used to work at Sugar, helping the Molinas with the bookkeeping, but that's an aspect of my parents' story that almost doesn't feel real. Mom never talks about Dad. His passing is a hard subject for her.

I did hear Isabel asking Mom once what it had been like

to fall in love with someone from Sugar. It was an innocent question from an overly nosy but still beloved family friend, but Mom showed no leniency. It was the first time I heard her snap at anyone who asked her about Dad.

"Gabriel wasn't *from* Sugar," Mom corrected her. "He worked *at* Sugar. There's a big difference. It's not like he was one of them."

Hearing Seu Romário bring Dad up so out of the blue now makes me wonder what it must have meant to him back then, to see one of his employees fall in love with a Ramires...

He continues. "There was one time when Gabriel tried to carry a large bowl of buttercream and he—"

Mom bolts up from her seat.

"Is this why you asked to speak with me? So you could marvel at the similarities between my child and her father?"

"How dare you raise your voice?!" Dona Eulalia shouts.

Seu Romário nervously gestures for Mom to stay.

"Please, please, I meant no harm."

She squints at him for a long second and sits down again, this time right on the edge of the seat.

"We're forgetting the *true* reason why we're here," Dona Eulalia says. "Pedro worked hard on fixing that wedding cake with the client's last-minute demands! It was a beautiful cake, Father. The Ramires girl marched straight to it!"

"Why did Pedro try to carry out the layers assembled," Seu Romário says, "despite the specific instructions I left to wheel them out separately?"

Pedro's face looks pinched. I can't believe he just got called out in front of us. "The driver was late and I was trying my best to hurry the order out the door."

"Excuses," his grandfather retorts, and the tips of Pedro's ears, sticking out from under a mat of cake-covered hair, turn bright red. "Always the same excuses. When are you going to learn to follow my instructions?"

"Grandpa—I mean, Chef, I didn't mean to—"

"I'm not going to argue with you now." Seu Romário makes an impatient hand gesture. "Eulalia, Pedro, leave me alone to speak with the Ramires."

Pedro is out the door in the blink of an eye, but Dona Eulalia lingers.

"Father, I thought we agreed that it would be better if Pedro and I—"

"*Leave.*"

She obeys, although not before one last nasty look at us. And the moment she's gone, it's like witnessing a magic veil come off. Seu Romário's shoulders hunch, like he'd been trying to seem stronger in front of his family.

"Now that we can talk privately," his voice cracks, "I'd like to express my deepest... My most... Alice, your mother—she was—she didn't deserve to go like that."

A painful sob swells in my throat, threatening to escape. I can't believe I'm about to cry in front of him. I can't believe I'm about to let myself melt, when all I want... All I want...

I want to *scream* at him.

I want to ask him why he was so cruel to Grandma all these years.

I want to blame him for every single time he made her cry. But, I can't.

I can't yell at Seu Romário, not when he has tears in his eyes.

"I know we've had our differences, but, believe me—" He

pulls a handkerchief out of his shirt pocket and wipes his eyes. "Believe me how I regret that Julieta—that she—"

His shoulders shake like a trembling mountain, threatening to crumble, and I look to Mom. Her lips are pressed tightly together while her face turns redder and redder. Her nostrils flare out with every breath she takes, sounding like she's starting to hyperventilate.

"You hated my mother," Mom says, her voice raspy with all her barely contained anger.

"I've known her ever since we were children, when our mothers let us play together while they worked on the Salt and Sugar recipe." He breathes hard as if searching for the best words. "Despite everything, I *respected* Julieta Ramires."

Seu Romário suddenly bursts into loud, sorrowful tears.

And Dona Eulalia flies back into the office.

"You've upset him!" she accuses Mom.

I notice Pedro is back at the door, looking stunned. Behind him, a multitude of curious bakers and customers crane their necks, not daring to step too close, but still trying their best to listen in. When he looks at me, I see the confusion in his eyes. I guess he didn't know the news about Grandma.

A sob escapes Mom's mouth like a hiccup. I want to pull her out of Sugar, but I'm stuck to the ground, unable to save her or myself from this mess.

"How can you say that, after all those years of tormenting her!" Mom shouts at him.

"Get out!" Dona Eulalia yells. Her face contorts with so much wrath that tears roll down her cheeks.

Pedro hurries to stand between Dona Eulalia and Mom to keep his mother away from us.

Mom shoves the chair back when she gets up to leave. I jump out of the way at the last second as it smashes into the wall, causing some of the certificates to come crashing down, glass shattering all over the floor.

"GET OUT!" Dona Eulalia screams, a vein bulging in the middle of her forehead.

Mom takes a step closer to the desk.

"If you cross me, if you point fingers at my daughter, if you try anything against my business, I'm not going to hesitate to fight you," she says, looking straight at Seu Romário. "You may say you're sorry all you want, but that doesn't erase the years of pain you caused my mother. The feud still stands. My mother didn't live her life in vain!"

Mom's words sound like an official declaration of war.

6

SATURDAY, APRIL 23

I find Mom in Salt's kitchen the next morning.

There are no customers yet, which is very unusual for a Saturday. But I hope that just means most people don't know we've reopened.

"You're up," she says, glancing at her wristwatch.

"I couldn't sleep anymore."

The kitchen is warm and fragrant with fresh bread—pumpkin bread, baguettes sprinkled with oregano, brown bread covered in sesame seeds. I notice the fresh bouquet of sunflowers sitting under Great-grandma's fubá cake recipe. Grandma used to leave those flowers for her mother, like the recipe behind the glass on the wall was a shrine. Now, the flowers are there to honor Grandma for the first time.

Mom catches my surprised glance.

"Why don't you go grab some stools?" she says. "Let's have breakfast in the kitchen."

Mom is already setting things down on the wooden counter when I come back with the stools.

Sweet potato. Mashed yams covered in beef jerky. French bread. Butter. A warm bowl of couscous. It's like she's trying to feed an army.

"I'm not very hungry," I say.

"It's not like you to refuse breakfast," she says with a wink. And my heart stops, because Mom winks just like Grandma used to. "And you barely ate last night. You need sustenance."

I join her at the counter, trying not to think about how without a third stool at the center to balance our family out, the counter feels much wider than it is.

Our breakfast begins quietly, just the hum of the fridge in the background.

I add butter to my yams, and the spoonful melts in my mouth, warming me up from inside out. I scoop up the little cuts of beef jerky individually, leftover from last night, chewing on them with my eyes closed. I let the salty flavor spread over my taste buds to wake them up one by one.

I then pull my bowl of milk couscous closer, breathing in the cinnamon-fragrant steam. I try to focus on chewing, but the ache in my heart doesn't go away.

I can't go on pretending that we didn't have that confrontation with the Molinas last night.

"Mom, I wanted to say… I'm sorry."

"There's no need for apologies," she says, slowly slicing a loaf of bread.

"I didn't destroy the cake on purpose. I went over there to tell them to stop laughing. To stop being loud when Grandma had just—"

I still can't say it.

Mom takes a sip of her coffee—black, no sugar—then puts it down.

"Forget about last night." She nods at the dishes in front of me. "Your food is getting cold."

How can I forget about last night? Seu Romário burst into tears in front of us and told us he respected Grandma. None of it makes sense.

The fridge starts sputtering, like it's choking on unspoken words, and Mom launches it a wary look. "I can't have you breaking on me now," she mutters.

"What did Seu Romário mean last night?" I ask, and the way Mom's shoulders tense up tells me she doesn't want to talk about this any further.

"Eat, Lari."

"What did he mean?" I insist, putting my spoon down.

The bells in Salt clink softly, and Mom rushes into the bakery, almost like she's glad to escape me.

"Good morning. How can I help you?" I hear her say.

I go join her. I may not be a baker, but I think I should at least start taking orders.

Standing in Salt is a customer I haven't seen before: a white man probably in his late thirties, tall and fit in an expensive-looking black suit. He only half glances at Mom, his unusually light blue eyes scanning the room.

"Good morning," he says after a few long seconds, like he's just remembered to reply.

He doesn't look like a tourist—there's no camera hanging around his neck—so maybe he's a new neighbor looking for breakfast before heading to a Saturday morning business meeting.

Mom frowns a little, but she's holding the smile.

"Welcome to Salt," she says. "Let me know if you'd like to try a sample."

"Will do," he says, sticking his nose in Grandma's flour jars.

When he finally approaches the main counter, he goes straight to inspect the goods Mom's already put on display this morning. Empadões sit behind the glass, the round, perfectly golden brown pot pies loaded with shredded chicken and green olives.

People usually know what they want when they walk into our bakery. Five loaves of bread. Shrimp empadinhas. Maybe some lunch quentinhas, the warm to-go box filled with couscous and carne de sol. But the man seems unhurried, browsing more like an inspector than a shopper.

"These are my favorite," I say, pointing to a tray of coxinhas, doing my best to welcome him like Grandma would have done. "They are filled with catupiry cheese. Would you like to try a sample?"

"What are you doing?" Mom hisses at me in a low voice.

"I was hoping I could help at Salt today."

"Lari, no—" Mom begins to say, but the man suddenly stops browsing, and her attention shifts back to him. "What can I get you?" she asks him with another smile.

He pulls a business card out of his suit pocket, which he then hands to Mom.

"My name is Ricardo Pereira," he says, flashing a smile that's more teeth than cordiality. "I'm a lawyer representing the supermarket Deals Deals. We're looking into purchasing a spot in the neighborhood to open up our new cafe and I'd love to make you an offer."

7

Deals Deals appeared in the heart of the neighborhood two years ago.

The whole construction was fast, like the building and massive parking lot popped out of nowhere in the middle of the night. Car traffic was even rerouted to benefit them. Foot traffic on our streets emptied, too, our potential new clients and tourists falling for their gimmicky events.

On their first Christmas here, they had a guy dressed as Santa Claus land with a helicopter on their parking lot. People were *stunned*. It gathered hundreds of customers and TV crews.

"This year, I'm closing the factory!" Santa announced to everyone listening. "I sent the elves on vacation, because I'm shopping at Deals Deals and so should you!"

After that, neighbors gathered at Salt one evening to discuss the future of the neighborhood. Everyone came. Well, everyone *except* the Molinas.

"Go upstairs," Mom told me when they arrived. "Don't you have homework to do?"

"I want to join the meeting," I whispered to her.

"This isn't child's play."

She said those words in front of everyone like I was a stubborn kid asking to stay up past her bedtime. I was about to protest, but Grandma agreed with her.

"Listen to your mother," she said, not even giving me a chance. And it *hurt* more than the humiliation of being treated like a baby in front of our neighbors.

I whirled around, making for the stairs, but when Mom's attention shifted back to the group I hid in the shadows, listening as she read from an article about Deals Deals and their controversial market experiments around South America, how they settle in neighborhoods like ours and lower their prices against the products family-owned establishments already offered.

Companies like these have a large enough safety net that they could run their store at a deficit, just so they could tank small businesses with no way to compete. They take down businesses like Salt and our neighbors' one by one until there's nothing left.

It was the first time I heard the term predatory pricing, and I pictured wolves stalking prey. Sharp claws. Baring teeth. For a moment, I even forgot I was angry with Mom and Grandma. I just felt so...*scared* for Salt. For everyone.

"We can't let that happen to us," Mom said. "I propose we only buy from each other. If we stay loyal to our neighbors and we don't give Deals Deals any business, maybe then they'll go away."

I watched the neighbors huddle together at Salt's counter, each signing the boycott. But when Dona Marta's turn came, the local florist, she panicked.

"They'll retaliate!" she shouted.

"So what?" Seu Floriano, the espetinhos vendor, said. "They're threatening me already. My booth is at the very end of the feirinha, and they want to expand their parking lot to the street directly behind it. But I won't let them win. We must stand together. Let them know we won't go down without a fight!"

"You can't let them intimidate you," Grandma said, trying to soothe her friend.

"It's easy for all of you to say," Dona Marta said. "But you still haven't seen what they can do! They're building a greenhouse behind Deals Deals! A *greenhouse* with every plant possible that will replace my business! Julieta, just you wait until they come for you. When they expand their bakery and you can't compete with the hundreds of cheap factory-made bread loaves they'll pump into our neighborhood, you'll know what I mean! A boycott will do nothing other than anger them. I thought you had a *real* plan when you invited us tonight."

It sounded like a threat. Worse. It sounded like a prophecy, and I saw anguish in Grandma's eyes for the first time in my life.

I think that's when I first started thinking of Salt as my responsibility, too. Everything I knew was at risk. Everything I loved. My life in the bakery. My neighbors. I didn't want to lose any of that. I knew I had to do something, I just didn't know what.

So, when the neighbors were gone, and when Mom and Grandma withdrew back into the kitchen, I tiptoed to the list. Carefully, dutifully, I put my name down.

Lari Ramires.

8

"Salt isn't for sale," Mom says emphatically.

"Aren't you interested in at least hearing our offer?" the man asks, his voice as sticky as honey.

"No, thank you." Mom slaps his business card on the counter and crosses her arms over her chest. I cross mine, too. "Like I said, Salt isn't for sale."

"You see, there are many great spots for a cafe in this neighborhood." The man looks over his shoulder at the street, like he's scanning his options, and maybe it's my imagination, but his eyes linger on Sugar for a second too long. "But I *love* this building in particular. I'd hate to pass on such a well-established place without even giving it a chance."

The way he says *love* sends a chill down my spine, like my home is a prime steak he's dying to sink his teeth into.

"We're not for sale," I reiterate Mom's words.

His blue eyes slowly turn to me, and I feel goose bumps run up and down my arms.

Mom's hand is on my shoulder in warning. "Sorry to disappoint, but for the third time, we're not for sale," Mom repeats to him, her voice perfectly controlled, but her hand is clammy against my skin.

"Keep my card," he insists with another toothy smile. "If you change your mind, come by my office. I can't offer you a lot of time to consider it since we're negotiating with other places. But, let's say…give me your answer by the end of May?"

"No, thank you."

He cocks his head, that smile still plastered on his face. "Okay, maybe that's too soon. I understand your hesitation. How about the end of June? Around St. John's Day? That gives you two full months to think this through. Does that sound fair?"

"*Fair?!* Didn't you hear my mother say we're not selling?" I snap, and Mom gives my shoulder another squeeze.

"Feel free to call or email if you have any questions in the meantime," he says, unbothered by my tone. After a quick nod at Mom, he leaves as quietly as he walked in like the wolf he is, the bells above our doors barely even making a sound.

Mom's hand drops from my shoulder and she exhales. "Go get dressed."

"Why? Are we going somewhere?"

"You are. Dona Selma invited you to visit her at Vozes."

Vozes is the nonprofit community center Dona Selma runs, where they teach kids and teens many after-school programs free of charge. They also run a free day care, and Grandma and I used to volunteer there every weekend. But ever since Grandma got sick, I haven't been back. Mom starts saying how it's important we return to our old routines, but I'm only half listening, because through the window I see the Deals Deals guy crossing the street, making his way to Sugar.

I run to perch behind our window display, my heart pounding.

The Molinas didn't sign the boycott list, and I've always wondered if they do business with Deals Deals. Knowing how awful and treacherous and selfish they are, I bet they do.

"Is he going to make the Molinas an offer, too?" I ask Mom, my breath fogging up the glass right as he steps into Sugar.

When I turn to look at her, I catch her picking his business card up, studying it, and a sudden wave of fear shoots through my body, like the card itself could hurt her.

"Mom!"

She drops the card, startled.

"Go get dressed!"

But before I can move, there's a commotion right in front of Sugar. I whirl around in time to watch the Deals Deals lawyer scurrying out of the bakery, Seu Romário bellowing at him from the doorstep to go away. Dona Eulalia and Pedro struggle to stop Seu Romário from chasing the man all the way down the street.

"Larissa, don't leave Dona Selma waiting." Mom snaps her fingers to get me to focus. "Your grandmother would have hated letting Vozes down."

"You want me to go to Vozes? *Now?*"

She must see the panic in my eyes, because her face softens a little. "They can't force me to sell Salt. You understand that? *I* don't want to sell Salt."

"I know, but what if he comes back? I need to be here to

defend Salt." My thoughts are spiraling with fear. "I think I should start helping you out. He probably thinks you're all alone. But I'm backing you up from now on. Salt is my responsibility, too."

I grab a dish rag to start wiping counters, but Mom yanks it from me.

"Salt isn't for you!" Mom raises her voice. "It's *not* your responsibility."

"But—"

"Your grandmother and I worked hard to ensure you didn't have to work at Salt. *School* is your responsibility. It's your vestibular year and I never see you studying anymore. Maybe you don't care about my sacrifices, but have you no consideration for your grandmother's?! She fought her entire life to give you what she didn't have herself! A better future! How can you be the first Ramires to go to college, if you don't show dedication?"

I feel the sting of tears, but I take a deep breath to hold them back.

"I do care," I say in a low voice not to upset Mom even more. "I'll study more. I'll start this very moment."

"No, go to Vozes." Mom rubs the spot between her eyes like she's trying to soothe a headache. "Dona Selma is waiting. You'll study when you get home."

"Alright," I give in, walking past Mom toward the stairs.

"Lari, wait."

I stop at the bottom steps.

She sighs. "I didn't mean to yell."

"I know." I try to smile to put her heart at ease.

Neither of us knows how to be without Grandma, but we'll have to find a way to be stronger, especially now that Deals Deals is sniffing around our doorstep.

9

SATURDAY, APRIL 23

Normally, the streets would be full with tourists straight from the airport in Recife. I grew up watching them point their cameras at everything, from lazy cats sleeping curled up on the doorstep of a boteco to the kites in the sky.

But the only tourists I see on my way to the bus stop are two women lingering outside an atelier, taking selfies in front of the hanging frevo umbrellas. And that's about it.

I get a wound up feeling in my chest, worried that Deals Deals is up to something again. There are festivities coming up in Olinda. St. John's parties are big in the northeast, starting as early as May going all the way into July. What if the supermarket puts together another event that's diverting commerce to them? Is the boycott enough to keep us safe? My neighbors have refused to buy from Deals Deals, but what about the tourists?

We rely on tourists to boost our local economy. That's something even little kids around here repeat before they learn what the word *economy* means. But it's not like the tourists even know our predicament. And if they did... Would it mean anything to them? Would they back us up?

I make my way down the street and I feel like crying, noticing everything that I didn't want to see this past year, once Grandma's health started to decline.

There are more and more empty storefronts. The shops that have remained standing, most selling lace and leather sandals, seem deserted, doors and windows wide open like they're trying to coerce new customers and tourists the same way they invite the cool sea breeze inside on muggy days.

Meanwhile, new businesses have popped up. Fancier. People from outside our neighborhood are taking over establishments that once belonged to Grandma's friends. The old florist's shop is now a store selling designer sunglasses.

Sunglasses!

Things around here are changing fast. Too fast. It makes me feel powerless, like I'm letting Grandma down.

She grew up in this neighborhood. She knew it like the back of her hand. And still, during our walks, she'd stand by the church and look out at the blue-green Atlantic ocean stretching into the horizon like it was her first time taking in the view. Like she was a tourist, pointing out every detail that caught her eye, every little thing that made her smile.

When I asked her why she did that, she told me that it was important to fall in love with one's neighborhood over and over again.

It's strange being back at Vozes without Grandma.

Every Saturday morning, we'd come to deliver a batch of bread, Mom staying behind to take care of Salt. Grandma would often linger for a few hours, chatting with Dona Selma, while I helped the volunteers with some of the games and activities at the day care.

When I step inside, Dona Selma is coming out of the kitchen.

My breath catches in my throat.

Today, she's in that flowy yellow dress that pops against her dark brown skin, the one Grandma gifted to her. She said the color looked like it held all the sunshine in the world.

The memory makes me smile and want to cry at the same time.

A man steps out of the kitchen behind her, *Silveira Construction* written on his polo shirt. She gives him a disappointed smile when they shake hands.

"I'm sorry I can't be of more help, senhora," he says on his way out.

She spots me in the back and her eyes light up.

"Lari! You're here!" When she sees the box of bread in my arms, she rests her hands on her hips. "I told Alice not to worry. You Ramires women are too stubborn. But, thank you. It's greatly appreciated."

I peer over her shoulder at the kitchen entrance. It looks like a hurricane went through the room. There are puddles everywhere. All the furniture has been pushed to one side, covered in dust, while part of the wall and tiles are ripped open to expose pipes like a gaping wound.

"What happened here?" I ask.

"It's a mess, I know. We've been having issues with our old pipes for a while but kept postponing repairs. And now the problems have caught up to us. I feel there's a life lesson in here somewhere, no?" She chuckles sadly.

"How are you cooking for the kids?"

Dona Selma launches the stove a mournful look. "We can't cook anything here. I'm bringing some food I prepare at home, but God knows I should stay away from the stove. We're relying heavily on donations, now more than ever."

She steers me out of the kitchen.

This is a disaster. Most families rely on Vozes being a free all-day day care service. How will they go on if they're not able to feed the kids?

"What's going to happen?" I ask her.

"I'm gathering price estimates from construction companies at the moment, but we can't afford anything just yet." She gives my shoulder a comforting squeeze. "Don't worry. Maybe we'll do a fundraiser event. A potluck with community leaders and small business owners, perhaps?"

I can't help but feel like I let Vozes down. I haven't been back in so long.

"I'm really sorry. I want to help."

Dona Selma takes the box of bread from my hands. "You're already helping."

The sound of children playing in the back playground reaches us, and suddenly my eyesight blurs with tears. Dona Selma smiles, pulling me into a side hug.

"How are you this morning, love?" she asks. "Last night was tough. I've already heard rumors about the meeting in Romário's office… I wish I'd been able to stop your mother, but I think Alice needed closure."

"Closure? More like she wanted to set everything on fire."

"Was it that bad?"

"Bad is an understatement." I let out a long sigh, and she gives me an understanding look. "But I'm more worried about Salt's future. It feels as if Grandma was the last force keeping us safe."

I tell her everything about this morning's encounter with the Deals Deals lawyer and Dona Selma listens, her expression growing more and more grave. When I'm done, she holds my hands in hers.

"Julieta knew this was a possibility," she says. "Don't let it scare you. That's what they want—to make us all feel cornered. But you aren't alone, Lari. There's a whole community linking arms against them."

The first tears roll down my cheeks.

Our financial issues aren't new to me—they became clear around the same time the first signs of Grandma's illness started. January of last year. Exactly one year after Deals Deals arrived.

Grandma wanted to continue working at Salt as if nothing was wrong, but she couldn't keep up. She'd get dizzy and so sleepy her eyes closed even as she kneaded dough. She was stubborn, always saying things were fine, until the day she fainted.

We rushed her to the hospital.

And then...

Well, it was all in plain sight. Grandma was sick. She started going to the doctors more and more frequently. There were days when Salt didn't even open. We were either at the hospital or Grandma was too exhausted to work and Mom wouldn't leave her side.

I *desperately* wanted to do something to help. I could've just run the counter, since anyone Mom tried to hire asked for more money than she could offer. But Mom swatted me away every time, repeating her mantra: "You're going to be the first Ramires to go to college!" And according to her, that's where all my energy needs to go, even if my own home is starting to fall apart before my eyes.

When things got really bad at the bakery, Grandma had an idea that she was going to apply to the Gastronomic Society, a prestigious culinary school and cooking society. If she got accepted as a student, even though she was good enough to be an instructor, she would've been able to participate in their big annual cooking contest. The type of contest that's televised—that changes people's lives. Winners have gone on to start their own restaurants and earn Michelin stars!

Grandma said that's what Salt needed. To be put on a map. Like it was a definitive way to keep us afloat.

But the entrance exam was three months ago, right as Grandma started feeling *really* sick. She didn't get accepted. Mom was furious that a baker as experienced as Grandma was turned down.

"What Salt needs is to get better catering opportunities to give us a boost and introduce us to potential new clients," Mom said. "We can't get our hopes up with dreams, with things that aren't within our control like cooking contests."

But there were no events to cater, except for the one Sugar stole from us.

Grandma had to be hospitalized in March and Salt closed its doors entirely. Still, she kept on studying to join the GS, hoping to try again next year. The past few days at the hospital, Grandma always had her recipes scattered over her bed, studying whenever she had a chance.

But she never got to see that dream come true.

I sob in Dona Selma's arms. She holds me close, rubbing my back.

"Grandma had so many dreams," I say, my heart breaking into one million pieces. "Was there ever... Was there ever any chance? Was she just being a dreamer, like Mom said?"

"There's nothing wrong with dreaming, love. Your great-grandmother Elisa was a dreamer, too. Didn't she dream the inn she'd inherited could become a bakery? She dreamed of building a home for herself and Julieta. A home that's your mother's and yours now. Against all odds, here you are now, living that woman's dream."

Dona Selma holds me by the shoulders so I'll look at her. When I meet her eyes, I can almost let myself find comfort in her words. But how can a dream survive in the face of so many obstacles?

10

Professora Carla Pimentel claps her hands to startle sleepy students awake on Monday morning.

"Listen up!" she says. "I know everyone is stressing out about the last quiz, but I have good news for you. I've spoken with a few concerned parents, and I thought it would be nice to give everyone a chance to earn extra credit."

Pimentel glances at me and I get the sinking feeling in my stomach that she's saying this specifically for me. Concerned *parents*? This feels a lot like something Mom would do.

"So, here's a little challenge for you," she says, turning around to write an equation on the whiteboard. "Whoever manages to answer this can get an extra point on last Friday's quiz."

The quiz I left halfway through to go to Grandma's funeral.

My stomach twists. I don't want my teachers, especially Pimentel, to think that Mom has to babysit my grades. Math is my best subject anyway, and I even compete in math contests against other schools.

Diego, Paulina, and Talita all leap to their feet. I guess the end of the semester is a bit of a wake-up call for everyone. Luana stands and strides to the whiteboard like she's a model on a catwalk. When she walks past my desk, she turns up her nose, and her Ariana Grande–style ponytail swings like a pendulum, nearly smacking me in the face.

As much as I don't want to do this challenge—and as embarrassing as it is to admit—I want to make Mom proud. She has been laser focused on my grades since the first grade. I understand that's just her way of saying that she loves me, but time and time again, I've wondered whether there's more for me than studying for mathematics contests and the vestibular. To Mom, the only thing that matters is carving a path toward college—becoming the *first* Ramires to go to college—even if I'm not sure that's what I want to pursue...

I let out a heavy sigh, pick a blue marker, and begin writing beside my classmates. We all work at a steady pace, the astringent smell of the markers burning the inside of my nostrils, and as rusty as my mind feels today, my hand moves like muscle memory.

It doesn't take too long until I start to feel numb.

Numb is good, right?

My hands stops.

Friday night in Salt's kitchen, I had felt the opposite of numb. I felt closer to Grandma than I ever had before. Before I burned myself with oil, there *was* a connection. Something happened. Something I can't explain, like cooking had linked me to her.

Giggling pulls me back to the present. I glance over my shoulder and see my classmates rush to the windows. Pimentel looks up from grading at her desk, her big glasses slipping to the tip of her nose.

"What's going on?" she asks, alarmed.

"Pedro is outside running from the doorman!" Luana announces.

Pedro is...*what?*

I join everyone at the windows.

Our classroom is on the second floor, and at first, all I see is the narrow path between the back of the school building and the fence. Then I see the doorman, Seu Vicente, running with his attendance list in hand. He's always stationed at the school gate, jotting down the names of the kids who are tardy or trying to play hooky. Many of us have perfected ways to avoid him over the years.

When Seu Vicente is out of sight, Pedro comes out of his hiding spot on the other end of the building, dragging a ladder along, and everyone cheers like he's Indiana Jones escaping the huge boulder.

I roll my eyes.

"Pedro Molina, don't you dare!" Pimentel shouts. "Get down this very moment! I mean it! Do not climb into my classroom!"

I return to the whiteboard, trying to focus, but with everyone cheering him on, and Pimentel on the verge of an anxiety attack, I can't focus on solving the last part of the equation.

"Professora, the prodigal son returns!" I hear his voice in the back.

His fans—I mean his friends—run to pull him through the window. They act starstruck, welcoming him back to school.

Some swoon, like Luana, all heart eyes. Pimentel looks frazzled, as if she's about to collapse.

"You're like Romeo," Luana says, all smiles. They went steady in fifth grade. Everyone says they'll get back together one day.

Who cares?

He dramatically takes her hand and kisses the back of it. Luana looks like she's about to melt.

I've had enough of this. I turn around and bite down on my lower lip, trying to get back in the zone. But the mental image of Pedro perched on the window is still stuck in my mind like a bad rash.

"What. A. Genius," I say.

And instantly I know I've got his attention.

"What's that?" he says behind me.

I inhale sharply, but Pimentel reprimands him before I can say something.

"Pedro, go to the principal," she says. "What you did is unacceptable! You could have fallen and broken your neck!"

"If you answer the equation, you can get extra credit," Luana tells him, and he flashes her a smile.

"Go to the principal," Pimentel repeats, but Pedro is still staring at the equation above my head. Now that he doesn't have cake all over his face, I realize he's changed a bit. Those Molina light brown eyes are usually bright and mischievous, like his brain is constantly looking for a good comeback. But now they've cooled off. Hardened. There's a general tiredness in those eyes, the type that maybe isn't just physical. Like wherever he went these past few weeks, maybe it wasn't a good trip.

When he pushes his bangs off his forehead—he's in *serious* need of a trim—his gaze flickers back to me. I look away before he thinks I was staring.

"May I answer it?" he asks our teacher.

"You want to answer the challenge?" Pimentel sounds pleasantly surprised.

"I missed some quizzes and I really need extra credit. May I answer it?"

He makes puppy eyes. The others back him up, begging her to let him. A flash of vanity crosses her face when she adjusts her glasses. She seems to forget his rude interruption for a second and looks proud of herself for finally getting *everyone* interested in mathematics. "Well," she hesitates, and then smiles, "go for it."

Pedro grabs a marker and scoots next to me to start working.

"But you're headed to the principal as soon as you're done—" Pimentel's voice gets drowned out with the cheers that erupt from Pedro's friends.

His hand flies on the whiteboard as he answers line after line. He's as sharp as always. Even Pimentel is starting to look dazzled. It reminds me of all the times she's tried to convince him to join the mathematics club. Thankfully, he didn't. He knew I'd be there.

"I bet I can finish it before you, even though I got here late," he whispers to me.

So he thinks he can challenge *me*?

"Bring it."

Behind us, our classmates start placing bets, and just like that our rivalry is back, as if he had never left.

11

MONDAY, APRIL 25

School is how Pedro and I deal with our families' feud.

On test days, we compete to see who gets the highest score. We're always on opposite teams during gym. Even during lunch, we're vying to see who gets to the line at the cafeteria first. Always competing. Always trying to make a point.

Today's battlefield is the whiteboard.

"You sure know how to cause a scene..." I say under my breath.

Pedro exhales. "I wasn't going to say anything, but speaking of scenes, care to explain why you crashed into me the other night?" he says, leaning in to be heard above all the cheering behind us. Just the sound of his voice makes my skin crawl.

"You mean when I *accidentally* ran into you?" I give him a pointed look.

"Was it really an accident?" He squints at me.

I hate that I can smell the scent of guava frosting from his family's bakery on his clothes because we're standing so close, sandwiched together between our classmates at the white-board.

"Leave me alone." I give him a little shove with my shoulder to get more space between us, but I end up knocking the marker out of his hand.

Our classmates begin accusing me of cheating.

"I swear I'm not—" I begin to say, but Pimentel shakes her head at me.

"No fighting," she warns.

My cheeks warm up with embarrassment. *Great*. Now even Pimentel is siding with Pedro.

Pedro grabs another marker, giving me a death glare from behind his bangs.

"Was that an accident, too?" he asks.

"*Yes*."

"Then why didn't I hear an apology?"

He doesn't deserve one. But I know he'll just use this against me if I refuse.

"Sorry," I say in a low voice, the words coming out like pulling teeth. "For the cake, too."

Pedro scoffs. "No, you aren't."

The blood in my veins feels like liquid fire.

"I know how to take responsibility. Unlike you, who refuses to admit to sabotaging my family. I know your family started those lies about rats in Salt's kitchen so you could steal the wedding gig from us!"

Pedro looks like he's about to retort, but our classmates get even rowdier behind us. Now they're rooting for Diego, who seems to finally be on the right track answering the equation.

He's so happy he does a dramatic lap around the classroom to hype himself up.

"So that's why you crashed into me," he says, not a question. "I knew you could get petty, but I never thought you— Never mind." He scoffs. "We didn't steal the client. She contacted us. She was always going to need a second caterer for the cakes and pastries. We were just doing our job."

"But I saw your bakers loading *empadinhas* into the back of the van. Don't deny it."

"You know what? Salt has no patent on empadinhas. Any bakery can—"

Diego is now doing celebratory cartwheels and he crashes into the first line of desks. There's a big commotion behind us to rescue him.

"Salt and Sugar have always had a deal, and you know it," I say. "It's such a Molina thing to backstab people when they're the most vulnerable. Like Grandma always said, trust neither thin-bottomed frying pans nor Molinas…"

Pedro looks a little taken aback. I don't know if he'd heard this saying before, but I think I got to him this time.

He's quiet for a while, a hand raised to answer his equation, but he exhales, turning back to me. "Believe it or not, it really was a one-time situation. The client commissioned empadinhas from Sugar because it was too last-minute to find a replacement for Salt. It's not our fault."

"How convenient," I say the words slowly. "In that case, maybe we'll start offering wedding cakes to our catering clients too!"

"Time's almost up!" Pimentel announces behind us. "Diego, are you alright?"

"You call us backstabbers, but you know what I'm starting to think?" Pedro lowers his voice to an angry whisper. "I think you're envious of Sugar. At first, I thought your mother sent you over when I was carrying the wedding cake. But revenge is more your thing, I think."

His words sting.

I hate the smug look on his face, thinking he figured me out, my *nefarious* plans to take his family down.

I hate the way he smirks.

I hate everything about him. Even his bangs that keep falling over his eyes.

"How dare you question my morals, when everyone knows *your* family never even signed the boycott against Deals Deals? Speaking of which, what did that lawyer want at Sugar?"

Our classmates are back cheering for Pedro, urging him to finish the equation before me. He does a little double take of the situation, throwing them a fake smile. But when he looks back at me, I realize I caught him off guard with my question.

"How do you know he came by?" he whispers.

"I saw him leaving Sugar."

"I saw him leaving Salt," he retorts like it's a big "gotcha" moment.

We stare at each other for a long second, his breathing stirring strands of his bangs.

He doesn't need to answer. I know when he's trying to hide that he's worried. He's the most arrogant person in Olinda, so he wouldn't be asking me about Deals Deals if he weren't terrified for Sugar. That lawyer must have made an offer to them, too.

We size each other up before going back to work.

I'm nearly finished answering the challenge, when I notice that Pedro's marker begins to fail. He swears under his breath, cycling through more dry erase markers.

I double my speed, reaching the last line of the equation. I can already taste victory, when Pedro's arm suddenly crosses over my vision, trying to get a marker to my right.

"Watch it!" I complain.

When Pedro finally moves out of the way, I realize what he's done. His shoulder erased half of my equation. And now he looks from my ruined work to my face, his mouth turning into a fake, exaggerated O.

I clench the marker in my hand so tight it hurts.

"Pedro, did you do that on purpose?" Pimentel asks, peering over my shoulder.

I whirl around to look at her.

"He did!"

"Sorry," he says, a hand on his heart, and the barely contained smirk tugging at the corners of his mouth. "Seriously, Larissa. I didn't mean to."

"Liar!" I protest.

"Lari, he already apologized," Pimentel says. "Now go on you two. You have one minute left."

Trembling with anger, I rush to finish the part of the equation Pedro erased. I can't believe this. He's barely back and he's already a nightmare.

"Now you know what it feels like when someone destroys your work, even if it was, like you said, an *accident*," he whispers to me.

And before I know it, I'm running a hand over his equation and erasing part of it.

The cheering quiets. It's like time stands still.

Pedro crosses his arms over his chest and leans against the whiteboard, like this was the reaction he was trying to get out of me all along. His eyes accuse: *You're vengeful. QED.* Like it's proof I tripped him Friday night.

Pimentel hurries over to us. "That's enough. Pedro, you already got your two minutes under the spotlight. I'm taking you to the principal."

"What about *her*?" he nods toward me, indignant. "She just erased my equation out of spite because she knew she was going to lose to me."

I laugh. "I was going to win!"

"Guys, this was not a competition," Pimentel says, already looking exhausted. "This was just a challenge for anyone interested in getting extra credit." She scratches her head with a pencil as she examines our work. "Look, you would have solved it if you answered with this part of Lari's solution and that part of Pedro's. If only you helped each other, instead of all this fighting, the equation would have been solved."

Helped each other?

"I didn't know we could ask for help," Diego whimpers.

"I'll die before I ask for Pedro Molina's help," I say under my breath.

"What was that, Lari?" Pimentel asks.

"Nothing."

Pedro glares. He heard me alright. I shoot daggers at him with my eyes.

The bell rings, and Pimentel goes to inspect my other classmates' equations. They were also unable to finish it.

Diego drops down to his knees. "Please, Professora, I need

this extra point! My parents are going to kill me if I can't get my grade up!" Pimentel's class sure has a way of leaving people desperate.

She sighs at his begging. "Alright, listen up. I have an idea. Class is over, but if you guys at the whiteboard could team up for a minute to put this solution together, I'll offer you all the extra credit," she says.

My classmates look back at Pedro and me expectantly. But working together means having to work with *him*, and that— that's impossible. It's *treason*.

"I can't work with him," I tell Pimentel.

"And I can't work with her," he echoes.

"Can the rest of us solve the equation as a group without Larissa?" Luana asks Pimentel, patting Diego on the shoulder to comfort him.

I glare at Luana, and she raises a perfectly tweezed eyebrow at me in defiance.

"No, *everyone* needs to work together," Pimentel says.

Diego looks hurt. "Pedro, it's just for one minute," he begs, his hands clasped in front of him. But even though Pedro clearly feels bad for him, his answer is still no. Diego then turns to me. "Please? *Please?!*"

I feel all eyes on me. Waiting for my answer.

"Sorry. I can't."

My classmates let out an annoyed grunt, and Diego dramatically rolls into a fetal position on the floor, looking as upset as when my homemade lollipop chipped his tooth years ago.

"In that case," Pimentel says, looking disappointed, "I'm sorry everyone. Class dismissed."

12

During recess, I stand outside the principal's office, shifting from foot to foot.

Pimentel has been in there forever with Pedro and the principal. I know Principal Oliveira *talks*, but recess is nearly over and there's still no sign of this meeting wrapping up.

"No wonder no one wants to be friends with her, she only thinks of herself," Luana said as she pushed past me to exit the classroom. Her words have been playing in my head ever since. And to think that we liked to play dress-up together when we were little. Her mom uses their living room as a hair salon, and Luana used to swipe brushes and makeup for makeovers that turned both of us into macaws, her fingertips smeared with bright eye shadow that left fingerprints all over her mom's furniture. She'd always take full blame, even when I tried to defend her.

Now she hates me. Everyone does. Even though Pedro refused to work together, too.

I grab my phone as I wait, pretending to text someone so

I can try to ignore my classmates hissing "Salty" at me as they walk past.

No wonder no one wants to be friends with her.

Tears start to fill my eyes. I wish I didn't care what these bullies think. But I can't deny that I *do* care. I need to fix this disaster. Besides, my classmates shouldn't have to pay for the consequences of my feud with Pedro.

After many chewed fingernails, the door finally opens.

I catch a glimpse of Pedro's back and Principal Oliveira's expression, staring at him like she's trying to solve a difficult puzzle.

Pimentel steps outside, closing the door behind her. I guess the principal isn't done with Pedro yet.

"I wanted to apologize for earlier," I say. "For the way I behaved in your class."

She seems surprised to see me lingering in the hallway, but she smiles. "I appreciate your apology, Lari."

"I wanted to ask… Is there… I don't know… Is there any way you could reconsider giving extra credit?" I feel my cheeks already burning with awkwardness, but I add in quickly, before Pimentel thinks I'm being selfish, "Not for myself, for my classmates. Could they still get credit?"

She tilts her head. "Why couldn't you work with Pedro when I asked you? It was just an equation."

I glance at the principal's door behind her.

"Because he's my enemy."

Pimentel raises her eyebrows, disappointment written all over her face. It's not a look I normally get from a teacher. And I hate it. It feels like I just got a bad grade.

"*Enemy* is a strong word," she says.

I think of Mom screaming at Seu Romário last Friday. I think of Dona Eulalia yelling at us. I think of all the rumors, lies, and accusations.

This isn't just a rivalry. Pimentel doesn't get it.

I shrug. "That's what he is."

She thinks for a while, her glasses catching the light of the fixture directly above her. She glances from her books to me and a curious expression crosses her face. "What if I told you there's a way you could help your classmates earn extra credit?"

It feels like a balloon is inflating in my chest.

"Really?" I cough to smother my excitement. "I mean, really?"

"I got a request from Principal Oliveira to encourage more third-year students to join our clubs. Would you be interested in joining one in exchange for extra credit? You used to be so involved in extracurricular activities these past few years."

That's a bit of an exaggeration, but I was the president of the mathematics club up until last year. I mostly gathered members to prep for all the math competitions we entered throughout our first two years of high school. But I'm retired now. If you are a third-year student, in your last year before college, you never stay for extracurriculars, *unless* they're review sessions for the vestibular—the college entrance exam.

"I know this is your vestibular year," she adds, as if reading my mind, "but Principal Oliveira and I think it would be a great benefit to show our students, especially you third-years, that there's more to your final school year than studying."

Mom would *so* disagree with that…

"You'll give everyone extra credit if I join a club?"

"Yes. This one club in particular." She pulls a flyer out of her textbook. "They meet only once a week. This afternoon, in fact. So it wouldn't be too much of a hassle. You'd still have the rest of the week free to study." She must sense my hesitation because she continues, "They're about to lose a member. And they're so swamped with commitments, Lari. Joining them would be a great thing to do. What do you think?"

She beams her brightest smile at me.

Mom would never accept it. Any free time goes to studying for college. The only place where she lets me spend any extra time is at Vozes. Even sleep sometimes doesn't make a lot of sense to her. *Sleep later. You're young. You'd stay up all night watching TV if I let you, so why not studying?* All to become the first Ramires to go to college.

I hadn't given joining a club a thought, but maybe it could be my crumb of freedom this year.

Monday afternoon. Yeah, I like the sound of that.

No one tell Mom.

"Sign me up," I say with a smile.

"Fantastic!" Pimentel sticks the flyer in my hand, suddenly in a hurry. "I knew I could count on you. And, remember, you have to attend the club until the end of this semester for it to count as extra credit!"

She takes off as fast as Jessie and James getting kicked into the horizon at the end of every *Pokémon* episode.

I breathe a sigh of relief. The conversation turned out better than I expected. And there are only two months left in the semester.

I turn around to head to my next class when the principal's door opens again.

I halt, holding my breath.

"We're not finished. Please, sit down."

"I already said I'm sorry," Pedro says, still in her office. "You gave me a demerit. Fine. I don't care. Can I go now?"

"Sit down."

Pedro sounds a little exasperated. He's always played the "I'm too cool for school" role, but the way he's addressing the principal today is bordering on rude.

He plops down in the chair in front of her desk, forgetting to close the door all the way. I step closer, squeezing myself against the wall.

"...not to mention that you were gone for *weeks* without giving much notice," Principal Oliveira continues as if listing his crimes. "I don't know what to do with you."

"If you're going to expel me, better do it quick. I have to head home for work."

"I'm not going to expel you," the principal says.

"Why not?"

"What do you mean 'why not'?" She pauses, and I can tell that she can read him better than he thinks she can. "Filho, how else am I going to give you your diploma and that recommendation letter to the Gastronomic Society?"

What? Pedro wants to get into the Gastronomic Society? I had no idea. Isn't he Sugar's golden boy, a *prodigy*? Why go to culinary school when he already brags that he's the best cook in town?

"I'm not going to apply anymore," he says, nonchalant.

"What changed your mind? Last time we talked, you said you were going to tell your family about it."

"I did."

She looks surprised. "And?"

"And…" I see Pedro's fingers drumming on the arm of the chair. "It went so well that Grandpa kicked me out," he says in a fake cheerful voice.

I take a step back from the principal's office, overwhelmed with a feeling like I've intruded too much. So that's why he was gone. I hate Pedro, but—how could Seu Romário kick out his own grandson? What's so wrong with wanting to join the GS?

I'm still in the hallway when Pedro storms out of the principal's office, nearly crashing into me. For a second, he looks at a loss for words, perhaps even embarrassed. Then he pulls sunglasses out of his pants pocket and puts them on.

"Is it possible that you missed me so much that you're spying on me now?" he says with a smirk, pushing past before I can reply, causing me to drop the club flyer Pimentel gave me.

I grumble under my breath. "Miss him…"

The recess bell rings, and students begin rushing down the hallway back to class. I crouch down to pick up the flyer. My fingertips have barely flipped it over, when I see the words:

COOKING CLUB
President: Pedro Molina

13

I could barely concentrate during the rest of my classes. I blink and it's suddenly the end of the day and I'm standing in the cafeteria with the cooking club flyer wrinkled in my hand.

I don't even know why I'm doing this. It's not like I can win Luana, Diego, and the others over with extra credit like Pedro used to do with Sugar's cream-filled sonhos when we were kids.

Besides, I can't join a club where Pedro is the president. I should just bail and go home. Maybe if I continue begging Pimentel this week, she'll let me join a different club.

I'm about to leave the cafeteria when laughter travels to me from inside the kitchen. Someone turns on music. And then there's the roaring of a blender. It's a delightful kitchen cacophony reminding me of the way Salt sounded when Grandma was around...

I decide to poke my head in the kitchen to take a peek before I leave.

Just a peek won't hurt. Grandma taught me to see kitchens as magical places, where everything turns into delicious memories. I want to see what sort of magic they cast at the cooking club. It doesn't mean I'm staying.

The moment I cross the threshold into the kitchen, I feel as if I just discovered the most amazing secret. Like Alice tumbling down the rabbit hole into Wonderland, falling more and more in love with a world where it feels she doesn't belong.

I should leave, before it's too late. But I can't take my eyes off the three students in aprons gathered around a metal counter that's covered in bowls of fresh fruit. They have their backs to me, talking over each other while picking fruit and tossing slices into the blender. I spot oranges, strawberries, bananas, grapes, mangoes, apples, pears, and cashews on the counter. There's a bottle of milk, too, and a bag of sugar. They look like they are making smoothies, disagreeing on what to add mid blending.

I thought maybe one of Pedro's closest friends, like Luana, would be here, but I don't recognize these three. I don't think they're third-year students like me. Maybe second-years?

I watch as a girl tries to take a container with strawberries away from a guy. She's a little shorter than me. Her complexion is a smooth, cool shade of black, and her long braids are tied loosely at the nape of her neck. The guy is very tall— the tallest person in the room—with swoopy, Poe Dameron hair, and little piercings going up and down his ear, the silver glinting against his light brown skin as he moves.

"Let's stick with the recipe," she says, but even as she blocks the blender with her hands, he still manages to bypass her to add strawberries to the smoothie. She grunts in frustration and the boy does a celebratory dance with brega funk steps, shrugging his shoulders in rhythm as music blasts from a phone on the counter. I'm guessing it's his.

The third club member is another boy who seems more interested in watching the others bicker. He takes a step back and places his elbows on the counter, chin on his hands, looking amused. His straight hair is messy and sticks out on one side of his head like he just rolled out of bed. It seems dyed a jet black shade, which makes his white skin seem very pale. He's giving off huge Timothée Chalamet in *Little Women* vibes. A perfect Laurie.

Dancing Boy manages to elbow his way past the girl one more time and adds a scoop of sugar to the blender, despite her protest. He slaps the lid on and blends the smoothie. When he's finished, he pours himself some of the light pink mixture and takes a sip. The other two wait.

"Misericórdia!" he shouts with a grimace, and the girl laughs at him—a belly laugh that tells me they're close friends—playfully shoving him aside. "Why is this thing turning out so sweet every time? *Blegh!*"

"I told you so!" She launches him a smile that puts a dimple in her cheek. "It's because you're adding too much sugar every time. You never follow recipes."

"Sure, I wasn't supposed to add strawberries, but I followed the instructions Chef texted us exactly. It's the right amount of sugar…" Poor Dancing Boy looks decidedly nauseated, one hand on his stomach. "The kids will probably like it…?" he wonders, sounding doubtful himself.

"They won't," the girl says, frowning at him. "And Chef will never let us serve them anything that's not sweetened perfectly. You know him."

The three of them exchange a glance that tells me they may bicker a lot, but they all agree on that. This Chef of theirs is a perfectionist and I know just who they're talking about. Who else would make fellow students in a cooking club call him *Chef*?

"Is he even coming today?" Dancing Boy asks.

"I sure hope not," I accidentally say out loud, and the three of them turn around, startled.

"You nearly gave me a heart attack!" Dancing Boy says, dramatically clutching his chest.

The other guy perks up, curious, and the girl looks surprised to see me.

I take a step back. The magic in the air that drew me into this kitchen starts to fade. I shouldn't be here. All eyes on me, my skin begins to crawl. If they're friends with Pedro, anytime now, they'll turn hostile.

"I didn't mean to scare you," I stammer, and I'm seriously considering bolting, when the quieter boy gives me a disarming smile.

"Are you here to join us?" he asks. "I'm Victor."

"I'm Cintia," the girl says, a little shy.

Victor comes round the counter with a hand stretched out to shake mine, cutely formal. I hope I don't start blushing.

Too late.

"I'm Paulo Cesar. But you can call me PC," Dancing Boy says, running his fingers through his hair like he's checking it's still swoopy.

I realize with an increasingly giddy feeling that they don't know me. Or they haven't recognized me yet. Regardless, I'm not "Salty" to them. I'm just a potential new club member.

"Hi," I say, still a bit worried to say my name.

"Do you know how much sugar we're actually supposed to add to the smoothie?" PC asks me.

I nearly choke. "You're asking me?"

He looks at the others, confused. "Why not?"

And then it hits me.

This is the *cooking* club. Where people are expected to, you know, cook! How did that slip my mind when I read the flyer? My attention zoned in on Pedro's name and that's all I could think about! And now the three of them look at me expectantly, waiting for my answer, because they don't know I've never made smoothies before!

If I say something wrong, I'm sure they'll tell Pedro, who'll then turn my life into a nightmare. *What true Ramires can't even make a* smoothie?! I can hear the rumors already.

"The smoothies are turning out *way* too sweet," PC explains.

I'm sweating. My mind cycles through one thousand catastrophic scenarios involving the blender.

But then I think of Grandma. I remember a conversation I overheard between her and Mom once when they were making mango and coconut smoothies. Grandma was telling her that you don't always need to add sugar if you're blending ripe fruit.

I look at the fruit on the counter. I'm not sure they're all ripe enough. But here goes nothing.

"Why don't you..." I squint at the blender, and the three of them do, too, like we're all trying to break a tricky code. "...try omitting sugar? Ripe fruit is sweet enough."

I'm surprised at the authority in my voice. *Good!*

"Great point," Victor says.

"Really?" I hope I don't sound as desperate as I feel.

PC quickly dumps the contents of the blender in the sink, rinses it, and brings it back to the counter. "Alright, let's go for a super basic recipe," he says, then adds oranges, a few mint leaves, and a bit of milk to the blender. No sugar. When he turns the blender on, it roars as loudly as my anxiety right now. Once it's finished, he strains the milky orange content into four glasses.

"Bottoms up!" he says and all three of them drink the smoothie at the same time.

My hand shaking, I lift the glass to my lips.

If this is soup, let me see you drink it, Pedro's taunt rings in my ears.

This time, I take a sip. Orange citrus comes rushing over my taste buds like a refreshing wave, naturally sweet.

"This is good!" I say and this time I can't hide the relief in my voice.

"So good!" Cintia agrees, raising her eyebrows.

Victor nods, too busy gulping down his smoothie to say anything. That's a good sign when it comes to food.

I still can't believe that nothing bad happened. Nothing went wrong.

"You're a genius for pointing out that thing about ripe fruit," PC says. "Do you want to try making something more elaborate?"

He's already steering me toward the blender.

My confidence suddenly soars, and I start adding other fruit to the leftover contents in the blender, filling it to the brim with slices of mangoes and strawberries, like I've seen

Grandma do when she was preparing "summer smoothies," a medley of different citrusy flavors that combined so well.

PC, Victor, and Cintia flank me, watching wide-eyed.

"She's like the smoothie whisperer," PC jokes.

I reach for more milk, following my instinct, and fill the blender to the brim to compensate for all the extra fruit I added. Who knew that blending fruit would be this exciting? I watch all the bright, colorful pieces of fruit stacking up in the blender, looking like a beautiful mosaic.

"Sorry I'm late—" a voice begins to say behind us.

I'm so startled, I end up pressing the blend button. *Without* the lid on. The contents of my smoothie masterpiece go splattering all over us.

Victor pounces on the blender to turn it off, but it's too late.

I turn around slowly to find Pedro Molina glaring at me, the front of his pristine uniform covered in chunks of fruit.

He peels a piece of mango off his forehead.

"I want to know who let Larissa Ramires in my kitchen!"

14

"I have an announcement before you leave," Pimentel says the next day.

Déjà vu. But I don't think we're in for another equation challenge. I didn't tell her how much of a disaster the first club meeting was, but I told her I couldn't do it anymore. For the second time in one week—and it's only *Tuesday*—I feel like I disappointed her.

If I'm honest, I've disappointed myself. There was this brief moment when I almost felt like I belonged at the club. It was the first time at school when I felt a little more at ease. But after the smoothie disaster, even if Pedro wasn't there, I'm sure I'd get voted out before I could even add my name to their sign-up sheet.

I glance at Pedro. He still hasn't confronted me about the club, but I'm bracing for the moment he does. He looked like I'd gone there to sabotage him. And now he's probably plotting payback.

He sits two desks away from mine, slouched, staring at the

ceiling fans. Luana taps him on his shoulder and nods toward Pimentel, but he yawns in response before putting on his sunglasses, looking like a knockoff Steve Harrington in *Stranger Things*.

Pedro probably senses my staring, because he suddenly looks at me, lowering his sunglasses to the tip of his nose. Luana follows his gaze, giving me her best death glare.

I avert my eyes.

Pimentel continues, "Before you leave, Principal Oliveira has asked me to remind you that if you still haven't started, you should get to submitting your college applications."

I gasp, turning a few heads nearby.

Ignoring my classmates' looks, I frantically rummage through my planner and come across Mom's round handwriting, reminding me to get my applications wrapped up. She even doodled the face of a bespectacled curly-haired girl with stars for eyes. That's me, I guess. Well, the version of me she envisions, starry-eyed about college.

I get a horrible sinking feeling. I thought I had more time.

Diego raises an anxious hand.

"What if I don't know what major I want to declare?" He asks the question I've been wondering myself.

Pimentel gives him a comforting smile.

"I know it's difficult," she says. "Figuring out your future careers is a daunting task, but I suggest you consider what you love. Maybe you'll find the answer there."

I catch Pedro rolling his eyes, before he hides them again behind his sunglasses.

I wish I could talk to Grandma about this. Only a few days before she had to be hospitalized, we took a walk together.

We slowly made our way uphill toward the feirinha, a set of booths in front of the sixteenth-century white and yellow cathedral, the Atlantic ocean to the left, the water dark blue in the drizzly twilight.

"Have you told Alice that you don't want to study economics?" Grandma asked me out of the blue.

"You should be tested for telepathy," I joked, heading deeper into the market. "No, I haven't told her yet."

The familiar cooking warmth coming from the booths soothed my anxious thoughts, like entering a labyrinth of barbecued, breaded, deep-fried treats. Acarajé bursting with shrimp. Grilled fish covered in lime juice and raw onion rings. Coxinhas loaded with shredded chicken and potato. Pastéis heavy with extra minced meat and olives. Coconut and cheese tapioca. Crepe sticks, too, prepared on demand right before the customers' eyes, the batter cooked like a waffle and filled with chocolate or doce de leite.

"Why not, love?" Grandma asked as we passed Dona Clara's booth, where she was scolding Isabel for letting the cooking oil burn for the hundredth time.

"She took me to visit an accounting firm the other day."

"And?"

I stopped in my tracks. "It was awful."

Grandma smiled to comfort me, taking my arm to gently lead me through the booths. "You should tell her how you felt."

"I can't."

"Tell her you don't want to be an accountant," she insisted.

I was grateful for the pause in conversation when we reached Dona Valeria's misto quente booth, where we or-

dered her famous grilled sandwiches with pan-fried morta-
dela, minced garlic on gooey, melting cheese, the type that
stretches on and on when you bite into it. They're messy, but
you gotta enjoy them. Forget your manners. Throw your
head back, even if you're precariously dangling off the stool
to get all the stretched cheese into your mouth, Matrix style.

I'm an ungraceful foodie, what can I say, but at least I always enjoy every bite as it should be savored. Like Grandma
taught me. But it wasn't long until she gave me a pointed look,
and I knew she wouldn't let our conversation go.

"When I think about going to college to study economics, becoming an accountant, staying all day in a firm like
that," I said, thinking about the stark contrast between that
thought and the flavorful bite of misto quente in my mouth.
"The idea tastes like…nothing. It's so bland."

I took another bite, the gooey cheese warming me up.

"I know you want to make your mother happy, but you
need to be happy, too. And if accounting isn't for you, your
mother will understand. I don't think she knows you're un-
happy."

"I don't know. I don't get Mom sometimes. She says she
wants me to have choices. Because she didn't go to college
herself. But then she tells me to go to college to be an accountant just like Dad wanted to be. She wants me to be the
first Ramires to go to college." I sighed. "That's…a lot of
pressure. And she's not leaving me with any choices at all.
She just wants me to be this *perfect* person."

"You don't want to be *perfect*?"

I looked at Grandma, and we both laughed.

She squeezed my hand, and I felt her wrinkly skin against

mine. She was so cold, even though it was a warm night. So fragile.

"Just talk to her like you talk to me," she repeated. "It will be fine. Your mother loves you. She just wants what's best for you."

I groaned, already dreading that conversation.

"As long as you're with me, I'll be fine," I said, and I meant it with all my heart. It's the only thing I knew for sure. "I'll apply to study econ like Mom wants. And becoming an accountant isn't so bad, is it? I'll do Salt's taxes! How does that sound? I'll take care of you!"

Grandma gave me a look she'd been giving me since she got her cancer diagnosis. Staring at me like she was trying to memorize my features, savoring the moment. It was the same way she was starting to look at everything around her. At Salt. At the market. At our neighborhood.

Like she was going to go away and didn't know whether she'd be able to come back.

"There's something I need to explain to you," she said. The ominous tone in her voice was like a storm approaching in the horizon.

I knew she had been seeing more doctors. The specialist kind. I didn't like the look in her eyes when she got home from those appointments.

"Please, don't think about these things. Just be here with me," I said.

I rested my head on her shoulder, the half-eaten misto quente in my hand.

Grandma nestled her head against mine.

"I'm here with you."

15

FRIDAY, APRIL 29

The beef pastel I picked up at the cafeteria is oily and filled
with more air than meat. After one bite, I put it down. It
tastes like filial tears and parental disappointment.

I bring up Federal University's website on my phone and
skim over the half-filled-out application form. I don't know
how many times I've tried to finish it, only to give up. Sadly,
the box for declaring my major has been blank long enough
for me to know it won't suddenly decide to fill in itself.

I will have to put something down eventually. *Right?*

Pimentel suggested we should think about the things we
love and maybe that will help us decide a major. But what are
the things I love? I look at the pastel in front of me. I'm not
loving the cafeteria's food, that's for sure. Even Isabel's worst
pastel at the feirinha is better than this one.

I *love* good food. Can someone sign me up to just eat?

I turn my phone off.

PC, Cintia, and Victor suddenly plop down in the chairs
in front of me. I look around, waiting for Pedro to finally

confront me about what happened at the cooking club earlier this week, but he's nowhere to be seen. PC unceremoniously reaches for my abandoned snack and takes a bite without asking. He makes a face.

"Now I know why you aren't eating this," he says with his mouth full.

"We come in peace," Cintia says quickly, probably catching the annoyed look on my face.

"We want to know if you're coming back to the club on Monday," PC says.

Last time I saw them, they were frozen to the spot in the kitchen, their uniforms covered in chunks of fruit. I assumed they'd never want to see me again.

"Why?" I ask.

"Because we need you," PC says, and then tilts his head toward his friends. "Well, *they* need you. My family is moving back to Caruaru because of my dad's new job, so I'm taking midterms early and leaving soon. We all know I'm irreplaceable, I know, I *know*, but I kinda need to be replaced, so, can you take my spot at the club or not?"

They're *officially* asking me to join? This doesn't make any sense.

"You know who I am, right?" I ask cautiously.

PC raises an eyebrow at me. "We know. A clumsy smoothie whisperer. And you still haven't apologized, by the way. Do you know how hard it is to remove strawberry stains from white fabric?"

"I'm Larissa Ramires," I say, and I add quickly, "I'm sorry about that whole mess."

"We know who you are," Cintia says with a sheepish smile.

"And you *still* want me back?" I frown. "Aren't you Pedro's friends?"

"No one's showed up until you did," PC explains. "We're a very intimidating club. It's only for the strong, and this school is filled with *cowards*." He hisses the last word at a group of first-year students walking nearby and they all jump. "So, it's not like we can ask anyone else to join. Help me, Larissa Ramires. You're my only hope."

Victor chuckles at the Star Wars reference and PC looks quite proud of himself. I cross my arms over my chest, leaning back in my chair to study them, because this is all too good to be true.

"Does Pedro know you're here?" I ask.

Cintia brushes her braids off her shoulder and leans in, suddenly conspiratorial.

"He said it's okay if you join," she whispers.

"Pedro—what?" My voice comes out high-pitched, and Cintia gestures for me to keep it quiet.

"He said you can join, as long as you stay out of the way, and don't tell anyone he said that, and...what else? Ah, I remember. Act pretty much invisible," PC explains doing magician hands.

I blink. "Pedro *Molina* said that?"

"The one and only." PC smiles, flashing the charming gap between his front teeth.

"Why is he suddenly so okay with it?" I squint at them. "Tell me now if he put you up to something. This is payback for the wedding cake, isn't it?"

The three of them look at each other, confused.

"What wedding cake?" Victor asks, chiming in for the first time.

This has to be a trap. They're being too nice.

"Whatever you're trying to do here, I'm not falling for it!" I say.

I get up and leave before the whole cafeteria turns into some kind of High School Musical flash mob singing a mean song about me.

There's a line of customers waiting to put in their order at Salt.

Mom's on automatic tonight, going back and forth from the ovens, to the baskets of bread, to the cash register. I tried helping her earlier, when I grabbed tongs to fish out bread from the baskets, but she yelled that I was just procrastinating and causing her more trouble at Salt.

So I stay out of the way.

I'm doing homework at the counter, instead, even though Mom complains I'll get coffee and food stains on my textbooks. But studying upstairs in my bedroom is too lonely, especially on a Friday night, when having nowhere to go and zero friends to text somehow hits different than on the other days…

If Grandma were here, she'd be the only friend I need. She'd find a way to convince Mom that I studied enough. She'd order espetinhos from Seu Floriano's booth at the feirinha, who'd always send extras because he had a crush on her. Bell pepper and onion skewers dripping with garlic hot sauce and a little lime. Chicken and steak skewers wrapped in bacon. And a side of farofa so we could dip the skewers and feel the crunch of kasava flour soaking up juices from the meat. We'd then sit on the sidewalk and watch the neighbors coming and going, and we'd eat together, laugh, and wonder about the future of her favorite telenovela characters...

It hurts to think about her. More than anything.

"Saudades, Julinha," I hear Dona Selma say, her old nickname for Grandma, and the sadness in her voice matches the ache in my heart. She has one hand lightly touching the sunflowers under the fubá cake recipe.

She turns around and comes back to join me at the counter, peering over my shoulder to look at my notebook.

"*Ave Maria!* Do you understand all these things? These numbers and symbols?" She shudders playfully, sounding just like Grandma.

"I'm not a fan of geometry, but, yeah," I say.

"It seems difficult."

"It's alright."

Dona Selma suddenly grabs my face with both hands and plants a proud kiss on top of my head that nearly makes me fall off the stool. The gesture is so unexpected, it steals a smile from me I didn't know I had to offer. "No wonder your mother always says you'll be the first Ramires to go to college!"

Mom comes out of the kitchen with a fresh batch of French bread, the delicious aroma filling the bakery.

"Don't praise her too much, Dona Selma," she says. "She's been slacking off lately. She didn't even get to retake a quiz and now her grade will look bad, more like my grades when I was in high school—now guess who didn't get to go to college?"

All the customers waiting in line glance at me, and I feel myself shrink, shrink, shrink with embarrassment until I'm a grain of sand.

"I'm still number one in my class…" I say in a small voice.

Mom puts the tray down a bit too forcefully.

"The Molina boy is number four in your class. I heard Eulalia bragging about it at the feirinha. *Four*, like it's a good thing. But then she said that he's number four, even though he missed school. Imagine if he hadn't." Mom glares at me from behind the counter. "Larissa Catarina Ramires, I've been warning you to take your studies seriously, but you don't listen to me. Now that boy is giving you a run for your money."

Now I'm smaller than a grain of sand. I've reached subatomic levels.

I look over my shoulder with a bitter taste in my mouth, and lo and behold, there's Pedro Molina standing on Sugar's doorstep with Seu Romário.

I know it's not exactly his fault, but I can't help but feel a wave of resentment for the way Mom always scolds me when she thinks he's doing better than me at school. It doesn't matter if other classmates occasionally get higher grades than me. But, God forbid Pedro Molina does, it's like the end of the world to Mom.

I watch him trying to entice uninterested passersby with a tray of bolo de bacia samples, the golden cakes catching the blinking lights behind him. He looks like he's in pain. He presses a hand to the small of his back, trying to stretch, and when he thinks no one's looking, he slouches, resting his back against the wall. But then Seu Romário pokes him in the ribs and Pedro quickly goes back to standing at attention.

Some of my resentment wanes. Just some, though. I guess his family can be strict with him, too.

"Alice, don't be so hard on her," Dona Selma says, patting me on the hand to comfort me. "She's number one. That's a good thing, isn't it, Lari?"

I try to smile, but I feel like a banana peel that's been tossed, slipped on, cursed at, and pushed to the curb.

"She's doing well because I watch her all the time," Mom goes on. "She has no responsibilities other than school, but if I don't tell her to study, she just sits around. So lazy. I don't know who she takes after. Her grandmother was like a working ant. Never stopped. And so was her great-grandmother." She pauses, her nostrils flaring a little. "And so was her father."

Now *that* hurts. Mom's bringing up the whole family to make a point of how useless I am?

"I've offered to help you at Salt," I say.

Mom frowns at me.

"Who's talking about you working at Salt? What can you even do here? You can't bake."

"If you taught me—"

"You're a *student*!" Mom cuts me off. "Your job is to study. I make sure that's your only concern. And you should count yourself lucky, instead of looking so miserable! Do you know how many kids your age don't have the same privilege? Your own father didn't!"

I don't know when I got off the stool.

But in the next moment, I'm already out on the sidewalk, Salt's door slamming shut behind me.

I sit by the side of the church, away from the bustle of people near the feirinha, where kids mill around the popcorn and churros cart. It would be the cherry on top of an already horrible night if anyone caught me crying...

The patio has a low wall, and, below, the houses' lights twinkle like a constellation in this drizzly evening, sloping down, down, down the steep streets until they meet the beach. The view is breathtaking. It used to be Grandma's favorite spot in the neighborhood.

I wish she could be here with me now. Grandma always knew the right thing to say. But now all I have are Mom's angry words that keep replaying in my head. *I don't know who she takes after.*

Well, Mom, neither do I!

Because I'm a Ramires who can't cook. And I wonder what that says about me. There are days, like today, when I feel like that's actually the reason why Mom and I have such a hard time understanding each other. I don't have those experiences in Salt's kitchen with her like she had with Grandma. Experiences that I'm sure Grandma had with Great-grandma, before. All the things that make the bond between us Ramires women stronger.

Now more than ever, I need Mom. And I like to think that she needs me, too, even if she's too proud to admit it.

Another wave of tears runs down my cheeks.

The wind is picking up, sending my hair flying in all directions. It stirs the St. John's strings decorating the side of the church and a few flags get yanked off, spinning up and down, surfing the air current.

I track one with my eyes as it mischievously wraps around a tourist's ankle. He gives his leg a little shake, and the flag gets blown off again. When he looks at me, I realize with a gasp that he's no tourist. It's Pedro.

I quickly wipe my face with my hands and get up to leave, my blood boiling.

"What do you want?" I say, not bothering to hide my anger. "Why are you following me?!"

He looks a little uncertain, and I know he can tell I was crying. I see the way he frowns, at a loss for words, studying the situation to figure out the best way to destroy my spirits even more.

"I heard you have some sort of deal with Pimentel," he says, crossing his arms over his chest. "To help out our classmates if you join my club. Is it true?"

I match his stance.

"What if it is?"

We've been in this staring contest for longer than I'd have liked.

Pedro sighs. "Larissa, I've had a long day, so I really don't want to waste my evening fighting with you. My friends told me you didn't believe them, so I just came by to let you know that as president of the cooking club, you're welcome to join us."

"*What?*"

He shrugs, still awkward, like he's trying to make himself accept his own words. "I'm not going to be the reason someone fails Pimentel's class. So…go ahead and join the club. Just stay out of my way, okay?"

He nods at me and leaves, headed back to Sugar.

"Stay out of *my* way!" I shout at his retreating back.

Goose bumps cover my arms, and I realize it's not only because it's windy. This could be the solution to my problems with Mom. I could actually learn to cook at the club. I could surprise Mom one day and show her I can help her out at Salt, without causing more problems. Learning to cook could be a real bridge between us.

The only issue is Pedro.

I can't let him find out I don't actually know how to cook. But if we stay out of each other's ways, how hard can hiding my secret be?

16

MONDAY, MAY 2

"You're late," Pedro accuses the moment I step into the cafeteria kitchen.

So much for ignoring each other...

The others look up, excited to see me, only for Pedro to yell at them to get back to work.

"What's going on?" I ask Cintia, who looks overwhelmed when she walks by me on her way out of the kitchen carrying cardboard boxes. Victor is on her heels, carrying a tall stack that makes him lose his balance. I straighten the boxes for him just in time, and he beams a smile at me that gives me warm fuzzies.

"We're taking these to the bikes," she says from the cafeteria.

"Bikes?"

Cintia doesn't have time to explain. I'm turning around to go follow everyone out, but PC grabs me by the shoulders. "Can you keep an eye on that pot of brigadeiro?" He nods at the stove behind me, looking absolutely frantic. "Also, wel-come!" he adds brightly on his way out.

I stumble toward the stove in a daze.

"I...can," I reply to the empty kitchen, and I hate how un-certain I sound.

I stare at the bubbling brigadeiro.

The chocolate paste can be eaten hot out of the pan with a spoon. It can be rolled into a truffle and covered in sprin-kles. It can also be used as frosting on cake. But we don't sell it at Salt—that's a Sugar recipe in our neighborhood—so I feel like I shouldn't be near it at all.

I stare at the empty cans of sweetened condensed milk on the counter and I'm already starting to hyperventilate.

I look over my shoulder, expecting Pedro to come back into the kitchen to yell at me. But he's gone to the bikes with the others carrying those boxes. I take deep breaths to calm my thoughts. It's not like I cooked this. PC just asked me to keep an eye on it. That's fine, I guess. I'm not breaking the decades-old pact.

It's just...brigadeiro.

The bubbling increases. "Wooden spoon," I say to my-self, remembering what Mom said that night at Salt. I begin stirring. And then I stop. What if I'm not supposed to stir it? The bubbling intensifies, like the mixture is answering my question.

I go back to stirring, and the brigadeiro quiets, as if ap-peased.

Sweat is already running down my back. How hard can watching brigadeiro be? I think about Mom's scrambled eggs and I remember that yes, it's hard not letting food burn. I pull my phone out of my pocket in a panic and look up tips on how to know that brigadeiro is ready.

"…when it stops sticking to the bottom of the pan," I read.

Oi?

How can something not stick to the bottom of a pan when it's literally condensed milk? Will it float up like a cloud or something? Like *magic*?

The kitchen slowly fills with a strong aroma of chocolate. An elated smile spreads on my lips. *It's working.* I haven't ruined PC's cooking. If I'm extra careful, like following the instructions to solve a mathematical problem, I think I can do this cooking thing.

The pan suddenly hisses at me.

I blink, startled.

I think I spoke too soon.

I try to turn off the stove, but the flame grows instead. It only takes a moment for me to turn the knob the other way to lower the flame, but it's too late. Brigadeiro sticking to the sides of the pan starts turning black and brittle, and no matter how much I scrape at it with the spoon, that beautiful chocolate smell turns burnt.

I look at the door in a panic, praying PC will come back.

My heart matches the music he left playing in the background, and I stir faster, trying to unstick the mixture, or whatever unsticking means, before I burn it all.

I turn the stove off even though I'm not sure this thing is ready or not and reach for a plate to begin transferring the bubbling, spitting brigadeiro before I ruin it for good. But the pot is heavy, and I have a weak grip on the handle with my left hand. My wrist begins to cramp.

My right hand holds the plate, which is getting increasingly hot with the steaming brigadeiro I'm dumping on it.

I leave the pot on the stove and turn around frantically to go place the plate on the counter, which sends some brigadeiro spilling onto my hand. I curse at the sudden pain and I instinctively let go of the plate.

I watch it fall in slow motion and shatter at my feet, sending brigadeiro *everywhere*.

My eyesight blurs with tears. I've made a complete mess!

I turn around to grab a rag, but my hip bumps the pot handle, knocking it sideways, and the remaining brigadeiro spills on the hot burner, bubbling and smoking.

"Oh my God!" I kneel down to wipe the floor with the rag before the others come back, holding back tears. My hand is throbbing and red, but I ignore the pain.

"What happened?" Pedro rushes round the counter.

I didn't realize he'd come back.

"I—I just—" I stammer, pushing myself to my feet, but my injured hand hits against the side of the stove, and I curse again in pain.

"You've burned yourself!" He gestures for me to hurry to the sink. "Go put that hand under cold water."

Where have I heard this before?

"I'm fine," I say.

"No, you're not," he retorts, turning the faucet on himself. "This is my kitchen. I can't have anyone getting injured and not getting first aid."

I bite down on my lower lip, making a point to keep eye contact with him as I place my hand under the stream. The burned spot on my skin stings even more in contact with cold water, but I don't let him see me sweat.

Pedro turns around to inspect all this brigadeiro on the floor, one hand pressed against his forehead like he's getting a migraine. "I step away for one second and you've already made a huge mess."

"Don't start," I say quietly.

"How's your hand?"

My eyebrows shoot up in surprise. *He's concerned?* The skin is still throbbing, but I flex my fingers to show him I'm okay.

"I'll live."

"Then now you can start explaining how the heck my kitchen ended up covered in brigadeiro." His eyes shine furiously.

Nope. I was wrong.

The others walk in, and their jaws drop when they see the mess all over the floor. I blush with humiliation.

"I'm so sorry," I say to them. "I'll clean this up."

"Don't touch *anything* else," Pedro says. "If I didn't know your family, I'd think you can't cook. Are you trying to sabotage my kitchen or something?"

I stop, balling my hands into tight fists.

"Who says I can't cook? It was just an *accident!*"

"You're being too harsh," Victor says, going round the counter to stand next to me. "So what if she burned that pot of brigadeiro? These things happen. Lighten up. This is a club. We're not professionals."

Pedro's face gets so red, I know Victor's struck a nerve.

"So this is just all fun and games?" Pedro barks. "This isn't just a club where anyone can kill time after school. The organizations we work with depend on us and deserve respect. I'm not about to let just anyone join and cook less than perfect food." He scowls at me. "This club means a lot to me. Please, don't drag our families' issues into it, if that's what you were doing. That food you saw in boxes, and the brigadeiro you burnt, we donate to NGOs in the community. A lot of families rely on these meals. So whatever problems you have with me, my family, or Sugar, I'm begging you, Larissa, just don't do anything to ruin the work we do here."

Does he actually believe I'm that *horrible* of a person? I feel tears prickle at the back of my eyes.

"I would do no such thing. But of course you would think the worst of me!"

I whirl around and I flee before he sees me crying.

17

My hand hurts and I'm still shaking with anger, but the sting of Pedro's accusations is much worse. He's always quick to jump to conclusions about me, and usually I don't care what he thinks, but this time he hit where it hurts. I would *never* hurt my community just to get payback.

I turn left at the corner drugstore and begin going uphill, headed home, when I spot Mom and Dona Eulalia shouting at each other in the middle of the street. I halt, my heart in my throat.

"You're vile!" Dona Eulalia shouts, one finger in Mom's face. "That's what you are! *Vile!*"

"Get out of my face," Mom yells back. "You're the only vile thing in this neighborhood."

I'm afraid this could get physical. Despite my trembling legs, I run to Mom's side.

She's so surprised to see me, it's like she forgot I stayed at school this afternoon. She swings an arm around my shoulders and begins steering me back into Salt, practically dragging me away from Dona Eulalia, who keeps yelling behind us.

Mom closes Salt's door in a hurry, and for a second I worry Dona Eulalia will try to force her way in, but after hitting the door once with her open hand, she turns around and marches back into Sugar.

"Is this still about that wedding cake?" I ask, my heart thumping in my chest.

Mom sits at the counter, massaging her temples. Her top bun is coming undone, strands of hair falling at the side of her face.

"Eulalia is just throwing a fit because she heard I met with the client she stole from us. Dona Fernanda, remember? Her daughter was getting married."

I gasp. "You did? Why?"

"To talk about the lies Eulalia spread." I must look as worried as I feel, because Mom makes a face like I'm chastising her. "I had to. You know how those lies tarnished your grandmother's final days."

A lump forms in my throat. "What did she say?"

"Dona Fernanda gave me a chance to explain," Mom says, tying the apron around her waist, one with sunflower patterns she sewed herself, "and not only that, but she brought up that her daughter wants to throw a birthday party next month. They're considering hiring us for it."

"*Really?*"

"It sounds like they will. They had hired Sugar, but I told them we could commission doces, too," Mom says, a tiny bit pleased with herself. "Justice, at last."

I drop my smile.

Pedro and I already argued over those empadinhas Sugar baked when they stole the last gig from us. Now we'll steal their gig and bake *their* recipes?

I don't think we should do this.

Besides, this isn't like Mom. She isn't vengeful. Why fight the Molinas the same way they fight us?

"Dona Fernanda is going to send someone to inspect our kitchen to put her daughter's heart at ease," Mom says, her eyes twinkling for the first time in months, "but I could tell she believed me when I told her it was just Eulalia sabotaging us. Filha, we'll get to cater again! I should start preparing sample platters with brigadeiros and beijinhos immediately!"

Mom rushes into the kitchen, eager to start working, even though Dona Eulalia was calling her names minutes ago. This burst of energy is great, like newfound hope, but I worry about the fallout. Judging by Dona Eulalia's reaction to the news, they won't accept losing the client to us.

I follow Mom into the kitchen.

"Can't we find a different gig? This will make things worse with the Molinas."

"Don't let them scare you. It's time the Molinas have a taste of their own poison. *They* started the rumor. You remember how hurt your grandmother was? I'm not an unfair woman. I'm not out to steal anyone's job, but I must clear your grandmother's reputation. *Salt's* reputation. If the client decides to give me another chance, I won't refuse it."

She's already made up her mind.

It will be Salt's first commitment without Grandma. One more reason why I desperately need to learn to bake. It's not fair Mom has to carry this big responsibility on her shoulders alone.

"I'll help you with anything you need," I offer.

She halts, poking her head out of the pantry to look at me. "How was your review session today? Will it be a weekly thing?"

We haven't discussed our last fight or apologized to each other. We just pushed things under the rug. So I'll tell her I'm attending review sessions, instead of the truth—that I'm learning to bake so I can help her. This way, we won't fight like that again.

"It went fine. And, yes, it will be weekly," I say.

She smiles, and it's the first genuine smile I've seen in so long. I smile back, that painful lump swelling in my throat. Mom goes back to rummaging in the pantry.

Without Grandma to mediate things, lying has become the only bridge between us.

18

TUESDAY, MAY 3

The next day, I sit doing homework at Salt after dinner.

Some customers are at the counter, too, absentmindedly dipping buttered tapioca beijus in their coffee, catching the evening news on the TV perched on the wall. The newscaster drones on about more rain and flooded roads. The wet season is starting early this year, he says, with record-breaking rains setting off mudslides.

Mom catches me looking at the screen.

"Focus on your homework," she says, looking over my shoulder at the lab report I've just finished. She shakes her head. "If you had a computer, it would look so much better, wouldn't it? This is very disorganized. You should staple these notes."

I shrug. "I think it looks fine."

"No. Go get these pages stapled. Your grandmother kept a stapler in the office."

She waits until I get up and drag my feet all the way around the counter and into Grandma's old office.

"Mom?" I call out, looking through the things on the desk. "Where is it?"

"On her desk!" Mom answers from the bakery.

The surface is covered in cookbooks. No stapler here. But I don't want to push it and tell Mom I couldn't find it. She'll just march in here and find it sitting in plain sight with her mom magic. I'll get in even more trouble.

I plop down in the office chair. There's the faintest perfume in the air, like citrus, rose, and...tomatoes. I smile to myself, thinking of how Grandma sometimes smelled like tomato sauce after a long day in the kitchen.

"Have you found it?" Mom shouts from outside, startling me.

"Still looking!"

I open up a drawer in a hurry, and a ton of bills pop out like a jack-in-the-box. When I reach to pick them off the floor, I realize one is a disconnection notice, the electricity company threatening to shut off our power if we don't pay by the end of June.

"The stapler is on the—" Mom begins to say, her voice sounding much closer than before.

I don't have time to hide the bills. Mom walks up to me and calmly gathers everything, then stuffs them back into the drawer.

"Mom, is everything okay? These bills. There's a disconnection notice."

She doesn't look at me. "It's nothing. They're bills."

"Yes, but there are so many."

"Debt is common when you run a bakery."

"I know."

Mom looks at me, her jaw tense. "So there's nothing for you to worry about."

But then I spot it.

The Deals Deals business card. I reach for it, but Mom snatches it up before I'm able to grab it. She stuffs it in her pocket, trying to pretend that it isn't odd at all.

"Why did you keep that?" I ask her. "We're not considering selling Salt, are we?"

"It's just a business card," she says, and it doesn't go unnoticed that she didn't answer my question. Mom grabs the stapler off a filing cabinet and presses it into my hand. "Now stop dillydallying and go finish your homework."

Mom's working so hard to keep Salt's kitchen spotless for Dona Fernanda's inspection and working on cake and doces samples, I wonder if booking the job is more important than it seems.

Why else would she resort to stepping on Sugar's toes to get the gig?

It's not just a matter of clearing Salt's reputation, is it? If this is also our only chance to pay all these bills, Mom would do whatever it takes to save the bakery. What will happen if we can't get the job, though? If we can't cover these bills?

Just a business card, she said.

And I want to believe her, but I can't help but feel like Deals Deals is breathing down our necks, ready to pounce when we're cornered.

19

We gather at the club for an emergency meeting on Thursday.

Pedro was a jerk last time I was here, but no matter how long I glare at him, he'll never apologize for treating me the way he did. Especially now that Mom is trying to win that birthday gig Sugar had already booked.

"Sour starch, Parmesan cheese, water, vegetable oil, milk, eggs… And salt, of course," he reads aloud the ingredients we'll need today. "We're making pão de queijo and packaging fresh fruit this afternoon."

This cheese bread has always been a favorite at Salt, pairing well with hot, chocolatey coffee. Growing up, I used to linger in the kitchen watching Grandma roll the dough into small balls with her hands. Once in the oven, they'd filled the entire bakery with a strong cheesy aroma that attracted customers all the way from Alto da Sé.

It sounds odd to hear Pedro read out the ingredients now. I wonder if he's chosen this recipe to poke at me. Sugar doesn't sell pão de queijo. In our neighborhood, this is a Salt-exclusive recipe. He's good at hiding his true intent, though, reading the recipe like it's any other.

"Why can't we bake these on Monday?" I whisper to Victor.

He leans in to answer. "Someone contacted Pedro last-minute to help with their event this afternoon. So we're sending these to them."

"Enough chitchatting and get to work." Pedro glares at Victor and me, as if PC and Cintia aren't right behind him chatting about the future of Star Wars. "Everyone get to work. I'll be in charge of inventory, because the vegetable supplier is coming by later this afternoon."

He disappears into the pantry.

"Good luck," Victor whispers to me, before he joins Cintia on one end of the counter to start assembling fruit medleys. I launch them a wistful look. Dicing fruit sounds easier than baking pão de queijo...

PC tugs my sleeve to join him at the stove.

"We were in a rush last Monday," he says, placing a big pot in front of me. "But today I'll get to train you personally. Consider that a great honor."

"I'm so sorry about the mess...*again*." I'm still embarrassed about the brigadeiro disaster.

PC makes a hand gesture like it's all in the past. "It happens."

"Will he humiliate me every time it does?" I nod at the pantry.

PC chuckles. "*Yes*. But don't take it personally. He's just trying to make sure we're safe in this kitchen. Principal Oliveira puts a lot of responsibility on him for being the president of the club and a professional baker, you know? That's how we get to work unsupervised by a teacher." He then mouths, "Thank God!"

I hadn't thought of it this way. As much as Pedro irritates me, I have to admit it makes sense that he is extra hard on us to follow safety rules.

"Now, forget Monday. Today is a new day!" PC says, turning on his phone to play music. The first chords of "Anunciação" by Alceu Valença fill the kitchen, a song that Grandma used to sing out loud every time she heard it. The lyrics carry so much hope and promise, they help set the tone to an afternoon of baking.

PC hands me the recipe Pedro left on the counter.

"You'll fit in sooner than you realize. Trust me," he says. "Can you get a bottle of oil? I'm going to fetch the milk cartons in the cafeteria for later."

"Where is the oil?"

PC gives me a playful wink. "In the pantry."

The pantry? But that's where Pedro is.

PC leaves before I'm able to beg him to switch tasks with me.

I take a deep breath. Just ignore Pedro. If he says anything, ignore, ignore, ignore. That's my mantra today.

I gingerly walk into the narrow room in the back of the kitchen filled with canned food, produce, and bags of flour and grains. Pedro is at the very end, a tall silhouette in the semidarkness, illuminated only by the light spilling from the kitchen. He's busy, squinting at the shelves and writing things down on a notebook, so maybe he won't even pay attention to me.

My stomach does a little flip with nerves.

When I reach for the light switch, the hanging fixture doesn't turn on.

"The bulb is dead," he says in a monotone, but the moment he looks up from his notebook and realizes it's me, he quickly turns around, crouching down to start inventory of the bottom shelf.

I try to find the bottle of oil in the shadows, but I don't know where things are. I'm taking too long, accidentally knocking things off the shelf as I search.

"What do you need?" he asks, a little annoyed.

"Vegetable oil."

He begrudgingly points with his pen at a spot over his shoulder.

Great.

I head deeper into the pantry to go fetch the bottle of oil. I'm carefully navigating around him, when Pedro says:

"Your mother is willing to do just about anything to destroy my family's livelihood, isn't she?"

I grit my teeth. "What did you just say about my mother?"

He stands up, leaning back against the shelf to put more distance between us.

"Your mother can't wait to see Sugar go under. And that's after bragging to everyone in the neighborhood that Salt is leading the boycott against Deals Deals to protect family-owned businesses. Can you be more hypocritical?"

I'm shaking. "How *dare* you?"

Pedro's expression, his features shadowed, is stony cold. "I almost didn't believe when I heard a rumor that Dona Alice is baking birthday cakes to show the client, but I remembered you said Salt should consider baking pastries. I thought you were poking at me, but it was a real threat, wasn't it? How foolish am I? After you lectured me about those empadinhas we baked at Sugar?"

But it wasn't a threat. All my family has always done is defend ourselves from their greed and treachery. Sure, I don't agree with Mom's methods this time. But I can't tell him that.

"*Your* family stole the client from us first," I snap back at him.

I hate that my voice trembles.

I hate that I feel like I'm about to cry and that he probably can see it.

I turn around to leave, but I get a second wind, whirling back around.

"For the record, my family does support small family-owned businesses! We're brave to face the wolves! Can you say that about your family? You guys didn't even sign the boycott!"

"We didn't sign your list," Pedro says, his voice still calm and steady, "because it never got to Sugar. But it doesn't mean we aren't boycotting Deals Deals, too."

I'm ready to keep arguing with him, but his words throw me off.

"You are?"

"Of course!"

We stare at each other. An awkward silence stretches on, and I get this weird feeling in my chest. Like why are we even still fighting in this pantry?

"I don't need to explain myself or my family to you," Pedro says, breaking the silence. His eyes look past my shoulder at the bottles of ketchup I knocked over when I was looking for the oil. "And if you're going to work in *my* kitchen, you better start memorizing where things are."

His patronizing tone irks me.

"You know what, I don't believe you're boycotting Deals Deals. You don't look like you're struggling like the rest of us. Your great-grandmother must really have gotten enough money from betraying my great-grandmother all those decades ago. Or maybe you're in cahoots with Deals Deals! Who knows what your family is up to. But it says a lot that you still have a big staff, while our neighbors are closing doors up and down our street!"

His mouth opens like he's still searching for the best words. *"What?!"* is all that comes out.

"My family's business is hurting," I say. *"We* don't get enough customers now. *We* don't have multiple bakers at our disposal. There are bills piling up. And we can't even afford to rent a catering van, while your family was showing yours off on the night my grandmother died! I'll *never* forgive you for that!"

I turn around to storm out of the pantry, but I trip over a bag on the floor, falling over it. It rips open, sending a cloud of wheat flour all over me.

Pedro has a coughing fit with all this powder in the air.

"How is it—" *cough* "—that you're always—" *cough* "—so clumsy?!"

My throat is raw, my eyes are watering, and I cough like my body is trying to expel a lung. I scramble to get up, and the moment the flour settles, I open my eyes. I'm back on my

feet. Pedro is right in front of me. And I realize he's holding my hand.

He looks down at our hands, startled, and immediately
lets go.

I've stared at him for one second too long, and now my
face feels hot like a sunburn.

I scurry out of the pantry, glad that it's dim so he can't see
my red face. My heart is beating so fast with embarrassment.
That sudden physical contact between us was…weird. I keep
waiting for something cosmically bad to happen, like a red
meteor crossing the sky.

"What the heck happened?" PC asks me, noticing all the
flour on my hair. "And where's the oil?"

The music he's playing on his phone was so loud, I guess
he didn't hear Pedro and me arguing in the pantry.

I slap my forehead. "No! I forgot!"

PC launches me a curious look.

"No need to explain," he says, heading into the pantry
himself. He returns with the bottle of oil. "Let's get back to
work."

Still a little dazed, I help PC pour oil into the pot with
water, and then we wait for it to start boiling.

"Newbie, are you listening?" PC asks, and judging by his
tone, he's been trying to get my attention for a while.

"Ah, sorry, what did you say?"

He raises an eyebrow at me. "I asked if you want to be in
charge of stirring?"

"What?"

"Stirring," PC repeats, amused. He cocks his head to look
at me. "Come on. Something happened. You are covered in

flour. Chef was covered in flour when I went to get the oil. I'm dying of curiosity!"

"Nothing happened," I reply, my voice rising a little with nerves. "We just… We argued a little. And, please, I know you're on his side, but can't we just, you know, focus on cooking?"

"Sure," he says, looking like the "keep your secrets" LOTR meme. "Sorry, I'm just giving you a hard time. And he is my friend, but I'm not on his side. I mean I'm on your side, too."

I blink. "You are?"

"I did beg you to join the club on my knees, didn't I?" PC nods at the pot. "Now, do you want to be in charge of stirring or not? I think we can start adding sour starch."

I instinctively take one step back, dread filling my chest. A bag of flour already ripped open and Pedro and I held hands. That's my cooking curse for you.

"I see what you're doing," Cintia says to PC, joining us at the stove. "Stop trying to dump all the work on her."

"Excuse you. I'm *training* her." PC nudges me in the arm. "Add in sour starch."

But I'm still frozen. I only have to stir, but it suddenly looks like rocket science. And on top of that, what if that gets out to the rest of the school, that I need cooking training? What would they start saying about Salt if they heard that I can't bake?!

I need to start acting like a pro, and fast.

"I don't need training," I say quickly. "I can cook. I'm from Salt, remember?"

"I never said—" PC looks confused at the prickly tone in my voice. I hear it, too, and I kick myself mentally for it.

"Okay. If you're annoyed about arguing with Pedro, take a little break. But you're helping with kneading later!"

"That's exactly it." I'm still sounding too defensive. "I need a quick break. I'll help out more later." I look down at the recipe. "N-now you add sour starch."

Victor turns around from the counter where he's packaging one last bowl of fruit, and hands me the bag of sour starch. Still panicky, I hand it to Cintia like it's a hot potato.

PC and Cintia exchange a look before he grabs a bowl and dumps sour starch into it. He then pours the boiling water and oil over the sour starch.

Cintia stirs the mixture in the bowl until it thickens and turns to clumpy dough. When she begins to strain, she starts adding milk. PC reaches over her shoulder and adds a pinch of salt. They make such a great team.

"Have any of you made pão de queijo before?" I ask.

"Just the ready mix type," Victor admits, scooting closer to join us.

"Don't tell Chef that," PC says, looking at Victor with feigned horror. He then nods at me. "And, yes, I have. My grandmother loved these, but she baked them with Minas cheese, instead of Parmesan."

Baked. Past tense. I guess just like me, PC's cooking influence comes from his grandmother. He smiles at me, bittersweet saudade tinging his features a little. And I know exactly how he feels.

"I've worked on similar recipes," Cintia says, "but I prefer cheddar pão de queijo."

PC looks horrified once again.

"Cheddar?!" he shouts. "I do not recognize pão de queijo if it's not Minas or Parmesan cheese."

Pedro comes out of the pantry, and my heart skips a beat. He doesn't make eye contact with me, but his hair looks grayer than normal from all the flour. He just mumbles on his way out of the kitchen that the produce guy is outside and he's going to meet with him.

Maybe he didn't perceive that moment in the pantry as strange as I did. It's like nothing happened. Well, *because* nothing happened. Good.

I try to relax a little.

"I think it's cool enough now," Victor suggests, and Cintia touches the batter. Dough sticks to her fingertips, and she starts kneading it in the bowl.

She must have a lot of experience, because after a while, she knows without checking the recipe that it's time to crack an egg over it. After more kneading, she adds grated Parmesan cheese.

Then Cintia stretches her hands out, and as if talking telepathically, PC knows to pour a film of oil on her hands. It's mesmerizing, watching her rub her hands together, and then she picks up the dough from the bowl and plops it down on the counter.

Victor leans in to whisper to me, "The dough isn't ready. It's too sticky at this stage. That's why she's going to use oil to manipulate it."

"I know," I lie and he smiles at me with a nod.

Using the heel of her hand, Cintia continues folding the batter onto itself. It's magical, watching it fold and unfold, like the carranqueiros at the open market working with clay and turning it into statues.

"It's like art," I say, and realize I've said it out loud when the three of them look up at me. I feel my face getting hot. "Like...sculpting?"

"True!" Victor says with another of his smiles. Why is he so nice to me? I thought they'd all have turned on me the moment they realized I'm Pedro's lifelong enemy. But they're going out of their way to make me feel welcome.

"Your break's over. Now you knead, newbie," PC says all of a sudden, startling me.

"Me?"

"Yeah, you," he insists.

My hands are shaking, but this time I don't step away. "Sure," I say. "Kneading. Very...simple. A common thing in baking."

"Right..." PC glances from the dough in front of us to me. "Go ahead."

I take Cintia's place at the counter, stretching my hands out so PC can grease them with oil, too.

I try to emulate Cintia's work, squeezing the heel of my hands into the dough. I thought it would feel more like Play-Doh, but there's elasticity to the batter, and I keep finding pockets of sour starch hiding inside.

Pedro's voice and what I assume is the supplier's travel into the kitchen. They sound like they're discussing the club's needs for the rest of the month.

"So the principal lets him order whatever he wants?" I ask.

"In general, yes. She gives him a budget and lets him purchase things for the club with his best judgment," Cintia explains. "She has a lot of confidence in him. As long as we don't mess with the cafeteria cooks' work and leave the kitchen clean and well organized, she'll let him stay in charge."

I remember overhearing the principal was planning on writing him a recommendation letter to the Gastronomic Society, probably describing the work Pedro does in the school's kitchen.

"Is he really going to apply to the Gastronomic Society?" I hear myself asking, like a hiccup. They look at me just as surprised. "I mean, I don't really care, I just— I overheard him talking about it with the principal." I try to fix the situation, but it's too late. PC is already giving me the same look he did when I stepped out of the pantry.

"You heard that?" PC says, lowering his voice, despite the warning looks from Cintia for him to stop talking. "What? We can tell her. Did he say it was a secret?"

"I don't think he wants you to share his stuff with her," Cintia whispers back. And adds quickly, "Or anyone else. Nothing personal, Lari."

It's none of my business. But, if I'm honest, I've been curious about everything that went down between him and his grandfather. "I'm not telling anyone," I say.

"She's not telling anyone," PC backs me up. He doesn't wait for Cintia's approval to spill the tea. "Look, I don't know if he'll still apply. Pedro had a huge argument at home in April, when he told his family he wanted to join the Gastronomic Society."

"I don't get it. What's so bad about culinary school?"

"Well, he also wanted to change things at the bakery, and his family didn't like the idea. I mean, his wish to join the GS says a lot about his baking philosophy. The GS is *the* place to experiment and learn about different cuisines. They're big on reinterpreting old dishes. But his family's business wants to stick with tradition, the sort of recipes that get passed down through generations. It would be unheard of for anyone to even think about changing the menu, and that's what Pedro proposed to his family, so…they clashed."

I guess Seu Romário is even more unreasonable than I thought.

Pedro's voice drifts into the kitchen again.

"Don't bring it up with him, please," Cintia begs in a whisper, glancing nervously at the door. "He's a very private person. He only told us because Victor overheard part of an argument between him and his grandfather." She launches Victor a chastising look.

"It wasn't on purpose," Victor says, raising his hands. "Pedro himself told me to go pick up extra bolo de rolo and other stuff for the centro cultural that day."

"He was gone for two weeks after that," Cintia adds, breathing out a heavy sigh.

PC looks worried, tapping a finger on the counter. "We had no idea if he'd ever come back."

"Do you know where he went?" I ask.

PC shakes his head. "No. No one knows."

I'm beginning to understand why the Molinas all seem so raw lately. How Dona Eulalia's public displays of anger are even more over-the-top than usual. The way Seu Romário almost sounded regretful when he gave us his condolences. And Pedro's sudden antics at school.

When I'm done kneading, PC grabs a baking pan and

greases it. Everyone coats their hands with oil again and starts making small balls with the dough. I copy them. It's a *lot* of work—no wonder Mom is always so stressed-out.

When I place one ball next to one Cintia's finished, Victor taps mine lightly with his finger to separate them. "You gotta give them some space to grow," he says.

Something about the way he talks puts butterflies in my chest. I look at him, a little surprised, and he smiles. If only he could be in my class, then school wouldn't have been so difficult all these years...

"Just like with today's youth," PC says, making Cintia groan at the joke. "What? You don't agree?"

When we're done making the pão de queijo balls, PC hands me the tray and I take it to the oven. Mission accomplished!

A hitch sits in my throat. Nothing went flying. Nothing spilled this time. Except for the incident in the pantry, everything went okay. I can't believe I just baked!

"Oh my God, are you about to cry?" PC says, although not in a teasing way. He walks right up to me and passes an arm over my shoulders for a hug. "I always cry when I bake good food, too!"

Just then Pedro steps in. He halts for one second, looking a bit confused at all the hugging.

"Everything good?" he asks, putting a clipboard down on the counter.

"Yes, Chef," they reply in unison.

He glares at me.

"Yes, Chef," I join in, half-hearted.

"Then let's clean the kitchen while the pão de queijo bakes."

We spend the next forty minutes wiping counters and sweeping the floor, until the timer on the stove beeps.

"It's ready," PC announces. "You go, newbie. Get the tray out of the oven."

I stumble a little as I walk to the oven. "Don't forget the mittens!" Cintia warns.

"Right," I say under my breath.

I put the mittens on and open the oven door. Warmth escapes out like a hot breath, and I lean back a little, reaching into the oven to get the tray with freshly baked pão de queijo. The buns have risen nicely, golden brown and fragrant like Parmesan cheese.

I walk slowly, one foot after the other, to place the tray down on the counter. I know I must look ridiculous, but I'm not risking dropping it. This is the very first batch of bread I've ever helped bake.

When I place them on the counter, more stubborn tears fill my eyes as I gaze at the pão de queijo rolls. I try to blink them away before Pedro notices them.

"Aren't they beautiful?" Cintia says, beaming at the tray. When she looks at me to offer a smile, dazzling dimples appear in her cheeks.

"Who made these?" Pedro asks, pointing at the line of bread that's the least consistent in size.

"I did," I say.

He looks up at me, finally making eye contact since the pantry.

And I feel my stomach drop like he's just found out my secret.

"I like Lari's style," Victor says, and I notice how he casually slips between us, like he's trying to defuse the tension in the air. "They don't need to all be the same size. People have different appetites. Sometimes you want just a little pão de queijo. Sometimes you're so hungry you want to go straight for a humongous one."

Relief washes over me.

"That's what I was going for, yes," I lie. "And that's something CIA students do sometimes. You know, Culinary Institute of America." Pedro's still giving me an incredulous look. I don't know if Cintia or PC buy into it, but Victor looks a little amused, watching me with curiosity. Maybe I've stretched the lie too much. But in my panic, I double down. "You didn't know? Aren't you a *baker*?" I challenge Pedro.

Pedro shakes his head. "Whatever."

Victor reaches for one of the pão de queijo rolls I made. Instead of taking a bite out of the poor, crooked thing, he hands it to me. "You should try your creation first," he says.

My hands are trembling a little when I take the roll. It feels hot against my fingers, steam swirling up.

My heart beating faster and faster, I bite into the pão de queijo.

The crust is crunchy and deliciously savory, and the crumb is surprisingly stretchy and cheesy. It tastes like afternoons at Salt. Like Grandma's comforting words. Old flavors I know too well. But, when I take another bite, I taste something new.

This misshapen pão de queijo that I rolled myself, it shows exactly who I am. What I am. A novice baker. The cooking club's newbie with an impish thumb for disaster. But, most importantly, it tastes like kitchen camaraderie.

When I look up, I realize Pedro's picked up one of the pão

de queijo I rolled. He takes one bite, and for the briefest second, I see the tiniest of smiles.

He realizes I'm looking at him and puts the roll down on the counter.

"I'll deliver them on my way home," he says, already packaging the rolls into boxes.

"Are you sure you don't need help?" Cintia asks.

"Yeah. I didn't help you guys with the baking today, so I'll be in charge of delivering these."

"Really?" PC insists.

"No problem. Go home."

The others say their goodbyes and stream out of the kitchen. I go grab my backpack, and I'm on my way out when Pedro stops me.

"I need to talk with you," he says, crossing his arms over his chest.

And just like that, the magic of eating the first pão de queijo I helped bake dissipates like vapor.

20

THURSDAY, MAY 5

We take the bus home together.

It's not like this has never happened, ending up on the same bus, usually when Pedro leaves his bike at home. But we've never sat side by side like this. It's awkward. And wrong.

For the first few minutes, every time someone enters the bus, we duck behind the seat in front of us, making sure no one we know sees us together.

"Couldn't we have talked at school?" I whisper to Pedro, still annoyed that he's making me do this.

"I'm late to make this delivery." The boxes with pão de queijo, fresh fruit, and bottled water are stacked high on his lap. "And we're headed in the same direction, so... I'll be straightforward with you. I'm not happy with you in my kitchen."

I squint at him. "What do you mean?"

"You make a huge mess every time. I don't know how things are at Salt, but at Sugar and at the club, we have high standards."

I roll my eyes.

"You can keep this performance evaluation to yourself."

I stand to go sit somewhere else, but the only seat available is directly in front of him. Darn it. I guess that's as far as I'll be able to go.

"That's not all I had to say—" Pedro tries to lean forward, but he's pinned down by the boxes. "I just wanted to make sure we finished what we started in the pantry."

I whirl around to look at him, my face hot.

"We started *nothing*."

He looks at me from behind the boxes. "You slandered my family," he begins to say, but the man sitting to my left is starting to stare. He's not a neighbor, and he probably doesn't know our families, but Pedro gives me an impatient look like I'm the reason why others are eavesdropping on us.

I begrudgingly return to my old seat next to him.

"And none of those things are true," he continues in an angry whisper. "That catering van you saw isn't even ours. The client sent it to pick up our order. She deducted it from our payment. We'd never use it to offend your family, so I—" He clenches his jaw, like he's summoning patience. He exhales and tries again. "I apologize."

I don't think Pedro's ever apologized to me in my entire life!

"You—what?"

"Even though it may not look like it to you, we feel Deals Deals's impact just as much as everyone else in our neighborhood. Some of our bakers have already left because they got jobs at the supermarket. We're cutting back on expenses. We have one thousand leaks we can't afford to fix now, all because we're following the boycott your family started. And I'm not complaining," he adds, putting his hands up to show he's not trying to fight me with that last comment. "I agree with the boycott. We can't give that supermarket any more business than they already get."

"Why are you telling me this?" I ask.

"So you'll quit trying to steal our clients. Play fair. It's hard enough having to deal with Deals Deals."

So much for getting an apology out of a Molina...

"*Play fair?* You're the ones spreading lies about Salt!"

"How many times do I have to tell you we didn't do that?"

"You did! Who else would have?"

Pedro leans back like he's done with this conversation.

"It's impossible talking with you," he looks away.

"Likewise."

We spend the rest of the trip sulking in angry silence. When we finally get to our stop, I exit quickly and begin to make my way home.

I only make it a few strides before hearing a thud behind me. I look over my shoulder. He's dropped one box, and now he's having a hard time picking it up while balancing the others, one leg extended to push the box closer to him.

I keep on walking. If a neighbor sees us, what will they think? That we're suddenly friends? Friend*ly*?

Another thud. I know another box has gone down without looking. Pedro curses.

I can't help him. I can't. I really—

I turn around with an annoyed grunt, every fiber of my being already regretting this.

Pedro's hair is in his face as he juggles the boxes in his

arms, but I see the surprise in his eyes when I pick one box up, place it on top of the box he's already holding, and I grab the third one to carry myself.

"Where are we headed?" I ask.

He's already looking defensive. "I don't need help."

"You're going to risk damaging the food? I'll take this one. You carry the others." I stare at him. "Where are we going?"

Pedro thinks for a while, studying the situation.

"To the senior center."

I follow him a few paces behind, making sure no one in our neighborhood notices that we're together, going up and down the steep streets, past colorful houses with fruit trees in their gardens, the branches hanging off low walls.

He enters the senior center, where they're putting together a dominoes tournament this afternoon. Elderly members of our community mill about the tables, the ivory-colored tiles clicking when they shuffle them. A big board behind them lists the competitors.

Pedro signals for me to place the box at the gate and leave. But it's too late.

A woman in her late fifties wearing a bright pink dress walks up to him. I think she's Dona Clara's cousin—I've seen her around the feirinha before, helping out Dona Clara when Isabel isn't at the booth.

"I'm so sorry I'm late," Pedro says to her, putting the boxes on a table. "I've brought pão de queijo, fruit, and some bottled water. Do you think they'll like it?"

The woman doesn't answer. She goes straight for a hug. A real hug.

"Filho, how happy I am that you're back! When your mother told me you'd left Olinda, I couldn't believe it! How could you do this to us? You left without saying goodbye!"

"Sorry," he says, sounding like her hug is a bit too tight.

"How have you been? You were missed," she tells him.

"I'm okay," Pedro answers, averting his eyes.

"No. Look at me. How are you?"

"I'll...be okay," he says with a smile that reaches his eyes, and she smiles back, satisfied to get an honest answer out of him.

And I'm *stunned*.

I've never seen Pedro Molina show this much affection to anyone. *Ever.* Not even his family. And the way she looks at him, like Grandma used to look at me, is just—it's like he's a completely different person.

Not the golden boy, above mistakes, like his mother thinks he is.

Not even a Molina.

He's just a boy. A beloved boy who cooks for the senior center in our neighborhood.

"And who's that over there?" the woman asks, squinting at me.

I duck behind the wall before she recognizes me, crawling behind the tables until I'm out on the sidewalk.

I dart through the alleys in between ateliers, dodging tall carrancas, hammocks, and paintings on display outside. I only stop when I find myself at the back of a group of tourists waiting to enter the Sacred Art Museum.

I slip inside and lean against the wall, breathless. My heart is beating so hard I can feel my pulse in my ears. What if she recognized me?

When I finally catch my breath, I turn to leave, just as someone is walking through the doors.

Pedro and I collide painfully.

His sunglasses fly off his shirt collar when he tries to steady himself. Luckily, they land unscathed on the cobblestones. I'm letting out a breath of relief when an oblivious tourist steps right on them.

Hearing the cracking sound the glasses make when they break *hurts*. Pedro and I both flinch.

I crouch down to pick them up. One of the arms is bent and the lenses are cracked. I can't help but feel guilty—if I hadn't run into Pedro, they'd be intact now. He sticks his hands in his pockets, moving next to a big window looking out at the feirinha. Even though he's trying to act like he doesn't care, his expression is strained.

I rush after him, holding the sunglasses out for him. "I'm so, so sorry," I say. "Please, let me pay for them."

"It's fine," he snaps. "Toss them in the trash. I don't care."

Somehow I get the feeling these sunglasses mean something to him. I put them in my bag when he's distracted. Maybe I could try repairing them. It makes me think of the wedding cake I destroyed in front of Sugar. No wonder he doesn't want me around the club.

"Pedro, I know you hate me… And I know we disagree on a lot about our families' businesses. And I *know* I am clumsy, but I promise I won't destroy your kitchen. I'll—" I take a deep breath. "I promise I'll follow your rules."

He glances at me, the late afternoon light bathing the side of his face with a golden hue as the sun sets.

"You will?"

"Yes, Chef," I say, and he makes a face like he thinks I'm teasing. "I mean it. I'm not at the club just because Pimentel asked me to be. I'm serious about it. I don't know if you know this, but I work with an NGO, too. It's called Vozes, and they really need help. After seeing the work the club is doing, I was wondering if the cooking club could get involved with Vozes, too."

I explain Dona Selma's predicament with their kitchen, and to my surprise, Pedro listens to me. No fighting. No bickering. And for the first time in the seventeen years we've known each other, we have a real conversation.

"We'll cook for Vozes," he says.

"Really?"

"Yeah," he smiles. "Why not?"

I'm so happy I could actually hug him.

And that's... Weird.

We both avert our eyes, smothering the moment.

"And just so you know, Dona Yara wasn't wearing her glasses," he says. "She thought she saw you, but I told her she was mistaken."

"She believed you?"

Pedro gives me a knowing look. "Why wouldn't she? What would we be doing together?"

"Ah, right."

Pedro scoots a little to make room for me at the window. From our spot, we notice that city workers are already setting up the big yearly St. John's bonfire in front of the church, although festivities don't start until next month.

"Grandma always looked forward to seeing that bonfire every year," I say.

He looks at me. "Yeah?"

"If she were here, she'd be watching it getting assembled, drinking too much quentão with her friends." I chuckle to hide the pain this memory leaves in my chest. I can almost smell the hot mulled wine just thinking about it, fragrant with oranges, cloves, and cinnamon.

My eyes sting with tears.

Pedro looks like he wants to say something, but one of the bonfire logs collapses, startling me. I instinctively grasp his arm. He looks down at my hand, and I let go, my heart beating wildly in my chest.

"Are you okay?" he asks.

I turn around to hide my flaming-hot face. "Do you want an espetinho?" I ask to change the subject.

"You're asking me out?" he jokes, looking as smug as always.

"*No.* It's just a thank-you for agreeing to help Vozes. And… Well… I feel bad about breaking your sunglasses."

Pedro looks a little disconcerted. "You don't have to."

"Have you tried Seu Floriano's espetinhos? I haven't had one in ages."

Pedro looks like he's going to refuse, but he nods instead. "What the hell. Who says no to Seu Floriano's espetinhos?"

"Wait behind the museum? I'll bring you one. We can't risk being seen together."

"Of course not," he agrees.

I exit the museum and cross the street into the feirinha. But the espetinho vendor isn't at his usual spot. Even the banner is gone.

"Where is Seu Floriano?" I ask Isabel, who's sitting behind Dona Clara's booth, her eyes glued to her phone.

"Gone," she says.

"Gone where?"

Isabel finally looks up, hoops dangling from her earlobes. She glances at Deals Deals in the distance, at the encroaching neon lights.

"*Gone*, amada."

21

I enter the Deals Deals parking lot like I'm stepping onto a cemetery of fallen businesses, all my neighbors' dreams buried under concrete.

"Larissa, wait!" Pedro shouts behind me. "I thought we were meeting behind the museum. Where are you going?!"

"Seu Floriano lost his booth!" I tell him, whirling around. My voice is hoarse with anger. I point at the supermarket. "*They* did that to him!"

Pedro looks from me to the neon lights on Deals Deals's facade. "I didn't know."

I storm off in the direction of the supermarket. I just can't stand around while they poach us one by one!

I step inside, Pedro right behind me.

This place is massive, cameras everywhere, TV screens announcing deals, and singsong voices coming through the speakers. Customers bustle in and out of aisles with full shopping carts, oblivious to the ghosts all around them.

It doesn't take long until we spot Seu Floriano, right where

Isabel told me he'd be. He stands in the back, an apron around his waist, helping at the butcher section with his brother. I thought I could rescue him, as if he'd been taken prisoner or something.

But I can't even summon the courage to say hello. The words are stuck in my chest like sharp rocks.

When he glances at me, I turn around and rush past Pedro. He hurries to keep up with me. "Wait. You're not going to talk with him?"

"He was Grandma's friend! He was her biggest supporter in boycotting Deals Deals and now he's succumbed to them." My heartbeat is pounding in my ears. "I want to help him like Grandma would have done. But I can't. I'm too scared. What am I even doing here? Are we next? Will they bury Salt and Sugar under concrete, too?!"

Pedro looks stunned. "I—when did you start caring about Sugar?"

That's all he has to say? His need to poke at me at every situation shouldn't surprise me, but now is not the time. And I should know better. Why am I saying all this to him? Why am I showing vulnerability to a Molina?

"Forget it," I say, headed for the exit.

I try to find my way out of the supermarket, but instead, I wind up in a section where country music comes through the speakers. I'm stuck behind a big group of customers. "Welcome to Olinda's Feirinha" is written on a banner hanging from the ceiling, two neon lanterns shaped like bonfires flanking the words.

The supermarket opens into a big area designed like a food court, where booths sit side by side to create corridors with strings of paper balloons hung high above the customers' heads, mimicking our neighborhood's feirinha.

They claim to sell comidas típicas—tapioca, acarajé, mungunzá, canjica—at half of the price these same products go for at the real feirinha. And the employees behind the booths wear costumes. The women are in chita dresses with bright patterns, and they dot their faces with fake sun-kissed freckles like they work the land. Some people even wear the typical leather hats of the Sertão region.

My face burns with anger, because this faux feirinha is a mockery of my neighborhood. A garish caricature of our northeastern heritage. Is that why we're getting so few tourists and new clients lately? If it goes on like this, what will the June festivities even look like for the rest of us?

I find myself backed against a wall of baskets filled with baguettes, milk bread, croissants, broas, and broinhas. I watch the stream of bakers going back and forth from the kitchen, bringing out trays covered in sweet cakes, savory cakes, quiches, and breaded and deep-fried party bolinhos.

This is Deals Deals's bakery, I realize.

Some of the bakers go through the crowd passing out samples, which people gobble up happily.

"Will you stop running like this?" Pedro says behind me, sounding a little annoyed. "Just forget this place. Let's go home."

"Why are you still following me?" I snap at him.

"Because you—" He makes an impatient gesture. "It's late, and your mother will worry."

"Like you care."

"*She* cares. Do you want to get grounded? How are you going to help Vozes if you can't stay for the club?"

I let out a sigh. "You...got a point."

After managing to make me stop, it's like Pedro finally notices the supermarket. He looks up, a little startled, at the hundreds of breads and cakes all around him. Some are well-known at Salt and Sugar. Deals Deals is clearly trying to imitate the way we decorate the packages with straw ribbons and dried flowers.

"They're trying to replace us," I say, pointing at the bolo de bacia they're selling in boxes.

Pedro picks up a box with his fingertips, like he doesn't want to fully touch it. "No wonder no one was buying the ones Grandpa baked last week. Look at how cheap the price is."

"Would you like to try our corn cake?" a baker offers us.

I stare at the round samples on her tray.

"No, thank you," Pedro answers.

"I'll have one," I say.

"What are you doing?" he mouths to me.

"I'll prove this can't possibly match the corn cakes we sell at Salt." I wink at Pedro, and he watches me take a bite like I'm holding a ticking bomb instead of cake.

I'm determined to hate this sample.

The cake doesn't have the touch of magic that Grandma's and Mom's fairy hands give the dishes they prepare. It doesn't have the savory tone of Parmesan cheese that they add to my family's recipe. But, if I'm honest, the corn cake at Deals Deals is...good.

And I'm heartbroken.

I wanted their recipes to taste horrible and remind me that there's no way they could compete with Salt. But for the price, the corn cake isn't bad.

The customers purchasing them seem happy. Why wouldn't they be? Many of these families don't get paid enough. These *are* good deals. They'll feed their families well this month.

The screen on the back wall starts cycling through announcements. *Deals Deals's bakery now offers catering services,* it says.

My eyesight goes blurry with tears. "I never thought I'd say this… But… For the first time I don't wish Grandma were here. Seeing that her worst nightmare has come true would break her heart."

Pedro looks conflicted, like he wants to say something, but the words don't come out. And then his eyes suddenly zone in on something past my shoulder. He goes pale.

I turn around to follow his gaze to see Seu Romário Molina across the bakery.

"What's Grandpa doing here?" Pedro launches me a worried look and runs to join his grandfather.

Seu Romário seems so intent on talking with the bakers behind the counter, he hardly notices Pedro approaching him. A baker there offers him a sample, and I see Seu Romário grab a slice of bolo de rolo, which he then hurls across the room.

The whole room of Deals Deals bakers and customers gasps.

"I don't want your bolo de rolo!" Seu Romário bellows, while Pedro holds him back. "I'm not afraid of you leeches! I'm not selling Sugar! Do you hear me? NOT. SELLING. SUGAR!"

Seu Romário looks like a cornered animal lashing out to defend himself. I wonder if Mom feels this cornered, too.

Pedro pulls his grandfather away from the counter, while the startled bakers call for security. And in the confusion, Pedro looks back at me. Just a brief moment. And I feel like this is the closest we'll ever come to understanding each other.

I see it in Pedro's eyes.

We're both up against something that's far bigger than our families' feud.

22

SATURDAY, MAY 7

Saturday morning, I get home from Vozes to find Mom and Dona Eulalia in yet another screaming match in the middle of the street.

A small crowd of neighbors has gathered to watch this time.

"There's no way I'll work with you!" Dona Eulalia shouts at Mom. "I'd rather sell Sugar to Deals Deals than work with a Ramires!"

Her words are so raw, my whole body freezes. *She'd rather sell Sugar than… What?!* I should do something, but I feel as if suspended in midair, my breath stuck in my throat. Even Pedro, who was just then rushing out of Sugar, halts the moment he hears his mother's words. The shock in his eyes matches the way I feel.

I hadn't had a chance to talk with him about what happened at Deals Deals. He kept himself surrounded by people at school yesterday, almost using his friends as a shield so I couldn't approach him. I was hoping he could put the feud aside for one second and help me figure out a way to save our bakeries, but that plan goes up in smoke as our mothers scream at each other.

"So you'd rather be a traitor to your own neighborhood?" Mom yells at Dona Eulalia.

"I'm not a traitor!" she bellows, spit flying out of her mouth. Pedro runs to his mother's side, trying to convince her to go back inside, but she pulls away from him to shove a finger in Mom's face. "How could you do this to my family? You're the traitor! You're a *liar!*"

Pedro looks at me from behind his mother like he's begging me to intervene with my mother, too, and I snap out of my daze to loop my arm with hers.

And just then a car drives by. A big *D* logo on the side.

Mom and Dona Eulalia are so busy yelling at each other, they don't notice the Deals Deals lawyer sticking a camera out of the passenger's window to photograph building facades. I'd recognize his bone-chilling grin anywhere.

Pedro sees him, too, and I know we're thinking the same thing. When Pedro turns back to me, I see fear in his eyes. He has to know we won't survive if our mothers keep fighting like this. While we're distracted by petty fights, Deals Deals watches the flames rise with amusement.

The lawyer nods at me in greeting before rolling his tinted window up. It makes my skin crawl.

"Mom, please!" I shout, tugging on her arm. "Let's go home!"

Mom finally gives in. And Pedro persuades his mother to return to Sugar, too.

Back inside Salt, Mom dashes into the office and I follow.

"What happened?" I ask, still shaking after seeing the lawyer, but Mom ignores me.

She sits at the desk, opens a drawer, and begins pulling bills out, studying them one by one, and circling deadlines with a red marker. I sit down in front of her desk.

"Mom."

She looks up, a hand wrapped tightly around the edge of the disconnection notice we got from the utility company.

"Dona Fernanda came by when you were at Vozes," she says, her voice trembling a little.

"The catering client?!"

"I got the job."

But she doesn't sound as happy as she should. After the fight that just happened outside, I know there's another side to this.

"I'm guessing Dona Eulalia got fired…?" I ask.

"No." Mom takes a deep breath. "Dona Fernanda wants Eulalia and me to work together."

"What?! We can hardly coexist on the same street!"

Mom's hand closes into a fist, crumpling up half of the bill accidentally. "You know, Lari, if I could step away from this commitment now, I would. But what choice do I have?" She stares at the disconnection notice. "I need to cover these bills. And I want to make your transition into college comfortable." Mom tosses the paper aside in an angry outburst that's so unlike her, breathing hard through her nose. She shuts her eyes, like she regrets the gesture. "I'm sorry… I'm sorry…"

I'm at a loss for words. This isn't good. I know we need the money, but this could escalate the feud even more. Now isn't the time for fights, not when Deals Deals is sending cars to photograph our bakeries.

"When Dona Fernanda came to inspect Salt, Eulalia ambushed her," Mom explains, like she's also trying to understand how the heck we got to this point. "She barged into Salt and saw the pastry samples I baked for the client. Someone must have told her." I get a wound-up feeling in my chest, because I wonder if Pedro told his mother how I said Salt should start considering baking cakes, too. "It was a nightmare, filha. Eulalia threw a fit in front of the client, telling her we were baking their recipes to steal their job, like the hypocrite that she is. I brought up the empadinhas they baked when they stole the wedding gig from us, but of course Eulalia put the blame on the client, acting like she wouldn't have done that had the client not requested empadinhas from Sugar..." Mom shakes her head. "I was so embarrassed. Dona Fernanda was mortified, so she thought it would be best to have both of us catering together to avoid any more issues between our bakeries. She'll pay more if we work as party planners and coordinate at the venue, instead of delivering things separately..."

"Party planning?"

Now I'm *really* worried. I know Sugar has dipped their feet in party planning in the past—I saw their flyers a few years ago, promoting their services—but this will be a new experience for Mom.

"I'll learn. Dona Selma used to host many parties and she already promised she will give me pointers," she says, but I must look unconvinced, because her chin trembles a little, her own anxiety starting to show. "Dona Fernanda could have fired both of us on the spot, but she didn't. Instead, she offered me a new opportunity. I'll do everything I can to make it work."

"Mom…" My chest feels so tight.

I should be apologizing—maybe Dona Eulalia wouldn't have totally believed the rumors about the doce samples Mom baked had I not told Pedro we had the right to bake them—but I can't do that without letting her know I clashed with him about the client.

Mom doesn't like the idea of the two of us going to the same school and I hide how bad our arguing gets. I don't want to worry her even more, so she thinks the feud only exists right here. On our street. And that Pedro and I ignore each other at school.

"I *have* to take the job," she repeats. "We need this. I just hope your grandmother and Gabriel can forgive me."

"Mom, there's nothing to forgive. You're fighting for us. Grandma and Dad would have done the same."

Mom presses her thin lips together. She gives me a tiny nod.

"Eulalia will have to swallow her pride," she says. "I don't know how, but she and I will have to make this work for everyone's sake."

She goes back to writing down bill deadlines, and my stomach churns with nerves at Dona Eulalia's words, shouting for everyone to hear that she'd rather sell Sugar than work with Mom.

If she's true to that promise, how are we ever going to keep Salt afloat? It'll be impossible with a new Deals Deals cafe sitting right across the street from us.

There has to be a way to make things smoother between our families.

And just like that, a solution comes to me.

It's an idea that makes me feel like a traitor to my family

for even thinking it, but it is in our best interest—Pedro's and mine—to make sure our mothers can work together. To be buffers between them.

But the thing is, after everything that went down today, could I convince him to work with *me*?

23

When Pedro looks up from cooking, I can already tell he's *this* close to starting a vote to kick me out of the club in retaliation for the mess with the catering client.

"Can I speak with you outside?" I ask him.

I don't wait for his answer before turning around. I head back into the empty cafeteria, pacing around with anxiety. When he finally steps outside of the kitchen, relief explodes in my chest. For a second there I thought he'd just ignore me.

"I'm busy," he says, crossing his arms over his chest.

"I promise it will be quick." I begin by acknowledging the elephant in the room. "We still haven't talked about what happened at Deals Deals. Is Seu Romário okay?"

Pedro's eyebrows shoot up in surprise. "You sure have some nerve. You're asking me if my *grandfather* is okay?"

"I am."

"No, he's not okay," he says, getting angrier and angrier. "If you really wanna know, he's been sick. He's constantly worried about Sugar. And now your mother stole a job from us, so you can imagine how things are going at home."

"My mother didn't—*ugh!*" I take a deep breath to calm myself. "She went to the client to clear Grandma's name, who then decided to give us another chance. Your family will cater, too. We're supposed to work together."

"Alright, I'm done here," Pedro says, turning his back on me.

"I'm not trying to pick a fight with you," I add quickly. "Please, just listen for one second?"

He looks at me, a fierce expression in his eyes. "What do you want? Are you here to apologize for your mother and let me know Salt is butting out? If not, there's nothing I want to hear from you."

My throat goes raw. But I'm not chickening out now.

"I want us to be mediators between our mothers."

"*What?*"

"To ensure they can work together," I explain.

I hate that he's already laughing. But I push forward. "Deals Deals is coming after Salt and Sugar. I wouldn't ask if this weren't urgent, but we have to do something."

My words only make him even more indignant. He squints at me like he can't quite believe this conversation is even happening. "Don't assume you know what goes on at Sugar," he says. "Do me a favor and only speak to me when absolutely necessary at the club this afternoon, alright?"

"Pedro, wait." I put a hand on his shoulder to stop him, and he flinches like I just burned him. "Sorry, I... We *need* this job, too. If we can't pay our bills, I worry... No... I'm... I'm *certain* that Deals Deals will back us into a corner. Correct me if I'm wrong, but if you guys also rely on this job to keep Deals Deals away, shouldn't we... I mean... Shouldn't you and I do our best to make it work?"

"Sugar was just fine until your mother sabotaged us," he says.

"That's not what you said the other day."

He frowns. "You misheard me."

"Why are you acting like nothing is going on?"

"Because *nothing* is going on," he shoots back.

I'm getting tired of this endless ping-pong match between us.

"Nothing is going on?" I cross my arms. "Then why is your grandfather furiously throwing pastries around at Deals Deals? Why is your mother shouting in the middle of the street that she'd rather sell Sugar than work with my mother?" My shoulders slump. I don't know how else to convince him. At least he's still waiting at the door, even if he's not looking at me. "You and I both know this job is important. Our families rely on it. And now the client says she'll pay more if our mothers work together... I... I'll admit I didn't personally agree with Mom's decision to bake pastries, but we were desperate. Pedro, without this job, we're both left at the mercy of Deals Deals. And they're not merciful."

He finally turns to face me, looking me dead in the eye.

"Would you help *me*, if I were the one coming to you with this idea?"

His question hits like a ton of bricks.

"It...would be a hard pill to swallow," I admit, but I add in quickly, "You have every right to be mad at my family. But all I know is that I don't want to lose my home. And I don't care if I'm humiliating myself now. I had to do something."

"I'm not trying to humiliate you." He scratches his head anxiously, leaving his bangs a cloud of messy curls atop his forehead. "I also didn't…you know…agree with my mom's decision to bake empadinhas for the other gig. I wasn't home when it happened. But I also don't blame her for having done that. There aren't a lot of catering opportunities lately, and they pay well, so…"

Never in one million years I thought he'd say this.

"I guess we've been butting heads over our mother's decisions, even though we don't agree with them," I say. "Isn't it time to stop arguing with each other over things *we* didn't do?"

Pedro nods, averting his eyes. "Okay, *if* I agree that we should work together, what are you even suggesting exactly?"

My heart swells with hope. "We could work as a bridge between the bakeries. Help our mothers see reason when things get complicated. They wouldn't, you know, *know* that we're doing that. But behind the scenes there's a lot we could do to mediate."

Pedro is silent for a second, deep in thought. But then he smirks. "Wasn't it you who said the other day that you'd die before asking for my help?"

I laugh humorlessly. "Yes, you're speaking to the ghost of Larissa Ramires."

He looks like he's about to laugh, but then he catches himself. "Can you promise me one thing?" he says.

"What?"

"Just please tell me if you think your mother is about to cave to Deals Deals." I must look confused, because then he says, "And I'll promise you the same. Diplomatic reciprocity, right? I need to know things in advance. I need time to think up plans B, C, D in case everything starts to implode."

I think of the lawyer's business card that Mom kept. Is she holding on to it because she's considering it as an option? I don't think that's the case, but if I tell Pedro about it, what if he tells his mother and grandfather? Knowing the Molinas, they could see it as proof that Mom is considering selling Salt. In a panic, they could try selling Sugar first. Now *that* would be the final nail in Salt's coffin.

Trust neither thin-bottomed frying pans nor Molinas.

No. I can't tell him about the card. I'm not betraying Mom.

"I promise," I say, and despite all my reasoning, the lie leaves a bitter aftertaste in my mouth.

"I know I'll regret this," he says, letting out a heavy sigh, "but, yeah, we can give this plan of yours a try."

"Really?"

"For now, yeah."

He stretches a hand out to me and I grab hold before he can change his mind, my heart beating out of my chest. We both look down at our hands. At the symbol of our truce. For better or for worse—for better, I hope—this is probably the first time since Great-grandma Elisa and Dona Elizabete that a Ramires and a Molina have *willingly* brokered an alliance.

Does Pedro realize the weight of this moment, too?

FRIDAY, MAY 13

I don't know what Pedro said to convince his mother, but the next day, Dona Eulalia asked Mom if they could talk.

Mom was unsure about it, but I suggested they meet at the feirinha—neutral ground—to figure out each other's boundaries (no more recipe stealing!) and their party planning responsibilities over powdered milk–covered açaí bowls.

Thank you, Pedro!

And thank you, açaí, for being so distractingly delicious and setting the tone for their conversation!

It all went fine, or as fine as you get when you're in a decades-old rivalry, because for the rest of the week, they work without any fighting. Mom will bake salgados, and she'll be in charge of finding a good florist and looking up designs for the party's decor. Dona Eulalia will bake a birthday cake and doces, and she'll book a live band and hire more waiters, too.

We're finally starting to make some progress. And not just in the neighborhood. At school, too, there's been a shift in the way people treat me. Well, in the way one person in particular treats me.

Pedro must have told Luana that I joined the cooking club after all, because she's stopped poking at me. She even let me go ahead of her in the cafeteria this week, and when her turn at the cashier came and she couldn't figure out what flavor of geladinho she wanted, she asked for my opinion. Almost like a friend, no?

Gum-flavored, I said.

It's not like we're back to doing each other's makeup like when we were little, but this feels like the beginning of better times.

I just hope that all of this positive progress isn't fleeting.

24

MONDAY, MAY 16

Another Monday at the club arrives.

When I step into the kitchen, the usual music is blasting, although a bit louder than Pedro normally allows. Speaking of Pedro, he's at the stove with PC, boiling spaghetti noodles, although it's more like Pedro is multitasking between checking if the noodles are al dente *and* pouring PC a glass of orange juice like he's his personal waiter.

"Chef, don't be so stingy and pour it to the brim," PC insists, snapping his fingers at Pedro. Does he have a death wish or something?

And, much to my surprise, Pedro sighs impatiently and obliges.

I'm certain I've stepped into the Twilight Zone, where PC gets to boss Pedro around and lives to tell the tale, but then I notice the banner Victor and Cintia unfurl to hang on the wall. Cintia holds it up, while Victor grips the chair she's perched on, and PC yells at them to straighten it and that they could have spent a little more to buy better paper.

The banner reads "Don't go, PC!" and my heart does a little somersault.

I was so distracted all week making sure Mom and Dona Eulalia's meetings went smoothly, I totally forgot today is PC's last day at the club. And that means I didn't bring the farewell gift he requested: a box of Salt's famous pão de queijo.

PC looks over his shoulder, lazily sipping orange juice, and notices me standing petrified at the door.

"Where's my gift?" he asks, a bright smile spreading over his lips.

Pedro looks up, too, seemingly grateful to get PC's attention away from him.

"I suck," I admit.

PC's expression falls. "You forgot?!"

I just nod, hanging my head.

"Wow. My last day, and that's how I'm treated?" PC says, more to himself than to me, but I still feel awful.

"I promise I'll make it up to you!" I say, but PC is still pouting.

"Just be grateful we're already treating you like a king today," Pedro mumbles to PC, and I think that's the first time ever he's come to my rescue on anything at school. I smile, which makes things even more…awkward. Pedro looks away, his ears getting a little red.

"I know how you're going to make up to me," PC says, once again in a good mood.

"Yeah?"

"I was supposed to dice onions, but I hate how the smell of raw onions stays under my fingernails, so you'll do that for me," he says, more like an order than a question.

"So you're just going to pester me and do zero cooking this afternoon?" Pedro asks him.

PC passes an arm over Pedro's shoulder. "Exactly!"

Pedro's shoulders slump and PC tugs and tugs at his sleeve, asking one million times whether Pedro will miss him a lot when he's gone, even if every time Pedro answers the same way. "Not one bit."

Cintia and Victor finish fastening the banner and join me at the counter.

"What are we making today?" I ask them.

"We're preparing a few different dishes," Cintia says, already sounding tired. She's in PC's class and he must have been bossing her around since early this morning. "Would you like to help with the black beans?"

"Sure…" I say.

"It's not like a full feijoada," she adds in quickly, perhaps picking up on my anxiety, and I try my best to keep a straight face like I've totally cooked black beans before and would have had no problem cooking a full feijoada dish…

"Sounds good," I say.

I spot Pedro's chef hat on the counter—a joke gift from PC the other day, which Pedro refused to wear—and I plop it on my head to at least look a bit more like a cook. I don't know if they suspect anything, although Cintia at least talks with me like I'm experienced. Still, I need to be careful. Truce or no truce, I can't let Pedro catch a whiff of my lack of cooking skills. It would be too humiliating.

"It's just a little something we want to serve with rice, in case some of the kids don't like spaghetti. Victor already cut linguiça toscana and I'm going to fry them now. PC was going to dice onions, but I guess you've become his next victim, so maybe you could start dicing them now?"

I frown. "Who's this for?"

Pedro turns to look at me, noticing his hat on my head. A tiny smile tugs at the corner of his mouth. He must think I look ridiculous, but I don't care. "We're cooking for Vozes today," he says. "If you're okay with that, of course."

My heart shoots to my throat.

"Is there a problem?"

"Ah, nope. No problem," I lie.

Although this is exactly what I'd discussed with Pedro when I brought Vozes up earlier this month, it feels too soon. Too...*official.* I've never helped at Vozes as a cook, and all I can think about are ways my cooking curse can ruin everything. I'll need to be *extra* careful this afternoon. I can't let Dona Selma down.

I stare at the cardboard box filled with onions.

When I look up, I catch Victor watching me. He scoots closer.

"I like the hat," he says.

I strike a pose to divert some of my anxiety. "Does it look cute on me?" I joke.

"Yes, it does," he says, dead serious.

And I just—

The way he looks at me—it's like he can see right through my act. How come he doesn't call me out in front of everyone? I don't get it. But instead of becoming more defensive, I realize I actually feel safe around him, like he's my lifeline.

Maybe I'll regret trusting someone I barely know. But I sure need a friend now.

"How dicey should this onion be?" I whisper to him, try-ing to sound casual. I think he can hear me shouting "HELP!" in my mind.

"Just cut them small like this." He holds his fingers just a centimeter apart.

"That's…what I thought. Just confirming."

He gives me a thumbs-up.

And I'm back to staring the onion down. Onions are no-torious for making people cry. But if I cry this afternoon, I hope the reason won't have anything to do with my impish thumb. *Please.*

"You probably should give that knife a try," he says.

"Ah, yes," I grab a big knife and try chopping the onion in half, but the blade gets stuck in the middle.

Victor laughs quietly. "You have the most intense expres-sion I've ever seen of anyone cutting onions," he says. "And that knife is probably blunt."

He grabs another knife and hands it to me with an encour-aging smile. "Thank you," I say.

"Why?"

"Just thank you."

Victor's eyes light up. How can a person be so breathtak-ingly cute?

"Lari, I was wondering if—" he begins to say, but Pedro suddenly sticks his head between us like a giraffe.

"What's with the chitchatting in my kitchen? We got work to do!" Pedro scolds, his face flushed from all the burners going on at the same time. "Where are my diced onions? What is this?" he picks up one of the halves of the onion I struggled to chop. "Who taught you these knife skills?"

I guess the honeymoon phase of our alliance is officially over. If it ever even began.

"There's nothing wrong with my knife skills." I hold my chin up.

"Take it easy," Victor says to him, but despite the nonconfrontational tone, I feel the tension building in the air.

"I'm responsible for everything that goes on in this kitchen," Pedro says matter-of-factly. "The school trusts me to keep you guys safe, correct?"

"Correct," Victor says, sticking his hands in his pockets.

"So I'll call anyone out if it looks like they're about to chop one of their fingers off." His eyes flicker back to me. "If you're dicing onions, tuck your fingers in like this." He balls his hand into a fist. "Peel off the skin. Like that. And then you can cut it in half now. Section these, too. And holding the sections together like this, begin dicing them together."

We stare at each other, like a challenge.

The pressure cooker whistles loudly, startling us both.

"I *know* how to dice onions," I say, coughing to clear the knots in my throat. "This knife was just blunt."

"Then get one that's sharp and hurry up." Pedro turns around to go tend to the stove. When he grabs a dish rag to wipe his fingers off, I notice a scar on the side of his hand. It reminds me of the day he called me out in front of the neighborhood kids for making flower soup. He had just cut himself in Sugar's kitchen.

I wonder if that's why he was being a jerk about my knife skills. If he was actually looking out for me, even if in his own arrogant way.

I don't know if Victor can hear my heart going off the rails, but he leans in and whispers, "Don't let him get to you," before heading over to help Cintia.

I try to focus on chopping onions for the next few minutes, working like Pedro showed me. His instructions were spot on. When I'm done, I bring the diced onions to Cintia and Victor, who start browning them with the sausages.

Pedro smacks a few cloves of garlic with the blade of a knife and tosses them into the pan that Cintia is stirring, and the kitchen fills with a mouth-watering aroma. I start to relax. This smells like home.

"I'm getting hungry," PC says, peering over the frying pan. "Is there anything more delicious than the smell of sizzling onions, garlic, and sausages?"

I smile. When I lift my eyes, I catch a silly grin on Pedro's face, too.

We both immediately drop our gazes.

"The beans are ready," he says, opening the pressure cooker.

Cintia pours the fried sausages, onions, and garlic in with the black beans. Victor hands ground pepper to Pedro, who seasons everything himself. When he's finished, they all take a taste.

"I feel like there's something missing," Cintia says. She glances at me. "What do you think, Lari?"

Put on the spot, my whole body tenses up.

I think about the way Grandma would often sneak me a spatula of something deliciously doughy to lick clean when I was little, and she'd whisper, "What do you think is missing in this recipe?"

In those little, conspiratorial moments, I started thinking more and more about my answer. I began suggesting things like ground pepper, olive oil, a dash of lime. Grandma's eyes twinkled, listening carefully to my suggestions, but I doubt she ever used any of them. I think she just wanted to make me feel included.

I try a spoonful. The black beans are almost sweet with the caramelized onions. The browned garlic, a little crunchy, gives the dish *so* much flavor. But there is definitely something missing...

"Basil," I say. The word comes out like magic. *Thank you, Grandma.*

PC, Victor, and Cintia look at me like they agree we should give it a try. I see the surprise in Pedro's eyes, too. Because he knows I'm right. I'm shocked I was able to think of it before he did, and a sense of pride washes over me. This time, I wasn't pretending to know what I'm doing—it was a real suggestion. I almost feel like an actual cook as I watch the leaves fall into the pot.

Pedro swallows another spoonful and smiles, his eyes catching mine. And I realize that despite the feud and all our bickering, if Pedro and I can find common ground in these moments, bonding over delicious food, our alliance is intact. I don't want to get my hopes up, but for the first time in a while, I feel safe against Deals Deals.

25

When we're done packaging quentinhas, we all head to the
parking lot to make our way to Vozes. Everyone makes a bee-
line for the row of bicycles chained to the side of the building. And I realize there are only four bicycles…and five of us.

"Wait," I whisper to Cintia. "We're not taking the bus or
something?"

"We'll bike."

"But I don't have a bicycle."

"You don't? Guys, Lari will need—"

She's barely announced my predicament when Victor rides
up to me.

"I can give you a ride," he offers, and Pedro's bicycle makes
a horrible screeching sound when he stops next to us.

"Ooh, looks like we got ourselves a Prince Charming,"
PC teases, and I'm blushing so hard I wish I could dig a hole
through the pavement and hide there forever.

"Thank you." I take Victor's hand, who helps keep me
steady as I sit down behind him, the box clutched under my

left arm. "You're lucky it's your last day," I mouth to PC, gesturing like I'd kick him otherwise.

"Make sure you hang on to your box," Victor says to me.

"I promise it's safe."

"I trust you."

His words fill my chest with butterflies. I really can't tell if he's flirting with me, or if he's just a nice person. Regardless, I'm not mad about being so close to a guy as cute and kind as Victor.

"Ooh, there she goes blushing again!" PC announces.

Cintia gives him a stern look. "That's enough."

"What did I do?" He shrugs.

I catch Pedro staring at me, and his scowl scares off the butterflies. "Lead the way," he says to me, making it sound like I'm holding everyone back.

I explain to them what streets we should take to get to Vozes. And, of course, because Pedro has to make my life difficult no matter what, he argues about the fastest way to get there.

"We should go through Avenida Coqueirais instead," he says.

"Why can't you listen to me? I've been going to Vozes my whole life."

Pedro pulls out the map on his phone and shows everyone that Vozes is on the other side of the Avenida Coqueirais tunnel.

"There's a new bike route cutting right through. Why not follow it? It's safe from traffic, if that's what you're worried about."

"Didn't you ask me to lead the way?" I retort.

We continue to argue as rain starts pouring down. PC yells that he's not waiting at this parking lot one second longer and letting the storm ruin his hair.

"Just follow her instructions already," he begs.

And Pedro gives in.

It's true, heading into the Avenida Coqueirais tunnel would have been easier. But that wasn't the problem. The truth is that I can't take that path.

I don't tell them that's where Dad died.

It was a motorcycle accident. I found out about it when I was a kid. I didn't know a lot about Dad then—it has always hurt Mom to talk about him—and I still don't. Just enough to avoid the avenue the same way Mom does. The same way Grandma did. Making a detour here, another there. Avoiding the tunnel. Avoiding the darkness.

The extra blocks we ride to get to Vozes stretch on and on.

There are big puddles along the way, and we weave around rush hour cars. I lower my head to avoid getting my glasses wet, but it's useless. Bright car lights are double their size through my rain-streaked lenses. Now and then I check that the box is safe, keeping a hand on Victor's shoulder for balance.

When we finally get to Vozes, I squint through my wet lenses, guiding us to the side entrance. Victor pulls a pack of tissues out of his bag. "For your glasses," he says, extending one to me.

"Thanks," I say smiling. When I reach to take it, Pedro stomps forcefully in between us, his ears turning a purplish shade.

PC and Cintia exchange a look, and then we all head inside.

No one's around in the dining room. The kids' voices echo from the back of the house, the bustle of excited games, high-pitched laughter, and adults' lower tones coming through now and then to guide the activities.

"The kitchen is closed off, so we should assemble the quentinhas here," I explain, and I've barely finished talking before Pedro already starts unboxing everything. Sure, he's an annoying Molina, but he's proactive like an experienced volunteer. I'll give him that.

"Now look what the rain's washed into Vozes," Dona Selma says behind us.

And my heart skips a beat. In my panic to get through cooking today without any disasters, I totally forgot to tell Dona Selma I'd be coming by this afternoon. She knows nothing about the club—or my truce with Pedro.

He launches me a worried look, noticing Dona Selma's surprise.

I've *royally* messed up! It feels like I'm standing in front of Grandma, waiting to see how she'll receive this alliance with a Molina.

"I think you have some explaining to do," Dona Selma says to me.

I pull her into the broken kitchen, leaving an anxious Pedro behind. The others watch everything with puzzled expressions. I don't even know where to begin. My heart is beating out of my chest. So I start with the obvious:

"Please, don't tell Mom."

She rests her hands on her hips. "That's Romário's grandson."

"It's not what it looks like."

"What does it look like?"

"We're in a club together at school. The cooking club. And Mom doesn't know about it, so, please, don't tell her. It's not like we're friends or anything."

She raises her hands to stop me. "Breathe, love. You're talking too fast."

"Do you think Grandma would hate me? Am I a traitor?"

It feels like Grandma is here, now, hearing my confession. I desperately need her to say I'm not betraying my family.

"She would never hate you or consider you a traitor," Dona Selma says. "And neither would I."

"No?"

"How can you doubt?"

I should feel better, getting Dona Selma's blessing like this, but she's always been so understanding. Would Mom react the same way if she found out? I doubt it.

"Please, *please*, don't tell Mom," I repeat, my hands clasped in front of me.

"It's not up to me. You tell her, alright?" Dona Selma steers me out of the kitchen. "Now let's go see what you kids brought. I'm so curious. Did you help them cook, too?"

Pedro launches me a cautious look when we rejoin them in the dining room, and I try to tell him with my eyes that things are okay. He stretches a hand out to greet Dona Selma, but she gives him a hug, instead.

He blushes, a little taken aback.

"I don't care what your last name is. If you're here to help, I'll treat you like any other volunteer," she says. "Welcome to Vozes."

"I'm glad to be here," he says in a tiny voice, staring at his shoes.

"And who are you?" she asks the others, and PC, Cintia, and Victor introduce themselves.

"They're all members of the cooking club," I explain.

"Lari's friends are always welcome here," Dona Selma says. And I can't help but smile. *Friends.* I've never brought friends to Vozes before.

Coming here without Grandma was so painful at first. But now I'm not as alone anymore.

"I don't know how much Lari has told you about us," she says, "but Vozes started out as a place where music teachers volunteered to teach children how to sing, hence our name. We started a choir, and kids came from all over the metropolitan area in Recife and Olinda to join us. Soon after, we began offering dance lessons, too. Hip-hop, modern dance, ballet, forró, and frevo."

Dona Selma gives us a tour of the house. When we reach the backyard, we find the kids and volunteers are rehearsing a St. John's quadrille, enjoying the break in the rain. Judging by all the commotion, they're still learning the dance steps.

Pedro chuckles next to me.

Never in a million years would I have thought someone as annoying and impatient as Pedro would like children.

"Our house has become a bit of a headquarters for everyone around here," Dona Selma explains. "A second home. Artists from Alto da Sé come by often to teach kids and teens how to paint and sculpt. Physical education teachers help coach teams. And capoeira masters start circles. We have volunteers come by to tutor the older kids who are struggling with their homework. And while the kitchen is under repair, volunteers like your cooking club have been donating meals. Some of these kids have to stay with us all day, so we make sure they go home well-fed."

Pedro nods, looking impressed. "I wish I'd come by much sooner," he says.

"Lari's been with us since she was little," Dona Selma says, passing an arm around my shoulders. "She used to come here every weekend with her grandmother, bringing bread and other delicious salgados from Salt."

Pedro looks at me. For the briefest second, I don't see the usual wariness in his eyes. He just…studies me. My cheeks warm and I turn away.

"I'll get Sugar involved, too," he tells Dona Selma, determined. "We'll donate bolo de rolo and pastries."

Ugh. There he is. Only a Molina would think of volunteer work as a competition. I roll my eyes and head back to the dining room, while Dona Selma continues giving them a tour.

I've finished assembling the plastic tables for the kids when they return. Cintia looks dazzled. "This place is awesome," she says to me. "Thank you for introducing it to the club."

"Good job, newbie," PC says, patting me on the shoulder.

Victor pulls me aside. "Can I talk with you?" he asks in a low voice, and something about the hint of nerves in his tone makes my heart do a backflip.

"S-sure," I say.

"Outside?"

He turns to open the door that leads into the side garden.

"It's raining," Pedro says, startling me. I didn't realize he was right behind me.

"No, it's not," I say.

"It started again." He points at the window.

"It's barely a drizzle."

Pedro looks at a loss for words, but then he grabs a box of quentinhas and hands it to me. "What's so important that you can't discuss later? We're here to volunteer, remember?"

Victor offers me another of his cute smiles. "Another time then."

"Sure." I smile back at Victor, and sneer at Pedro for butting in.

"Get to work," Pedro says, clapping his hands to get us moving.

The volunteers start bringing the kids into the dining room, and I get a wave of excitement and nerves. This is the first time kids will try food I helped prepare! Please, cursed cooking, don't ruin anything today.

When everyone is seated, Pedro explains what we've brought today and we distribute the quentinhas. The kids listen eagerly, but a little girl at a table nearby pushes her meal box away. She seems to be about five, her light brown skin covered in adorable freckles like a constellation over her nose. She lowers her head, but her round, curious eyes dart right and left, looking like she doesn't want to be here.

Pedro notices her, too.

"That's Amandinha," Dona Selma whispers to us, letting out a heavy sigh. "She's struggling a lot. Her mother is unemployed, and Amandinha has to stay longer hours with us now. She's completely shutting everyone out."

"Should I talk with her?" I suggest.

"It doesn't hurt to give it a try," Dona Selma says.

"May I talk with her, too?" Pedro butts in again.

My back immediately tenses up. Judging by the way his grandfather has terrorized kids who play soccer too close to his bakery and the way his mother feels at liberty to criticize me—a *teenager*—so openly, I doubt someone like Pedro Molina will know how to talk to a kid.

Next thing I know, he's kneeling down next to Amandinha. They chat a little, and he opens her box with rice and beans for her, pretending to eat it all by himself like the Cookie Monster. She smiles, and I feel myself smiling, too, but in the end Amandinha doesn't give in. She pushes the box away from her even farther this time.

Pedro walks back to us, scratching his head.

"It didn't work?" Dona Selma says.

"No." He sounds worried. "She said she has a stomachache. I wish I'd brought boldo tea."

"I don't think boldo tea will help," I find myself saying.

I make my way to Amandinha's table. There's a big Snorlax plushie in a toy box nearby, and I pick it up. I crouch down next to her and sit the Snorlax in an empty chair by her side.

"Hi, I'm Lari."

She gives me the side-eye, pulling the Snorlax to herself. "That's mine."

"He's my favorite Pokémon," I say. I point at her quentinha. "You didn't like the food?"

Pedro suddenly takes the seat where the toy had been.

"I have a stomachache." Her voice is muffled, her face buried in the plump Snorlax.

"I have a stomachache, too," I admit. Pedro glances at me

like he doesn't know where I'm going with this, and she looks up from behind the toy. "Where does yours hurt?"

"Here," she says, pointing to her heart.

"Your chest?"

"And here," she points to her stomach.

"Like you have to use the restroom?"

"No." She shakes her head, getting frustrated with me. "I want my mom!"

Pedro looks at me, at a loss for words.

Tears streak her flushed face and she wipes her eyes with the Snorlax. Amandinha's words cut through me. I know the feeling of missing someone so much that my stomach hurts. The hollowness that spreads within me aches and aches, and I know that no amount of boldo tea would help.

Cintia and PC, who were walking right behind her chair, notice Amandinha crying. They crouch down near her, and Cintia offers her a hug. Amandinha rests her head on Cintia's shoulder, while PC rubs Amandinha's arm looking teary-eyed himself. Victor comes by with tissues for Amandinha, before having to leave again to continue distributing quentinhas to the other kids.

"What happened? Why is she crying?" Cintia asks Pedro and me, a wrinkle in between her eyes.

"She wants her mom," Pedro mouths to her.

"She'll come pick you up soon," Cintia says to soothe Amandinha, but the little girl shakes her head.

"I want her now!" Amandinha shouts.

"I wish you could be with your mom now," I tell her. "But I bet she wants you to be happy with your friends here at

Vozes until she can come pick you up." She shakes her head, clamming up again. "I miss my grandma," I admit.

Amandinha looks up. "She can't come pick you up?"

A painful knot forms in my throat. "She can't."

Breathe.

I try to smile, but I think it comes out a little crooked with trying to hold the tears back because Pedro jumps in.

"If you eat and go play with your friends, you'll see that time will go by faster," he says.

"I don't want to eat!" Amandinha snaps. "I'm not hungry! I miss my mom!"

"Amandinha, we understand," Cintia says, and PC nods along.

"I think about my grandma all the time," I admit to Amandinha. "And sometimes I don't want to eat. It's hard to swallow, right, when you feel sad and it hurts inside?" Cintia looks at me, offering me a comforting glance.

I catch PC dabbing at the corner of his eyes with the tissues that were supposed to be for Amandinha. He looks away, standing up abruptly. "Sorry, I think Victor needs help distributing the rest of the quentinhas," he mumbles quickly. "I'll be right back." He steps out of the room, rushing past Victor on his way out.

Cintia and Pedro notice he was getting emotional, too, because they exchange a worried glance.

I swallow the knot in my throat and continue, "But when I do eat, it actually feels like my grandma is with me. She loves cooking."

Amandinha looks down at the rice and beans. "My mom loves cooking, too!" Her voice rises with excitement. "She likes making rice and beans for my cousin and me. But I don't like rice and beans."

"Can I tell you a secret?" I whisper to her. "I didn't like beans growing up either. They looked like bugs to me."

"What?!" Pedro says, like I've just said the most sacrilegious thing.

Something about the genuine surprise in his voice makes her giggle. "What?" Amandinha echoes him, and we all laugh in surprise.

"But one day I decided to give beans a try, and I liked them," I say.

She isn't too convinced.

"Have you ever had boiled peanuts at the beach?" Cintia asks.

"I like boiled peanuts!" she says.

"Beans taste a bit like that!" Cintia says, and Amandinha looks at the quentinha with renewed interest. "Rice and beans will make you strong, too. That's probably why your mom likes it. You don't have to eat it if you don't want to. We brought some delicious spaghetti, too."

"But I think you're in for a treat with these beans," Pedro adds.

"You know, we made them," I say, giving Amandinha a wink. "And I added my Grandma's magic to them."

She widens her eyes in awe. *"Magic?"*

"Did you know some people have fairy hands? It means they make the most delicious food."

"You have *fairy* hands?" She looks at my hands like she's expecting them to sparkle.

I think about the flower soup incident again. I glance at

Pedro's encouraging smile. Doesn't he remember it? Doesn't he remember what a deluge of bullying he started that day?

"Me? No," I explain, my throat a little dry. "But my Mom and Grandma do. And I borrowed some of their magic so I could turn these bugs," I nod at the quentinha, "into delicious beans."

She pulls her meal box closer and happily starts eating.

Pedro gives me a wide smile of relief. But I don't return it.

"I'll go check in on PC," Cintia whispers to me, and after planting a kiss on Amandinha's cheek, she leaves to look for him.

We rejoin Dona Selma. "My, my, that's a miracle," she says. She turns around to help another kid open her quentinha box.

Pedro's looking pleased with himself. Sure, he's good with kids now, but I can't shake off the bad memories from when we were that age.

"Do you remember when we were kids and you bullied me about my flower soup?" I ask him.

"Flower—what?"

"I'd made a flower *soup* and you challenged me to drink it. And everyone at school started questioning my cooking and Salt's products," I angrily whisper at him.

He frowns, making a face like the memory is vague to him. "That was so long ago."

"It doesn't matter how long ago it was. It hurt my feelings," I snap.

I whirl around.

"Larissa—"

I don't wait to hear what he has to say. I gather the empty

quentinhas from around the room, my heart pounding at the bottom of my throat.

PC and Cintia head back into the dining room. The rims of his eyes are a little red, but he's smiling again.

"Everything okay?" I ask him.

"All good," he says. "It's just… That kid made me think of myself when I was her age. I used to miss my grandmother so much. I still do."

I know exactly how he's feeling.

PC looks like he's about to cry, but then shakes his shoulders like he's trying to make sad memories roll off his back like a blanket. He puts on his brightest smile and heads back to work, Cintia by his side. One second later, and he's already making a kid laugh with his jokes.

For the rest of the afternoon, we hand out more quentinhas, assist the other volunteers, and continue chatting with the kids, going from table to table.

I can't help but watch Pedro interacting with them, encouraging Amandinha to make friends, and acting like he wasn't a bully when he was their age. Like he still isn't a bully.

At the end of the day, when I finally come by to grab Amandinha's empty quentinha box, she waves me over.

"Lari," she says with her mouth full, "is Pedro your boyfriend?"

I nearly *die.*

Behind me, Pedro drops an armful of empty quentinha boxes, turning the brightest shade of red I've ever seen. We look at each other, and just the thought of us being together is too—

Heck, no!

I shake my head to rid myself of the mental image.

"Amanda," Dona Selma gives her a stern look.

"W-why do you ask?" I ask her.

"Because in the telenovelas, when people look at each other a lot, that means they're in love," she says matter-of-factly, a rice kernel sticking to her cheek. "You look at Pedro a *lot*. And he looks at you, too!"

Pedro starts coughing uncontrollably.

"I—I was just—" I try to explain myself, but I can't summon an excuse. "Ah, do you want ice cream? Be right back!"

I sprint out of the dining room, fully aware of the confused looks PC, Victor, and Cintia launch at me.

There's an ice cream shop at the corner. Grandma and I used to go there on our way home from Vozes.

Waiting in line, I shut my eyes with embarrassment and regret. I shouldn't have brought up the flower soup. Pedro looked so surprised that I still remember it. And, sure, it feels so small an issue compared to everything else. But it's not a small issue to me.

If he'd apologized then, or maybe if he'd told his friends to stop calling me Salty, would everything have been different? For the first time, I realize how tired I am of always fighting with him.

When I'm back at Vozes, Pedro approaches me.

"The club can't reimburse you for that," he tells me in a low voice, nodding to the ice cream.

"It's a gift."

He looks like he wants to say something else, but I dash past him to offer gum-flavored ice cream to Amandinha and the other kids.

"This one is my favorite, because it turns your tongue blue," I tell her, and she sticks her tongue out and goes cross-eyed trying to see if it's blue already.

"Thank you." She gives me a hug and skips away.

Dona Selma comes up to me in the garden.

"Amandinha hasn't opened up like this in so long, and she's actually playing with the other kids! Together, your cooking club did an incredible job. Cintia is so caring, her smile brightening our room on this gloomy day. Victor is a quiet boy, but so observant, always anticipating the kids' needs. PC is such a sweetheart. And, if I may add, you and Pedro look good standing together in my dining room," she says to me, and I must look defensive, because she adds, "There are things in this world that *are* bigger than your families' fights, Lari."

She echoes something I've started to notice myself. But how can I come to terms with all the resentment I still feel for him?

Pedro and the others join us outside. PC's eyes are glistening again. "I hate goodbyes," he says, his voice a little garbled.

Cintia wraps her arms around him. "Group hug!" she shouts.

I notice Pedro shyly joins us, looking away to hide the tears glinting in the corners of his eyes.

"Are you crying, Chef?" PC says, excited. "Don't cry! You'll make me cry!"

"I'm not crying!" Pedro dodges him, running down the garden, past the hibiscus bushes, with PC on his heels.

Amandinha runs toward us when she notices we're leaving. She glances at me and then tugs on Pedro's sleeve. When he bends down, she whispers something in his ear and dashes back inside Vozes.

"What was that?" PC asks.

"Nothing," Pedro says, averting his eyes when I look at him. "Just Amandinha being Amandinha."

PC sighs. "I'll miss the club too much."

I'm ready to sit behind Victor's bicycle again, when Cintia says, "Since it's late, we should probably head home. PC, Victor, and I live north of here."

"I still can give you a ride home," Victor says to me. "So we could talk."

I feel my cheeks getting hot again. In all the chaos of the evening, I forgot about that.

Pedro's bicycle makes that horrible screeching sound again when he breaks.

"You'd be going the opposite direction," PC says with a tiny, mischievous smile. He glances from Pedro to me. "Don't you two live across the street from each other?"

I see what he's trying to do. "I'll take the bus," I say quickly.

"Do you… Would you…like a ride?" Pedro asks me, although he's not making eye contact. His offer is so surprising. I wait for a dramatic clap of thunder and lightning above my head, but there are just cars honking outside in the rain.

"You don't have to," I say.

"I mean we're headed the same direction…" His voice trails off.

"Great!" Cintia says. "See you two at school. Ride safe!"

Victor looks a little disappointed, but he doesn't insist on giving me a ride himself. Part of me wishes he did, but I don't want him to go so out of his way just to talk with me.

"Can I have your number?" he asks, suddenly shy. "I'll text you later, if that's okay."

"Sure." I can't suppress my smile as I type the digits into his phone.

Pedro clears his throat, looking off to the side.

"You can't replace me, newbie," PC says to me, reaching for another hug. When I look at him, he grabs my face between his hands, squeezing my cheeks until I probably look like a puffer fish. "*But* you're the Smoothie Whisperer, and a natural talent like yours is a sign of great things ahead. Don't ever let anyone doubt that…and don't *you* doubt yourself." He releases my face, giving my cheek a loud goodbye kiss. "Let's stay in touch, okay? Next year, when I'm more settled, you better come celebrate the June festivities with me in Caruaru." He looks at the others. "All of you."

"I will." I get choked up. I didn't think I'd get so attached to him in such a short amount of time. "Safe travels, PC."

He looks at Vozes one last time, and waves goodbye to us.

"Alright. I'm outta here! Try not to cry too much when I'm gone!"

He rides off with Cintia and Victor, leaving Pedro and me alone in front of Vozes.

"That rascal…" Pedro says under his breath, brushing an eye with the back of his hand. When he notices I'm looking, he straightens his back. "I wasn't crying or anything."

"I should go," I say, turning around to open the side gate.

"You don't want a ride?" he asks, his words coming out quickly. If I didn't know him, I'd think he's anxious. "It's no big deal," he adds, suddenly nonchalant.

No big deal?

The rain is now falling harder, and Pedro's hair mats on

his forehead. He impatiently brushes his bangs off his eyes over and over.

I let out a shaky breath and hop on behind him.

26

MONDAY, MAY 16

How can someone so annoying smell so good?

The wind stirs Pedro's hair and balloons his shirt. I guess after years of preparing buttercream, melting chocolate with delicate precision, and kneading sweet rolls with his bare hands, the scents have remained on him like a second skin. He smells like Sugar's early mornings, when they fill their ovens with the first batches of bolo de rolo and coconut buns.

The rain pours down harder, and I'm soaked down to my bones. The road is flooding, hiding potholes and bumps, and even though I cling to the metal seat of Pedro's bicycle, every time he swerves through traffic, I'm this close to slipping.

He suddenly veers off to avoid riding into a massive puddle, and I wrap my arms around his waist with a panicked gasp.

I feel him tense beneath my arms. "I can't breathe if you're squeezing me like this," he says.

My face is burning up. I never thought I'd ever be this... *cozy* with Pedro Molina. "You almost sent me flying back there!"

He winces. "Can you not *yell* in my ear?"

I place my hands lightly on his shoulders. I've barely touched him, and Pedro's already twitching like that annoys him, too. So I let go, my fingers precariously wrapping around the metal seat again.

Pedro keeps on riding, this time more carefully.

He taps his shoulder. "It's okay to hold on to me. If you fall off, I don't want you going around saying I did it on purpose!"

I let out a tired breath, my hands going back to his shoulders. Accepting this ride was probably a mistake.

We travel past school, in and out of the streetlights along the way, and when the twinkling lights at the feirinha appear in the distance like the first stars in the night sky, Pedro stops. We both know we can't risk being seen together.

I hop off, darting for the protection of the drugstore's awning. But instead of riding straight home, Pedro leaves the bicycle resting against the sidewalk and comes to join me, the thick raindrops pelting the metal above us.

"Do you have a minute?" he asks.

We both glance uphill toward the bakeries. "What did I do wrong now?" I say, crossing my arms.

"You don't need to be so defensive." He looks like he just tasted something sour. "You're probably wondering why I offered to give you a ride home."

"Not out of the goodness of your heart, I guess?" I poke at him and Pedro shoots me an annoyed glance like he's regretting having stopped to talk with me.

"I just wanted to say that I had some time to really think about our alliance—"

"You already accepted it, didn't you?"

He raises his hands for me to calm down. "Relax. I haven't changed my mind. I just wanted to make sure that after working together at Vozes today, *you* haven't changed your mind. I know it was your idea, but are you still serious about this truce between us?"

"Of course!" I stare at him. "Why are you bringing this up now?"

"Well, I'm just worried that if our past issues still bother you a lot, then how can we help our mothers get along? I guess what I'm saying is… Well… I'm sorry."

I blink. His apology catches me entirely off guard.

"I'm sorry about that flower soup thing when we were kids," he continues, and I search and search for any hidden meaning, any malice in his words, but Pedro seems…disarmed. "You may not believe me, but I hate how we ganged up on you back then. It wasn't fair."

"You set all our classmates against me!" My voice shakes with pent-up resentment. "It's not fair that I had to deal with all of you on my own!"

"I'm sorry."

"You brought our families' feud to school and ten years later people still don't like me. They still call me Salty!"

Pedro Molina doesn't fight back. He doesn't try to deflect or deny my accusations. He just stands there looking at me, his clothes drenched with rain, droplets falling from the tips of his bangs, listening to every word I throw at him.

"I'm sorry," he says again. "You don't need to forgive me. I don't deserve it. And if you realized that it's too difficult for us to work together, I'll understand. As president of the cooking club, I'll tell Pimentel that you were involved enough.

Or maybe I'll tell her we're pausing activities or something. Whatever keeps everyone's grade safe, you know? And as for the truce, if you changed your mind about it, I'll still try my best to steer my mother in the right direction if any problem arises between her and Dona Alice. I give you my word." He looks embarrassed for a second, scratching the back of his head. "I mean…if the word of a Molina means anything to a Ramires."

I'm speechless.

I've never seen this side of him. This Pedro who gives heartfelt apologies and listens to me without trying to evade his responsibility in our fights.

Trust neither thin-bottomed frying pans nor Molinas.

Part of me feels guarded. Cautious. Scared of falling into a trap.

But part of me also wants to believe him. And if I'm being completely honest, that part is a lot stronger. Working with him at the club and at Vozes showed me a side of him I didn't know. A side that probably was always there, hidden behind our families' generational rivalry, only I couldn't see it. The truth is Pedro is a dependable guy—talented, too, I'll admit it—and he cares about our community and loves food just as much as I do.

"That means a lot," I say.

A tiny smile spreads on his lips. He actually looks relieved. "Even though we're enemies?"

"*Because* we're enemies."

And I realize how relieved I feel after finally hearing his apology, too.

"So…?" He kicks a pebble on the sidewalk, sending it

back onto the cobblestone street. "We'll go on working together or…?"

"Yes," I confirm. "At the club. And with our truce."

Pedro lets his smile widen. "I'm glad," he says. "Because I didn't want to break my promise to Amandinha."

"What promise?"

"She asked me to come back. Together, you know?" Pedro looks off to the side, a little embarrassed. That's a first. "All of us," he explains quickly, "Not just, you know, you and me. Cintia, Victor, and PC, if he weren't leaving for Caruaru. And I said we will. Don't make me break my promise to her."

Together.

My heart does a weird somersault, and I pounce on it, smothering it down. *Hush. Why are you beating so fast like this?*

We're silent for a while and the air around feels electrified. Staticky. I don't dare move. Or breathe. Does he notice it, too?

Maybe a thunderstorm is coming.

"I think you and I can learn to put our issues aside for now," I reiterate, feeling a little light-headed. Why does this moment feel so much like a dream?

"You know, it's actually a good thing, not just for Amandinha, if we do," Pedro says with a smirk. He steps back into the rain and swings a leg over his bicycle. "I think it's in the neighborhood's best interest that a Ramires works alongside a Molina. Maybe some of my talent will rub off on you and your bakery will actually learn to make something that tastes good."

He rides off.

"Don't flatter yourself!" I shout at his back.

27

FRIDAY, MAY 20

I'm half listening to Pimentel's lecture on Friday, when my phone buzzes with a text. I sneak a peek at the screen.

VICTOR: I didn't get a chance to ask you in person, but would you like to go to the party with me tonight? :)

My hands immediately start tingling with nerves, my fingers turning into icicles.

Victor is asking me out?!

No one has ever asked me out. I should say yes. Victor is cute and nice and he makes me smile. But my fingers only hover over the screen. I can't make myself type an answer just yet.

Every year around this time, our school puts together a big party to gather funds for the graduating class's ceremony. The theme is usually St. John's Day, but I've seen heart-shaped flyers getting passed around all week, so I'm guessing this year's theme will be St. Anthony's—Brazil's Valentine's Day equivalent. Somehow it makes a date with Victor feel like it's an even bigger deal.

I look up from the screen and catch Pedro on his phone, too, texting under his desk. And I can't look away. For a brief, strange second, I imagine a different scenario. Like Pedro was the one who texted me, instead of Victor.

I nearly fall off my chair.

WHAT IS WRONG WITH ME?!!!!

I curse under my breath, typing a quick answer back to Victor:

LARI: Sure! :)

Pimentel goes on and on in the background about trigonometric functions, but who cares about sine, cosine, and tangent when I can't calculate how in the world my mind betrayed me with a thought about going on a date with Pedro Molina?!

I rest my forehead on my desk to cool it off.

VICTOR: Awesome. Meet me at the school gate tonight at 6pm?

Pedro's desk is already littered with cards, his admirers practically hanging off his neck to convince him to go to the party with them. And I can't help but wonder if he's asked anyone to go with him.

Maybe, that's what he's doing right now...

Like I care!

I straighten my back and give my head a shake to avoid any more unwanted thoughts and continue texting Victor:

LARI: Sounds good.

The bell rings, marking the end of the day.

Pedro gets on his feet to leave, and there's a tiny nod of acknowledgment from him when our eyes meet, before he joins the stream of students headed out of the classroom.

And I nod back, my heart beating out of my chest.

I must have gone through every single piece of clothing I own before I collapse in defeat on a pile of discarded options.

Mom pokes her head in, immediately making a face at the mess in my bedroom.

"I'll organize everything before I leave," I say, breathless.

I'm still surprised that Mom didn't object to this party, so I don't want to push her buttons in case she changes her mind.

I didn't tell her this is actually a date. I don't know how I feel about it myself, and I definitely don't want to answer a thousand questions about Victor. But when I told her about the party, she encouraged me to go, saying it's my last year before college, so it would be good for me to go out.

The thing is…in what world would Mom think that going to a party is a good thing? True, it's Friday night, but every night is study night at the Ramires household.

I begin shoving clothes back inside my wardrobe in a hurry, but Mom stops me. She picks up a dress and holds it at arm's length to take a good look at it. The fabric cascades down in front of her.

"Why don't you wear this one?" she suggests.

It was Mom's gift to me last New Year's Eve, so we could celebrate the coming year in traditional white to attract peace.

I don't know if my New Year's magic is working at all, but if this truce with Pedro Molina is any indication, maybe it's starting to take effect?

Just thinking about him makes my pulse quicken.

When I glance over my shoulder at his window, I see that the lights in his bedroom are off. He must be at the party already.

"I think you should wear it," Mom insists.

I'm not a fan of wearing dresses, but I want to make her smile. She's barely smiled at all lately.

The dress shows a bit of cleavage, but not too much. It's also a tiny bit too tight around my waist but fans out perfectly, pleated down to my knees.

One look and Mom is unsatisfied, though. She steers me into her bedroom, where she uncovers her sewing machine, gesturing for me to take the dress off so she can fix it. Mom sews so little these days, I forgot how good at it she is. The machine rattles happily, as if recognizing she's back.

While I wait, I sit down on Mom's bed. There's a photo of Dad on her nightstand.

He was tall and handsome, very skinny, the type with bony legs and arms that didn't quite fill his clothes, looking a bit nerdy with those big, heavy-framed glasses. I smile, feeling a sudden twinge in my heart. How is it possible to miss someone I never met?

When she's done, Mom gets up from her sewing machine and hands me the dress.

"Try it on," she says.

Mom's adjustments were spot on. She not only has fairy hands for cooking, but she also has them for sewing. When I was younger, I remember finding old sketchbooks where she drew dresses and shirt patterns. A few times, she'd design and sew some of my outfits herself.

She's still not totally satisfied yet with the full result, though.

After wrangling my tennis shoes away from me, she makes me wear her golden brown strappy sandals. She also offers to do my hair, and normally I wouldn't bother with anything too complicated, but we spend so little time together, I gladly accept. She hasn't done this since I was little.

Mom braids my hair down my back, the plait wide in the middle, thinning as it goes down, interspersed with yellow flower clips.

When she's done dressing me, a measuring tape dangling around her neck like a scarf and her hands on my shoulders, we both stand in front of her wardrobe mirror to inspect my appearance. Suddenly, it doesn't matter how irritated I was when she first purchased it without asking for my opinion. Or that Mom's fancy sandals are chafing against my ankles. Or that my collarbone feels too exposed.

Because Mom looks proud. One hand on her heart, she sighs. "You look beautiful, filha."

I take one good look at myself in the mirror. There are stray curls escaping from my braid, catching the light of the lampshade next to me, looking almost auburn. This dress hugs and accentuates curves I didn't think worked for me. Even my glasses match my sandals. Mom sure has an eye for fashion, noticing the tiniest details.

For the first time, I *feel* beautiful.

Warmth creeps up my neck, and I see myself blush, but the red flush in my face seems less embarrassed…and more playful. Happy. I smile, and Mom does, too. It catches me off guard, seeing the higher tilt in the right corner of her mouth when she lets herself grin. The way mine occurs at the same time, like our smiles mimic each other.

People say I look like my father.

But, standing side by side with Mom, the mirror doesn't lie. I look like *her*, too.

The moment I arrive at school, my heart starts racing.

Standing by the front gate, I recognize other students and some of my classmates headed up the street, arms linked, already swaying to forró pé de serra songs traveling from the gym, the sound of accordions, zabumba, and triangle filling the air with excitement. The school's been transformed for the party. There's even a tall bonfire, the flames dancing in the breeze, creating a light haze of smoke all around. Delicious smells travel to me, like a symphony of barbecued flavors.

I hear someone talking behind me, and for a second, I think it's Pedro. But it's just some guy waving at a friend. I take a deep breath, still feeling a little uneasy.

Why am I doing this again?

I feel unsteady on Mom's sandals. The heel isn't even that high, but I wish they were flat. The strap around my ankle is starting to leave a blister, and now I'm really tempted to leave, but I spot Victor running up to me through the barbecue smoke, and the whole thing looks like a scene in a telenovela. The romantic lead coming to the rescue.

He's in a white shirt and black jeans, a red flannel jacket wrapped around his waist, and Converse on his feet. It's so strange seeing him in something other than our school uniform that I almost don't recognize him. A piercing glints in his eyebrow.

"You look *beautiful*," he says a little out of breath when he reaches me, taking a timid step closer.

"You look very handsome yourself," I say with a smile.

And then we're silent.

He looks at me like he's waiting for me to say something. But when I try to break the ice, he starts talking at the same time. We both chuckle. I don't think this can get more awkward. Maybe I'm not meant to go on dates after all...

"Go ahead," I encourage him to speak first.

"I was just saying I'm sorry I left you waiting. They needed me to help out at the grill last-minute, but my friend will sub for me now," he says. "I'll make sure you get a full supply of espetinhos tonight."

"That's alright."

"I actually was so nervous to ask you out." He takes a step closer. "I couldn't believe it when you said yes."

I don't know what to say.

Victor then stretches his hand out to me.

I stare blankly. And the realization that I am on a date hits me full force.

I think he can sense my hesitation. I don't want to hurt his feelings, but I'm so confused. I like Victor. Well, I want to like Victor. He's a good guy. This isn't a bad thing...going on a date with him.

What would Pedro think if he saw us holding hands?

I take Victor's hand in a hurry, running from my thoughts.

I can hardly hear a word Victor is saying while he guides me through the party, showing me the food booths and games his classmates have put together.

There's a lot going on at once, like stepping onto carnival grounds. Students set off fireworks. People dance around the bonfire. Lines stretch in front of the booths. It's dizzying.

I look up at the colorful flags hanging from strings above us and the banner "Arraial dos Estudantes" comes undone right as I walk under it. When the students closest to us scramble out of the way, one of them bumps into me and I get jostled back, ramming into someone else behind me. Wearing these heels, I can't keep my balance, but Victor keeps me steady with an arm around my waist.

Warmth rushes to my cheeks at our close proximity.

"You alright?" he asks me.

I'm about to mumble an apology when I hear a cough behind me. I turn around, and Pedro is right there.

Another wave of warmth flushes in my face, this one much stronger than when Victor pulled me away from the banner. I realize he was the person I bumped into. The candy apple Pedro was holding had fallen to the ground. The sparkly red bow that was fastened to the stick is the only thing he could salvage, which he holds pitifully.

"Oh no!" Luana says, mourning the loss.

I was so caught up in the moment that I didn't notice her. And judging by her hand on his arm, they've come together. She's in a beautiful short white dress and knee-high black boots. But, unlike me, she *knows* how to wear a dress and nice shoes.

I feel my smile disappear.

Pedro glares at me, looking even more dramatic in his all-black outfit. He's even wearing a jacket, despite the warm weather, all for the sake of trying to look cool. The worst part is that he does. And I hate it.

"I'm so sorry," I say about the candy apple, and I clumsily start rummaging through my purse to get my eyes off him, looking for money to pay for the damage.

Talita, who's in line for a food booth nearby, bursts out laughing. "Your sandal! You broke your sandal!" I look down. The strap must have broken when I ran into Pedro. It's humiliating, seeing it hanging off my ankle. And now they notice it, too. "Was it your first time on heels?" She's laughing so much she's out of breath. "That spin you did to catch yourself was literally the funniest thing I've ever seen! Salty, you're comedy gold!"

Hearing the old nickname makes me cringe.

"Leave her alone!" Victor snaps at my classmates. The anger in his voice is so uncharacteristic, I notice the surprised look Pedro gives him, too, his eyes tracing Victor's arm still around me.

I don't know why, but I scoot away from Victor, hobbling because of my shoe. I'm caught in a hurricane of thoughts, as if I owe Pedro an explanation why I'm with him.

Despite Victor's attempt, some of my classmates join Talita in laughing at my clumsiness.

Luana launches me a nervous look. "Come on, Talita. Stop it," she says, but the people in line are all laughing now, following Talita's lead.

"Shut up!" Pedro barks at them, and the students calling me Salty look at him, startled. I'm startled myself. "Stop calling her that. It's just a freaking shoe! You should apologize to Larissa, and while you're at it, thank her for convincing Pimentel to let you earn extra credit! Did you know she's the reason why you aren't failing?"

All the mocking quiets. But I flee before they can restart or I die of mortification.

I'm almost at the gate, blinking away tears of embarrassment, when Victor and Cintia reach me. They're both out of breath, Cintia clamping a straw hat down with her hand to keep it from flying off.

"Lari! Are you okay?" she says. I didn't know she'd be here tonight. "I was running the darts booth and I saw everything."

Victor looks worried, like he doesn't know the right words to make me feel better. The broken sandal is still hanging off my ankle. I'm so angry trying to unstrap both my sandals with my free hand, I nearly trip again.

I glance at Cintia, who offers me an arm for support, and this whole thing would be comical if it weren't tragic. I let out an exaggerated whimper and the three of us laugh.

"So much for wearing something nice," I mumble and Cintia wraps a comforting arm around me. "God, I'm so embarrassed." I press a hand to my forehead.

"They're all jerks. Please don't leave," Victor says. "I promise the night will get better. I know you're barefoot, but I'll give you a piggyback ride anywhere!"

True to his promise, he promptly turns around for me to perch on his back. Cintia looks surprised, struggling to hold back laughter.

"Okay," I give in. "I'll stay, but you don't need to carry me."

Victor grabs my hand and Cintia's, pulling us back into the party.

We sit down at a table in the gym, where we can watch the band play. Victor leaves us for a moment with the promise of bringing delicious food to make up for the night so far.

"I didn't know I'd see you here! Did you come with Victor?" Cintia asks, wagging her eyebrows like she's channeling PC.

"Sort of," I say, leaving out that this is a date. I don't know why I lie. "I don't always come to parties. This is...my first one, actually."

Cintia takes off her St. John's straw hat and playfully plants it on my head. "I'm also not a fan of parties." She leans back, watching with a pained face as students begin gathering for a quadrille. "I was signed up to dance with PC, but then he moved to Caruaru, and now I'm stuck having to dance with some guy I don't even know." She squirms in her chair, looking nervous. "I'd skip it, but I don't want to ruin the quadrille..."

I place the hat back on her head.

"If I signed up for more of these school things, maybe I'd have more friends."

Cintia launches me a small smile. "You have me."

Just then, Victor returns with an armload of food. *And* flip-flops. He places the sandals in front of my bare feet like an offering. "There. Just like Cinderella," he says with a sheepish grin.

I'm so stunned, I don't know what to say.

"Where did you get these?" Cintia asks for me, looking impressed herself.

"Some girl from your class, Lari," he says, nodding toward the quadrille. "She said you could borrow them."

My eyes flicker to the students gathering near the band. "One of my classmates offered them?! Who?"

"I'll point her out if I see her again."

I can't imagine who'd have done that, after half my classroom just laughed at me. Part of me is cautious when I put the sandals on, but they fit perfectly and there's nothing wrong with them. Warm fuzzies spread in my chest. I glance at the students in the distance again, hoping to spot who my guardian angel is.

"I gotta go. The quadrille is about to start," Cintia says, standing up as Victor takes her seat. "Save a skewer for me, will you?"

"No promises," he says.

She playfully flips him off and rushes away to pair up with a boy in a similar hat and a yellow flannel that matches hers— the other quadrille couples all wear matching colors, most of them younger students, I think. I watch her take position in line, facing her pair. She's beautiful in cropped jeans, and her high heels complement her quadrille outfit, making her legs seem longer, her calves toned.

"You're not joining them?" I ask Victor.

"Only if you dance with me," he teases.

I raise my hands in defeat. "No, thank you. I suck at dancing."

"I suck, too. We'd make quite a pair."

"After nearly falling off my heels earlier, I'll pass on any more opportunities to break my ankle."

"Fair enough."

Victor places a buffet of St. John's delicacies in front of me. A cup of mungunzá, the maize kernels swimming in a thin, heavily sugared porridge. A plate of canjica—dense, creamy-like pudding, and bright yellow—covered in a dusting of cinnamon. He's brought a cluster of fragrant espetinhos, too! Beef, chicken, and golden brown, crispy coalho cheese skewers which Victor says he grilled himself. I understand why Cintia wanted one!

We eat so much, messy and chatting about all the delicious flavors with our mouths full, that I forget about my early embarrassment. When I'm done, I feel like I'm about to burst, so I just lean back and listen to Victor talking about the different ways he was fanning the grill, trying to make sure the steaks retained the smoky flavor and remained juicy.

His excitement is too cute. When he looks at me, his lips bright with food grease, I can't help but smile.

"My grandmother would have loved you," I say.

"Yeah?" he smiles.

"Because you love food."

Victor wipes his mouth with a napkin, his eyes lighting up. "Who doesn't?"

"True. But you're *excited* about food." I take a deep breath, feeling slightly melancholy after this buffet and good conversation. The full-stomach blues sure hit different.

One of the flower clips in my hair falls on the table and Victor picks it up. He smiles, handing it back to me.

"Is it a sunflower?" he asks me.

"Yeah. They were my Grandma's favorite flowers," I say, clipping it back to my braid. "Now they're my favorite, too."

Victor is quiet for a while, his friendly eyes studying me. "Would you like me to bring you something else? Maybe another skewer?"

"Thank you, but I'm totally full." I watch the way he turns to look at the food booths nearby. I think he's tempted to try everything, the same way Grandma was every time we visited the feirinha. "I never asked you why you joined the cooking club," I say. "Do you plan on working in the food industry when you graduate next year?"

He starts stacking up the empty plates in front of us. "I hope so, although not as a cook. I want to write about food."

"I didn't know you're a writer!"

"Not yet." He smiles. "But one day, who knows. I want to travel and eat different dishes. But more than writing about food, I'm interested in the people making it. The people eating it."

That explains the way he observes us at the club more than he talks, his eyes curious, as if photographing the moment, analyzing us with journalistic interest.

"You'll be a great writer."

"I hope to write something about you one day."

I straighten my back, a rare spark of vanity making me feel good about myself. "What would you write?"

"That you're the type of person who's definitely going to remember everything you ever eat."

I laugh. "Oi? Is that good or bad?"

Victor laughs with me. "You'll find out, I guess!" He studies me for a second. "How about you? Do you want to be a baker or...?"

"Me?" I wave my hands. "No."

"Why not?" He looks genuinely curious. "Doesn't your family own a bakery?"

I look him dead in the eye. "You know I can't cook, right?"

For such a big secret, the words come out so easily when talking to Victor. And as scary as telling the truth is, I actually feel relieved to say it out loud. I needed to tell someone the truth.

"I've seen you cook," he says plainly.

"Yeah, but… I had zero experience before joining the club. You knew, right?" Now I'm starting to think maybe I misread the way he helped me out at the club.

"I had a feeling," he admits.

"Do you think Pedro knows?"

Victor frowns. "Why do you care so much what he thinks of you?"

"I don't want him to use it against me," I say, my voice rising a little with nerves. "Sorry. I just… It's complicated. I want to learn to cook, but at the same time I don't want Pedro to find out that I'm the only one in my family who can't cook. Please, don't tell anyone."

"I won't. And I get it… But have you ever considered a career as a baker, even if you're not as skilled as you'd like to be now?"

"No, I'm going to be an accountant." Victor looks like he wasn't expecting that answer at all, so I quickly change the subject. "The quadrille is starting! Cintia looks miserable. Should we go rescue her?"

I try to laugh to smother the weird feeling building up in my chest that comes every time I think about studying econ in college. I still haven't even submitted my application. Mom will murder me when she finds out.

There's clapping and cheers all around, and I realize people are responding to the way Luana pulls Pedro along to join the quadrille.

He digs his heels in, but she moves behind him and pushes him to take position as her partner. And I realize they're not going to be just any couple. They'll be the bride and groom in this quadrille's faux wedding ceremony!

"That's the girl," Victor says.

I whip my head to look back at him. "Who?"

"The girl who gave you her flip-flops."

"*Luana?* Pedro's date?"

Victor nods. So Luana helped me? Does that mean she's overcome her grudge against me? She did defend me against Talita, and it makes me wonder if her closeness with Pedro has anything to do with this.

As if sensing me staring, her eyes meet mine across the gym, and she offers me a tiny, friendly nod, before putting on a straw hat with a white veil and hooking her arm with Pedro's. And my elation at finding a friend in her suddenly dissipates a little, giving way to a tight feeling in my chest the moment Pedro beams his most telenovela smile at her.

Victor leans in and asks in a low voice, "Did running into Pedro upset you a lot earlier?"

"Ah, no." I try to smile to hide my uneasiness. "I'm...used to arguing with him."

"I actually never fully understood why you two can't get along. Shouldn't all the animosity between your families stay in the baking world?"

I stare at Pedro across the room, the way he laughs and twirls Luana so many times she looks dizzy. And a nagging thought creeps up. We've been fighting for seventeen years.

But if the feud had stayed in the bakeries, like Victor said, would Pedro have been the one to invite me to this party? If the feud had died out by now, we'd have grown up closer, living across the street from each other. I could have been the one dancing with him now.

Pedro and Luana go on dazzling everyone with their chemistry. What a beautiful couple they make. And my heart breaks into tiny pieces. A feeling I'd been smothering all night catches up to me, knocking the breath out of me, threatening to spill over.

I realize that the reason why I kept looking for Pedro when I arrived was because I wanted him to see me. To notice me, like he notices Luana.

And I hate that I feel this way.

I hate that this date… That my *first* date wasn't with—

Pedro pulls Luana close to him, and she raises one of her legs against his hip. Hello, this isn't a tango. I could never dance like that. For someone who didn't look like he wanted to dance at first, Pedro happily spins Luana now, showing off his forró skills, their bodies moving together gracefully, so…in sync.

"Lari, are you crying?" Victor asks, surprised.

I wipe my face with my fingertips, surprised myself. "It's probably just the smoke from the bonfire," I try to put on a smile again, sounding a little hoarse. "My eyes are stinging a little."

Victor looks from me to Pedro, his expression still tinged with concern. "Did I say something wrong?" he asks.

"Maybe I should leave." I get on my feet and Victor stands, too.

"Would you like me to get you an Uber?"

"No, no… I have a cab driver who I can call."

I slip out of the gym with the excuse to call Seu Alcino, the cab driver who was close friends with Grandma, but I take the chance to catch my breath outside. I lean against the giant heart-shaped prop where couples have been taking photos all night.

What's wrong with me? I'm on a date with the nicest guy in the world, and all I can do is resent the fact that Pedro Molina wasn't the one who asked me out?!

After calling Seu Alcino, Victor joins me outside and we make our way to the front gate to wait.

"Tell Cintia I'm sorry for leaving early?" I say, a little embarrassed. "I don't know why the smoke is bothering me so much tonight."

Victor is silent for a moment, deep in thought. "Lari, I feel like I messed up somehow."

"What, no. Tonight was perfect." I pat him on the arm. "Thank you for inviting me."

"You're a great person." He stands in front of me, looking like he's about to get on his knee and propose or something. "I'd like to hang out with you more often, if you want. Maybe… Maybe go on a proper date? You and me? Go somewhere people don't make you sad."

I'm so startled by his words, I take a step back.

"I understand you're graduating this year," he adds, quickly, "and you have the vestibular to focus on, but if you give me a chance, I'd consider myself so lucky."

Never in one million years I'd have thought Victor would have asked me to go on a second date.

A second date would feel like we're officially *dating*. I think.

I've never dated anyone. I've never even *kissed* anyone. If I could pick the person I'd like to have these experiences with, I'd hope it could be him. Victor is kind, thoughtful, and he kept my secret even before I confessed it. He wants to make sure I'm somewhere people don't make me sad. I know *he* would never make me sad.

But, if I'm honest, I just don't think I'm interested in him this way.

"I'm sorry…" I say. His expression falls, and I feel horrible for disappointing him.

"I understand."

"I think you're a great person, too, but I… I don't see us becoming anything other than friends."

Victor gives me a self-conscious smile. "That's okay. I'm glad we're friends."

I still feel terrible, though. Victor opens his arms for a hug, and I step into them. It's a little awkward but nice. It'd kill me to lose his friendship. He already means a lot to me.

I see a shadow out of the corner of my eye, and my heart skips a beat when I realize it's Pedro. When we make eye contact, he turns around, headed back to the party.

I go after him. "Pedro, wait!"

"I didn't mean to interrupt you guys," he says quickly, not making eye contact.

"You aren't."

Pedro stops. He looks from Victor to me. "You're leaving?" There's an edge on his voice.

"Yeah. Before I turn into a pumpkin." I mentally kick myself for the corny joke. I blame Victor for calling me Cinderella.

"I just wanted to say sorry about what happened earlier. I'd already told them to stop with the jokes. I'll talk with them again." He stares at me like there's something else he wants to say, but he just stands awkwardly, like Victor's presence is putting him off.

The smoke-filled breeze blows in suddenly cold, bringing down a thin drizzle that stirs his hair and makes me shiver. Pedro must notice, because he takes his jacket off, offering it to me.

And the gesture is so *unexpected*, I just stare at it, unable to react.

"Aren't you...cold?" he asks. I still don't know what to say, so he puts the jacket back on, looking a little disconcerted himself. "Alright. Get home safe."

"Wait. I forgot to give you these!" I pull his sunglasses out of my purse. "I fixed them. Sorry it took me so long."

Fireworks go off from the party when Pedro turns to look at me again, the sky streaking with bright stars. He takes a step closer, looking stunned, and our hands brush when he takes them, sending goose bumps down my arm. "*You* fixed them?" he says, like he can't believe his eyes. When he looks at me, there's a longing in his expression that makes the whole world stop. "Thank you."

Now I'm the one who's stunned.

"I—I'm—"

"Lari, your cab is here," Victor says behind me.

I catch the way Pedro's eyes flicker to him, almost resentfully, before he looks back at me. We stare at each other for a long second. And I don't know what's going on. I don't understand the sudden shift in the world. In the way I feel about him. All I know is that I wish… I *wish* things had been different.

I wish the feud had never existed.

And I really, *really* wish one day I'll be able to tell him all this.

"I gotta go," I summon the words, my voice sounding distant even to me.

"See you at the club on Monday?" he says.

"See you at the club."

28

MONDAY, MAY 23

As I'm heading down the stairs Monday morning, running late for school, I hear a loud popping sound like a firecracker. Mom screams.

I hurry into the kitchen, where Mom is on the verge of tears, staring at the huge mixer she uses for preparing big batches of batter.

"It's dead," she cries. "The mixer is *dead*. It was working fine a minute ago, and then suddenly it just gave up!"

I look from the mixer, filled to the brim with batter, to Mom's flushed face. "Can't we call someone to fix it?" I suggest.

"I got this thing fixed six months ago, and the lady said that I was better off getting a new one. Like I have money for that—" She stops midsentence, shaking her head. "Don't worry about this. Go catch your bus or you'll be late for school."

Every inch of the kitchen is covered in trays of perfectly golden empadinhas, coxinhas, potato croquettes, chicken rissoles that Mom's going to freeze in preparation for the event coming up in two weeks. This is definitely the biggest catering order Salt's ever gotten, and Mom's not even close to being done. She juggles her time between baking for Salt, baking for the catering client, and party planning. Not to mention long meetings with Dona Eulalia at the venue, who likes to micromanage *everything*.

And the client isn't helping either. Every other day, Mom gets word that Dona Fernanda's daughter wants something different, so Mom has to make everything over again. Pedro told me she's the same way with Sugar, asking them to make things like petit gâteau and crème brûlée, despite the contract specifying Sugar only offers traditional recipes. At least we have plenty of extra food to donate to Vozes.

But what are we going to do about the mixer? While the one-month deadline seemed doable at first, it's now looking nearly impossible. Mom tries not to show it, but I see her struggling. She's not used to this routine. Mom and Grandma used to prepare for events—*way* smaller ones—in forty-eight hours of baking. But this birthday party is massive. And Mom and Grandma never had a client who changed her order frequently and wanted party planning on top of catering.

"Let me help you," I offer. "Tell me what to do, I'll follow your instructions exactly."

"Larissa, go to school," Mom says instead, kicking me out of the kitchen.

My heart sinks. How is Mom going to pull this off without a working mixer? And what happens if we don't get another big catering gig after this one? How will we fend off Deals Deals then?

★ ★ ★

The moment I arrive at the club, I smell guava jam. And every time there's the sweet smell of guava in the air, there's—

"Pedro," I say.

I just *knew* he'd be in the kitchen early. He's cooking alone, and he gives me a tiny glance of acknowledgment before shifting his attention back to the pot he's stirring. His posture is tense, his back to me.

The shift I sensed at the party last Friday is still here. Something's changed between us. Something that's hard to ignore.

I join him at the stove, leaning against the counter next to it.

"I'm just melting some guava before our meeting," he says, lowering the heat. He's still not making eye contact. "Every time I get a chance, I have to practice my family's bolo de rolo recipe."

"That smells good."

I look from the bubbly red guava to him, and I sense he doesn't want to be alone with me. Or maybe it's me who feels we shouldn't be alone, like I could start thinking about us the way I did at the party.

"You left early on Friday," he says as if reading my thoughts.

"I did."

He finally looks at me. "He's a nice guy. Victor, I mean," he smiles, although it's forced and doesn't reach his eyes. "Congratulations."

"Why 'congratulations'?"

"Because he's... You two..." It's odd to see him at a loss for words. "Isn't that what you're supposed to say to new couples?"

He thinks I'm with Victor? If I didn't know him, I'd say he's jealous. I laugh, but that only annoys him more.

"What's so funny?" he asks.

"Should I congratulate *you* for marrying Luana?" I joke.

Earlier today, I finally caught Luana alone to return her flip-flops—after a whole morning of her friends gushing over the wedding quadrille—and thanked her for the gesture. "I always have them handy when I go to parties," she said like it was nothing, but I know it's her peace offering to me. Not the flip-flops, but the little secret that even she struggles with high heels, too.

Pedro stops stirring. "You know that wasn't a real wedding, right?"

"And Victor and I aren't a couple," I say plainly.

"I thought—" Pedro hesitates. He goes back to stirring. "Never mind."

I notice the slight tug in the corner of his mouth. A smile? A smirk? I give my head a little shake before I get caught up trying to figure it out. I need to focus on why I came here early, not on deciphering misleading signals.

"I need to ask you something," I say, already feeling a little jittery, and Pedro turns the stove off, giving me his full attention. It makes me even more nervous, honestly.

"Did something happen?"

"The mixer at Salt broke and Mom can't afford a new one," I say. "It's a lot of batter to mix by hand."

"Yeah, no kidding. I do not envy you." He fills a glass with water and takes a sip.

"There's no easy way to say this, so I'll just be blunt." I

take a deep breath, summoning courage. "Can we borrow Sugar's mixer?"

He chokes.

"Please?" I add.

Pedro puts the glass down, wiping the water he spilled on his shirt with a dish rag. "I thought all I had to do was keep my mother from fighting yours. You never said anything about dealing with your broken equipment."

"I know I'm asking too much, but if Mom can't finish her work in time, we're doomed."

"Then there's a chance the client will ask Sugar to take over the part Salt can't finish," he thinks out loud. "Thank you for letting me know."

He stares at me with those eyes that resemble his grandfather's. My *enemy's* eyes. I feel the blood draining out of my body.

"I didn't tell you so you could use it against my family! I thought we had a *truce*. If Mom loses the job, drowns in debt, and then is forced to sell Salt to Deals Deals, what do you think will happen to Sugar? Do you think you can compete against that supermarket? Is that what you want?!"

This is Pedro Molina. Of course that's what he wants. I can't believe I thought otherwise. *Trust neither thin-bottomed frying pans nor Molinas.* Everything about him, his very name, tells me he'll betray me. But after these past few weeks at the club, cooking together, I thought he and I could—

I thought we—

He looks stunned.

"Larissa, I'm not this evil monster you apparently still think I am. I was just pushing your buttons. And I'm not ignorant.

I'm not letting Deals Deals get to Salt just because of a broken mixer." I stare at him and he waves his hands awkwardly, adding like an afterthought, "*So* they can't get to Sugar."

I could cry. "So you'll help us?" I ask.

"I'll text my mother and see what I can do."

I feel awkward for having doubted his character. And he looks irritated that I did. "I'm sorry I yelled. I—"

He unfastens his apron on his way out of the kitchen, still looking a little miffed. "Get to work. We'll need to prepare a lot of bread dough today."

I head to the counter, where the ingredients for baking bread sit waiting for the rest of the club members to arrive. Wheat flour, water, salt, and yeast. Straightforward ingredients, but why does it feel so daunting?

Maybe because it's not just bread. It's my family's *livelihood*.

Even though my stomach is knotted with anxiety over the broken mixer situation, I pick up the recipe. After pouring all the ingredients into a bowl, I use a wooden spoon to stir. But I'm a bit clumsy and get flour on my uniform.

When Pedro walks back into the kitchen, I ask, "What did your mother say?" The question comes out so fast, it sounds like one big word.

He grabs the apron he was wearing earlier and holds it out for me. I try to fasten it, but I'm so nervous, I keep dropping the strings.

"May I?" he says, offering to fasten it for me.

"S-sure."

He stands behind me, carefully tying the apron around my waist for me, so gentle while I stand like a statue, my heart pounding at my ribcage.

"How do you manage to be so careless?" he mumbles. He then flexes his fingers toward the spoon and I hand it to him. "You're going to hurt your wrist if you mix bread dough with a spoon. Use your hands."

He looks at me like I'm a complete amateur. Well, I am, but I don't want him to realize that!

"I know that. I was just distracted and picked up the spoon because… I wasn't thinking." I stick my hands in the bowl quickly, and my fingers sink into the batter. It's like squeezing mud at first, but the more I knead, the batter slowly thickens.

Pedro sprinkles a dusting of flour on the counter. "Knead it on the counter now," he instructs.

"But what did your mother—"

He gives me a pointed look, so I stop asking and transfer the dough to the counter, where I continue kneading. Pedro watches me for a while.

"Try folding it as you pull the batter toward you."

I try to do as he says, and still he isn't happy. He stands next to me, his shoulder touching mine, and takes a section of dough to show me how to properly fold it. Warmth travels through my body at our close proximity and I feel out of breath, but I press my lips together to hide the feelings bubbling up.

"I called my mother and said that she should go check in to see if Dona Alice is able to keep up with the order, because I heard rumors that your mixer broke."

I look at him. "Rumors?"

"Isn't that how our families communicate?" He shrugs. "I said she should go see if the rumors are true, because if they are, maybe we should let Dona Alice borrow our mixer, in case Mom wound up having to pick up her slack and still be paid for only half a job done."

My heart feels like it's about to burst with joy. Never in my life I thought I'd be so grateful to him. "I don't even know what to say. Pedro, *thank you.*"

He looks a little flustered. "No need."

"Thank you," I repeat. "One thousand thank yous."

We're staring at each other. Perhaps longer than we should. And I want to tell him that he's saving me and my family. When suddenly—

My eyes travel to the beauty mark above his lips.

"I wish you didn't look so surprised I helped, but, yeah." He swallows. "You're welcome. I mean, it's no big deal, and we've known each other our whole lives, so why can't we be—"

Pedro never finishes his sentence because Cintia and Victor walk in.

"Are we late?!" Cintia screeches, craning her neck to look at the clock on the wall. "I didn't know we were meeting early...?"

I catch the surprise in Victor's expression. The way his eyes travel to the dough we're kneading. The tiny, sad smile that forms on his lips, like he's only now fully realizing something.

I look down at the bread dough and I see my hands are resting under Pedro's, caked in raw batter. A jolt of adrenaline and something—something *brighter*, and electric, and dizzying runs through my body. I pull my hands out, and it's only then Pedro seems to notice we were touching this entire time. He steps away from the counter in a coughing fit.

"What is this for?" Victor asks, going straight to the pot with guava filling. "A Romeo and Juliet recipe?"

My face gets hotter.

"A Romeo and Juliet recipe requires cheese. Do you see any cheese around here?" Pedro snaps at him, wiping his fingers with a dish rag.

"You don't need to be so sour," Cintia says.

"Let's get the meeting started," Pedro pushes past Victor to take position at the counter, still flustered. "We have a full afternoon ahead of us."

I have no clue why Pedro is being so short with Victor. Cintia must see the confusion on my face, because she leans in to whisper, "I think they argued at the party," nodding in their direction.

"What?" I whisper back. "When?"

"I think after you left. Do you know why?" She looks worried.

I shake my head no. What would they even argue about?

I try to focus on the meeting, but my mind keeps going back to the way Pedro looked at the party when I returned his sunglasses. The longing in his eyes.

Stop.

I sharpen my focus.

"Vozes is having a fundraiser event in two weeks," Pedro goes on, his voice distant, like I'm listening from behind a thick wall. He's avoiding eye contact with me again. "It's important everything goes well. They need the funding to start construction in their kitchen."

I find myself noticing little details about him. The way he projects his voice, trying to mimic his grandfather. The way his curls are a lighter shade of brown at the tips, tucked behind his ears.

"We should contribute to their potluck with a cake," Pedro continues, "maybe a bolo de rolo?"

At the sound of Sugar's flagship recipe, I snap back to reality. He's Pedro *Molina*. Not some cute, brooding boy.

"We shouldn't bring bolo de rolo," I say. Cintia and Victor turn to look at me. Pedro crosses his arms over his chest, eyeing me from the other side of the counter. "It's almost June. Can't we make something more seasonally appropriate?"

"Like something with corn? Corn cake?" Victor suggests, and Cintia nods in approval already.

"I don't like corn," Pedro says, flatly.

"Are you saying that just because it's my family's specialty?" I glare at him.

And he glares back. "No. I just don't like it."

"The kids will like it," I insist, thinking of Grandma's corn cake recipe. "It's sure to be a success."

"I like corn cake," Cintia says, siding with me, and Pedro grimaces, as if witnessing his crew mutinying against his leadership.

"We're not making corn cake for the fundraiser," he says.

The three of us start bickering. We can hardly hear each other over all the shouting, when Victor waves his hands above his head to get everyone's attention. "How about we make *both* recipes and decide which one is the best?" he suggests.

We fall silent.

"Like a bake-off?" Cintia says, already excited. "I *love* that idea!"

Pedro and I stare at each other. "Are you okay with that?"

he asks me, the old hint of arrogance in his voice again. Like he thinks I can't possibly win against him.

And I just can't back out of a challenge. "Are *you?*"

"Alright. Let the best recipe win." He sticks a hand out to me.

I shake it.

And I try not to think about how good it feels wrapped around mine.

29

MONDAY, MAY 30

I was so quick to jump into a challenge with Pedro, I didn't think straight. How am I going to win a bake-off against him? I've never baked a corn cake before—let alone baked *anything* on my own. And Pedro is called the golden boy for a reason.

For the rest of the week, I considered asking Victor for help, but it just felt...wrong. We haven't properly talked since our failed date, and I don't want it to affect our friendship.

I'm sure Cintia would have helped me if I asked. I've been meaning to tell her my secret, too, and I know she also wouldn't tattle to Pedro. But all week she's been busy in the library, sitting down throughout recess with some of her classmates. I found out she's the best student in her class, so I guess with the midterms coming up soon, she must be extra busy tutoring students. I didn't want to be another reason for her to worry.

So I spent the week pestering Mom to bake Grandma's corn cake recipe. I wanted to watch her and secretly take notes, but Mom refused every time I asked.

When she sees me lingering by the kitchen this morning, the day of the bake-off and my final chance at getting any pointers from her, she gives me a stern look.

"I'm not baking that corn cake!" she says before I'm able to ask.

"Why not?"

"There are recipes even I can't touch, Larissa. I need you to respect that."

This recipe reminds her too much of Grandma. But it reminds me of Grandma, too, even more than any other recipe. And that's exactly why I want to learn how to make it.

"You're always procrastinating," Mom says, diverting the conversation. "If you get up early, go study. Don't just stand in the kitchen."

I feel shut out.

Forget the recipe. I just wish we could spend time together, like the night she helped me get ready for the party.

"Okay..." I say, dragging my feet.

"If I were in your shoes, I'd be so excited about going to college, but you act like it's a burden. You'll be the first Ramires to go to college. Do you realize what a privilege that is? Your father dreamed of studying economics. He had a real talent. And you share the same skill. You're the only one in our family who can finish what he started."

Her words aren't anything I haven't heard before, but now the pressure feels unbearable. "Maybe I have my own dreams," I mumble.

And I realize it was loud enough for her to hear. I regret the words immediately. I've never been open like this with Mom.

"Go to school," she says, not looking at me. I dart out of
Salt, hoping she'll forget my honesty.

As soon as I step outside, Pedro comes out of Sugar. And
right away I know something is wrong. Pedro doesn't go for
his bicycle. His hair is disheveled and he's not in his uniform.
Instead, he's wearing jeans and an inside-out shirt, like he
tossed it on in a hurry.

Seu Romário is right behind him, and Pedro turns around
to offer him a hand. His grandfather normally swats anyone
offering help away. But this time, he takes Pedro's arm and
leans against him, letting Pedro guide him to their car.

Dona Eulalia comes up behind them, and I immediately
recognize the look in her eyes. It's the same one Mom had
when she pushed Grandma's wheelchair in the hospital—a
strained expression as she steered, careful to navigate Grandma
through the busy corridors, one million worries behind her
eyes that she was never going to share with me.

"He's in pain," Mom says next to me. I didn't realize she'd
come out to the sidewalk.

We watch the Molinas climb into their car. When Seu
Romário leans back in the passenger's seat, even from afar I
can tell his breathing is heavy.

A couple of customers that were headed to Sugar stop on
the sidewalk, looking worried at the scene. "We're not opening this morning!" Pedro shouts from the car.

Dona Eulalia takes her place at the driver's seat, but the car
is unresponsive. She tries again and again, and the car fails her
every time. She squeezes the steering wheel tightly, like she
could strangle it for disobeying her when she needs it the most.

I see the fear in Pedro's eyes when he looks to the right and realizes I've been watching with my mother all along.

I think of the times when Grandma couldn't sleep in her infirmary bed, the discomfort in her chest leaving her out of breath, gasping. No matter how many times I begged the nurses to go check in on her, running from the infirmary to their office over and over, the nurses told me they were already doing everything they could.

It was terrifying.

It was infuriating.

It was—

A horrible, *powerless* feeling I don't wish on my worst enemy. How I hoped, and hoped, and prayed someone would make Grandma's pain go away.

"Mom," I put a hand on her arm. "Your car. Please, let them borrow it. *Please.*"

Without a word, Mom runs up to them, holding her car keys out to a surprised Dona Eulalia. Pedro glances at me, and I try to tell him that everything will be okay with just my eyes.

"I need to get my father to his doctor—" Dona Eulalia begins to say, her words tripping over her panic. "He's not well."

"Alice," Seu Romário begins to say, but he chokes. He's too agitated, a hand pressed to his chest.

"Father, stay calm, we're taking you to the clinic," Dona Eulalia says.

Mom grabs Dona Eulalia's hand and presses the key into it. "Go."

Dona Eulalia makes a sound like a whimper, her lip curling like she's trying not to cry.

The Molinas get into my family's fusquinha—the word *Salt* written on the doors—and drive off. They're long gone, and Mom and I are still standing in the middle of the street when we realize a small crowd of neighbors has gathered nearby, whispering to each other and glancing between both bakeries.

I feel like I just swallowed a bunch of sharp pebbles. Why are they staring at us? Because we helped the Molinas? Because, despite the feud, we showed that we care? Rivalry or no rivalry, what cruel person would deny another human being help?

Mom snaps out of it and taps on my shoulder. "Go now. It will be a miracle if you don't get a demerit for being late."

She hurries back into Salt as if running from the neighborhood.

30

Pedro doesn't show up for any of our classes for the rest of the day. I guess that means the bake-off is canceled this afternoon.

I spend the morning wondering if I should get his number from Cintia or Victor to text him about Seu Romário, but it didn't seem appropriate.

It must have been difficult for Mom to help the Molinas today. I mean, it was the right thing to do, and I don't think it was ever a question for her, whether to help or not. But that's the man she's hated her whole life. I guess seeing him as anything other than the pain he's caused must have been confusing.

I know it's confusing to me.

Seu Romário could make Grandma lose her temper in a heartbeat, even though she was the most patient woman on earth. He challenged her over and over, leaving her feeling like she wasn't herself for yelling, for getting angry, for letting him get to her.

But he's also...

Someone who must have respected Grandma to some extent, enough to give us his condolences. And I don't know what to make of these different versions of him. Which one is the truth? The man who made Grandma cry, or the man who cried over her death?

Cintia practically jumps at me the moment I walk into the club.

"There you are! Were you going to forfeit the bake-off?"

"I didn't think we were having it today," I say.

She looks confused. "Why not?"

I have no idea if she heard about Pedro's family emergency this morning, and I don't know if he wants to keep it private. I'm racking my brain for a quick excuse, when Victor says, "I just texted Pedro and he's on his way."

That has to be a good sign! Pedro wouldn't be coming if his grandfather were still at the hospital. Relief washes over me.

Feeling a little more at ease, I notice the way Victor's dressed this afternoon. He's changed into one of those neon yellow shirts, black shorts, and knee-high black socks like he's a soccer referee.

Cintia catches me staring. "I told him it wasn't necessary," she says, rolling her eyes. "But he never listens."

He flashes his brightest smile. "Don't I look cool?"

"Why are you dressed like a ref?" I ask.

Victor suddenly blows his whistle, making Cintia and me wince. "In the spirit of friendship!" he says, getting more and more excited. "It's important to remain friendly during bake-offs, you know, and I'll make sure that's the case today."

"It's only because he got that whistle from a claw machine

last night and didn't know what to do with it," she whispers to me, covering her mouth with a hand. She then glares at him. "Victor, the whistle is so not necessary. You're going to give us all a migraine."

Despite her chastising, his childlike excitement doesn't wane. "Just seeing if it works in case Lari and Pedro start arguing."

"What if I start arguing with *you*?" she snaps.

Cintia is on edge today. I catch a glimpse of all the books she's borrowed from the library—most of them on trig—and the mass of textbooks and study planners peeking from inside her open backpack. Maybe she's stressing over school?

"Everything alright?" I ask her in a low voice, while Victor is distracted, squinting into the whistle.

She gives me a sheepish smile. "I'm okay. I just didn't sleep well last night."

"Any reason in particular?"

"No," she shakes her head, noticing I caught a glimpse of her study material. "It's nothing."

It doesn't seem like it's nothing. "Let me know if you want to talk about it."

"Thank you for offering. I think I'm just overthinking stuff. I'll be okay," she says, suddenly busying herself with reorganizing her books so she can get her backpack to zip. I hope I'm not making her feel uncomfortable, so I don't hover.

I take the chance to pull Victor outside with me. "I just wanted to make sure you're okay. That we're okay," I say to him.

Never in my life would I have imagined myself standing with a cute boy dressed as a referee in an empty school cafeteria after turning him down at my first date. But the truth is, I don't have many friends. I don't want to mess things up with the few I have.

He gives me a genuine smile in response. "Lari, we're okay," he says, and I probably make a worried face, because he adds, "I promise you we're okay."

I don't deserve Victor.

"I heard something about you and Pedro arguing after the party..." I begin to say, and he looks a little embarrassed.

"It was nothing," he says, just like Cintia earlier, so I squint at him skeptically. Victor takes one step back, looking like he's considering bolting back into the kitchen. "We talked and we're friends again, so don't worry."

"Wait," I say, and he stops by the door. It's strange that they argued, but I shouldn't push it any further. Whatever happened, I'll trust Victor's belief that they're back to being friends. And I'm so relieved he's still my friend, despite the slight awkwardness between us. "You, Cintia, and PC mean the world to me. Thank you for accepting me just the way I am, even though I splattered smoothie all over you guys when we first met."

He bursts into laughter.

Just then a blur darts past us into the kitchen like an arrow. Victor and I exchange a confused glance. Neither of us noticed him entering the cafeteria.

"Pedro?" I say, following him inside.

He's focused, traveling back and forth between the pantry, the fridge, and the counter to gather the ingredients for his family's bolo de rolo recipe. Tubs of guava paste, wheat flour, sugar, eggs, and butter. He doesn't say a thing. That's how I know he's upset.

I want to ask him how everything went at the doctor's, but he's making such a point of getting his mise en place ready, I stay out of his way. His single-mindedness reminds me of Mom's a little.

"Lari, your ingredients!" Cintia says, yanking me back from my thoughts. "Hurry!"

The bake-off!

I pull Grandma's corn cake recipe out of my pocket with a trembling hand, reading the ingredients:

Sweet corn, cornmeal, vegetable oil, eggs, baking powder, Parmesan cheese, and cinnamon.

I'm supposed to blend everything and my stomach is already knotted with nerves, because the last time I tried using the blender, disaster struck. And that's not even my only problem. I realize that the bullet point indicating the Parmesan cheese doesn't specify the amount!

How did I not notice this before? All these years competing in mathematics contests, Pimentel trained me to look for all the key elements to solving equations, but I failed at reading Grandma's *favorite* recipe?

Victor blows his whistle, and I nearly have a heart attack. Pedro jumps too, letting a bowl fall to the floor.

"What did you do that for?" he barks, getting another bowl from the shelf. "This is a kitchen. Not a soccer field!"

Even Cintia, who wasn't a fan of the whistle either, looks surprised at Pedro's outburst. Something tells me they're not as okay as Victor seems to think they are, but then again... Pedro had a stressful morning.

"He didn't mean to startle you," I say, defending Victor.

Pedro looks like he wants to chew him out some more, but after a few tense seconds, he finally makes eye contact with me. He seems embarrassed by his outburst.

"I'll stop with the whistle, if it's really that annoying," Victor says, his tone still amiable.

"Sorry. I'm just..." Pedro exhales, averting his eyes. "I'm sorry. Let's get this thing started?"

"No worries," Victor says, flashing Pedro a smile. "Alright, the rules of the bake-off are simple. Lari and Pedro will have exactly one hour to prepare their recipes. There's no tripping allowed in this bake-off. No name-calling. We're all friends here, so let's stay friends after this. At the end, all club members will try the dishes and vote on the one that should represent the cooking club at the Vozes fundraiser. Will it be Lari's corn cake? Or Pedro's bolo de rolo?"

I look at Pedro, and he launches me the tiniest glance back.

Victor pulls his phone out of his pocket and sets the timer for one hour. "Ready? Set! Go!"

The countdown begins.

I place Grandma's recipe in front of me on the counter and I go back to my previous dilemma. Parmesan cheese.

"I got this," I say to myself. "As long as you're with me, Grandma."

I take a deep breath and focus.

If this were an equation, my hands would know what to do before I even thought about it. But it's not like I haven't encountered tricky tests before. I try to approach baking like it's a bonus question during a math contest. I can't let it overwhelm me. So I begin by getting some of the ingredients out of the way. I'll worry about the Parmesan cheese later.

I pour cornmeal into the blender, ignoring my shaking hands. I then try to crack the first egg the way Grandma used to, hitting it with a quick flick of the wrist against the side of the blender. But my hand isn't as swift and the whole egg breaks, spilling its contents all over the counter.

"Problems?" Victor mouths to me, casually sliding over to my end of the counter, pretending to just be observing my ingredients. He knows my predicament.

"I'm okay," I say in a low voice, egg slime dripping between my fingers.

"You can do this." I tear up at his words.

I reach to get another egg from the carton, but I slip on something on the floor. I nearly fall, but Victor catches me just in time.

I look up at him, embarrassment making me blush. After a few successful experiences in the kitchen, I thought I'd broken my curse. Maybe chipped at it a little. But, no. I still have my same old impish thumb. And it's foolish I thought it could ever be any different.

I turn my head in time to catch the look on Pedro's face. His eyes go from Victor to me, before focusing back on his work, a muscle twitching in his jawline. He doesn't say anything, but I know he must think I'm a joke. Why did I even accept a challenge against a guy who's been baking since he was a baby?!

I steady myself, straightening my uniform. "Thank you," I say to Victor.

"Don't lose heart," he whispers with a smile, and heads back to his stool beside Cintia's. She gives me a thumbs-up.

I pick up another egg from the carton and try cracking it. Finally, a combination of hitting the egg carefully against the side of the blender and then finishing it off with a spoon works, although I'm left having to pick pieces of egg shell out of the batter.

Meanwhile, Pedro is already working on his cake's filling!

I pour the can of sweet corn into the blender, followed by vegetable oil, and cinnamon. Now there's only one last ingredient:

Parmesan cheese.

And I'm officially stuck.

Grandma, what should I do?

I think about her serving this cake at Salt, the slice still warm, the aroma of corn filling the whole bakery like the branches of a tree stretching in all directions. It tasted buttery, and savory, and with just the right hint of sour, which I guess came from the cheese. It was perfectly salted and spicy, cinnamon's contribution to the taste.

My heart beating quickly, I close my eyes and grab a fistful of grated Parmesan cheese.

I may not have Grandma's fairy hands, but maybe there's a way to coerce some of it, like magical kids in stories do, their powers finally blooming to life in times of great need.

The guava perfume coming from Pedro's cake is intoxicating. The layers are perfectly thin and rolled with guava filling. And the sugar on top looks like a dusting of crystals.

I mean, of course it looks amazing. The Molinas have been

baking this same recipe, not one sugar granule more or less, for *decades*!

While my corn cake... Well, it is golden yellow, as it should be. The steam swirling from it has that signature cinnamony, cheesy aroma. But the cake came out a little burnt on the sides because I forgot to grease the pan. Even the corn cake they sell at Deals Deals looks better than mine!

I catch Cintia and Victor staring at the burnt spots, and a horrible hollowness spreads within me.

"I'm really sorry," I apologize before they try it.

"It will still taste delicious," Cintia says with a supportive smile.

Pedro picks up a knife and goes for the corn cake right away, but he seems to think better of it. He puts the knife down and looks at me, making intentional eye contact for the first time today. "Do you want to cut your cake?" he asks me.

I take a deep breath and cut a slice, taking a bite of the very first cake I ever baked by myself.

I taste the warmth of cinnamon right away, reminding me of home, and I look for the memories that this recipe has always provided. Grandma's Sunday morning cooking with her neighborhood friends, chatting and gossiping. Salt packed with customers. Children begging their parents for another slice.

But then the flavor veers abruptly into all the Parmesan cheese I added with my eyes closed, and I'm left feeling my way out in the dark, none of my old memories there to guide me. This cake has a much stronger cheesy flavor than Grandma's version.

Although it isn't bad, it's *not* Grandma's recipe.

My eyes sting with tears. I look away before the others notice I'm hurt.

Cintia hands me a slice of Pedro's bolo de rolo, and I stuff my face with it quickly, letting the tanginess of guava roll over my tongue, washing over any hint of the Parmesan in my corn cake. The crunch of sugar granules is perfect. The delicate layers miraculously hold together. No wonder this cake has been Sugar's pride for generations.

I see Pedro nibble on his slice of corn cake, and he quickly puts the plate down. He hated it.

"What are we taking to Vozes for the fundraiser?" Cintia asks. "Should we vote? Who votes for the corn cake?"

Pedro and I both come from families of bakers, but while he can recreate his family's recipe perfectly, I can't recreate mine. *What am I doing?*

"My cake isn't right," I say, stopping them from voting.

"Don't worry that it burned a little bit," Cintia says, failing to hide that she's just trying to make me feel better. "I think I understand the flavor—"

My face goes hot. "I don't need pity votes."

Her eyes widen with worry. "It's not a pity vote."

"I messed up my grandmother's recipe!"

The tears I'd been holding back freely roll down my face. I keep thinking of Mom yelling at me every time I offer to help at Salt, reminding me that I can't bake.

"It's still a good cake," Victor says, but I don't want to hear it.

"I'm a fraud!" I say. "I can't cook! I can't bake! I can't—I just can't!"

I'm shaking. The whole kitchen spins and spins around

me. There. I've just told them the truth. Pedro Molina will tell his family, who will make fun of Mom for my lack of cooking skills. After all this time in this kitchen, did I even learn *anything*?

Pedro's silence is starting to irritate me. I bet he's judging me, maybe calculating how exactly he'll use this against me.

"I'm sure you already suspected it," I say to Pedro, and it makes me even angrier that he looks surprised. "Are you happy now?"

"Why would I be happy?" he asks.

"Because I'm from a family of bakers and I don't know how to bake!"

Pedro just stares at me.

"Lari, look… You can bake," Cintia says, conciliatory. "You just did."

"I make a mess every time."

"We all make messes when we're learning," Victor says.

"You don't get it!" I step away from them, before they convince me that this pitiful cake I just made, my homage to Grandma, is any good. "I'm a disgrace to the whole Ramires family!"

I hide my face behind my hands, my shoulders shaking with every sob I fail to hold back.

"Can you guys give us a minute to talk?" I hear Pedro say to Cintia and Victor.

A moment later, I feel someone stand directly in front of me.

"You're not a disgrace," he says.

When I drop my hands, it's just us. Had this happened one month ago, it would be the biggest humiliation of my life.

But he's not laughing at me. He's not judging me. He's not looking smug. And I begin to realize that *because* of the feud between our families, he's the only person who understands why I'm upset. Why this recipe matters so much to me.

"I'm sorry I lashed out at you," I say, wiping my face with my sleeve.

He hands me a glass of water, and the moment I take a sip, I realize it's sugared. An old remedy after crying. Like you could coat sadness with sugar and make it better.

"Don't worry about it."

"Did you know?" I ask him. "That I couldn't bake?"

He takes my empty glass and places it in the sink. "I didn't," he says. And then he hesitates, averting his eyes. "Maybe? I've known you long enough to know when you're hiding something."

"Please, don't tell your family!"

Pedro frowns. "Why would I do that? It's none of my business. None of *anyone's* business."

He acts like he's always been this way. Like I have no reason to think he could use this as fodder to our families' feud.

"The old Pedro Molina would probably laugh at me before running to tell his mom all about how the *Salt* girl can't bake," I say, and I can hear the bitterness in my voice.

I hate to throw accusations at him again. But I can't take it back. Every time I think I'm overcoming my resentment toward him, more comes bubbling up.

Pedro thinks for a while, looking contrite. "I'm sorry I hurt you."

It makes me feel awkward. "Forget what I said. It's fine."

"No. I agree with you. And you need an apology." Pedro's

shoulders slump, and I know he's feeling put on the spot, too, but he doesn't break eye contact with me. "I thought people would think I'm cool if I acted exactly like my grandfather. I thought if I antagonized you and proved I was better than you, maybe I'd *feel* better myself." He takes a step closer, his eyes sincere. "But I'm telling you now, I'm not that guy anymore. I don't *want* to be that guy anymore. I'm not going to use your cooking against you, like I did when we were children. I actually respect that you're learning to cook. I really do. That suggestion to add basil leaves to black beans, that was brilliant. You may not have experience, but you love food. And you *know* food. You have no idea how I admire you for it."

I wasn't expecting him to say all this.

"You…admire me?"

Pedro's ears go red. "Yeah, I do," he says. "I can't help it."

We stare at each other, and I get the feeling that Pedro both wants to say something else and is waiting for me to speak, but we're just stuck waiting for the other to make the first move. My heart feels derailed. I want to tell him that I've learned to admire him, too. I want to tell him that sometimes, when I think of him, my chest feels too small for all the pent-up feelings, but—

I can't say any of that.

I can't *feel* any of that.

I think he gets it, because he offers me a tiny nod and turns around to start cleaning utensils in the sink.

I should leave now, before it's too late. Before he sees that I'm confused about us. But I end up sitting on the counter next to the sink, while he washes dishes.

"That flower soup incident when we were kids, I think

it bothered me so much because you were right," I admit. "Back then, when you challenged me to drink it, to prove that it was really soup, I knew I'd never be able to. Because I'd never even made soup at home. I just played with flowers, trying to imitate Mom and Grandma, but I didn't know the first ingredient."

"Aromatic ingredients go first," he says like the know-it-all he is.

I splash him with the sink hose.

Pedro raises his hands in defense, the tips of his bangs dripping. Next thing I know, he splashes me with water, too. We laugh, both drenched. I think it's the first time we've ever laughed together. And it feels…right.

But then I spot my cake on the counter.

I never thought I could feel so resentful about a recipe. No wonder Mom's been avoiding it, too. Only Grandma knew the amount of Parmesan cheese that goes in the batter.

"I'm sorry," I say. "I was crying about a cake, when you and your family went through a lot this morning. Is Seu Romário okay?" Pedro averts his eyes like he'd rather not talk about this. "I shouldn't have brought him up—"

"No. It's okay. He'll be fine. It was his blood pressure," Pedro explains. "Mom and Grandpa were talking about Sugar, and he got upset. It's this whole Deals Deals thing. But thank you for your help this morning."

"Let me know whenever you guys need to borrow mom's car again," I say.

Pedro looks a bit surprised, but he smiles. "Thank you."

I'm about to hop off the counter, but there's water everywhere, and I nearly slip again.

"Be careful!" he says, placing both hands on my waist to help me down. My hands grip his shoulders. And the moment we make eye contact, it's like we both realize how close we are. I feel like I just collided with the sun.

Pedro steps away from me, looking flustered. "I need to get back to Sugar soon. I should start packing up."

My heart sounds like a samba school.

"I'll help," I mumble. I'm grabbing a plate of corn cake while Pedro carries the bolo de rolo to the fridge, when I slip on leftover egg yolk still on the floor and come crashing into him. Pedro tries to catch me, and both of our trays upend onto each other. We fall together, trying to keep the trays safe.

"Oh God! I'm so sorry!" I reach for a dish rag dangling from the stove.

Pedro reaches for the same rag.

And the moment his fingers wrap around mine, the world stops.

I should pull back, but I don't want to break the physical contact between us. Warmth spreads under my skin, the same glow I got when he was showing me how to knead bread. He leans closer. And I'm leaning in, too. Our mouths nearly touching, I feel heat traveling from his lips.

And then a flash of doubt crosses his face. A little feverish exhale escapes his mouth when he turns away from me.

What just—what just happened?

I'm stunned, trying to process everything. Pedro looks just as confused, his expression strained like he's agonizing over his thoughts. He clumsily picks up the trays of corn cake and bolo de rolo, now all mixed together. He shoves a piece of the mixture into his mouth like he's doing it just to avoid talking.

But then his eyes light up.

"Oh my God!" he says with his mouth full. He grabs another piece of corn cake stacked with bolo de rolo, holding it up to show it to me, like he's just made a great discovery.

"What?" I ask.

"You gotta try this," he says.

I'm so nervous that I don't think I can make myself eat, but I take the first bite—

Salt and sugar mix in my mouth, the two tastes meeting like a kiss.

"It's... It's..." I can't find the right words.

"*Perfect,*" he finishes for me. He's so close, his eyes locked with mine and that silly smile on his face.

WHAT'S WRONG WITH ME?!

My conflicted thoughts must be written all over my face, because he suddenly looks worried. "You don't like it?" he asks.

"I'm sorry. I can't—I gotta go!" I push myself to my feet, grabbing my backpack on the way out, as I practically run away from the kitchen, past Cintia and Victor in the cafeteria as they call out to me.

I still feel tingles running up and down my back while I wait for the bus.

It's just the cake, I tell myself.

Both cakes were perfect when combined. That's what this weird, intoxicating feeling in the middle of my chest is. Right?

31

I avoid Pedro for the rest of the week. I don't even let myself think about him, burying myself in homework anytime he pops up in my head.

Mom has no idea what's going on, but she's glad to see me studying late into the night. She even brings me a platter of salgados for fuel. That's how I enter June. Studying geometry so I don't need to think about anything else.

We're still in a feud. Our families have been at it for generations. I can't forget that just because Pedro and I almost kissed. That's the one point of reference I must *never* lose track of.

During recess on Friday, I sit down to use one of the library computers to fill out my college application.

I'm determined to finally get it done. I'll choose economics. No more excuses. No more room for doubts. And there are so many great reasons if I choose this path. 1) I'd be finishing Dad's dream, like Mom hopes. 2) I'd become the first

Ramires to go to college, like Mom wants. 3) I won't disappoint Mom.

My fingers inch toward the keyboard. I stare at the box prompting me to declare my major. And it stares back at me.

I blink, groaning in defeat.

Despite all the pros, every time I try to make myself choose economics, I feel like I'm making a bad decision. The idea still tastes as bland as ever. And I can't help but wonder if... If I had what it takes to pursue my family's legacy, would I?

Neither Mom nor Grandma saw me as their successor. Maybe they never saw potential in me. I bet all they saw was my cooking curse. And they knew I better find a career for myself elsewhere.

But *if* I had what it takes to follow in my family's footsteps, what would I be doing now? Would I be sitting in front of this college application? Or would I be interested in studying cooking, like Pedro? The thought is so far from my reality, I can't help but chuckle. *Me?* Going to culinary school...? I shake my head.

I pull up the Gastronomic Society's website like I'm trying to prove a point to myself. This was never meant for me. I tell myself it's just a joke at first, like playing pretend. Like mashing flowers together and calling it soup. But the moment it loads, I know I can't go back to the economics application waiting behind the web browser.

My eyes scan all the photos of the different classrooms, students in aprons, kitchens packed with delicious ingredients, teachers celebrating their restaurants' success, Michelin stars... And a simmering starts in my heart.

I frown, noticing this doesn't feel new.

It was there when I was a toddler sneaking into the kitchen. It was there as a kid, as I played with my flower recipes. It was there the day Grandma died and I stood alone at the stove. And it was there the moment I started at the cooking club, this feeling that quickly envelops my whole chest with warmth.

I let it reach every part of my body this time.

I let it guide me.

I move the cursor across the screen toward the application form, and it's both scary and exciting at the same time, like the breathless moment before a roller coaster drops—

A hand on my shoulder startles me. I turn to see Cintia. "I didn't know you were here," I say, mentally kicking myself for forgetting Cintia's been practically living in the library lately.

I hate that I was hiding from her, too, slipping back to my loner days. I search her face for any signs that she knows about my near kiss with Pedro. But Cintia just sits down at the computer to my right, giving me a playful warning glance.

"Don't run away," she says.

"I wasn't…planning to." I hear the hesitation in my voice.

"Very convincing," she teases to lighten the mood, but the worry in her eyes betrays her. "I feel like you've been avoiding me since Monday."

"Don't take it personally. I'm avoiding everyone." *Especially Pedro.*

"Why, though?"

"I didn't know how to cook before I joined the club, and I'm embarrassed. I was going to tell you. I'm sorry about all the setbacks I caused with my clumsiness, when you thought I knew what I was doing."

Cintia's eyes are understanding, but I still feel bad. "Lari, there's nothing to be embarrassed about."

"My family owns a bakery," I say, my anxiety from earlier reemerging, reminding me that my college application is still waiting for me. "All the women before me were famous bakers. And I'm...not. That bothers me."

"Because you don't feel like you're going to be a good baker like they expected or...?"

"Ah, no," I say quickly, and Cintia's eyebrows shoot up. I can hear the bitterness in my tone and I'm sure she does, too. I take a deep breath to center myself. "There's never been any expectation about me becoming a baker. My mom doesn't want me to—I'm not going to be a baker. That's all."

"What's that then?"

She points at my screen, her finger hovering above the word *application*, where the cursor rests. I pull my hand away from the mouse and Cintia gives me a knowing look. I'd forgotten about the Gastronomic Society's website. Now I can't hide the evidence.

"I'm not applying or anything," I say. "My grandmother was going to. I was just curious."

Cintia's expression falls when I mention Grandma. "I'm so sorry, Lari. I know she passed away recently. My condolences."

I feel a twinge in my chest. "How do you know that?"

Her eyebrows knit together, and she closes her eyes for a second, like she just gave herself away. When she opens her eyes again, she seems apologetic. "Pedro told us," she admits, and then she adds quickly, "Don't be mad. It wasn't like gossip or anything."

Just hearing his name makes my pulse quicken. "He did? He told Victor and PC, too?"

"Yeah, he, well… He wanted to let you know personally that it was okay to join the club, after you showed up that day we were making smoothies, but I think you two had a fight that week, so he asked PC, Victor, and me to talk with you instead. And he asked us, you know, to be nice because you were in mourning." Cintia presses her lips together, still agonizing over letting this piece of information slip. "Not that we wouldn't have been, but more like… Pedro just wanted to make sure we knew you were upset. Don't be mad at him. Are you mad?"

I thought he'd put them up to something that day, but Pedro was just being…thoughtful? I can't believe this. He hasn't acknowledged Grandma all this time. Not once. It's strange to hear he told them about her.

"I'm not mad," I say, and Cintia relaxes a little. "Thank you for telling me."

"He's not a bad guy, Lari." She turns back to her computer. "But something tells me you're starting to notice that…"

My heart does a little backflip. What does she mean by that? Maybe she doesn't know about the near kiss, but is it written all over my face that my feelings for Pedro are super confusing now? Out of instinct, I open my mouth to protest, to say she's wrong, but I find that I—

I can't deny it. She's right.

I've noticed he's not a bad guy.

I've noticed more than that.

I've noticed sometimes I get butterflies in my chest when he stands close to me.

I shake my head before I start noticing more things I shouldn't, and my eyes zone in on the website Cintia pulls up on the computer. "The Mathematics Regionals!" My voice rises, grateful for the distraction, and the librarian shushes me. "Sorry," I mouth to her, before turning back to Cintia. "Are you going to apply?"

The regionals feel like a lifetime ago. It takes place every December, but the application deadline is mid-June. Every year, I'd hear Mom pestering me to sign up, saying it would look good on my résumé to get mathematics gold medals when I applied for my first internship at an accounting firm. Entering my last year in high school helped me dodge the contest this time—now that Mom thinks my full attention should be on prepping for the vestibular—but I guess I just traded one application stress for another...

"I need to tell you something," Cintia says, and she thinks for a second, like she's looking for the best way to say it. "I totally knew you before the club. Well, sort of. Before I transferred here this year, I used to go to a school that sent students to compete at the regionals, too."

"Ah, you competed?"

"No," she says quickly. "I went to root for my friends. And I watched you destroy them every year."

"I'm not sure if that's good or bad..."

Cintia laughs quietly. "It's good. I love my friends, but it was actually fun to watch you beat everyone." Her eyes light up with excitement, like the memory is still vivid to her. And that blows my mind. I've never seen anyone get this excited about these contests...other than Pimentel and Mom, I guess. "We all thought you were like Beth Harmon in *The Queen's Gambit*."

I can't help but laugh, and the librarian shushes me again.

"I'm serious," Cintia says, lowering her voice to a whisper. "We all felt you made those equations seem so easy. You always got in the zone so quickly. It was scary. In a good way, I mean. I've always wanted to ask you how you managed to just…shut everyone and everything out and focus on the equations when you were on stage."

I lean back in my chair, thinking about how numb I felt during those competitions, even though Mom was in the audience watching me. They made me feel fake, like pretending to be someone I wasn't. I craved Mom's smile in the end, when they announced me as the reigning champion. But, getting the work done felt like…

Like one step closer to going into economics.

If I continue examining how I felt during those contests, I know I'll only complicate my mission to finish my college application today even more. So I change the subject. "Are you going to compete this year?"

Cintia perks up in her chair, looking like I just announced a bear is about to sneak up behind her. "No. Yes. I don't know." She turns to the application in front of her. "I thought if I looked at the form one more time today, I'd know the answer."

I remember how uneasy she was the other day at the club and all the mathematics textbooks she was carrying in her backpack. "Wait, is this what you were overthinking?"

She shoots me a guilty look. "Yeah."

She's top of her class. I see the way students go to her for tutoring. I think she'd be great at the regionals. "You don't want to compete?" I ask, looking from the screen to her, the way she moves the cursor to the application form like she wants to take the first step, but can't.

"I do!" she says, her voice rising, and the librarian says if we're loud one more time, she's totally kicking us out. "And I don't," Cintia explains in a whisper. "I'm not a huge fan of standing up on a stage like that, everyone looking at me while they project my work on a giant screen. Just the thought of people watching me develop solutions makes me queasy." She shudders. "I thought I could finally muster the courage this year, but I can't. And the worst part is I told my parents I would. Now I feel like I just…disappointed them. I didn't do any of the things I said I would. I didn't introduce myself to Professora Pimentel, even though I heard she preps students for the regionals. I didn't even join the mathematics club. Instead, I joined the cooking club."

I frown. "Why the cooking club in particular?"

"Because cooking relaxes me. I don't like being put on the spot and kitchens have a way of making you feel safe, protected… You know what I mean?"

A knot forms in my throat when I think of Salt. "I do," I say. "Cintia, I think your worries are valid. I'm a little stuck myself making college decisions, but if this is what you want, why don't you give it a try?"

She pulls her hand away from the mouse. "You know, PC had a plan. He signed me up for the quadrille because he bet that if I could dance in front of everyone, then I could answer equations in front of everyone, too." She rolls her eyes. "He wasn't even there for the quadrille in the end…"

"But you danced!" I point out. "You didn't back down."

"It's different, though." Her shoulders slump. "I guess leaving the quadrille a dancer down was worse in my mind than dancing in front of everyone. And even though it made me anxious, at least there were other people dancing, too. Pedro was there. The regionals are totally different. It would be just me on stage against some other kid."

"How about I introduce you to Pimentel?" She's already shaking her head again, but I continue, "Just listen to this. I know it's scary, but she'll help you. She helped me. And she'll quiz you so many times until December you'll learn to get in the zone faster." Her round dark eyes shine like she's picturing herself achieving it. "She's a great teacher. And I'll help you, too. You've been cheering me on at the cooking club all this time, so it's time I support you, too."

"Lari, I don't know…"

"Just talk with her, at least? No strings attached."

"Okay, I could talk with her—" she begins to say, and I'm already getting up and prompting her to come with me to the teacher's room, the librarian is looking like she'll fulfill her promise when she sees all the commotion. "Lari, no promises!"

Cintia shakes Pimentel's hand when I introduce them, and she glances at the end of the hallway like she's seriously considering bolting. But Cintia and Pimentel are kindred spirits. Their love for mathematics is contagious, and for a moment I forget my college worries, and I just listen to Cintia discussing her goals and Pimentel's anecdotes about her time in college. But then I start to wonder… Is this what Pimentel meant when she said we should consider the things we love when we're declaring our majors?

I know I'll never muster the same enthusiasm for economics.

In the end, Cintia agrees to send in her application—she can decide later whether she'll compete or not in December—but at least she's taking this first step toward her dream with Pimentel's support.

When we leave the office, Cintia looks like she's floating. The bell rings, ending recess, but before I head to my class and Cintia to hers, she stops me.

"Lari, you said you're struggling with your college decisions, but what about Salt?"

What about Salt?

It's like she read my mind.

She continues, "You clearly *love* baking. You've never considered becoming a baker? Applying to culinary school? Working at Salt?"

"I'm too cursed in the kitchen to follow in my family's footsteps. I'm probably going to study economics... I mean, even if I don't totally care for it, that's what my mom wants for me."

Cintia crosses her arms over her chest. "For someone who feels that way, you sure have a special relationship with cooking and baking. Maybe you're just scared to admit it, Lari. Maybe you're anxious about trying something new and challenging. Trust me, I get it. But don't you think cooking would make you happy? Happier than becoming an accountant, at least? I've seen you in the kitchen. You always come to life. Much more than when you participated in those mathematics contests."

My brow furrows as I consider her words. "But shouldn't I follow a career in something I'm already good at? I don't have my grandmother's fairy hands, so how could I ever be a baker? How could I ever apply to culinary school?"

She sighs.

"You don't need them to cook. And they're definitely not a requirement for you to apply to study cooking, at least." She winks at me. "The only thing you need to do is send in your application."

32

SATURDAY, JUNE 4

"Surprise!" Mom shouts when we turn the corner.

A sign featuring UFPE in big block letters lies ahead of us. The Federal University of Pernambuco. I'm speechless, and I wish it were for the right reason. I have a weird feeling like there's a beeping device screaming I'm about to run out of oxygen.

"I thought it was time we visit the campus together," she says with a smile. "Did I surprise you?"

When Mom had asked me to come with her to Recife, I jumped at the opportunity. I know she's been busy prepping for the catering event next weekend, and I figured maybe it was her way of saying she needed a quick break this Saturday morning.

I thought we'd visit Boa Viagem beach to drink coconut water and watch people shuffling up and down the palm tree–lined calçadão, like we used to when I was younger. I pictured us crossing the well-lit avenue and heading into their feirinha—that sea of turquoise-colored tarp one step away from the sandy beach—to gawk at the art, dresses, and jewelry sold at booths with big white buildings towering over us. I imagined us lining up to try delicious coconut and cheese tapiocas, bolinhos de charque, and washing everything down with the sweetest sugarcane juice. We'd come home re-energized, the smell of salt on our skin.

I was wrong.

Mom cranes her neck to peer out the window, driving slowly into the campus. Her eyes are wide and full of wonder, like a kid at an amusement park, still deciding which will be her first ride.

"Look. *Look!*" she says, pointing out the window.

I try to summon the same excitement, but Mom is too amazed to notice I've failed.

"So many students apply every year..." Mom marvels. "This place, Lari, I just know it will be *freedom* for you. It will be your independence." She talks as if I am trapped in my current life. "You know, studying here will make you so happy. It will help you figure out what type of person you are. That's so important, filha."

But I already am happy. And I know the type of person I want to be.

I want to be a baker.

The revelation comes to me crystal clear.

My heart booms in my chest, and I get that feeling of standing high, high above a swimming pool, looking down at the water from a diving board. *I want to be a baker.* My inner voice is loud. The clearest it's ever been. It hits me in a dizzying rush of feelings.

I want to be a baker.

I *am* a baker.

I've always known it, like finding out that the warmth under my skin was my own blood running in my veins all this time.

I picture myself applying for the Gastronomic Society, and just the thought puts a wide smile on my face. Mom notices it and nods in approval, thinking I'm finally getting excited about college.

"The vestibular sounds so scary," Mom says. "I could never do it. But I have total confidence in you. You study every day. You even go to review sessions in the afternoon, don't you?"

She pauses, waiting for my answer.

"I do," I lie.

"See? You always do your best and I know you'll earn a spot here."

"But what if… I don't fit in?" I ask.

"You'll fit in," Mom's voice rises a little, like I spoke nonsense. "You're your father's daughter. A talent like his, like *yours*, is a great asset to any school. This university would be lucky to have you. You'll be the first Ramires to go to college."

Sometimes I feel like that's all we have left. These college plans she wants me to fulfill. The milestone in our family. Without it, I worry there's nothing left that ties us together.

When I joined the club, part of me hoped that learning to cook could act as a bridge between us. So I could finally bake side by side with Mom in Salt's kitchen. Like it was all that simple. A matter of working on a recipe together.

But now…

How can I tell her the truth? That all this time I've been

trying to connect with her, the more I've distanced myself from her plans for my future?

Mom parks the car and we begin our walking tour. I follow her around, a bit dazed, as she points out the different buildings. I realize she's rehearsed a little for this trip.

She takes me to a lake on campus. There are picnic tables nearby, and she points at a spot under one of them. When I crouch down next to her, I see G + A carved into it.

"Gabriel and Alice?!" I say with a gasp.

Mom's eyes are bright with saudades. "This is where your father and I met," she says.

Mom tells me that when she was my age, her friends often hung out near this lake. And that's where she met Dad. He was only seventeen and he had lied about his age to get a job as a gardener on campus so he could linger by the classroom windows and listen to lectures.

It was his dream to go to college, but without a high school degree, he couldn't even apply to take the entrance exams. When students went to buy their study sheets at the Xerox room, he'd pretend to be one of them, so he could read the material, too. That's how he honed his talent in mathematics.

"As an economics student, you'll be taking most of your classes here," she says, proudly pointing at a building where students step in and out in a constant stream. "Gabriel dreamed of this building day and night. Isn't it amazing to think you'll be studying here soon?"

I listen to her, perplexed. I'd never known these things about him. More clearly than ever, I understand why Mom puts so much pressure on me to finish Dad's plans. So his dreams weren't for nothing.

I feel a deep twinge in my chest. Guilt. How do I tell Mom this isn't what I want? She'll be so disappointed in me...

There's a computer store nearby that catches Mom's attention. Before I can say anything, she heads inside, leaving me behind.

"Mom, wait!" I can barely keep up with her.

"My daughter is a future economics major," she says to a bored-looking employee. "I want her to have a good, reliable laptop so she can work on her projects." But before the guy can even give her a suggestion, she points to a laptop on a shelf nearby. "I'll take that one."

I stare at the price. We can't afford this. "I don't need a laptop," I say quickly, but Mom isn't listening.

"Your handwritten reports look unprofessional," she says, striding to the cashier to get in line.

I rush after her. "I can just use my school's computers."

"But you don't always have access to them. And what will happen when you start college? All your classmates will have laptops. I don't want you to be the only one who doesn't."

"Mom, you're not listening."

She whirls around to look at me. "What are you saying?" And I freeze.

I remember Grandma's words. *Talk with your mother. Tell her how you feel.*

"Don't get mad," I begin, and Mom's face scrunches up.

"What should I be mad about? Everything is fine."

Nothing's been fine for so long.

Mom stares at me, waiting for me to talk. It's like the night of Grandma's funeral, Mom and me standing in the bakery in front of Great-grandma's recipe, uncertainty stretching on and on in front of us.

"I'm sorry, senhora, but your card was declined," the cashier says, and she jerks around to look at him.

"Try again," she says.

"I've already tried twice."

"Then try a third time," Mom says in a low voice.

"It's declined." He waves the next customer over, ignoring Mom's pleading eyes.

She snatches her credit card and rushes outside. I go after her. "Mom!"

She stops only when she's reached the economics building again. "Do you understand now?" she says. "Do you understand what this all means to me? To *you*? It's not just college, filha. It's—It's *everything!* It's my sole consolation that you'll never have to fear anything. That you won't be buried like I am under a pile of bills! That you'll be free. Freer than your dad and I ever were!"

My heart breaks. Even though I want to help her run Salt when school is over, how can I argue against financial problems as serious as what we're going through? She won't listen to me. Not until Salt is no longer in the red.

"Did you want to say something?" she asks.

And I just can't bring myself to tell her the truth. "No."

Mom launches the computer store one last, hurt look. "Then let's go home."

That night at Salt, the Deals Deals cars are once again on our street.

We watch them go up and down, up and down, like they're

scouting the region. Every time they swarm like this, one of my neighbors packs up and leaves the next day. There are so many empty storefronts now, like snuffed out candles. Without their store lights, the neighborhood just gets darker and darker.

Now that we've entered June and the deadline the lawyer gave us is approaching, I feel like the shadows are longer. If we show vulnerability now, *any* at all, they'll swoop in. Is the catering gig Mom's getting ready for even enough to keep them away? Why does she still look so cornered?

I see her shudder, walking away from the window display like she's thinking the same thing. She goes behind the counter and turns on the TV. I'm still watching from behind the window display when I hear the journalist on TV mention the Gastronomic Society. I whirl around to look at the screen with a gasp.

He's interviewing the winner of last year's cooking contest, mentioning how winning has impacted her life. I rush to the counter, nearly tripping. The winner goes on explaining that her restaurant got starred reviews and attracted more customers with the investment money and new contracts. She's now a world-famous restaurateur!

"If Julieta were here, she would show all these fancy chefs what traditional, good food is like," Dona Clara says from her stool at the counter beside me. Isabel, who's squeezing a lime wedge over their shared plate of quibe, nods in agreement.

Mom scoffs, looking away from the TV. "She wanted to bake her favorite corn cake, and she would've won!" she tells Dona Clara, and for the first time I hear clear resentment in her voice. I thought that being the practical woman that she is, she just didn't like these types of contests in general. But it looks like Mom actually holds a personal grudge against the Gastronomic Society. She gets a second wind. "Had they not slighted her, the best baker in this whole city, she would've won! But my mother didn't fit their profile. They enroll these rich, well-traveled kids who barely know a thing about cooking and tell everyone they're genius chefs making *art*. I see their photos on the internet, where it's more about them and less about the food they make. Of course my mother never stood a chance. She'd make them all look bad with how good she was!"

"Opportunities like that don't come around at our neighborhood," Isabel muses, getting a rare look of approval from Dona Clara.

It hurts to see Mom is so biased against the Gastronomic Society. Can't she see that the cash prize and the attention the winner gets from the cooking community would have been a tremendous help to Salt? Grandma knew this. Had they accepted her, we'd be safe now, not so reliant on one catering job that's already taking a toll on Mom. The dark circles under her eyes are even more prominent now.

The interviewer ends the segment with an announcement that this year they're opening up to nonmembers for a brand-new contest format. A *family* cooking contest. There's a minimum of two contestants per entry, encouraging couples, parents, and siblings to join. I nearly choke, because the contest is on the twenty-third. The day before the deadline

Deals Deals gave us. It feels like one last chance to make a difference against the supermarket.

"It's a *scam*," Mom says right away. "They want to include everyone, but in the end, do you think one of us would win? I bet they've already picked one of their students. It would look bad for them if they lost to one of us."

I launch Mom a pleading look. Because this is it. The best shield possible against Deals Deals!

"Shouldn't we at least give the contest a try?" I beg. "Let's send in an application!"

Dona Clara and Isabel look expectantly from me to Mom.

"Your grandmother must have filled your head with non-sense dreams about the Gastronomic Society. She was an amazing baker, and they didn't even accept her as a student. You see how it's all rigged? We'd be better off trying the lottery. The probability of winning would be higher," she says, making a point of turning the TV off like it's her final say in this.

Mom will never listen to me. Call me foolish for being a dreamer like Grandma, but what's so wrong with at least *try-ing*? Maybe the contest is rigged. Maybe it's a scam. But we won't know if we don't give it a try.

A sunflower under Great-grandma Elisa's recipe falls at my feet, and I get goose bumps up and down my arms.

A sign.

What if this is Grandma telling us that we should go for it?

"If we win, it would show Deals Deals once and for all that they can't mess with us," I plead with Mom one last time. "The cooking world would rally behind us. The Gastronomic Society would *never* let a supermarket chain get to the winner of their cooking contest. And even if we don't win, there's all this TV attention during the contest. We could start speaking up about the situation in the neighborhood!"

Mom raises a hand to stop me. "*We?* If *we* win? There's no 'we' here. You don't bake."

"I know a thing or two—" I stop, feeling like I just gave myself away. "I mean I know I could *learn* a thing or two," I measure my words carefully like how I measure flour at the club. "You just have to show me how to bake one amazing recipe, and we could enter the contest together. We could stand up in front of all those cameras and tell them that Deals Deals is making everyone in the neighborhood go under."

Dona Clara slams her hand on the counter. "Do it, Alice! Show them what Salt can do!"

For one second, Mom looks like she's considering my idea, getting intoxicated with my excitement, but then her eyes travel to my textbooks on the counter, and it's like they're a reminder of everything she's always hoped and dreamed for me. Everything that I could lose, if I'm not one hundred percent focused on school.

"You're studying for the vestibular," she says. "I didn't sacrifice so much for you to get distracted with a contest that's already a lost cause. You're not a baker. And you have no business getting involved with these things. So spend your time wisely. *College* is your lottery ticket, filha."

I place the sunflower back in the vase, fighting back tears.

When I turn around to grab my books and head upstairs, I spot Pedro leaving Sugar. He takes off on his bicycle, wind stirring his hair. And just like that, I have one of my wildest ideas so far.

What if Pedro and I enter the Gastronomic Society's cooking competition together? I know the contest is for families, but then again… Aren't Salt and Sugar kind of like estranged sisters?

33

MONDAY, JUNE 6

I arrive early at the club Monday afternoon, catching Pedro alone. He goes red the moment he looks up. He's been avoiding me, too. "I have to do inventory," he announces, super skittish, ready to dash into the pantry. But the finished list is on the counter right in front of me.

"Pedro, do you have a moment?" I say.

He turns around gingerly. "What's up?"

He must have been working on his family's bolo de rolo recipe again, because the kitchen smells deliciously sweet, bringing back dizzying memories that I try to shove out of my mind.

"There's something I need to ask you." I take a deep breath, summoning courage. "Did you know the Gastronomic Society has a yearly cooking contest?"

His demeanor changes, immediately guarded. "Yes," he says, shortly. "It's for members only."

"Not anymore. And I think we should—" I fidget with the dish rag on the counter. "I think we should enter together."

Pedro looks at me like I've just spoken gibberish. "What?"

"I'm serious. We need a way to keep Deals Deals from coming after us once and for all."

"And you think that contest is the answer?"

"Yes!"

After getting kicked out of his own house for wanting to apply to the Gastronomic Society, I'm sure it must be difficult for him to even think about getting anywhere near that dream again. He's already shaking his head.

"I don't know..." he says. "This is a lot to think about. And it's really hard to get first place in a contest like that, too... I'm not sure it's the best solution against Deals Deals."

"But we could at least give it a try."

"You and me?" He shakes his head again. "Entering a contest together? If my mother finds out—"

"Our families don't need to know if we don't win," I say.

He squints at me. "And if we do?"

"They'll be mad, but it will be for a good cause. Think about it this way. The contest would show our families that the bakeries are safe against Deals Deals. And winning as nonmembers would get a *lot* of press attention directed to our neighborhood. It could attract more business for all of us." I walk up to him. "And if you were to change your mind about applying to the Gastronomic Society, winning would show them your potential as a future student."

The way his eyes sharpen tells me I've crossed the line. "Who said I wanted to apply?"

"I overheard you talking with the principal about it..."

Pedro turns away from me. "I can't do this."

"Pedro—"

"This is a big ask," he cuts me off, getting annoyed. "You have no idea what a hornet's nest this is for me. If you want to join their contest, go for it. But I'm out."

"I can't join alone," I say at his back.

He turns around. "Why not?"

"The contest this year is for families," I explain. "Mothers and daughters. Cousins… You get the picture. My mother won't be my partner. I figured since you and I have a common goal, shouldn't we join together?"

Pedro's ears go pink. "How are *we* a family?"

I feel myself blush, so I stare at my feet.

"There's an option for couples," I say, my voice tiny with embarrassment. "I already…checked."

Pedro is silent for so long, I look up to make sure he hasn't left the room without me noticing. It's awkward enough that we've been avoiding each other since we nearly kissed—in this exact same spot—last week. And now I'm asking him to join a contest with me, pretending we're…you know…*together*?!

Why do I feel like I'm actually asking him to be my boyfriend or something?

His ears have gone from pink to a bright shade of purple in a matter of seconds. He must feel like I'm asking him to be my boyfriend, too.

Pedro opens his mouth to say something, and I never get to hear his answer because Victor and Cintia arrive. He quickly steps away from me to start our meeting—the Vozes fundraiser is later today, and we have a lot to do.

I sit down on a stool by the counter, my heart pounding.

When Cintia comes to sit next to me, she's unaware of the electrical currents traveling all around the kitchen. Pedro chatters on, sounding a little hoarse, and when she asks me if something happened, my heart slams against my chest so hard I'm sure she can hear it.

When we get to Vozes, the house is packed. Community leaders bustle about inside, while the kids' choir gets ready to perform.

We go straight for the table in the back, where other dishes are assembled. Guests have brought their favorite recipes for the potluck, and we carefully place our double-layered guava and Parmesan corn cake next to them. Victor and Cintia liked it so much when they found it in the fridge, they insisted Pedro and I recreate it. Leaving out the details of our little accident, we adjusted the recipes to make both layers blend better when they stack.

Tiny arms wrap around my waist.

"Amandinha," I say, returning the hug.

She smiles, looking up at me. "You came!"

"Of course I did!"

"I made him promise you would come back," she admits, glancing at Pedro, who's busy assembling more plates and cups.

"He told me."

She gestures for me to kneel down.

"Is it a secret?" I ask her.

Amandinha nods, and then says in my ear:

"My mom got a job."

"Wow!" I give her another hug. "That's really great! I'm really happy for you."

"She said she'll get me a Barbie!"

I think of Mom trying to buy me a laptop and my heart aches at the memory of her embarrassment. "You take really good care of that Barbie," I tell Amandinha. "I know she'd give you more dolls if she could."

She smiles. "She's going to make delicious food just like you guys do!"

"Yeah?"

"I told her about your grandma's fairy hands!"

Dona Selma taps Amandinha on the shoulder, and she waves goodbye, skipping to go take her spot in the choir.

"I'm glad your club could join us today," Dona Selma says, and Pedro shows her the cake we've brought.

I still can't believe it's a cake that I helped bake.

Last time I tried baking Grandma's corn cake, it felt wrong that I couldn't make it like I remembered it. I had baked it looking for her and couldn't quite find her. But, in the magic of cooking, the recipe took a detour and led me elsewhere. Not to Grandma, but to myself. And then after a little slip and a near kiss, the recipe reinvented itself and turned into perfection.

I'm nervous to hear what Dona Selma will think of it. I swallow down the sorrow that Grandma will never try anything I baked myself.

Dona Selma tries a slice, and after just one bite, she starts passing plates around to the guests standing nearby, urging them to try it.

"This is amazing!" a woman says, and the other guests all respond the same way, looking like they're about to melt along with the flavors in their mouths.

"Your club baked this?" another guest asks, impressed.

"Pedro and Lari came up with this recipe together," Cintia explains.

"This is a Romeo and Juliet, isn't it?" Dona Selma asks.

Pedro looks at me, suddenly shy. "It does fit the requirement. The layer of corn cake carries a lot of Parmesan cheese and with the sweetness of the guava, you do get a Romeo and Juliet recipe."

It feels like a dream, seeing the way everyone smiles when they try our cake. The kids are bouncy, their mouths full. Some of the guests giggle, cake crumbs on their lips. Volunteers give each other side hugs, midchew.

Dona Selma stands in front of the kids' choir to speak a few words. "I wanted to thank everyone for making this fundraiser a success," she says, and the room cheers. "Thank you for dreaming this dream with me, every day. Because of you, we'll be able to fix our kitchen so we can continue doing the work we do here." More cheers and clapping. Dona Selma is starting to look tearful, her eyes bright. "This has been such a difficult time for our community. Such a difficult time, personally." Her voice cracks a little, and the painful lump that forms in my throat tells me where she's going. "I lost my best friend recently." Her words feel like a punch in the gut. When Dona Selma locks eyes with me, I'm stuck to my spot, breathless, trying to hold back tears. "She was an incredible woman who believed in dreams, too. She believed in my dream. She was a fierce supporter of our Vozes, and wherever you are, Julieta, I thank you for never letting go of my hand. This song is for you."

People all around raise their glasses to honor Grandma. Victor, who slides next to me, gives my shoulder a supportive squeeze. Amandinha appears and hands me a sunflower before running back to take her position in the choir. The kids sing "Oração" by A Banda Mais Bonita da Cidade, a song that's like a prayer, just like its title, describing how hearts aren't as simple as we think, how they're big enough to store even what pantries can't.

And I can't take this.

I'm not ready for final prayers or goodbyes.

I slip out of the room, headed into the side garden, ready to run away like the day of Grandma's funeral, but the door opens behind me.

"There you are," Pedro says, joining me.

I smile to hide the pain inside, but tears begin rolling down my cheeks. A gust of wind blows Pedro's bangs over his eyes, and when he brushes the hair off, I notice the slight tremor in his hand.

"Lari, I know I'm very late, but is it okay if I give you my condolences?" he says. "I feel like a jerk for not saying anything earlier. I've actually tried to bring it up a few times."

His words catch me off guard. I only realize now that I had been hoping he'd acknowledge Grandma's absence to me. Because as much as our families hate each other, Grandma was one of our community's beating hearts. Just like Seu Romário is.

"You're not too late," I say, my voice cracking.

"I'm so sorry. I'll never forget the way she was there for me when I needed help."

The tears won't stop. "What do you mean?"

Pedro gives me a sad smile. "When I was ten, I found a family of stray cats living in that alley behind the ateliers, you know, and I was worried the kittens were too thin, so I kept taking milk from Sugar to feed them," he tells me, his eyes glistening. "But Grandpa caught me and forbade me. Dona Julieta saw me crying, and without saying anything, she brought me scraps from Salt. Raw chicken, ground beef, any time she baked empadinhas or coxinhas, she'd leave me a bag on the windowsill, and I'd take it to the cats. It was like a secret between us. She never said anything to Grandpa, and I fed the cats until they were strong and went away. I'll always be grateful."

Grandma never told me about this. But that's—that's such a Grandma thing to do.

"Thank you for telling me." I fling my arms around him, burying my face in his chest to muffle the sobs racking through my chest.

I feel him tense in surprise, like he did that night he gave me a ride home in the rain, but he doesn't pull away. He holds me, letting me nestle against him. Letting me cry in his arms, one hand rubbing my back.

"I don't want to say goodbye to her," I tell him.

"You don't have to."

I don't know how long we stay like this, standing next to the hibiscus bushes, the rain falling over the garden, curtaining the world all around us.

34

Pedro never told me if he'd enter the contest with me, but I take his silence on the subject to mean he won't.

I can't ask Mom to join me—she has too much on her plate as it is. But Grandma would not have let me give up this easily! So I'll find a new partner. Maybe Cintia or Victor would agree…

For now, I try to figure out what my entry dish will be, and I spend the rest of the week studying Grandma's old recipes. I'm sprawled in bed, recipes stacked up all around me in Grandma's handwriting, when someone knocks on my door.

I bolt upright, hiding the recipes under my bed.

Isabel pokes her head in. Just from her face, I can tell something's wrong. "You should go talk with your mom," she says.

"What happened?"

"She was taking everyone's orders and then she got a phone call, started yelling, and locked herself in Dona Julieta's office."

I run down the stairs two steps at a time, my heart beating

out of my chest. The atmosphere in the bakery is tense. A few customers stand uncertain on the other side of the counter.

I hurry to the office door. "Mom? Everything okay?"

After what feels like an eternity, she opens the door.

"Tell everyone to come back another time," she whispers before closing it again.

When I turn around, shaking, the customers are still looking at me. "S-she's not feeling well," I stammer.

"We understand," Isabel says in the back, already opening the door to usher everyone out. She mouths "call me if you need anything" before she leaves.

Alone in the bakery, I head back to the office. "Mom, they're gone. Can I come in?"

The door clicks open and I step inside. Mom sits at Grandma's old desk, bills assembled in front of her like a tarot card reading. And judging by her expression, our fortune is bleak.

I sit down in front of her.

"Dona Fernanda just called to fire us," Mom says, blunt, and it's like all blood drains from my body. "They're hiring Deals Deals instead."

"What?!" I shout. "No. No. She can't—"

"She can and she did," Mom cuts me off. "It's very unprofessional, but it happens. She'll pay for whatever I had already prepared, and that's it."

"But the party is in two days!"

"I know. But Deals Deals has been feeding her rumors that we've been having sanitation problems at Salt all this time and hiding it from her. That Eulalia and I could ruin her special day with one of our 'infamous fights.' That we're unreliable and won't deliver in time. And...that I personally don't have experience as a party planner..." Mom smiles sadly. "Now that last rumor isn't a lie."

"You did an amazing job! You worked day and night!" I say, my voice rising with indignation. "*Deals Deals* said all that about us?!"

"They started the original rat rumors, Lari," Mom says, getting back on her feet with an impatient gesture. "It was them all along. And Dona Fernanda's daughter doesn't want any more stress. Even if her mother believes us, this is still her party. There's nothing else I can say or do to convince them that our kitchen is safe. And I'm sick and tired of this. I'm so tired."

I'm speechless. I shake my head, willing this moment to be a nightmare I'll wake up from any minute now. Everything will be okay. Mom and Dona Eulalia had already put everything together so well. The freezer at Salt is filled with frozen salgados, ready to get baked and deep-fried for the party.

Mom pushes past me in a hurry, like she's trying to escape all our bills. I follow her into the kitchen, where she pulls out all the trays filled with food she'd prepared and dumps them into a big trash bin.

"Mom, stop! Don't do that! We may still be able to convince them!" I grab a tray from her, but Mom dodges me and throws more empadinhas in the trash. I watch helplessly. When there's nothing else left in the freezer, she grabs a carton of eggs and gets ready to cook.

She cracks the eggs over a plate, catching the yolk between her fingers. She whisks the egg whites, her hands moving with quick, precise strokes. She's done this so many times in her life, she doesn't even need to look down at her work, and still the egg whites grow into a white cloud, never spilling, obedient like they recognize my mom's hands.

The sound of the whisker hitting the bottom of the plate is almost hypnotic. And I know—this is how Mom copes. How she numbs the pain.

"We should apologize to the Molinas," I say, my voice coming out like a croak.

The whisker hits the rim of the plate a bit more forcefully. When Mom looks at me, her eyes are so bright with anger, it scares me. "Why do I have to apologize?" she asks.

"We owe it to them. We accused them of starting the rat rumors," I say.

Mom lets the whisker fall right on top of the cloud of egg whites. "I owe that family absolutely nothing!" She's visibly trembling. "Sure, they aren't to blame *this* time. But they are behind countless other rumors. Do you want me to pretend those didn't happen? Where are *my* apologies for all the pain they've caused?" She looks down at the ruined egg whites, throwing her hands up. "Now look at this. I'll have to start all over again!"

"Mom, I'm sorry—"

"Larissa, *leave!*"

I hurry out of the kitchen before she can yell at me again, my thoughts spinning like a hurricane. We got played by Deals Deals. I bet they thought they could use our feud to their advantage, pitting us against each other, ready to swoop in the moment one of us felt vulnerable. And I fell for it.

How can Mom not wonder if we've been misled in other ways? Maybe she just doesn't want to give the Molinas the benefit of the doubt. She's too proud. It would also mean admitting that we falsely accused them of slandering us.

All this time, I thought we were different. I thought we were just trying to defend ourselves against the Molinas. But I now understand my family can be just as responsible for keeping this vicious cycle spinning.

How many times in the past were we the ones inflicting pain? How many times did I perceive an attack, when the Molinas were actually *reacting* to something we did first?

Attack. Retaliation. Attack. Retaliation.

It no longer matters who or what even set the feud in motion. All that matters is the next step. Will the cycle ever end?

35

THURSDAY, JUNE 9

I wait for Pedro in the back of the corner store as the sun sets.

When he finally arrives, he stands on one side of a shelf, half-hidden behind bags of couscous flakes. I stay on the other side, pretending to browse, so none of our neighbors will think we're together. And it kills me that we can't even talk openly, that we have to hide in our own neighborhood. Like we're doing something terrible.

"Dona Fernanda fired Mom," I tell him.

"She just fired us, too," he says.

"Pedro, there's something you need to know." My voice shakes with anger. "I just found out that Deals Deals came up with the rumor about rats in Salt. They were trying to make us fight with you." I ball my hand into fists to hold back the sudden urge to scream. "I'm so sorry for accusing you and your family. I'm so, *so* sorry."

He marches round the shelves to join me. Standing near a wall of herbs, we're in a shadowy hidden nook in the dim store, alone in our aisle.

"I need your help," he says, looking as confused and angry as I feel. "I was thinking, if you're okay with it, the cake we brought to Vozes could be our entry dish."

"Our entry dish...?"

"I think it's a winner, don't you?" he says. "Unless you don't want me anymore. I mean—as your partner. At the Gastronomic Society." I just stare at him because I don't think I heard him right. "What should we write in the contest application? That we're dating or...?" He coughs. "Because of the 'family' requirement, you know?"

I feel myself blush so hard I must look bright red. "Right, right..."

"So...?"

"Yeah, we're dating—I mean *write* that we're dating." I blink, trying to focus. This still feels like a dream. I just told him we accused his family wrongfully, and he still wants to team up with me?! "Are you serious about entering the contest with me? What about your mother and grandfather?"

"I haven't been more serious in my entire life. Mom is too worried about Grandpa's health to consider anything like this, and Grandpa is sick, so I can't ask him. I have a feeling he wouldn't trust me enough to be his partner, anyway..." He offers me a sad smile. "But now that we can't cater anymore, Sugar is in trouble. I need to do something. I have to do this for my family, and there's no one I'd trust to enter this contest with more than you. You're fighting for your home, too. You're the only one who understands the way I feel now."

My heart aches for him. He's only seventeen. He shouldn't have to feel the weight of running his family's business.

"We'll win," I say, and deep down I try to convince myself, too. "And when we do, Salt and Sugar will be safe."

Pedro stares at me for a moment. "Lari, you'd tell me, right?"

My heart skips a beat. It's the first time he's called me by my nickname. "Tell you what?"

"If your mom decides to sell Salt now that things are falling apart. Remember our original truce? The deadline for the Deals Deals offer is in two weeks. We have to stop our mothers if they begin to cave, okay? This contest will be for nothing if one of them decides to take the offer."

I open my mouth to tell him that Mom still has that lawyer's business card, when our mothers' raised voices outside the store make us jump.

For a terrifying minute, I'm sure Mom has followed me and sees who I'm talking to. Pedro looks just as startled.

But it's just the feud. Our mothers are yelling simply because they've crossed paths on the sidewalk and don't have the catering gig to force them to coexist anymore.

"I should never have worked with someone like you! You didn't know the first thing about party planning! You're ruining Sugar's reputation with your incompetence and I *know* you must have said something to Dona Fernanda's daughter to get me fired! She was perfectly fine with Sugar catering alone for her birthday before you went and ruined everything!" Dona Eulalia accuses Mom. "Now she's not even answering my calls! What did you do, Alice? Tell me!"

"Now why would I do something that hurts my business?!" Mom retorts. "We were catering *together*! I'd be sabotaging myself, too!"

"Because you're already in talks with Deals Deals to sell Salt! I know it! You couldn't care less about the job and decided to take Sugar down!"

I glance at Pedro, worried he'll believe his mother's words. "It isn't true," I tell him. "Deals Deals must be behind these lies, too, putting pressure on your mother."

He doesn't look at me, his eyes still glued on the fight outside.

"You're a snake, Alice!" his mother goes on.

"Get out of the way!" Mom shouts back.

"You've always known you were going to sell out, haven't you? Admit it! If I find out you've been discussing with Deals Deals from day one, while you had the whole neighborhood fooled with that boycott you started, I'm selling Sugar first! I won't be made a fool of! I'm not leaving this godforsaken neighborhood with nothing!"

This is a nightmare.

We wait until our mothers go their separate ways so we can come out from behind the shelf. But even when they finally step away from the store's entrance, Pedro and I still stand staring at each other. I can't help but feel like we're getting swept back into the feud. And now I'm too afraid to move.

I can't make myself walk away from him before I know what he's thinking. And somehow I feel he's wondering the same about me. When we hear the shuffling of customers nearby, Pedro grabs my hand and pulls me into another empty aisle.

I need to tell him about that business card. About the way Mom keeps it clipped to the disconnection notice like it's an emergency number, but after hearing Dona Eulalia's threats, I'm stuck in an overwhelming dilemma.

Is it safe to expose *all* of my families' vulnerabilities to this boy who has always been my enemy?

I gave him my word. I promised I'd warn him if I noticed Mom was about to cave.

But if Dona Eulalia gets so much as a whiff that Mom is considering selling, she could take it as the sign she's been waiting for to sell Sugar first.

I feel small.

I feel like a coward.

"I have to go," I say, my throat dry like sandpaper.

But he looks into my eyes, his fingers entwined with mine, and I can't leave.

"I'm sorry," I say. Without thinking, I wrap my arms around him.

"I'm sorry," he says in my ear, sending a shiver down my back.

We say we're sorry a thousand times, not just for things in our past, but also for things to come. We stash up on our apologies, because we're children of a multigenerational feud. We brace for the day when our families will clash again. When they'll make us hate each other. And even worse, when we'll feel compelled ourselves.

But just for this brief, magical moment, we're together.

We hear more customers approach the aisle. We need to separate. Hide. Hide our feelings. But his arms are still around me, one hand on the small of my back, pushing me against him. My grip doesn't loosen either.

Three seconds until someone will catch a glimpse of us. I don't want this to end.

Two seconds. I know he's aware of the countdown, too.

"Lari," he says. A tiny word like a sigh. My name. But it sounds so powerful in my ears, I feel intoxicated. I look up, and that longing is back in his eyes. And it scares me.

One second.

We peel away just in time, and I sneak out of the store first, a tightness in my chest. His warmth still on my skin. Tears sting my eyes. *Mom has never said she'll sell Salt,* I repeat mentally. *All she did was keep that lawyer's business card.*

Then why do I feel like a liar? Like I'm betraying Pedro's trust?

I'm hit with a sudden wave of emotion—terrified of losing Pedro. But I try to push my worries aside. I *have* to—before I march back into that store and kiss him in front of everyone.

Pedro and I, together, will win this contest. When we do, it won't matter that my mother or his mother ever considered the supermarket's offer. Because by then Deals Deals won't be a threat to our neighborhood anymore.

It's odd to think our futures rely on a cake recipe. But isn't that the fate of all Ramires and Molinas?

36

SATURDAY, JUNE 11

Saturday night, the day Mom would have been catering Salt's biggest event ever, an old wine-colored Fiat Uno parks in front of Salt.

I see it all from my bedroom window.

Dona Clara climbs out, boxes and luggage stacked in the back of the car. She knocks on our front door with her cane, pulling a flimsy shawl over her shoulders. It's past work hours, but Mom's insomnia keeps her up and she opens the door right away.

Dona Clara seems in a hurry. She doesn't want to come inside.

One look at Grandma's oldest friend's car, and Mom bursts into sorrowful tears. The gesture is so abrupt, I clamp my mouth with a hand, my eyesight blurring with tears of my own. Because Mom never cries like this. She always contains her feelings, but this time she lets herself sob. I'm too scared to go downstairs. I can't take any more sad news. I can't take any more goodbyes.

"Who'll look after Isabel?" I hear Dona Clara say on the sidewalk. "No one will hire that careless girl. She's always daydreaming about telenovela actors and letting the cooking oil burn. It's my fault for not being harder on her. I didn't teach her well."

"Isabel is hardworking because of you," Mom says. "And I'd hire her in a heartbeat if I could."

Dona Clara pats her gently on the cheek. "You have your mother's heart." Her eyes suddenly shine with fear. "Alice, you've put up a good fight. We all have. But there's nothing else to do. Look at me now. I'm moving in with my little brother in São Paulo. He says he'll take care of me, but he can hardly look after himself." She squeezes her cane, leaning heavily against it. "My cousin Yara is stubborn. She's staying. But I give it one month, and she'll be joining us, too."

"Olinda won't be the same without you," Mom says.

Dona Clara's eyes are bright with tears when she looks at the houses, like she's trying to memorize our neighborhood. I duck behind my curtains to avoid detection. When I peer out the window again, she's back in her car.

"Accept their offer before it's too late," she urges Mom. She nods toward Sugar. "Before they take the chance, because *if* and *when* that happens, you and Lari will be left with nothing. Julieta didn't spend her days in that kitchen so her girls would be ruined in the end." She reaches out the window and squeezes Mom's hand, and they don't let go of each other until the last second. "Watch over Isabel for me? That foolish girl has no one in the world."

"I'll look after her like she's my own daughter," Mom promises.

Dona Clara drives off, her car's engine rattling and sputtering down the street.

I watch the taillights until they're gone.

37

WEDNESDAY, JUNE 15

There are no classes after the midterms, and I lie to Mom saying my teachers are running review sessions. Instead, I meet with Pedro at the cafeteria's kitchen to work on our cake. Sometimes Victor and Cintia join us to be our taste testers, after we explained to them we're up against Deals Deals.

Other times, like today, it's just Pedro and me...

Although we should keep our interactions limited to the kitchen at school, it's becoming harder and harder to say goodbye to him at the end of the day. I crave being around him. Every little moment.

I even crave his annoying know-it-all smirk when he brings coconut bread he baked at Sugar and it tastes like perfect, carefree mornings. "One day, I'll get you to have a sweet tooth like mine," he says.

And, above all, I crave his body's warmth. When we sit together in the empty parking lot after baking, shoulder to shoulder. For one glorious hour before heading home, it's just us, getting distracted with random stuff. Just talking. No feud.

No Deals Deals. No failed catering gig. No cooking contest anxieties. Just two new friends getting to know each other.

That's how I learn he can't watch horror movies because he hates getting startled.

He's a Trekkie. Nog is his favorite character, because he worked at his uncle's bar, just like Pedro works at his grandfather's bakery.

And he's a little more sentimental than he likes to admit.

He nonchalantly passes me a note this afternoon. I can't believe it when I see that it's a belated St. Anthony's card. It's not one of the heart-shaped cards that couples pass each other, but it's one celebrating our budding friendship.

"I couldn't give it to you on Monday," he mumbles, looking off to the side. "And then again yesterday. The others were around, and you and Victor wouldn't stop chatting about YouTube videos. I didn't…want them to…you know…"

Cintia and Victor still don't know Pedro and I are…whatever you call this thing that's starting between us. I'm sure they suspect, though, judging by the furtive glances Pedro and I get when we stand shoulder to shoulder at the stove.

I think of the card covered in hearts waiting in the depths of my backpack. I can't give that to him—what was I thinking?! I should have made a friendship one, too! And now he's looking at me like he's waiting for his card.

"It's not just any YouTube video," I say, quickly changing the subject. "Victor is thinking of starting a channel to talk about the dishes he tries. He's been showing me the ones that inspire him."

"What's the deal between you two?" Pedro asks out of the blue, making a point to look very immersed in watching the clouds.

He is *jealous. Has he been jealous of my friendship with Victor since the party?*

"I told you before. He's my friend."

"He likes you." Pedro looks at me this time, like he needs to see my reaction to his words.

"Why did you argue at the party?" I ask, instead.

Pedro averts his eyes again. "We didn't argue." He shrugs. "We just— He told me to leave you alone. To quit bringing our families' feud to school."

Victor was upset when he heard my classmates calling me Salty. It's good to have a friend who has my back. But I wish they hadn't fought.

"Victor really said that?"

"He likes you," he repeats like he's proving a point.

"What...did you tell him?"

He looks me in the eye. "I told him he didn't have to ask. I told him I—that he didn't have to worry."

I can't help but smile. "Did you suddenly learn to tolerate me?" I joke.

"No," Pedro says. "I learned to *like* you."

The words come so smoothly out of his mouth, my heart does a little somersault. And I think he startles himself, too, because he goes red. "Do you want to eat something that's not just cake?" he asks, changing the subject. "Maybe grab a coffee before we go home?"

"Coffee sounds good," I say, warmth spreading under my skin.

When I sit behind Pedro on his bicycle, my arms go around his waist. He doesn't twitch or tell me that I'm too close.

We find a lanchonete down the street from our school,

a small family-owned shop. Some teens wearing another school's uniform sit around plastic tables, so our secret is safe. Other patrons pull chairs outside to people watch, take selfies, and teach dance moves to each other while they eat.

It makes me think about Salt. The way it used to be before Deals Deals. Now I don't even know what's going through Mom's mind after Dona Clara left the neighborhood, urging her to sell Salt. And I can't stop thinking that Mom never told her she wouldn't.

"Lari?" Pedro says. His cutely disheveled face is right in front of me, trying to get me to pay attention to what he's saying.

"Sorry." I smile, getting off his bicycle. "What did you say?"

"I was just asking if you're hungry." He steals glances at the burgers other customers are eating in front of the lanchonete.

"Not really, no... Just a coffee is fine."

"I'll be back in a second."

When he returns, he places my coffee in front of me. "I never asked if you're coming back to the club next semester," he says, sitting down with his coffee. "You are coming back, right?"

"I hadn't thought about it," I admit. "I've been lying to my mother for so long about the club, I feel like I shouldn't anymore."

"Well, tell her the truth and come back next semester."

I hold my cup close to my face, watching him from behind it. He clumsily rips open three packets of sugar and dumps them in his coffee at the same time. But one of the wrappers dives into the mug. I watch him burn himself when he tries to fish it out, and he then proceeds to stir the coffee, slowly, methodically. He takes a careful sip, makes a face like it's still not to his taste, and tears *another* sugar packet. Only then does he look up and finally catch me staring.

"It wasn't sweet enough," he explains a little flustered.

"You'd think sweets would be the last thing on your mind when you're not working."

He feigns offense. "I've seen you eat. At least I don't add mayo to pizza," he says, making a disgusted face.

"When did you see me add mayo to pizza?"

"Remember that time we had that intercollegiate science fair, I think in sixth grade? You were eating pizza with a ton of mayo on it."

I feel myself blushing. I didn't realize he was watching then. "Well, I was experimenting with condiments. For science," I mumble into my coffee cup. "And for the record, mayo is *delicious*."

He shudders. "Whatever you say."

I take a tiny sip of coffee. The taste is rich and nutty.

Pedro puts his cup down. "Are you happy with your layer of our recipe?"

"I…think so? I keep wondering if the way I bake it maybe isn't as good as Grandma's original. All that Parmesan cheese is delicious, but…"

"Your recipe is *good*," he says. "You don't need it to match hers."

"But do I have the right to change something that's worked well for generations? I think it was Great-grandma's recipe."

"Honestly, I wish I had the chance to do something like

that with Grandpa's recipes." He looks at me like he's deciding whether to tell me something or not. He then pulls his chair closer, lowering his voice. "Do you know what it feels like to be in a kitchen that's just stuck, *frozen* in time? I've prepared the same dishes so many times, *always* the same dishes, I don't even know whether I like them or not anymore. That's my curse. I know it bothers you that you didn't grow up cooking, but I envy you. You get all this freedom to just grab a recipe and prepare it for the first time, or to reinvent it, make it your own. You can do whatever you want and not feel like you're offending anyone."

He looks off to the side, his arms crossed.

"Pedro...is that why you wanted to apply to the Gastronomic Society? Because you feel stuck at home?"

"That's a big part of it."

"Is that also why you...left?"

He leans back in his chair, getting defensive. "I shouldn't have brought that up. Why ruin a perfectly good coffee with bad memories?"

He lifts the cup to his mouth, taking a long sip to silence the subject.

"Sorry I asked..."

"No, it's fine. I just think it's pointless to talk about all that. I'm back, aren't I? So..."

He takes another sip.

I hate to think how lost he must have felt when his grandfather kicked him out, all because he wants to go to culinary school. I could have lost him for good then, had he never come back. I worry that if we don't win the contest, and Salt and Sugar close, I could *still* lose him.

When we're done with our coffee date (of sorts), Pedro gives me a ride home and drops me off by the drugstore. He's about to ride away when I put a hand on his arm to stop him.

I quickly pull the St. Anthony's Day card I made for him out of my backpack—hearts and all—and press it into his hand. "Don't read it now," I say quickly at the first sign of a surprised smile on his face, my voice shaking with nerves. "Just listen to what I have to say."

Pedro looks amused, trying to keep his smile contained. "I'm all ears."

I take a deep breath to steady my heart rate. "I've been meaning to say... It feels like history repeating itself a bit, you know? How we're making a cake together. And, well, I don't want things to end badly like they did for our great-grandmothers." He watches me with the cutest smile while I struggle to find the right words. But I don't want to give away too much of all the feelings I don't understand myself. "I—I don't want to fight with you anymore. When the contest is over, you know? I don't want to go back to how things were."

He looks relieved. "Neither do I."

We stare at each other for a while, soaking in our promise. I can't believe this is happening, but if it's a dream, I don't want to wake up.

I know it's not just up to us, though. And I guess Pedro is worrying about the same thing, because his eyes flicker to Salt and Sugar down the street.

"When are we telling them?" he says.

"One day, hopefully."

Pedro nods. "Deal."

"And feel free to change your layer of our cake, too," I tell him. Surprise lights up his eyes. "If you wish, of course. I'm sorry you feel stuck in your grandfather's kitchen. But you don't need to follow those traditions when we're baking our cake. Reinterpret your layer, just like I did with mine. We're already taking a huge leap with the cooking contest, and with being friends, so why not do that wholeheartedly in every possible way?"

He squints at me, like he's considering my suggestion.

"What are you saying, Dona Larissa?"

"I'm saying, be free to be the baker you want to be."

And don't go away again, please.

He looks at Sugar again in the distance, nodding along, slowly assimilating my words. "Be the baker I want to be…" he repeats under his breath. "But what if I actually can't make anything original and end up failing?"

"I never took Pedro Molina for a coward," I say, winking at him.

"Who are you calling a coward?" he jokes. "Alright. I'll give it some thought. But you have to promise me one thing."

"What?"

"That you'll come back to the club next semester," he says, riding off.

My words sit in his pocket:

I read somewhere that St. Anthony is actually the patron saint of lost things. So, happy St. Anthony's Day to you, who would have lost Pimentel's equation challenge to me had you not erased my work. I'm sorry about the cake. For the record, it was an accident.

Thank you for everything. I mean it.

L

38

SATURDAY, JUNE 18

By the time our tests are over, the neighborhood has put together its official St. John's party.

Neighbors bring their favorite dishes for the potluck and gather around the big bonfire in front of the bright church, where couples dance to the sound of accordions, zabumbas, and rabecas. Older kids light firecrackers, and the little ones play tag and run around with sparklers.

I convinced Mom to come, too. But she takes one look at Dona Eulalia making a plate at the buffet table and turns to head back home without a word. The way Dona Eulalia glares at Mom tells me someone—Deals Deals, most likely—must have filled her head with more lies about my family. *What now?*

"Mom, stay for just one minute," I insist, tugging at her sleeve. "Just *one* minute."

Her eyes go from me to Dona Eulalia in the distance. Their angry tension could slice the air.

"It's not the same without your grandmother," Mom says, leaving me behind.

I find a seat between Isabel and Dona Selma, who's playing the triangle along with the band. It's impossible not to notice that, one by one, we're disappearing. Grandma isn't here at her old spot, where she'd be drinking too much quentão and getting tipsy. Dona Clara isn't here to poke Seu Floriano with her cane to get him to ask her to dance. He didn't bother to come this year either, after losing his booth. So many neighbors are absent, driven out by Deals Deals or grief.

No, it's not the same without Grandma. It's also not the same without Mom.

I leave.

I'm almost back home when I spot Pedro rearranging the window display at Sugar. His white apron is tied around his waist, the sleeves of his black flannel shirt rolled up to his elbows. His hands and arms are covered in a dusting of wheat flour, like he's been busy in the kitchen.

He puts down a tray of sonhos, the round, delicate donuts the size of a fist and covered in confectionary sugar. He notices me staring from the sidewalk and crosses his arms over his chest. When we were little, we used to stick our tongues out and make faces at each other through the glass. Now, he signals for me to meet him by the alley and my chest fills with butterflies.

I only have to wait a minute before Pedro slips into the shadows with me. "Try this," he says, excited, a smear of flour on his cheek.

I bite into the sonho he brought for me. The jelly inside is still warm. So perfectly sweet and tart. It tastes like the pastry's name. Like a dream. "This is amazing! What is it? Passion fruit?!" I say, my lips covered in sugar.

"Correct! The inspiration came to me in a dream," he jokes, beaming at me. "I knew I'd give you a sweet tooth."

His smile is contagious. I haven't seen him so happy about baking in a while. Something must have changed since we last talked about Sugar.

I'm about to protest my developing a sweet tooth, when we hear Seu Romário calling out for him. Judging by the tone, he wants to slap the back of Pedro's head.

My blood goes cold, and the playful smile on Pedro's face vanishes immediately. He puts one finger to his lips, signaling for me to stay quiet, and leaves.

"Chef?" I hear him say.

My heart slams inside my chest as I listen in.

"You changed my sonho recipe?" Seu Romário yells. "Wait for me to die before you go around changing things in my kitchen!"

"Please, Chef, don't talk like this," Pedro's voice remains submissive.

"WHAT DID YOU DO TO MY RECIPE?!"

"I—I changed the filling..."

"YOU DISRESPECTFUL—!"

"I'm not disrespecting you!" Pedro shouts back, stunning Seu Romário into silence. This is the first time I've heard Pedro raise his voice to his grandfather. "I was just trying to offer something to our customers that Deals Deals doesn't already."

"You don't change anything at Sugar without my permission, do you hear me?" Seu Romário says, his voice low but trembling with so much anger. It's scarier than when he shouts. "You think I don't know you're dying to leave again? I know you don't care for Sugar. Why don't you go back to that good-for-nothing father of yours?"

Standing from my spot in the alley, I see Pedro run off.

I wait for Sugar's door to slam shut before emerging from my hiding place. I find Pedro unchaining his bicycle, fumbling to get it unlocked. He looks up, his expression pained like he's fighting back tears. He's so surprised to see me, like he forgot I was hiding next to Sugar all along.

"You...heard all that?" he asks, clearly embarrassed.

"Pedro, I'm so sorry." I take a step closer. "Don't listen to him. He didn't mean it. He's just angry."

"Do you want to run away together?" he offers with a sad smile. "Forget the bakeries, the feud, everyone and everything?"

"Pedro..."

I know he doesn't mean it, but I still glance at Salt and think of Mom all alone inside.

"I know, I *know*." He chuckles dryly. "Well, how about we run away for a few hours?"

I hop on behind him on his bicycle, and he takes off, pedaling quickly. The wind is blowing against us, like we're indeed running away from our lives. He only stops when we reach the beach, the salt in the air so heavy I can taste it. He chains his bicycle next to a coconut water stand, and after we purchase two cold coconuts, we sit on the sand, watching night fall over the Atlantic.

I don't know how long we sit in silence, our shoulders pressed together, sipping coconut water while staring at the waves lapping over the sand. But we stay long enough that the first stars begin to twinkle in the sky.

That's when Pedro pulls his phone out of his pocket and leans in to show me something. His head rests against mine and his hair tickles my forehead, sending goose bumps down my neck.

The website for a restaurant loads up, and there's the photo of a man in a kitchen, commanding everyone with a pirate-like aura about him, ears pierced, tattoos up and down his arms, wearing sunglasses just like Pedro's. *Exactly* like Pedro's.

"My dad," Pedro says. "And his restaurant."

"Your *dad*?"

He's so not the type of person I'd picture Dona Eulalia marrying. I mean, she's always tense and scowling at everyone. This man is laid-back, like he'd rather twist his hair into a messy bun than waste time brushing it.

Pedro looks at me. "That's where I went."

I notice the restaurant's address. "Curitiba? You went all the way *south*?" I can't hold back my surprise.

"When I told Grandpa about the Gastronomic Society, about wanting to apply to culinary school, I gave him an ultimatum," he says. "I asked him for permission to start baking my recipes at Sugar. And if he didn't think I was good enough, well, I said I didn't think I could stay home anymore." He laughs at himself, and it breaks my heart into one million pieces. "I actually thought he would have listened to me."

"Pedro, I'm so sorry."

He smiles like he's trying to convince me that he's okay, but all I can see is how sad he looks. How much pain he tries to hide with every smirk.

"My father left when I was a baby, and my mom and Grandpa talked about him like he was the plague... But what could I do? I couldn't stay in Olinda. My father was all I had." Pedro picks up a shell, hurling it at the ocean. A wave gobbles it up at once. "You know he actually doesn't even see me as his son? It's like I never existed. And still I went to him. How *naive* am I?"

"You're not naive," I tell him. "You hear me? Your father is the one at fault here."

Without answering, Pedro stands up, nodding at me to follow. We kick off our shoes and walk alongside the water, dodging the waves when they get too close.

"I would have given everything up," he says, looking out at the ocean. "*Everything.* If he'd said he was sorry, that he wanted to make up for all this time I didn't get to grow up with him, I'd have stayed in Curitiba." I hear the anguish in his voice, a self-loathing I'd never noticed before. "In the end, the only thing I got from him was his favorite sunglasses."

"*Sunglasses?*"

"He let me wear them when we grilled outside," he says with a coy smile. "I never returned them." Pedro sits down on the sand again, looking defeated. I sit beside him.

"It's okay to expect things from your father. You aren't in the wrong for hoping he'd have been there for you."

Pedro scoffs, staring ahead. "In the two weeks I stayed at his place, I actually realized that Dad and I aren't too different."

"Pedro, no."

"I'm serious. Listen, I was ready to abandon my family and my entire life, just like he ditched Mom. Just like he ditched me all those years ago. I left my family when they needed me the most. When I realized I didn't have a place with my dad either, I came back like the prodigal son," he shakes his head. "But I was still so angry with Grandpa, too. I had this plan that I'd get myself expelled from school, so I'd have no choice but to accept my life at Sugar once and for all..."

I'm so angry on his behalf, I could scream.

He looks at me, suddenly anxious. "Do you think Grandpa shouldn't have accepted me back?" he asks. "I do."

A stubborn tear rolls down my cheek. "Don't say that!"

"Why not? I turned my back on him, only to come back two weeks later like nothing had happened. I think Grandpa should have kept the door locked."

"You didn't turn your back on your grandfather. You had nowhere to go when he wouldn't listen to you."

"You don't get it." Pedro's eyes glisten with tears. "Grandpa taught me everything I know. I'm a baker because of him. And that's how I repay him? How *ungrateful* am I?"

I grab his hand so he'll see I'm right here with him. That he's not alone.

"You're *not* ungrateful," I say, fighting tears of my own.

"What am I going to do?" his voice cracks with the first sob. "How am I going to go home tonight? He doesn't want me. He told me to go back to my father. You heard him—"

It's like Seu Romário's words are finally registering in Pedro's mind, and he's starting to panic. I pass an arm around his shoulders, and Pedro stops crying just as quickly, wiping his eyes with his sleeve, like he doesn't want to cry in front of me.

"I'm okay now," he says, laughing a little. "I swear I am."

It worries me to see him shut off his feelings so quickly.

Pedro leans back on the sand, looking up at the stars. I lie down next to him. It's a rare clear June night. Not one cloud in the sky. We stay like this until it starts to get a little cold. Only the lights from the calçadão, where joggers and families pushing strollers go up and down, and the tall buildings facing the beach cast any glow on us.

"Thank you for running away with me for a few hours," he says, breaking the silence.

I turn my head to look at him.

And I realize he's been staring at me.

Without thinking, I reach for his hand while he moves toward mine. The gesture feels natural, like we've been doing it all our lives.

"You know I can't swim?" he says all of the sudden, his voice a little raw from crying earlier.

"You can't?"

"No one ever taught me."

"Well, I know how," I say. "Grandma taught me."

"You can swim in the ocean, too?"

"I can."

"And you aren't afraid of sharks?"

"A little."

He whistles, impressed. "You'll have to teach me one day."

"Deal." I smile at him.

We're silent again, Pedro's face shadowed, but he's still looking at me.

"Lari?"

"Yeah?"

"May I kiss you?"

My breath hitches and my heart beats faster. And it feels *right*, so right that it scares me. I see in his eyes that he knows there's no going back from this. That neither of us wants to return to how things were, which is the most dangerous thing that could happen when you're in a multigenerational feud.

"Yeah," I say.

He scoots closer, his head dipping. The moment I taste the sweetness of coconut water and the salt of the sea breeze on his lips, I don't want the kiss to ever end. One of his hands travels up, his fingers digging into my hair and resting at the nape of my neck. My arms fling around his neck, his warmth seeping from his skin to mine.

The waves are practically at our feet. I hear them lapping closer and closer as the pent-up, confused feelings I've been dodging all this time rush in my veins. He kisses me with an increasing urgency, like he's afraid this is his only chance to be with me.

His arm wraps under my waist to pull me closer to him. His lips then stray from mine, playfully traveling down my jawline, sending tingles down my back. I shiver and feel a kiss turn into a smile against the skin on my neck. And I smile, too, because this feels like a dream.

A wave finally touches our bare feet, startling us—

"Wait," I say, sitting upright and interrupting the most perfect moment.

Pedro looks worried. "Lari, I'm sorry. I shouldn't—I—"

"You did nothing wrong," I say. But I'm stunned that this happened. I wanted to kiss him, and I've been wanting to for a while now. But we can't be together like this. What would happen if our mothers found out?

I push myself to my feet.

Pedro stands up, too, now looking even more alarmed. "What's wrong?"

"We can't," I say.

"Who says we can't?" he asks, his voice shy.

"You know we can't. They'll never, *ever*, accept this."

He knows who I mean. "They'll have to."

"This isn't like our alliance, you know? We can't mediate *this*. We can't tell them to forget the feud and accept that their kids are...you know..."

"Together?" he finishes for me. And I must still look a little panicked because he frowns. "Lari, do you like me?"

He stands in front of me, the ocean breeze blowing his bangs over his eyes.

"I do," I admit, and I see the relief in his eyes. "That's why I'm worried for us. I don't know what will happen."

"I like you, too," he stands closer, bridging the gap between us. "And you said you like me, so the present is all that matters to me right now."

I brush his hair off his face. And I realize how I've been *dying* to do that all this time.

I lean in to kiss him again. Pedro gently holds my face in his hands as he kisses me back, his thumb brushing against my cheek to soothe my anxiety. I feel light-headed, like how I used to get after spinning around and around in place as a kid.

When we need to catch our breath, he hugs me close, burying his nose in my shoulder. My fingers wrap around the back of his shirt.

"I don't want to lose you," I say, fighting back tears.

He hugs me tighter. "We'll sort everything out with our families. I promise. I'm not going anywhere."

I want to believe we can, but nothing is easy when it comes to the feud. It's overwhelming, like the waves lapping against our calves.

Don't turn your back to the ocean, Grandma used to say. *You don't know when a wave will come and sweep you off your feet.*

39

SATURDAY, JUNE 18

It's hard to say goodbye, but after one last kiss when we reach the neighborhood, Pedro rides off.

I wait a second longer under the drugstore's awning before I start walking home, every inch of me electrified. I still can feel his lips on mine. Giddy, I spin in place, listening to the music coming from the St. John's party in front of the feirinha.

I've nearly reached home when I notice Pedro's bicycle right on Salt's doorstep. Something's wrong. I run the rest of the way, and my heart skips a beat when I spot him inside. His mother is here, too.

Now I know something must *really* be wrong.

I push the door open so frantically, the bells jingle with a panicked shrill.

Pedro looks back at me and his lips part, like he can't ask me the question he wants to in front of our mothers, whose faces are red and eyes are bloodshot like they've been crying angry tears.

Dona Eulalia threatens to come round the counter to fight

with Mom, past the invisible line between "Salt, the bakery" and "Salt, the Ramires' home" that everyone knows not to trespass, and Pedro holds her back.

A fine layer of sand dusts his hair and clothes. I'm pretty covered in it, too. If our mothers were paying attention, they'd see our secret hiding in plain sight, and I suddenly get a jolt of fear that someone saw us together and told them.

But our mothers continue yelling at each other like they don't even notice we're here. Maybe this isn't about us.

"I have proof you've been arranging to sell Salt!" Dona Eulalia shouts.

"Get out of my house," Mom says, her voice shaking.

Dona Eulalia holds her phone up, showing screenshots of texts. One quick glance shows me what looks like Mom saying she won't sell Salt for less than what it's worth. Dona Eulalia is so angry, she drops the phone and Pedro picks it up. While she continues accusing Mom, a text catches his attention. He reads it, his expression becoming more and more severe.

I want to grab him by the shoulders and make him look at me.

I want to show him that none of this is true.

I need him to believe me. But when he finally meets my gaze, there's so much fear and confusion in his eyes, I freeze on the spot.

I don't want to lose him.

"There's nothing wrong with hearing what they had to say!" Mom yells at Dona Eulalia.

And the floor could open up now and swallow me alive.

"I'll go to Deals Deals on Friday!" Dona Eulalia threatens. She pushes past me on her way out, and Pedro starts to go after her, but he suddenly stops. His eyes lock with mine, and I take a step toward him, but Mom stares him down. I feel his fingertips secretly brush against mine when he walks by me to follow his mother. Despite the gesture, an ominous cloud descends on my mood.

I turn to look at Mom, shaking. She's staring ahead, her eyes glinting with tears, the tips of her hair trembling.

"Those things Dona Eulalia said—they're not true, right?" My voice comes out like a croak. "Mom, tell me they're not true. Please." I feel like I'm burning up with a fever, Mom's silence making me angrier and angrier. "When were you going to tell me? Before or after you sold Salt?"

Mom's eyes flicker to me, furious.

"When were *you* going to tell me that those review sessions were a lie?" she snaps. "I spoke with your teacher this morning. She said there were no review sessions. There haven't been *any*. She said you were attending the cooking club. *Cooking*, Larissa?"

"Yes, cooking!" I shout. "And I'm actually not terrible at it, but you wouldn't know since you never bothered to teach me!"

"You lied to your own mother!" Mom yells back.

"I didn't want to lie to you," I say, the first sob escaping me. "But how can you look at me like I've just betrayed you over learning to cook when you're *selling Salt* and didn't even bother to tell me?! You can't sell Salt!" I choke on the words, panic flooding my chest.

"If I have to sell Salt, I—" Mom stops herself, her shoulders tensing up. She exhales. "I hate it when we argue. Believe me, I've tried everything. But, it's true, I listened to what Deals

Deals had to say," she admits, and I shake my head, because I don't want to believe it. "We exchanged a few texts. I needed to at least know what they had in mind for the bakery first. A cafe won't be so bad. They'll keep the building just as it is."

Anger makes my blood boil. "Grandma would never have let this happen!"

"Your grandmother told me to sell Salt, so don't assume you know what she would've wanted or not."

I don't think I heard right.

"Grandma—what?" I say, the words coming out like a gasp.

"Filha, I didn't want to tell you like this," Mom begins to say, but I don't want to hear it anymore.

This is too much.

Too unbearable.

The Grandma I knew—the Grandma I *know*—would never have told Mom to sell Salt.

It makes *no* sense.

I run up the stairs.

"Larissa!" Mom calls out again, but I rush into my bedroom and slam the door shut behind me. Pacing back and forth, I text Pedro.

LARI: Can we meet somewhere?

PEDRO: Are those texts forged? Is Deals Deals trying to make us fight again?

PEDRO: We'll fix this together. Don't worry. We'll fix this.

LARI: I'm so sorry.

LARI: The texts aren't forged.

PEDRO: They're not another lie?

LARI: I didn't know Mom was talking with that lawyer. I'm sorry. Mom had been acting strange for a while, but I had no idea she was actually talking with him.

PEDRO: Acting strange? What?

I stare at the screen, just the sound of my anxious breathing in the deafening silence. I should have told him earlier.

LARI: She kept the business card the Deals Deals lawyer gave her when he came by to offer. I didn't know how to tell you.

PEDRO: Why not?

He'll hate me for this. He'll hate me.

LARI: I didn't know if I could trust your family finding that out.

PEDRO: I wouldn't have told them.

LARI: I know!

PEDRO: Do you? Because it feels more like you didn't trust *me*.

LARI: I trust you. Pedro, I do! I promise you I do! I was just worried about what your mother would do if she found out. I was trying to protect Salt.

No reply from him. My heart is practically in my throat.

LARI: I messed up! But you have to believe me when I say I trust you.

LARI: Pedro?

LARI: Let's talk. I need to see you.

The dots go on and off, on and off, while I stare at my screen, breathless, until they disappear altogether. He's given up on me.

LARI: Please, can we talk in person? Let me explain everything.

PEDRO: I don't want to talk with you right now.

I hurl my phone across the room and curl up in bed, a pillow above my head to smother my sobbing. I don't dare look up to find his curtains closed, shutting me out for good.

I wasn't brave enough to tell him every time I felt Mom was acting strange. I wasn't brave enough to end the vicious cycle that keeps our families' feud spinning. All this time *I* couldn't see past the feud. I feared betrayal, but then I went and betrayed him first.

Those hours we spent on the beach still feel like a dream… Like something I imagined. But reality comes crashing down.

I'm losing my home.

And I've lost Pedro, too.

40

SUNDAY, JUNE 19

The next day, I spend the morning in my room to avoid another fight with Mom. Late in the afternoon, I finally build enough courage to go looking for answers. I go to Parque das Flores cemetery in Recife.

I make my way carefully around the graves until I spot the oak tree that shades Grandma's tombstone. It was the last thing I saw before I fled the funeral. The branches swaying in the cool breeze a few paces ahead of me. Just a tree. But it feels like a giant.

I approach carefully, trying to steady my breathing. I don't want to be angry at Grandma. I don't want to resent her. And yet I can't hold back the pain anymore.

Mom's words play over and over in my mind. *Your grandmother told me to sell Salt.* I shake my head. I tossed and turned all night, trying to understand why Grandma would have told Mom that. And it still makes no sense.

I keep thinking about something Grandma told me in early March when she was hospitalized. She said she'd dreamed I was little again, playing with the sugar bowl. "Did I tell you that back then I thought it was a sign?" she said. "A sign that you were meant for Salt. You were always in the kitchen."

I think that's when I knew for the first time that Grandma was...you know...

Rationally, of course, I understood she wasn't making progress. She was too weak for chemo. Her body wasn't producing enough urine. Her digestive system was stopping. Her abdomen bloated day by day. The doctors came in every night and pulled us aside to add a new organ to the list of compromised body parts.

Intestines.

Uterus.

Stomach lining.

Right kidney.

Lungs.

The disease spread quickly, rushing higher and higher. And I knew what came after her lungs. I knew she wasn't recovering, but I didn't want to believe it. Not with my soul. Because, like Grandma, I believe in signs, too. I believe in curses. But I believe in happy endings above all. The type you see in telenovelas, when characters recover from the worst tragedies, stronger and reborn.

But Grandma's sign about me, it would never be true. Because I was not meant for Salt. I was *never* meant for Salt. And we both knew it. Just like we knew Grandma wasn't making a miraculous recovery.

Maybe signs aren't real, after all...

And if they aren't, I guess I'm truly not meant for my own home. Where do I even belong?

When I crouch down to place a bouquet of sunflowers on her grave, I notice there are other sunflowers there already, maybe a day or two old. Someone who knew these were her favorite flowers must have left them. Maybe Dona Selma?

I trace Grandma's name on the tombstone with my fingertip.

"Ever since you left us, we've been in serious trouble," I say, fighting back tears. "Grandma, what did Mom mean? You told *me* you had dreamt about me at Salt."

I hate that she's not here to defend herself. To tell me that I'm wrong. That it's a misunderstanding.

To tell me that—

That she loves me. That it was just a bad dream. And she didn't leave us.

"I don't know why I'm here in this cemetery, like I could find you and convince you to come home and fix everything. As if you'd left because of an argument. As if this is something I could remedy with an apology." I gasp for air. "What did I do wrong? I'm sorry. Come back. *Please*, come back."

I cry for a long time before I'm faced with the truth.

Grandma isn't coming home.

She's gone.

And there's nothing I can do to bring her back, no matter how long I avoid saying goodbye.

A terrible wave of resentment washes over me, like Mom and Grandma must be punishing me for something. For not being a good daughter. For not sharing their talent for cooking. For being my family's weakest link. I was always doomed to be alone, wasn't I? I never belonged with them.

"Why didn't you teach me to cook? Why didn't you let me

take care of Salt? Why did you—why did you have to leave when we—when we need you the most? When *I* need you? You promised me you'd be with me. You promised me! So why tell Mom to sell Salt? Why did you give up on us? Why?"

I hide my face behind my hands to smother my yelling.

"Don't be so hard on your grandmother," a voice says gently behind me. I was crying so hard I didn't realize someone else was here. When I turn, a figure is silhouetted against the setting sun. I squint, trying to make out their face.

And then I quickly push myself to my feet so Seu Romário isn't towering over me. Without Mom by my side, I don't know what to do. I want to run. Last time I saw him, he was yelling awful things at Pedro. My heart races in fear.

"Maybe in the end she felt that closing Salt was the best for you and your mother," he says. "A chance to restart without her."

He motions closer to the grave, and I realize he's holding a bouquet of sunflowers just like mine.

"What are you doing here?" I ask, but he just smiles sadly and replaces the old sunflowers with the new bouquet he's brought. "You don't know Grandma like this! You're her enemy! How do you know sunflowers are her favorite?!"

He doesn't give me an answer. He just busies himself with the flowers, trying to arrange them neatly so they're not blocking Grandma's name. I wait in silence, trembling with nerves.

"When she got sick," he says at last, "I went to see her at the hospital."

I take a step back, dread filling my chest just at the thought of this man showing up in the infirmary room. "You had no right! What did you say to her? Did you *hurt* her?"

His eyes widen. "Larissa, no. *No.* I had to see her... I couldn't find the strength to tell her how sorry I felt... I couldn't... I couldn't speak... But I think she knew. I... I tell myself that she understood... And she... She confided in me. She told me about Salt. About the finances going bad. And she said she was going to tell Alice to sell the bakery. She was going to tell Alice to let go... To start a new life with you where you both were free."

Those are Mom's words, too. Could it be true, that Grandma confided in him? No, Grandma would never have. She didn't trust him.

But then again, the Grandma I knew also wouldn't have told Mom to sell Salt.

Now I'm not so sure whether I truly understood her at all. I don't know what to believe.

"I must admit it's also time Sugar closes doors, too," he adds. "In this economy, no one cares for homemade pastries. There's only room for big industrial bakeries. I was stubborn not to see it earlier."

A painful lump forms in my throat. If the head of Sugar is giving up, then there's no hope left for Salt—or the rest of the neighborhood. "You've fought for your bakery your whole life. How can you suddenly give up your own home?!"

"I'm no longer the man I was." His eyes linger on Grandma's grave for a second too long, and I get the feeling that he's saying it to her, too. He looks back at me. "My daughter is tired and she worries about my health. I had hoped my grandson would take care of Sugar, but I know he'll be gone again as soon as he graduates. He doesn't care for Sugar like I hoped he would, and I'm done fighting with him. I have no reason to hold on now."

I see the tears he's trying to hide. I know he hasn't totally given up.

He gently pats the grave next to Grandma's. *Dad's* grave.

"Gabriel was one hell of a worker," he says. "Couldn't cook or bake, but he earned his spot in my bakery."

I can't help but smile. I didn't know this. "Dad couldn't cook?"

"Gabriel? Not even a pot of rice. But that boy knew book-keeping like he'd been born an administrator. A real genius. He had a real knack for running Sugar like my mother. He saw it all like it was a special recipe none of us could read. If he were here, I know Sugar wouldn't be at risk. I miss him every day. I miss his advice."

I had no idea Dad meant so much to him. More than an employee. More than a protégé. More like a son, judging by the sorrowful glance Seu Romário gives his grave.

I used to wonder how involved Dad was in the feud, and what it must have triggered when he fell in love with Mom. Now I get the feeling there's more to my parents' story than Mom has ever been willing to tell me.

"You...miss my father?" I ask.

"Every day!" Seu Romário replies without thinking twice, and I hear so much pain in his words, it makes me tear up. "I even miss his clumsiness," he chuckles wryly, just like Pedro does. I guess it's the other way around. "Gabriel was the only one who ever understood me. Who understood my vision for Sugar. He believed in traditional recipes. He loved my mother's guava tarts. He cared for Sugar like no one ever will."

"Pedro cares, too," the words tumble out, and Seu Romário looks a little taken aback.

"How do you know that?" he asks.

Maybe I've crossed the line. I shouldn't speak for Pedro. But Seu Romário looks at me so expectantly, like someone who's grasping at straws, and I can't help it. "The same way you knew Grandma's favorite flowers," I say, and I see the spark of realization behind his eyes.

I came to the cemetery feeling so confused, but I wonder if maybe Grandma led Seu Romário to me, so she could be there for me, when I couldn't hear her through all the pain. To explain that she was just trying to keep me and Mom safe.

Seu Romário glances at Grandma's and Dad's graves and there's a tenderness in his eyes that renews my hope for the future. The feud could end one day. I just know it.

"Thank you for the way you loved Grandma and Dad," I say.

He suddenly starts sobbing. I wish I knew what to say. What to do to comfort him. But now that I know the way he truly feels, I don't smother my own tears like the night he tried giving us his condolences. We cry together.

"It's true!" he admits. "I *love* her, and could never tell her I did! And I loved Gabriel like a son. That's why I'm doomed to carry the guilt of losing them both for the rest of my life!"

He can't catch his breath, and I stand beside him, worried about his blood pressure. His crying has turned into something more painful. Something that looks like it's gnawing inside his ribcage, kept trapped who knows for how long. I wipe my eyes with the back of my hands, trying to encourage him to stay calm, to not let his grief overwhelm him for the sake of his health.

"Let me bring you some water," I suggest.

But he shakes his head no. "I lost them!" he cries again.

"You didn't lose them," I say, and I can hear the heartache in my voice. "Grandma's illness and Dad's accident took them. Please, don't blame yourself for things we can't control."

He shakes his head again, still having a hard time speaking. "I failed her! And I failed Gabriel! I—I sent my own godson away!"

Godson?! I'm so stunned, I stare at him, unable to say another word.

He grabs on to the edges of Dad's grave like he's afraid the earth will open up under him. "He's dead! He's dead...because of me!"

41

SUNDAY, JUNE 19

"Dad was Seu Romário's godson?!" No matter how calm I tried to become on the way home from the cemetery, the words burst out of me as soon as I see Mom in Salt's kitchen.

There's a scary intensity in the way she looks at me. The intensity of a secret long kept.

"It's not true," she denies, automatic. "Who told you this?"

After I walked Seu Romário back home to make sure he was okay after crying so much, he asked me to forget everything he'd said. He tried to backpedal, saying he considered Dad a godson, not that he *was* his godson, but I know what he told me at the cemetery was true.

What I don't know is why I'm the last person to find out my own father was practically a Molina.

"It doesn't matter who did. And you don't need to deny it." I take a step closer to Mom. "It's okay. You can tell me the truth."

Mom balls her hands into tight fists over the counter, her knuckles going white. "I thought I was protecting you," she says with a gasp, finally giving in. "Seu Romário has always been manipulative. He had asked your father if he'd like to be his godson, knowing very well Gabriel had no family left in the world. Made him feel like he was being adopted. All manipulation to make Gabriel feel morally obligated to Sugar forever, of course."

So it *is* true. I should be angry. But strangely, I feel an immense sense of relief hearing the truth about Dad's past with the Molinas. I realize it's because Mom and I—

We're talking with each other. *Finally.*

"Why didn't you tell me?"

"I didn't want you to grow up thinking that your dad was the enemy, too!"

"Dad would never have been the enemy to me. He could have had the Molina last name, and I wouldn't care. He's my father. I'd love him just the same."

Mom breaks down sobbing, her arms wrapped around herself. "I needed to protect his memory," she says, hyperventilating. "You say you'd still love him, but my own—my own *mother* saw him as a Molina! And you don't know how much suffering he and I went through because of it! I had—Larissa, I had to make sure there was no room for you to have the same doubts—*any* doubts—about your father."

My stomach churns.

"Grandma didn't like Dad?" My voice comes out so quiet with shock I'm surprised Mom hears it.

She nods, her eyes bright with tears. "She saw him as one of them. For a long time, she hated Gabriel."

This is too much. "W-why?"

"Because Gabriel believed that our bakeries were better off

as allies, rather than enemies. Because for a while, I believed that, too, and she blamed him for it." Mom bites down on her lower lip to hold back the pain from her memories. "One day, your father and I decided to bake the Salt and Sugar cake as a symbolic gesture. We were foolish. But Mother and Seu Romário caught us. They didn't understand what we were trying to do. Mother wanted him far away from me. The Molinas called him a traitor. So we left Olinda. We got married without her blessing."

The whole truth about our families' feud begins to wrap tightly around me.

Suffocating.

I look up at the ceiling, and all the fixtures are spinning, spinning...

"This isn't the grandma I knew..."

"I know it's hard to hear that the person you love the most has flaws, but honestly—Lari, it doesn't mean she didn't love you, and it doesn't mean you should stop loving her."

I don't know what hurts more. That Grandma hated Dad. Or that Mom thinks I would have rejected him had I known he was Seu Romário's godson. It all turns into one big, ugly ball of pain that sucks all the oxygen out of the room.

Clumsily, I climb over the back counter, knocking over some utensils, until I manage to swing the window wide open. I stay perched on the windowsill for a while, gulping the night's cold breeze that blows in.

"Lari, talk to me."

I turn to look at her. "What happened when you got pregnant? When she heard that you were going to have a kid with the man she saw as a Molina? Did she hate me, too?"

Mom looks taken aback. "Lari, no. Your grandmother *loved* you."

"I don't see how." I look away. "She hated Dad. She must have hated what I represented, too!"

"She fell in love with you immediately. Never doubt that. Please, it would kill me to think you're questioning your grandmother's love."

I jump down from the windowsill, feeling a little unsteady. The mental image of Seu Romário admitting guilt over Dad's death keeps running through my mind.

There's something she's not telling me about Dad's accident. Mom and Grandma always refused to take Avenida Coqueirais, always talking about the street in fear. But there was something else. Something I couldn't quite put my finger on.

"What exactly happened that day of Dad's accident?" I ask her.

Mom looks desperate. "Who's feeding you all these things?"

"What *happened*?" Tears roll down my cheeks. "I'm sick and tired of being kept in the dark."

She hangs her head, like the weight of this conversation is too much for her. "Your father, he… He came to speak with Seu Romário and your grandmother that night. He hoped they'd seal a truce when I got pregnant. He wanted your grandmother to be in your life. He hoped you could grow up in a world where you had your whole family together."

"And then…?" I ask, cautious, because at this point I'm not totally sure I want to know.

"That horrible man called him a traitor and told him to leave and never come back!"

"And… Grandma?"

Mom lets out a shaky breath. "She wouldn't hear him. I stayed at Salt, trying to get Mother to talk with me, at least. Gabriel went for a ride to clear his head. That's when he…he had his accident, and we… We lost him forever."

I cover my mouth with both hands.

Mom continues, as if in a numb trance, reliving everything. "Months later, you were born. And your grandmother tried to fix what she'd broken. She begged me to give our family one last chance. She swore she would never pull you into the family's business. To keep you free from this feud."

My heart hammers against my ribcage. *That* was my cooking curse all along. My family's guilt, keeping me away from the kitchen—away from getting involved in Salt—for fear I'd get hurt the same way Dad did.

Silent tears tumble down my chin.

Mom looks nervous as she watches me cry, like she doesn't know how to comfort me. "Don't cry, filha. Blame me. It's all my fault. I should have stopped Gabriel that night, but I couldn't. I let him ride off!"

It breaks my heart to hear her say this. "What happened to Dad isn't your fault."

"It *is* my fault. And I've stayed here all these years to pay for my part in his death! I fought for Salt. You believe me now? You believe I did everything I could against Deals Deals?!"

I look at her, the way her eyes are getting swollen, her expression tinged with regret and pain.

"Mom," I say to soothe her, trying to keep my voice calm although my heart feels like it's beating out of my chest.

"Selling Salt was the last thing I wanted. It makes me feel like your father's death, his suffering, his attempts at bringing the Molinas and our family together, were in vain. Like this bakery, this object of so much contempt, could just disappear like dust in the wind?!" She grabs my hand. "That's my guilt to carry when I break my promise to myself and sell Salt. But at least I know *you* will be free to follow your dreams."

"Mom, his death is not your fault," I say again. "You don't need to feel tied down by Salt and your guilt. You can go after *your* dreams."

"Your future is my dream!" Mom says. "You'll be the first—"

"No," I interrupt her. "What's *your* dream? You still can do anything you want," I say, pulling one of her notebooks closer. I open it on a page filled with doodling. Sketches she'd prepared for Dona Fernanda's daughter's party. There are floral designs. Table patterns. But there are dresses, too. Shoes. Things she absentmindedly doodled while on phone calls. "Look! You're so talented!" I say, but Mom closes the notebook. "I know you dreamed different things for yourself. Is that why Grandma felt she needed to tell you to give up on Salt? Because she wanted you to finally be free to find your path? Mom, you can open an atelier, if you want. Just don't sell Salt. I'd like to take care of things around here when I graduate. Let me take care of Salt. Just let me—"

"Larissa, no." She cuts me off. "This bakery is nothing but trouble. I wouldn't be a good mother if I let you inherit a hurting business. A pile of debt. I clung to Salt for as long as I could, but with the threat of losing everything, I can't leave you with nothing."

"But I—"

"You need financial *stability*. This offer with Deals Deals is the only option we have now. And then we'll restart our lives. You'll be the first Ramires to go to college!"

Mom's poured out her heart for me today. There's no point in hiding the truth now.

"I didn't mean to lie to you," I begin, "about the review sessions. About the cooking club. I didn't know how to tell you this… But I don't want to study economics. I don't want to be an accountant. Those were Dad's dreams. Mine are different. I want to go to the Gastronomic Society and be a baker. And I want to take care of Salt. And I—I wish you would give me a chance to make things right," I beg, my voice coming out so raw from all the secrets I hid from her. "I wish… I wish you supported me."

Mom looks tired.

I wait for her to yell that she knows what's best for me. I wait for her disappointment. But instead, Mom wraps her arms around me. And the gesture is so sudden that I'm frozen like a statue.

"I love you," she says. "I'm your mother. I'll always support you."

When the first sob escapes me, I can hardly believe it's mine. I make a horrible guttural noise in her arms. And suddenly the stone encasing me breaks. My chest feels like it's about to explode as I try to hold the tears back, but they're stronger than me. I bury my face in Mom's shoulder, shaking.

She hugs me tighter.

It's the hug I've been waiting for for so long. The hug that didn't happen months ago at the hospital, when they said Grandma wasn't recovering. The hug that didn't happen while we watched Grandma's disease spread. The hug that didn't happen at the cemetery, when they filled Grandma's coffin with sunflowers. The hug that didn't happen when we were back at Salt, just the two of us, the daunting challenge to go on with life without Grandma.

"I love you, too," I say. "I missed you."

"I don't expect you to understand my reasons, but I kept you away from the kitchen all this time because I didn't want you to get hurt like I did. Like your father did. I just wasn't counting on you being, well—you're too much your grand-mother's granddaughter. And I guess... I am not getting in the way of that anymore. I'm not going to keep a northeast-ern girl from learning how to at least make couscous."

"What?" My heart races. "You're going to teach me?"

"If you're serious about culinary school, do you think they'll let you in if you can't even make couscous?"

A grin overtakes my face. "I'm my mother's daughter," I correct her.

Mom gives me a teary smile. This feels like the beginning of finally bridging the way to each other. She picks up the bag of couscous flakes, flocão type, and hands it to me. "Now, the trick for getting couscous fluffy is—"

Everything suddenly goes dark.

"What happened?" I say, panic rising in my chest.

"The disconnection notice."

In the darkness that befalls Salt, it's like there's no room for hopes and dreams.

I sense Mom's anxiety for my future in the way she grabs a matchbox and shakily lights a few candles. She looks so scared and embarrassed when she turns to guide me out of the kitchen. "I can't let you inherit a bankrupt bakery. Make a future for yourself elsewhere, filha. Forget this place." Her voice is strangled with tears. "And I'll try to forget it, too. I'm going to that meeting at Deals Deals on Friday."

I could never forget Salt, even if I tried. I've come too far to give up now, so I dig my heels in.

"Can you show me how to make couscous?" I ask.

"I'm selling Salt, Lari," she says more emphatically. "I'm not getting in the way of you going to culinary school, but there's no hope for this bakery anymore. I'm not letting you sink your future with debt."

"Please?" I insist. "Just teach me to cook."

"Lari—alright," Mom gives in.

With trembling hands, she guides me in the semidarkness, showing me how to prepare the flakes in the smaller steamer with the gas stove. When the aroma of corn rises in the kitchen, Mom pulls me into a side hug. And I realize I'm not alone. Not only because I'm with Mom, but Grandma and Great-grandma are here, too.

Salt has always been a dream dreamed together.

Our bond will see me through, no matter what happens by the end of the week.

42

When I walk into the cooking club on Monday, music is blasting.

School is out for the winter break, but we were supposed to meet to wrap up activities and say goodbye. Cintia and Victor are at the counter, mixing cake batter. And I'm surprised to see PC standing by their side. It's like how it all started, that first day when I walked in to fulfill Pimentel's condition to earn extra credit.

I freeze at the doorway when I spot Pedro in the back, kneading—more like *pounding*—bread dough, his sleeves bunched at his shoulders, exposing his biceps.

A hot flush creeps under my skin.

"Smoothie Whisperer!" PC says meeting me at the door, his arms stretched out to pull me into a hug. All heads turn to me.

"PC! What are you doing here?" I ask.

"My family had to solve a few things in town and I came to get my transcripts. Did you miss me a lot?" he says, trying to sound cheerful, but judging by the nervous looks Cintia and Victor keep launching from behind him, I get the feeling that they all know what happened. Or at least that something happened. "Come. We need to catch up—" He's already steering me out of the kitchen, but I dig my heels in.

"I need to apologize to Pedro," I say.

"I don't know what went off between you two, but he's in an awful mood," PC whispers to me. "When I asked about you, he nearly sent me back to Caruaru. Trust me. This isn't the right time to approach him."

"I have to do this," I insist. I push past PC. "Pedro, can we talk?"

"Please, not now," Pedro says, not even making eye contact.

A painful knot forms in my throat. "I came to apologize."

"I don't want to hear it." Pedro unties his apron in a sudden movement, tossing it at the wall peg. "I'm out. Pack up and lock the door when you leave."

"Pedro, I know you hate me, but just give me one chance," I beg, trying my best to keep my voice steady. "One last chance? And then I'll leave you alone. I promise."

Pedro stops. He turns around slowly to look at me, his shoulders tense.

Cintia, Victor, and PC mouth good luck to me on their way out, so Pedro and I can speak privately.

I stand trembling. I knew it wouldn't be easy.

"I didn't know Mom had been discussing things with Deals Deals," I begin. "She wants to sell Salt, but I swear she hasn't accepted any offers yet."

He squints at me. "How can I trust you now, when you

didn't even tell me about your mother keeping a simple business card?"

"I'm sorry. I should have told you."

I hear his pain when he laughs in self-mockery. "Why was it so hard to tell me? We could have tried fixing things together. But you didn't trust me enough. Did I do something to make you doubt me?"

"I didn't tell you because..." I shake my head. "Because I didn't want to believe it myself, that my mom would ever sell. And because... I think... I think I *was* worried you'd tell your family and they'd go ahead and sell Sugar. But that was before. That was before I learned to trust you, I swear!"

Pedro stares at me. "But you still didn't tell me."

I feel horrible. But there's no way around it.

"Pedro, I'm sorry."

He shuts his eyes for a second, taking a deep breath. When he opens them again, they're filled with so much regret, it breaks my heart. I don't know if I can fix this.

"I can't help but think your mother was setting my mom up to fail, so she could go ahead and sell Salt first."

"You know that's not true."

"My family will go bankrupt." He shakes his head. "Do you understand why I'm— Lari, just tell me the truth. Were you...using me or...?"

"*Using* you?!"

Pedro looks conflicted. "My head is a mess now. And I... I don't get it. I thought you and I... Were you trying to distract me so your mother could sell Salt?" His voice is raw like he's been crying. I just stare at him in stunned silence. It kills

me that he can so easily go back to seeing me as a person capable of doing anything to hurt his family.

"Pedro."

"Was the contest a lie? You were never going to show up,
were you? I'd get there on Thursday and you'd be, where?
Helping your mother gather the paperwork for the Deals
Deals meeting on Friday? What I don't get is why would you
go so far to hurt my family. *Why?* Did your mother put you
up to this or—?"

"*Pedro!*"

I can't hold back the tears.

His eyes glisten, and he looks off to the side. I know he
hates showing vulnerability.

"Look at me," I say, and he looks up, his jaw clenched so
tightly like even making eye contact is painful. "There was
no plan against your family. I'd never do anything to hurt
you or lie to you like that. I didn't know this, but my mom
stayed in communication with Deals Deals because she wanted
to know what her options were. She was scared. We all are.
But she hasn't signed any contracts. Nothing. And I didn't
tell you about the business card because I was worried your
mom would find out and think exactly what she does now.
You know your mom—"

"Larissa, the worst isn't even that you lied to me," he says,
looking drained. "It's that after everything we went through
together, you're still biased against my family. How does that
saying about us go...?" He coughs to clear his throat. "*Trust
neither thin-bottomed frying pans nor Molinas*, isn't that right?"

I nod yes, my throat so knotted I can't breathe.

He chuckles sadly. "Was I ever anything more to you than just another untrustworthy Molina?"

Before I can answer, he storms out of the kitchen.

I hide my face behind my hands, but I can't stop the tears. I don't know how long I stay like that until I hear shuffling in front of me. I look up with a gasp, hoping he's back, but I see PC, Victor, and Cintia instead through blurry eyes.

PC tilts my chin up gently so I look at him. "I'll admit we eavesdropped a little. Sorry. But let me tell you this. Time will heal things. You've come a long way already, haven't you? Give him time."

"No." I shake my head. "It's not just any fight. This time I really blew it. I betrayed his trust."

"He'll forgive you," Victor echoes.

"Time has never healed anything between our families," I say. "It's only made things *worse*."

Cintia looks at me carefully, scrutinizing my face. "You've fallen for him, haven't you?" she asks.

"I love him," I admit, the words coming out natural and true.

They look at each other, smiling.

"Then what are you still doing here?" PC nudges me in the arm, like when he used to push me toward the stove. This time, he's nudging me out the door. "Go after him!"

43

MONDAY, JUNE 20

I run through the school corridors trying to find Pedro, until I realize that he may have left the building completely.

I rush to the parking lot, despite the pouring rain. His bicycle is still chained by the gate, but the back tire is flat. If he's headed home, he'll have to take the bus.

I turn around and race to the bus stop.

Water pools near the curb, already splashing onto the sidewalk with every passing car. Squinting behind my rain-streaked glasses, I spot a bus leaving. Pedro's probably on it! I wave my arms above my head for it to stop, but the bus doesn't slow down. The wheels hit the flooded spots on the road, sending a wave of dirty water at me as it passes.

I didn't know I could get even more drenched than I already was. Ankle deep in water, I chase after the bus, shouting, "STOP! PLEASE!"

But it's long gone.

My eyes are hot with tears and my forehead feels like it's

burning up. Everything spins. The trees. The houses. The flooded road. I crouch down, my head in my hands.

I blew it. It doesn't matter how many times I run after Pedro to apologize. If he doesn't want me around him, there's nothing I can do...

I don't know how long I stay like this. But eventually I realize the rain's stopped. I still see thick drops hitting the road, but they're not landing on me. Like I'm in a protective bubble. Like—

Pedro stands holding his jacket above my head like a makeshift umbrella.

I jerk to my feet. "I thought you left..." I say.

"I'm still here."

A dull ache spreads in my chest. "I'm sorry. I made a horrible, horrible mistake hiding things from you, and I'll spend the rest of my life apologizing if necessary, but—please, I'm not going back to the feud. I refuse to do that."

He stares at me, cautious, like he's trying to figure me out. "I don't want to lose Sugar," he says, letting his guard down a little. "I know that my grandfather, for his own health, needs to step down. But I want to show him that he can trust me to fight for it." I see the look in Pedro's eyes, the pain from needing his grandfather's approval. "And I will *not* fail. The cooking contest is my only hope. Are we still going to compete together?"

I fight back the tears welling in my eyes. "If you want," I say. "It's my only hope to keep Salt, too."

"How do I know I can trust you'll be there on Thursday?" he asks.

I bore my gaze into his, willing him to see the truth in my eyes. "I'll be there."

We're silent for a while, listening to the rain hitting his jacket above us.

I feel the old abyss widening between us, and I'm terrified things will go back to how they were.

"I hate this," I say. "What will happen to us when the contest is over? The feud goes back to how it was?"

Pedro remains impassive. I feel like this is goodbye forever. Like we'll never get the chance to talk again while the other is listening. *Truly* listening.

"Last time we talked, you brought up your father," I say, and Pedro immediately looks defensive. "I didn't have a chance to tell you how I wish I'd been there for you. To tell you that you're not ungrateful for having left home. And I don't know if I'm crossing the line here, but I think there's something you need to know. Something about your grandfather."

I tell him about my unexpected encounter at the cemetery with Seu Romário. Pedro listens to me, his expression frozen.

"I don't know if you knew about my dad's past at Sugar and the way he died," I say. "But your grandfather loved him like a son. Maybe when Seu Romário is being stubborn, when he yells at you to respect tradition, when he refuses to change, he's just trying to honor my dad's memory. Maybe he just wants to keep things the way my dad left them. It's all guilt, Pedro. He loves you."

Pedro averts his eyes. Another bus arrives.

"I should go," I say, fighting back tears. Pedro still won't look at me. "Let me know when you want to meet up to bake our cake for the contest?" Still nothing. A muscle twitches near his jaw. That's it. I've lost him forever. "Goodbye, Pedro."

I get on the bus quickly, without looking back, so he won't see me crying. I sit in the back and lean my head against the window, the glass streaked with rain. The A/C is blasting. I sit shaking, my arms wrapped around my waist, not just because I'm freezing, though. Because I feel like I just left a part of me behind.

I'm startled when Pedro sits down next to me, gently placing his jacket on my lap.

"You'll catch your death like this," he says.

My heart is beating so fast in my chest, I'm light-headed. "Why—why are you here?"

I put his jacket on, his scent immediately all around me.

"I thought I wasn't good enough for Grandpa, and all that time I had no idea he... He was feeling guilt over your father's death."

We talk some more about my encounter with his grandfather, and the long conversation I had with Mom afterward. He listens carefully, but there's bitterness in his eyes. Conflicted feelings. My heart breaks to see him like this.

"None of this is your fault," I say. "Your grandfather has been stuck trying to honor my father's memory. So has my mother."

He looks at me, his eyes bright with tears. "Thank you for telling me. I'm sure it was hard for you to hear all that from Grandpa, too."

"It was," I admit. "But now I understand him a little better."

Pedro frowns. "You do?"

"I understand he loved my grandmother and father," I say, and Pedro's eyes widen. "And that he loves you more than anything. He's made poor decisions, but I… I hope you two will find a way to mend things."

He stares at me for a long second, his eyes scanning my face, traveling over my lips, and I realize he's thinking about us, too. Measuring whether there's a chance for *us* to mend things. But I shouldn't get my hopes up. I hurt him, and he has a right to be guarded. I can tell he's judging whether or not he can trust me. My heart sinks when his expression hardens, because I know he still feels something for me, but he's fighting it.

Maybe PC, Victor, and Cintia were right when they told me to give him time. There's nothing else I can do or say. It's Pedro's decision now to give us another chance. Or not.

"What if *I* don't want an apology at this point?" he says. "What if it's too late for that? What if I'm tired of feeling like I'm never good enough?"

Pedro looks away, crossing his arms over his chest. I don't know what to say. Stubborn tears tumble to my chin and I look out the window to hide my face, too.

We continue the trip in silence. It hurts that I'm still wearing his jacket, his scent enveloping me with memories of the night at the beach, when it was just him and me, the neighborhood and our issues distant like the stars in the sky.

The bus swerves suddenly. Passengers scream. I stumble to the left, slamming into Pedro, and he passes a protective arm around me.

Passengers are craning their necks to see why the bus had

to swerve off like that, and we do the same. The bus driver
stands up, wiping his forehead with a hand towel.

"The flooding in the avenue is getting worse," he announces. "Cars are breaking down all along the road. I nearly
rammed into one!"

Just then I realize that I hopped on the wrong bus. This
isn't the route I normally take home. And this bus has led me
straight into Avenida Coqueirais. My blood runs cold.

"I shouldn't be here," I mutter, panic rising in my chest.

"Can't we go on?" a passenger asks, and others echo him.

The bus driver waves his hands nervously. "I'm not risking it. I'm stopping here."

People protest when the driver opens the door and steps
outside.

"What?" I shriek.

I peek through the window. There's water outside as far as
the eye can see. A couple of cars slowly try to make their way
through the river that the avenue has become.

A woman in a small car goes by, following behind a truck.
I watch her clutching the steering wheel, her head stuck out
the window to assess how deep in the flood her car is. She
has two kids in the back seat.

I've seen it happen many times. Smaller cars following
trucks in a false impression of safety in a flooded road.

"This is Avenida Coqueirais," I say under my breath, panic
swelling within me. "This is where Dad died."

Pedro's eyes flicker to me with a flash of fear.

44

MONDAY, JUNE 20

We're in the middle of the avenue, knee-deep in water that goes deeper as the road slopes into the tunnel. I hear a few people shriek behind me as they head for the sidewalk. A man slips in front of me, but a woman pulls him to his feet. He curses nervously.

I'm so dazed with panic, I didn't realize Pedro has been trying to get my attention. He holds me by the shoulders now, standing in front of me, his face so close to mine I can feel his breath on my lips. "It will be okay. I promise." He pulls the jacket I'm wearing closed, yanking the hood over my head. "Stay close to the other passengers and start heading to the sidewalk, okay?" I nod, already hyperventilating.

I take the first step toward the sidewalk when I realize Pedro isn't coming with me. I turn around with a gasp, my fingers grasping the back of his shirt. "Where are you going? You aren't coming with me?!"

Pedro looks at the car we saw drive past the bus. The one

with the woman and kids. "They'll get stranded if they keep going. I need to help them."

"No." I shake my head, tugging his arm. "Come with me."

"Lari, go with the other passengers!" Someone must have heard him, because I suddenly feel an arm loop with mine. A woman begins to steer me away. My grasp on his arm slips.

"Pedro!" My voice goes high-pitched with fear.

"I'll be fine! Go!"

I watch Pedro's retreating back as he ventures deeper into the avenue, waving his arms at the car.

My legs are heavy like lead, and my heart beats frantically as people help me get to the sidewalk. But I can't let Pedro do this alone. What if he falls? He can't even swim! I take a deep breath, once, twice, and I pull away from the group of passengers and rush back into the avenue after him.

I see the car begin to turn, making for the side of the road. The driver finally realized she can't make it to the flooded tunnel ahead. But then the small car hiccups. The engine lets out a few gurgling spurts and dies. I hear the woman's muffled screaming.

"The engine is flooded!" Pedro shouts. He hobbles, now waist-deep in water, toward the stranded family.

I'm no stranger to flooding—water pools quickly along the roads and trash-clogged gutters—but this... It's a like a *river* overflowing into the tunnel, the current growing stronger and stronger against my legs, threatening to sweep me off the ground.

"Pedro!" I call out after him, but he won't turn back.

"Help! My kids!" The woman's cries pierce through the storm, ringing of terror that curdles my blood. Pedro reaches her window, and the woman clasps his hands. She seems too scared to leave her car. "My kids! Please, save my kids!"

She turns to the back seat and grabs one of her children— I gasp. It's Amandinha.

Her face is angry and swollen from crying, and her little pudgy hands cling to her mother for dear life, fiercely struggling against being handed over.

"Amandinha, it's me!" Pedro says, and she looks up, recognizing him. "I volunteer at Vozes," he tells her mother.

Even though Amandinha trusts Pedro, she still doesn't want to let go of her mother. "Go with him, filha. Don't worry."

"No!" Amandinha shouts.

"I'll be right behind you," the woman says. "Go with him first. I promise I'll be right behind you."

The woman opens the door and Amandinha looks from her mother to Pedro in a split second of hesitation. Her grip loosens. It's the opportunity he needs to pull her out in one swift motion. Startled and separated from her mother, Amandinha kicks and wails, but at least she's no longer in the car.

Her mom then passes a little boy to Pedro. He's older than Amandinha, eight or nine years old. He doesn't fight Pedro, and I can see in his wide eyes that he understands the situation, that he's old enough to know exactly how much danger they're in.

Pedro has Amandinha perched on a hip, the boy on the other. "Come with me, senhora," he says to Amandinha's mother.

Her expression is frozen in terror. "My leg," she says.

He's stuck for a second, looking from her to the sidewalk, the kids in his arms. When he shifts a little to the side, I realize her predicament. Her left leg is up to her knee in a cast. There's so much dread in her eyes when she reaches for her crutches in the passenger's seat.

I rush to the car. "Lari!" Amandinha shouts in Pedro's arms, giving in to her fear and crying again.

Pedro turns around with a start. "Why aren't you on the sidewalk?"

"I'll take the kids," I say. "Help Amandinha's mother out of the car."

Pedro does a double take of the situation. Water is rising quickly.

"Hurry," I tell Pedro. "I'll cross with the kids. Help her."

"Tia!" the little boy cries.

"It will be alright," Pedro says, trying to calm him. "We'll make it. My friend here will carry you and your cousin. I'll help your aunt."

"You promise?" Amandinha asks.

"When have I ever let you down?" Pedro says, giving her a comforting smile.

Pedro finally hands me both kids. They're heavier than I thought they would be. Amandinha wraps her arms around my neck. The little boy wraps his legs around my waist. I hold them tightly, trying to find my footing. I take a few tentative steps back, steady, careful...

"Mainha!" Amandinha screams as we distance ourselves from the car.

"It will be alright," the little boy echoes Pedro, reaching to stroke her hair. "She is right behind us."

"What's your name?" I ask the boy.

"Pedro," he says in his tiny, scared voice.

"Pedro? That guy back there is named Pedro, too."

The little boy smiles like only children do when they find someone else who shares their name, forming an instant bond.

I take one step at a time, flood water pushing heavily against my knees. Panic is still making me dizzy, but slowly, I make my way to the sidewalk. People see me approaching with the kids, and they run to help, taking them from me so I can catch my breath.

I turn on my heels, hoping to find Pedro and Amandinha's mother not far behind me.

"Mainha is still in the car!" Amandinha shouts.

Far ahead, near the mouth of the tunnel, I see her mother attempt to get out of the car with her crutches. Pedro turns to carry her on his back. She clings to his neck, her legs held high to keep water from reaching her cast. He's making progress, slowly carrying her to safety, when he suddenly trips over something underwater.

The kids and people on the sidewalk scream.

And just like that the woman and Pedro go crashing down under the water.

I don't think twice. I jump back into the flooded avenue.

"Girl! Wait!" I hear a man's voice calling out. I look over my shoulder to see him running after me, but he's not alone. A long line of people have formed, holding hands to create a human chain. "Hold my hand!" the man shouts.

We grasp each other tightly, and slowly the chain of people stretches across the avenue. My eyes are glued to Pedro and the woman in the distance. He struggles to get back on his feet, while she clings to him, a streak of blood running from her chin down her neck. Pedro cries in agony, trying to keep them both propped up against the car.

"Help!" he shouts.

I push forward as fast as I can, an arm stretching toward them.

And then I can't go on any farther.

I look back to see why we've stopped, and so does the man beside me, our hands tightly linked in a vicious grip that threatens to break my fingers. We've pulled the human chain as far as it will go.

"Grab my hand!" I stretch my fingers toward Pedro.

"Lari! I can't!"

There's something wrong with his right leg. He's standing with his full weight on his left side, an arm wrapped around the woman to keep her balance, while she clings to the side of the car.

"You can do this! Come to me!" I shout, but Pedro and the woman are stuck in place.

I glance back at the man holding my hand. "I need to go to them," I say.

The rain has turned into a full-blown June storm, falling heavy, muffling our voices with the steady thrumming of thick drops pelting the river-like avenue.

The man's expression is strained. And I realize with a jolt of surprise that his eyes remind me of Dad's.

Eyes that I've never seen in person.

Eyes that I've known only through photos and newspaper articles that described his death. A dark, warm shade of brown.

In a flash, I see a motorcycle under all the water.

"This avenue is covered in potholes. I can't let you go on.
We'll call the firefighters!" he says, alarmed. Like Dad probably would have said in this situation. But instead of trapping
me in fear, this realization gives me courage.

"They can't wait any longer!" I wiggle my hand in his to
free it. "Please. I know what I'm doing."

The man seems conflicted. He looks from me to Pedro and
Amandinha's mother, his eyes wide with fear.

Somewhere down the human chain, someone's interlocked
grip breaks loose. But only momentarily. The man and I
get pulled back as they rejoin hands. The abrupt motion is
enough to let my hand slip free. I don't look back. I head toward Pedro.

A stray piece of trash underwater wraps around my ankle
and I lose my footing. I do a little lunge to keep from falling, colliding painfully against the car. The air gets knocked
out of me, and a million stars burst in front of my eyes. My
left knee burns.

"Lari!" Pedro's voice is panicked. He is still holding the
woman.

"I can't walk," she says, scared. "My leg." Her crutches are
lost underwater.

"I think I broke my foot," Pedro says. "I can't do this!"

"You can!" I say, but he won't look at me. His eyes are focused on all this water threatening to drown us. "We can do
this together!"

The man who was holding my hand before ventures closer,
leaving the others. He struggles to keep himself upright against
the current. "I'll carry you, senhora," he says to Amandinha's

mother, noticing the way she limps. He then looks at me. "Can you help the boy? Will you be okay without me?"

I feel a knot in my throat. But the courage in his eyes gives me strength. "Yes," I reassure him.

The man picks Amandinha's mother up and slowly heads back to the human chain.

"Lean on me," I tell Pedro. He's too panicked to move. "It's okay. Lean on me." I offer my shoulder for support. Pedro is still stuck, fear overwhelming his features. He's not listening, so I grab his arm and pass it over my shoulders. I then wrap my arm around his waist. "Let's go home," I say.

Pedro's eyes finally meet mine. And then he nods.

Step by step, we walk together toward safety.

45

The tiles covering the walls and floors in the hospital's waiting room are faded blue. I'd forgotten, even though not long ago I'd spent an hour or two here every day, getting homework done while Mom helped Grandma upstairs.

It feels like a bad dream I had a long, long time ago.

Pedro sits down next to me, propping his ankle up on another chair, a bag of ice wrapped around it. He was in so much pain, I was sure it was broken. Luckily, it's just badly twisted.

He's been quiet ever since we got here an hour ago. Now and then he looks expectantly down the corridor, and I know he's wondering if there's any way we could find Amandinha and her family. The hospital staff took the kids to a separate room, probably to wait for other family members while they run tests on her mother.

When we got Amandinha's mother to the sidewalk, she was alert and didn't seem like she had a concussion, but a crowd formed around her when they saw all the blood staining her collar. I remember her eyes searching frantically, traveling from face to face, until she found her children's. That's when she calmed.

Someone must have called for help when we were on the avenue, because not long after, paramedics were coaxing us into ambulances. I keep thinking about what she told her daughter and nephew. "I'm fine. This is nothing. It doesn't hurt. I'm sorry for worrying you." Just like Grandma used to say.

My eyes sting.

"If it weren't for you, I'd still be out there, stuck to the side of that car," Pedro says, breaking the silence.

I blink away tears. "That's not true. I know you'd have found a way to bring Amandinha's mother back to safety. You fulfilled your promise to her. And you were the first to run to her rescue. I don't know if I would have done the same."

Thinking about his bravery still sends goose bumps down my arms. It was selfless. *Too* selfless, perhaps. He forgot about his own safety. He forgot that he never learned to swim. It makes me wonder now if it's the same driving force prompting him to take full responsibility over Sugar's future. I don't want him to get hurt like... Like Mom has been hurt.

"I'm sorry," he says. "Your father. That avenue."

I push away bad thoughts. Pedro and I are both lucky things turned out okay. "Now you know why I always avoid it when we go to Vozes," I say.

"You were brave."

"Well, the only way through was literally through." I let out a tired sigh. "And I wasn't going to leave you."

Pedro swallows. "Thank you."

We stare at each other, my heart beating quickly in my

chest. He opens his mouth to say something, but someone's cell phone ringing at maximum volume in the hallway startles us. We both instinctively glance at the exit door.

"Should we wait for our mothers separately?" I ask.

"I'm fine with waiting together," Pedro says. "If you don't mind."

Knowing both of our mothers are coming feels a lot like waiting at the shore as a tsunami approaches.

"Are you worried about what they'll say? You know, because we were together?"

"No," he says, and the conviction in his voice is a little startling. But we've been hiding our increasing closeness for so long now, I realize I actually don't want to keep this up anymore. It's time I come clean.

We're silent again, watching—although not following— the telenovela playing on TV in the reception area, our eyes darting to the door every time a person walks in. He must notice I'm nervous, because he holds my hand. The gesture is so careful, almost reverent, it makes me feel warm inside, even though my clothes are soaking wet.

When I look at him, I hope he can see in my eyes how sorry I am to have betrayed his trust.

When he looks at me, I get the sense that he wants to say something. Something that scares him. Like he's worried I'll pull away afterward.

"I used to watch you when we were kids," he says at last, "the way your grandmother treated you. The way you seemed so happy at Salt. How well you did at school, winning all those medals. And it felt like you had everything. It's hard to say this…" Pedro frowns, looking regretful. "But I think I used to resent you."

I give his hand a little squeeze. "It's okay."

"Not, it's not okay. I felt belittled at home, but I had no right to lash out at you. To see you as my enemy. I'm sorry. I'm really, really sorry. I was just so confused."

"I'm sorry, too." I take a deep breath. "I wish we could put the past behind us."

Instead of responding, Pedro lurches to his feet and leaves the room, hobbling away on his injured ankle. I crane my neck, confused, to see where he went. One second later, he's back.

"Hi, I'm Pedro," he says, a hand stretched out to shake mine.

He's giving us a chance to start over. To begin anew.

I stand up to take his hand.

"I'm Lari," I say.

He smiles, his expression softening and his eyes lighting up. It takes my breath away. "Nice to meet you," he says.

"Nice—" I begin to say, but my mother's raised voice cuts me off.

"Larissa Catarina Ramires!"

46

I don't know how long Mom was standing there, but if she saw Pedro and me holding hands, she pretends she didn't. I don't know if that's better or worse.

She takes one look at my bandaged knee and runs up to me.

"It's—it's okay," I stammer. "It doesn't hurt."

"You're drenched!" she says, rubbing my arms.

"I'm okay."

She acknowledges Pedro, glancing at his ankle. I feel the questions she's keeping to herself for now. *How did you and Pedro end up together in a flooded avenue? Why were you together to begin with?* Mom may be willing to accept a future where I'm not following her academic plans, but a relationship with Pedro? *No way.*

"I was so worried," she says, her voice strangled with panic. "When they called me saying you were here… I thought… I thought of your dad and… I thought I'd lost you, too!" She pulls me into another hug, like she's afraid I'll disappear.

"I'm sorry. I'm safe. It's just a tiny cut on my knee."

Mom glances back at Pedro, who's standing awkwardly by my side. "You're hurt," she says in guarded concern for him.

Pedro's eyes flicker nervously from me to her. He smiles sheepishly, "I'm alright."

I stand in between them, holding my breath.

Mom looks like she's about to say something else to Pedro, but Dona Eulalia's arrival, bursting into the reception room like a hurricane, steals the opportunity. The moment her eyes land on Pedro, she lets out a pained cry, shoving her way to him.

When she pulls him to her, Pedro bumps his injured ankle on a chair and winces. She doesn't notice. Her hug is just as desperate as Mom's.

"My son!" she cries out, cupping Pedro's face in her hands until her well-manicured fingernails leave small crescent moon–shaped marks on his skin. "Are you in one piece? What happened?!"

"Mom, I'm fine," Pedro says, sounding a little smothered.

"You're not fine!" Dona Eulalia is starting to sound angry at him. "Look at this ankle! Is it broken? Where's your doctor?" Her sharp eyes turn to the nurses behind the desk, who all straighten their backs in response like meerkats. "Where's my son's doctor? I want to talk with a doctor!" She turns around to Pedro again, starting to cry. "Did you take anything for the pain? Are you in a lot of pain?! My son!"

"Let the boy breathe," Seu Romário says in the back.

And I see the blood drain from Pedro's face.

"*Grandpa?*" He takes a step away from his mother, trying to stand like his ankle isn't bothering him. "I mean, Chef. You shouldn't be here."

"How am I supposed to stay home when I hear my own grandson is at the hospital?" Seu Romário's eyes are accusatory, and Pedro immediately lowers his gaze.

His grandpa acts like he's angry with Pedro for getting hurt... How is this his fault? It's infuriating!

"Pedro saved a family today," I blurt out at Seu Romário. "He was a *hero*. That's how he hurt his ankle."

Pedro glances at me nervously like he'd rather I stayed out of this, but it's too late now. Mom's looking at me funny. Dona Eulalia grasps Pedro's arm like she's only now fully realizing the extent of what happened. And Seu Romário turns to me. He nods, letting my words sink in, and his expression softens when he looks at Pedro again.

"Are you alright, son?" Seu Romário asks Pedro.

"Yes, Chef," Pedro nods eagerly, and I can tell just the question means the world to him. There's a lot of unspoken concern in the way Seu Romário glances at Pedro's leg.

Dona Eulalia ruins the moment, stepping around them to confront me. "Why were you with my son?" she asks, indignant.

Mom pushes me behind herself, getting in Dona Eulalia's face. "You say one thing to my daughter and I swear I'll forget I'm in a hospital!"

"I'm not afraid of you!" Dona Eulalia shouts at Mom. "I want to know why my son was with your daughter! She put him in danger! I don't trust this Ramires kid!"

A hollowness spreads inside my chest. Dona Eulalia thinks I'm this horrible person, based on...what? Our family's feuding history? How can she accuse me like this?

"Mom, no one put me in danger. We took the same bus at

school and the flood happened," Pedro tries to explain. But his mother is so quick to jump to the worst conclusions. I now understand how Pedro must have felt when I didn't tell him about the Deals Deals lawyer's business card. Despite all the evidence in his favor, just for having Molina as his last name. Now his mother thinks I could have hurt him, all because my last name is Ramires. "Mom, please, let's go home." He tentatively walks toward the exit, urging his mother to follow him, but Dona Eulalia doesn't budge.

"Took the bus at school? *Together?*" Dona Eulalia snaps, her face going red. "Do you think I was born yesterday? I'm not going anywhere until I find out exactly why this girl is trying to hurt you!"

"She's not—"

"She already tripped you before! Did she trip you again?!"

Pedro shoots me a pained look, like he doesn't know what else to do to keep his mother from barraging me with these horrible accusations. And I can't even stand up for myself. I just hide behind Mom, trying to make myself small, even though I'm a head taller than her.

"Can we go home? *Please!*" Pedro begs on the verge of tears. "I'll explain everything on the way back."

"No!" his mother shouts, her angry eyes zoning in on his jacket, which I'm still wearing. "Are you—are you *friends* with this girl?" She says the word like it's an even more horrifying concept and starts wailing.

"Shut up!" Mom barks at her.

And chaos erupts.

Mom and Dona Eulalia shower each other with accusations past and present, while the hospital's staff struggle to keep them from jumping at each other's throats. Everything twists and turns, and it somehow all comes back to Deals Deals and our mothers vowing to sell the bakeries before the other by the end of the week.

I catch Seu Romário's eyes and he winks at me. Before I can decipher his meaning, he lets out a pained cry, clutching at his chest. A cry that seems a little too rehearsed, but it works, because all the attention shifts to him. Nurses rush in, and Dona Eulalia abandons the fight with Mom to help him.

Mom wraps an arm around my shoulders and begins to steer me out of the room. I glance at Pedro on my way out, and he gives me a desperate glance back, but there's nothing we can do now.

When we reach the parking lot, Mom turns around to face me. Her face is pale like she's just seen a ghost. "I don't know what you were doing with that boy, but promise me you aren't going to see him again."

"You do realize we go to the same school, right?" I joke, trying to lighten the mood, but it only makes Mom even more furious.

"He's a *Molina*," Mom says. "I don't trust him around you one bit. Whatever is going on between you two, end it now. Before it's too late."

LARI: Meet me by the church?

PEDRO: I just need to figure out how to climb down from my bedroom window with a twisted ankle!

It's close to midnight. I'm running down the deserted street, the wind blowing strong and heavy with a relentless drizzle. The feirinha has already been packed up. Not one soul around. I turn left at Alto da Sé, entering the church's side patio.

The ocean breeze blows salty air at my face when I sit down on the wall to look out at the darkness beyond. Tonight, the moon is hiding behind thick rain clouds the color of mud.

I don't know how long I wait, but when I hear quick footsteps approaching, I bolt upright. A tall silhouette enters the church patio. "Who's there?" I call out.

The shadow steps into the orange glow a moth-obsessed lamppost casts. "It's me!" Pedro says.

And I melt with relief. He walks straight to me, hobbling a little because of his injured ankle. I go to him, colliding into a hug. He lets out a little yelp of pain but doesn't let go, hugging me tighter.

"I was scared you wouldn't be able to come," I say.

"I'm here," he says in my ear, sending a tingling wave down my spine. He's trembling, despite the warmth traveling from his skin.

"My mother wants me to stay away from you," I tell him.

"My mother actually thinks we've been dating behind her back for ages." He chuckles to himself. "If only."

"Pedro, I… I love you." I feel my cheeks getting hot. Is it too soon to say I love him? "You don't need to say anything back. But after everything that happened today, I just wanted to tell you that—"

I hide my face in his chest.

"I love you, too, Lari." He kisses the top of my head, and relief washes over me.

We stand like this, his arms around me, for a while.

"I don't think I asked you," he says. "What changed your mind about me, after all? Was it my charming smile or my incredible baking that won you over?"

Although he's not far from the truth, I try to disentangle myself from our hug so I can give his arm a playful slap, but he doesn't let go of me.

"If you really wanna know…" I say, looking into his eyes. "I saw the things that mattered to you. And suddenly I was terrified of losing you. But what changed *your* mind about me?"

"When you crashed into me that night."

"What?"

"It's more like… I was so tired after coming home from Curitiba. While I was gone, I thought about the life I'd be leaving behind if I decided to stay with my father, and I realized I didn't want to leave my family, Sugar, the neighborhood… But if I came back, I knew things would have to drastically change. I knew I also couldn't go back to the feud. I was drained enough from arguing with Grandpa. And then you came out of nowhere when I was carrying the cake. I realized I wasn't totally sure if you'd done that on purpose, when in the past I'd have been positive you did. It was a small doubt at first, but it was enough for me to start questioning everything I believed about you. About us."

He plants a kiss on my lips. A kiss that's full of pent-up yearning, like he's trying to bottle this moment.

When I kiss him back, it's like a reminder of all the things I wish we'd realized sooner about each other, the missed opportunities to grow up together, fall in love, and start a relationship with our families' support.

I hate this constant reminder that everything is drowned in rumors and old grudges.

We drink up each kiss like it's our last, unable to escape the constant fear of being pulled apart. Our mothers are still feuding, after all. And Mom got so upset today thinking we're just *friends*. Imagine if she knew we're dating.

"I don't want to lose you," I say.

"You're not going to lose me."

I pull away to look into his eyes. "I want us to end the feud. At the contest."

Pedro frowns, a thumb rubbing my cheek. "We can't end a decades-old feud in one day."

"No. But we can start." I hold his hand. "I don't know if you're up for it, but let's bring our families to the contest. Let's show them we're stronger together."

He looks fearful, gazing out at the ocean. But when he turns back to me, his eyes are bright with new determination. "I'm with you. No matter what," he says.

And we kiss again, our lips sealing a promise to ourselves that we'll be brave.

47

When we arrive at the 1800s palace-style building on Thursday, the huge banner that hangs above the front stairs reads "Gastronomic Society's Cooking Contest." The street is lined with TV crew vans, and the place is packed with contestants and journalists.

I gawk at the front stairs, the big windows, and the blue-and-white Portuguese tiles covering the facade, which I'd only seen in pictures. This is all so bittersweet. I wish Grandma were here now.

PC gives me a quick shoulder massage like I'm about to enter a UFC fight. This is it. The moment we've all been waiting for. But when we reach the front gates, Pedro looks it up and down like he's about to face a giant.

"Is it just me or did this building suddenly get taller?" he asks.

"Don't be scared, Chef," PC teases, patting him on the back.

"Who says I'm scared?" Pedro retorts, but I see the sheen of sweat already beading at his temples.

We head inside, holding the box with our creation carefully. There's a stage smack-dab in the middle of the building, where contestants display their entry dishes on a long table. Fruit parfaits, seafood stews, skewered meats, breads... I look away before it all overwhelms me, motioning for Pedro to come help me set up our cake.

We open the box and slowly remove our two-layered Romeo and Juliet cake. Cheers erupt from the audience, and when we look down from the stage, PC, Victor, and Cintia have already taken their spots. They give us a thumbs-up and I wave back, smiling. But when I turn to Pedro, he's starting to look decisively green.

"You okay?" I ask.

"Of course!" He steps away, working on displaying our cake. The ruby guava melts into the cheesy corn cake looking like a flower sprouting in the sun-kissed earth. This is the best compromise between our families' bakeries. It's *perfect*.

I glance at the dishes next to ours. A team of contestants— father and sons, I think—assembles a pretty display of tall clay pots holding black beans and pork sausage. They neatly place many small bowls all around it, each showcasing a regional choice of condiment: vinaigrette, olive oil, hot sauce with chunky red peppers. My mouth begins to water just looking at it.

"They made feijoada," Pedro whispers to me, noticing I've been scanning the competition. "And down the table, did you see, they've brought moqueca. And over there, they have the most elaborate fruit basket I've ever seen!"

"I think the basket is edible, too," I point out. Pedro's face scrunches up with nerves. It's odd seeing his usual confidence give place to fear. "What's wrong?"

"Most contestants are Gastronomic Society students," he says, pointing out their jackets.

He's right. At least one person in each group gathered on stage has the Society's logo on the side of their jackets—a big, entwined *GS* in silver lettering. There are even full teams of GS-only competitors, like the triplets down the table. Even though the contest opened for nonmembers this year, outsiders were clearly intimidated.

Pedro and I are the only team that's entirely comprised of nonmembers.

He steps around and crouches behind the table. I crouch next to him. "Who are we hiding from?" I ask.

"Chef Augusto and Chef Lorêncio are here. They're cooking *gods*! On a par with Anthony Bourdain and Eric Ripert! They had a segment on a TV show I used to watch when I was little and now, look, they're judges!" he whispers to me, his ears going red. "I can't do this. I'm not good enough."

I realize that as cocky as Pedro is at school, he hasn't had any experience with contests. Who knew that all those mathematics competitions would prepare me for a cooking contest! I never thought I'd say this, but I'm grateful for Mom's pestering me to participate and Pimentel's guidance, because now I know what to do on stage.

"You *are* good enough," I say.

"I'm not."

Contestants to our left and right give us curious looks. "I've been in big contests before. And if there's one thing I learned, it's that you do yourself a disservice if you look like you've already lost." I get on my feet, pulling him along with me. "Show them you have nothing to fear."

"But I have *everything* to fear," he whispers to me.

"Remember the guy who climbed up a ladder to get to class? Why let a cooking contest get to you, when you're that guy?"

"That guy was being destructive and trying to get himself expelled. But this… This is my *dream*." He looks up at the vaulted ceiling, beams of sunlight filtering through the skylights. "I'll get lost."

He looks panic-stricken.

"Then we'll get you a map."

"*Lari*."

"*Pedro*. You belong here." He still seems unconvinced. "You're the best baker in our neighborhood. You were born for this. Don't let anyone make you doubt your worth."

He's silent for a while, and then he nods, agreeing with me. "Just for the record, you just said I'm better than you."

He just can't pass up the opportunity to poke at me, can he?

I slap his arm. "Just you wait until I join the Gastronomic Society, too."

A smile spreads across his lips. "You're going to apply?"

"Yes. And so are you," I say. Before Pedro can start protesting again, I add, "You said so yourself that this school is your dream. I'm not letting you give up. We both could study here one day."

I see that twinkle in his eyes again.

"Chef!" PC calls out from the audience, and about a dozen teachers look at him. He waves his hands, embarrassed, gesturing that he means Pedro. Victor and Cintia, standing behind him, frantically point at the front door.

Our families are walking in.

My heart stops. Because even though this was planned, it's still nerve-racking to see them together at the Gastronomic Society, moments before a contest they didn't know we'd be entering. Together. But we couldn't keep this a secret any longer. We had to make them a part of this contest, too. Because this isn't just about fighting against Deals Deals anymore.

It's one final attempt to bring our families together.

"There's no going back now," Pedro says.

Despite the worry in his voice, he grabs my hand. And I know that no matter what happens today, he'll be by my side.

And in a way...

In a way we've already won.

The feud, as far as Pedro and I are concerned, is over.

48

Pedro and I hurry down the stage together to talk with our families.

"Please, tell me this is a prank," Mom says when I reach her. "Tell me this whole thing is a terrible prank. The note you left saying you were entering a contest with Pedro Molina. And...*this!*" She glares at our entwined hands. "I told you to stay away from this boy!"

She motions like she wants to pull me away from Pedro, but I take a step back, dragging him along with me, and Mom's hand just hangs in midair. When I don't budge, her eyes ignite.

Pedro's hand feels clammy in mine. "Dona Alice, I can explain—" he begins to say, but his mother is already in Mom's face, drowning out his voice.

Pedro and I exchange a look. "I'm so sorry," I mouth to him.

Cintia sneaks past our fighting mothers to come nudge me

in the arm. "You guys are starting to attract attention. What if the judges disqualify you?"

She's right. People have started whispering, launching us annoyed looks.

When we decided to invite our families to the contest, we knew it wouldn't be easy. But we wanted to try to bring them closer. If they continue fighting like this and we get disqualified, we'll end up achieving the exact opposite.

"Mom, please, let me explain," I say. "We're here because we wanted to show Deals Deals that we can fight back. So we made a cake together, something that matters to us."

"What is this girl going on about, Pedro?" Dona Eulalia asks, glaring at me over Mom's shoulder.

"Please, just listen for one second," Pedro begs. "We figured that if we won the contest, it would help us keep the bakeries safe. Maybe the money won't solve all our problems, but the neighborhood will at least see we're together, and Deals Deals will, too. They'll think twice before threatening us."

"You know your grandfather can't take any more of this stress," she hisses. "We *have* to sell Sugar."

"I'd like to be at the forefront of things," Pedro announces. "I'll run Sugar."

"What's this about you running my bakery?" Seu Romário's voice booms behind us.

And my heart skips a beat. I wasn't sure he'd come.

We turn around to look at him. Even though he helped us end the fight between our mothers at the hospital, I realize his relationship with Pedro remains strained. These two still haven't talked.

Pedro glances from me to his grandfather nervously. I'm

still holding his hand, so I tap a finger on the back to encourage him. He taps mine in response. It's time to be honest with Seu Romário. To tell him how he feels, just like Grandma used to urge me to be honest with Mom.

"It would be an honor, if you'd still like me to run it one day, Grandpa," Pedro says, and adds quickly, "I wouldn't want to make you feel like I'm going about things in any way that displeases you. I respect your kitchen and I'm grateful for everything you've taught me."

Seu Romário squints at him. "Will you change my whole menu?"

"I'll respect your boundaries, but if you let me at least introduce a few new things…" Pedro hesitates. "I mean, if you don't want me to change anything, that's okay."

Pedro is shrinking again.

"Why are these new dishes so important to you?" Seu Romário asks, but for the first time, he doesn't sound defensive. He's giving Pedro a chance to explain. Like he's trying to understand his grandson.

I see the surprise in Pedro's eyes. "I wanted you to see that I can bake," Pedro says eagerly. "I—I know it sounds like I'm just trying to change everything you've done for Sugar, but I've always wondered if, you know—if I had what it takes to make you—" Pedro clears his throat. "Proud. Of me."

He lowers his gaze, while Seu Romário just stares at him.

"Peu, I didn't think you wanted to run Sugar," Dona Eulalia says, remorseful.

Pedro turns to his mother. "It's my home," he says. "I never meant to leave."

Mom finally manages to pull me aside. "I thought there

were no more lies between us," she whispers. "And yet you didn't tell me you were entering this contest. And now you're with this boy, too?"

"This is the whole truth," I say. "And I know you think we should close Salt, but I want to stay. Let me run it when high school is over."

Mom's eyes fill with hurt. "I already told you this. I can't keep you from going to culinary school, but I won't watch you ruin your future at Salt. Salt isn't just a bakery—it represents the feud, too. I'm not letting you get any more involved." She shakes her head. "No. Your grandmother was right. I'm selling Salt tomorrow. I must keep you safe from the Molinas."

"Selling Salt won't erase the way I feel." I glance at Pedro. His mother and grandfather flank him, listening in. "Give them a chance. We all have more in common than you think. And give *me* a chance too, Mom. If Pedro and I win this contest, you won't need to go to that meeting tomorrow." I look at Dona Eulalia. "And neither will you."

"*If* you win?" Mom nods at the contestants behind us. "Look around you. You're setting yourself up to fail. I won't let my daughter fail." She clutches my hand.

"You're right, I could fail today. And I'll fail a thousand times as a baker. But I'll keep on trying my best. Because this is what I want. This is where my heart is. Let me fight for Salt, Mom. Please? I can't do this without your blessing."

"Lari, what if this boy is using you—"

"Your daughter is the one using my son!" Dona Eulalia snaps at Mom. "What does this kid know about baking? My son grew up in the kitchen, while your daughter was too good for it, wasn't she? I never saw her working at Salt!"

"Eulalia," Seu Romário says, stopping her. He looks at Pedro, who instinctively lowers his eyes again. But, this time, Seu Romário taps his chin gently, encouraging him to keep his head high. "Just tell me one thing, filho."

Pedro swallows. "Senhor?"

"Are you really serious about Sugar? Or is this whole thing with the Ramires girl your way of calling attention to yourself after I disagreed with your ideas?"

Pedro straightens his back. "Grandpa, I'm not a toddler throwing a tantrum. Like I said, I respect your kitchen, but wanting to change things at Sugar, applying to culinary school, or joining a contest with Lari isn't an affront to you or our family's traditions. When we had that fight in April, I didn't mean to sound disrespectful when I said I didn't want to stay stuck in the past at Sugar. I just want to learn more, and maybe with time, you'll see that I care about Sugar just as much as—that I care just as much as Gabriel did."

I hear the tiny gasp Mom tries to suppress at the mention of Dad.

"What did you say?" Seu Romário asks him, taking a step closer, like a challenge.

Pedro doesn't recoil. "I know that you respected Gabriel's plans for Sugar. And I understand that maybe you're trying to keep Sugar the same way he left it to honor his memory. But I promise I won't cross your boundaries."

Seu Romário begins to speak, but his voice cracks, his eyes glistening with tears. Mom seems taken aback, and he turns to her. "Alice, how I regret that night Gabriel came to beg me to listen to him. I should have listened. I should have supported him. I should have supported you two."

I pass an arm around Mom's shoulders. Her whole frame is shaking, so I squeeze her tighter.

"All these years, you never said anything," Mom says, her words coming out like a gasp. "I waited and waited, and you never said anything."

"Gabriel was like a son. My son." He looks at Pedro and me. "There's too much hatred and misunderstanding in our families, but these kids are a breath of fresh air in this old feud. Go and enter the contest. For today, our bakeries are together once more, as they should always have been. As Gabriel hoped." He turns to look at Mom and Dona Eulalia. "Will you allow it, Eulalia? Alice?"

Maybe it's my imagination, but something about Dona Eulalia's resolve melts a little bit. "I will," she says.

But Mom still hesitates. I take a step closer. "Mom, please? Let me do this. I need your blessing."

Mom nods, her eyes conflicted.

And I fling my arms around her. "I'll fight to save our home," I whisper in her ear.

"I'll be cheering you on," she whispers back.

This won't be easy. It won't be like answering an equation challenge, showing Mom my stellar report card, or winning a mathematics contest. But that's why it will be even better. Because she'll finally see me doing what I love the most. She'll finally see me for who I am.

49

Pedro and I were so busy trying to convince our families to give us a chance, we didn't realize that a few cameras were zooming in on us.

It's mortifying, having our families' fight on a big screen for everyone—contestants and judges alike—to see. We head back to our spot at the judging table, mouthing apologies to the judges. I swear I can hear them thinking, *Why did we let nonmembers in again?*

An awkward silence spreads over the Gastronomic Society, and after what feels like an eternity, the contest finally begins. One of the judges approaches us.

"So you're…" She checks her clipboard. "Ah, such a young couple!"

I feel myself blushing. Pedro has gone bright red next to me, too. I try not to look at our families in the audience.

The woman leans in, admiring the cake we brought. "This is beautiful!" she says, grabbing a sample from the platter.

"Anything you'd like to explain about the dish before I take it to the other judges?"

She holds the microphone toward us. Our faces are projected on the big screen, sweaty and panicked, and I see myself go even redder like a giant tomato.

"It's a—a guava and Parmesan corn c-cake," Pedro says too quickly, tripping over the words. His confidence wilts in front of the dozen TV cameras pointed at us.

Our families and friends watch us expectantly. We can't fail now.

I step in, summoning all the training Pimentel's given me for mathematics contests. "I wish we could tell you that we created this two-layered cake to represent the bond between our families, however…"

I look at Pedro. His old confidence comes back at the right time. "…we're actually enemies," he finishes for me, and a buzz of surprise travels through the audience. "Well, our families are. They have been in a feud for generations, beginning with our great-grandmothers. Lari and I only started dating recently, and they *literally* just found out, so…yeah."

The judge gives us a nervous smile. "You two are very brave for entering our contest together and sharing the news of your relationship this way."

Pedro and I exchange a look. This is it. This is our last hope to bring attention to the problems in our neighborhood, and even though it's hard to find the right words when all these lights and cameras are pointed at us, I focus on the feeling of Pedro's hand holding mine.

I spot our families and friends in the audience. And I think of Grandma smiling at me from the kitchen counter at Salt.

I take a deep breath. I find my strength.

"I don't know if it's bravery or not, but we *had* to do something," I say. "There's a supermarket in our neighborhood. Deals Deals. They're a threat to all the small businesses. We bake our goods at our families' bakeries, and then they go and sell similar dishes for a cheaper price. Many booths at the Olinda feirinha have shut down because of them. Many family-owned businesses have had to close their doors. And now they're pitting our families against each other, because they want to buy one of the bakeries and replace it with a coffee shop. We don't want to lose our homes, so we hoped that if we entered this contest together and won, none of us would have to leave."

My throat is parched from nerves. I'm terrified of failing. But when I find Mom in the audience, she nods at me, standing sandwiched between Seu Romário and Dona Eulalia, her eyes bright with tears.

I feel an invisible link between us. Strong. A connection I hoped and prayed I'd be able to form with her one day, only it was there all along.

"Our cake represents the best our families' bakeries Salt and Sugar have to offer," Pedro says, addressing the audience. "Two layers. There's the savory, nourishing quality of Parmesan corn and the sweetness of a guava-drizzled cake that's a reinterpretation of bolo de rolo. Two flavors that are dominant by themselves, meeting to complement each other." He points at each layer. "Salt and Sugar. Just like our families' bakeries."

The judge smiles. "Thank you, kids. And what do you call your cake?"

I meet Pedro's eyes. Deciding on the name wasn't hard. But saying it out loud in front of our families could go either way.

"Romário and Julieta," we say in unison.

I see Mom and Dona Eulalia look at each other in surprise. Seu Romário turns around, disappearing into the crowd. Dona Eulalia goes after him. One second later, Mom is gone, too.

I want to run to them, but the judge is still asking questions.

"Ah, like Romeo and Juliet?"

"Y-yes," Pedro says. He glances at me, worried.

"What a moving story," the judge says. "Good luck to you both!"

The audience claps. She moves down the table to interview the other contestants.

"What happened?" I ask Pedro the moment the spotlight isn't on us. "Did you see them leave?"

"I think Grandpa was crying."

PC, Victor, and Cintia run to the edge of the stage and Pedro crouches to speak with them. They talk for a moment, then Pedro turns to rejoin me.

"Victor saw them enter a classroom or something," he says. "I'm afraid they're arguing again."

A horrible pang rattles in my chest. "Did we go too far, naming the cake after our grandparents?"

More judges walk down the table on stage, trying samples and writing down notes. We do our best to smile and answer all their questions about our cake, meanwhile my brain keeps yelling at me to go find Mom.

"I need to talk to my mother," I whisper to Pedro.

"Wait, I think the judges are deliberating now. We shouldn't leave the stage."

Pedro is right. I wait, shifting from foot to foot. Still no sign of our families in the audience.

The judges gather behind the stage, and after some private conversation, they come back and approach the microphone.

"This year the Gastronomic Society is proud to have opened its doors to the community. We've heard your families' incredible stories and tried amazing dishes tonight."

I search for Mom in the audience.

"Voting was difficult, but we're proud to announce the winner! Please give a big round of applause for…"

I see them! Mom, Dona Eulalia, and Seu Romário reappear in the back of the room just in time for the announcement. Pedro exhales in relief, spotting them, too.

"The Aguirre family with the Feijoada Island! Congratulations on winning this year's contest."

The audience claps and cheers. The fancy feijoada pot with side dishes has won. And I feel my heart sink all the way to my toes.

I've failed.

After everything… After lying to Mom for so long, I wished, and wished, and *wished* I could show her today that I'll be okay. That we'll be okay. But I've failed. And now Mom and Dona Eulalia will have no choice but to sell the bakeries.

We're stepping off the stage, but the audience hasn't stopped clapping. The ovation goes on, and much to my surprise, I realize people have directed their gazes to us.

"What's going on?" I hear myself ask, my voice distant, drowned out by their cheering.

"Lari," Pedro gives my hand a little squeeze, "they're clapping for *us*."

The judge who first interviewed us taps on the microphone. "I just wanted to say that the Gastronomic Society fully supports these kids' and their neighborhood's fight against that predatory supermarket chain. They may not have won the contest tonight, but they've won our admiration. We stand by family-owned businesses."

My legs go numb. I'm glad Pedro is holding my hand, because I feel like I could fall over.

My eyes finally find Mom.

In the middle of it all, I realize she's clapping harder than anyone.

50

In the chaos of trying to get off the stage, one of the judges asked to speak with us privately.

We mill about in a classroom, waiting with our families, but now Pedro and I are stuck with the aftermath of naming our dish after our grandparents. Mom and Dona Eulalia are sniping at each other again, looking close to turning this into a physical fight.

"My father's name should never be associated with your mother's! It's an outrage!" Dona Eulalia shouts at Mom.

"Why are you talking like it was *my* decision?" Mom snaps.

The contest was supposed to bring our families closer, not to widen the abyss between us.

Mom's phone rings and she turns her back on Dona Eulalia to answer the call. When Mom says, "Yes, Seu Ricardo?" the Deals Deals lawyer's name, Dona Eulalia immediately snatches the phone from her.

"Why is he calling you?" Dona Eulalia shouts. She presses Mom's phone to her ear, desperate. "Hello? HELLO?"

Mom yanks her phone back from Dona Eulalia's grip. Dona Eulalia lunges again, her face going red, and Mom shoves her back. Pedro and PC quickly squeeze themselves between the women to keep them apart, while Cintia and Victor make sure to fan a distraught Seu Romário.

This is a nightmare.

"Stop fighting!" I shout. "Please, just—*stop!*"

The shouting and accusations continue despite our pleas. But then Seu Romário stands up and everyone quiets. He walks toward the platter with samples of our cake and reaches for one of the slices. We watch him as he studies the cake and brings it to his mouth.

When Seu Romário takes the first bite, he bursts into tears.

"Father!" Dona Eulalia cries out. She starts fussing over him, but he waves a hand for her to let him speak.

"This is a great homage to an old recipe. I'm proud of you, filho," he declares, and Pedro's eyes glisten. I know he's been waiting so long to hear this. "When I was your age, I once baked a recipe with Julieta. It was the Salt and Sugar cake, the recipe our mothers created together."

"*What?!*" Mom exclaims.

"Father! I never knew…" Dona Eulalia says, shocked.

"You think you and Gabriel were the only ones trying to end the feud?" he says to Mom. "Julieta and I tried, too… Our mothers found out. We wanted to run away together, but I couldn't leave my mother behind. She needed me. She'd done everything she could to raise me, and I couldn't find the courage to fight for Julieta. And Julieta went back too, and she did her best to regain her mother's trust. Maybe, after our mothers passed, we could have come together again. We could have said it was all water under the bridge. But it's hard to swim against *so much* water. And then Gabriel came along and became involved with you, Alice. When you tried to bake the Salt and Sugar cake with him, I thought it would be heartache all over again."

Mom's eyes are bright with angry tears. "If this is true, if you loved my mother and tried to end the feud with her, why did you call Gabriel a traitor? He loved you as if you were his own father! How am I supposed to trust you will respect my daughter and your grandson's relationship now? That you won't hurt them, like you hurt Gabriel and me?!" she yells.

"I didn't want Gabriel to get hurt. I should have listened to him," Seu Romário says, his voice garbled. "Ever since Julieta passed away, my mind has been in the past, and I keep thinking about Gabriel, how everything would have been different, and he would still be alive, had I accepted you two. Had I not sent him away that night, he would be here now. I regret the way I reacted then. I deeply regret it, Alice. I was the traitor. Not Gabriel. I betrayed his trust when I turned my back on him and you, after I had promised him to be his godfather. I failed to be his family."

Mom presses her lips together, and I see her shoulders relax a little, her whole frame losing some of her defensive stance. I think she waited all these years to hear Seu Romário apologize for the way he treated Dad.

He looks at Pedro and me. "But I won't make the same mistake again. Eulalia, you're not selling Sugar tomorrow. If my grandson says he wants to run it, he has my blessing."

Pedro stands trembling next to me, like he's fighting back

tears. But then Seu Romário gives him a hug, the first hug I've ever seen between them, and Pedro melts in his arms.

"I don't want to disappoint you," Pedro says.

"You could never—you're my grandson." Seu Romário pats him on the back, failing to contain his own tears. "I love you."

"I love you, too," Pedro says. This time, he doesn't try to hide his tears. His shoulders shake while his mother rubs his back, looking teary herself.

Cintia stands beside me, and when I look at her, she smiles. Victor flanks me, too, and PC is right behind, sniffling. My heart feels like it's about to burst.

"I wish my grandmother were here to see this," I tell my friends.

"But she is," PC says.

"Alice," Dona Eulalia says, approaching Mom. "I didn't realize that my father and your mother… You know. I know it's been difficult, but maybe we… Maybe we could at least stop listening to rumors? Tell me the truth. Have you closed negotiations with Deals Deals?"

"No. I only scheduled a meeting for tomorrow," Mom says. She takes a deep breath. "And I apologize for blaming you for the rat rumors… I heard recently that it was Deals Deals who started them."

Dona Eulalia looks taken aback, but continues. "I'll never forget that you let me borrow your car to take Father to the hospital. I didn't know how to thank you then. So…thank you."

There's a lot of awkwardness in the way they apologize. And a lot of awkwardness in the way they stand next to each other, like they still can't believe they're in a room together discussing Grandma and Seu Romário's unrequited love.

Mom looks at me for guidance. "Is this really what you want? You want to run Salt one day?"

"Yes," I say with all my heart.

Mom lets out a shaky breath, her eyes bright with determination. She turns to Dona Eulalia. "Alright, Eulalia, what are we going to do to help our children? We must keep them safe. Do we team up one more time and refuse to sell?"

I feel an important shift in the room, like some of the painful knots in the fabric of our families' shared history are finally loosening. I look at Pedro, and when his eyes widen in response, I can tell he sensed it, too. I see the way our mothers look at us, the way they find common ground in their desire to keep both of us safe, and it fills my heart with hope for our future.

"You can count on me, Alice! But I'm not sure how we can stop Deals Deals from coming after them when we refuse to sell and let the kids run the bakeries. The Gastronomic Society said all that in front of the cameras about supporting our fight against the supermarket, but at the end of the day, those are just words. That's not enough to make a real difference, and I honestly don't think Deals Deals will care about this school's opinion." Dona Eulalia looks at Pedro and me. "I'm so sorry, kids. I don't know what else there is to do."

Just then the door opens and the judge who announced the result enters the room. Chefs Augusto and Lorêncio are right behind. Pedro goes even redder when he sees his idols, quickly wiping his eyes with his sleeves. The chefs hold the door open for a fourth person: a woman who walks in on crutches, with a bandage under her chin and her leg in a cast.

Amandinha's mother! And she's wearing a GS jacket!

Pedro and I look at each other, stunned. Chef Augusto pulls a chair out for her to sit down, but she refuses it to come give us a hug.

"When I saw you on stage, I couldn't believe it! This is incredible!" she says. "I wanted to thank you for saving my family during that flood. You'd already left the hospital when I tried to look for you."

"It was nothing, senhora," Pedro says, a little nervous. "We tried to look for you at the hospital, too, but the nurses didn't let us. Are you really alright? I was so worried you got a concussion. And Amandinha and her cousin, too? They looked so scared."

"I'm fine! No concussion! My family is fine thanks to both of you!" She beams at us.

Dona Eulalia comes to stand next to Pedro. "Who are you?" she asks Amandinha's mother.

"I'm Chef Rosa Luz. I teach here at the Gastronomic Society. These kids saved my family when our car broke down during the flood in Avenida Coqueirais!"

Amandinha said her mother got a job, but I had no idea she had become an instructor at the Gastronomic Society!

"My daughter told me so much about your cooking club, Lari," she tells me. I wave Cintia, Victor, and PC over to introduce them to her. She's stunned that we're all here, her smile spreading on a freckled face just like Amandinha's. "My baby admires you so much. All she does is talk about your club. How Cintia and Victor give the best hugs, how PC is so funny. And how Pedro saved her, of course." She looks back at me. "And you, Lari… She says you have fairy hands like your grandmother. She wants to grow up to be just like you. You helped her see that food is magical. I'm so grateful for everything you kids have done for my daughter and everyone at Vozes!"

I don't know what to say. I feel like a balloon is inflating in my chest.

"You shouldn't stay on your feet for so long, Rosa," Chef Lorêncio says, and Pedro nods in agreement, looking a little starstruck.

"I'm fine. The doctor said I'm fine," she says, nodding toward her co-workers. "Look, everything happens for a reason. I had to be here today to hear Lari and Pedro's message. I'm sorry you didn't win. I truly am floored thinking about all it took to enter the contest together," she says.

"All of us were impressed," the woman who interviewed us says. "I'm Chef Giselle Leal. These are Chef Augusto and Chef Lorêncio. Although you didn't win, we hope that won't keep you from competing again next year."

"I love your show!" Pedro says to them, unable to control himself, and they smile like they're used to enthusiastic fans. It's funny seeing him act like this for once, when he's usually the one with a throng of fans at school, acting all broody and nonchalantly cool.

Above all, it makes me happy for him. He's living his dream.

"Is that why you asked to speak with us? To remind our kids that they've lost?" Dona Eulalia snaps, not bothering to hide her hurt.

"I knew these types of contests can't be trusted," Mom sneers.

They nod at each other, and I bet they are starting to realize how they are more alike than they wanted to admit.

I know they are trying to keep us from any more hurt, but I feel put on the spot in front of the judges. Pedro goes bright red, too. I guess that is what we get when our mothers team up... But, you know what? I never thought I would feel so glad that our moms are embarrassing us with their outspoken protectiveness, because at least they are starting to side with each other more and more. That is the best sign possible!

"I wanted to congratulate your kids for entering the contest together," Chef Rosa says. "I know what a supermarket like Deals Deals can do to family businesses. I lost my restaurant to them, too, before I came to the Gastronomic Society."

"Those vultures at Deals Deals have had a clutch on us for a while now," Dona Eulalia says. "No matter what we do, they keep lowering their prices, stealing our customers from us. We tried *everything*."

"I'm very touched by your story," Chef Rosa says. "My colleagues here have left me in charge of managing their line of restaurants in Recife and Olinda, and we'd all like to offer Salt and Sugar a contract to supply their kitchens. Your cake is a powerful statement to big sharks like Deals Deals. There's a lot of strength in unity, and that's what I hope this dish will inspire. It's an homage to small family-owned businesses."

"Are you serious?" I exclaim.

When they nod yes, I feel like I'm about to faint, but Pedro scoops me up into a hug. He winces a little because of his hurt ankle, but now Cintia, PC, and Victor are lifting us in their arms, too.

In the back, Seu Romário passes around samples of our cake for Mom and Dona Eulalia to try.

They take small bites and immediately close their eyes, surprise and elation written all over their faces. My heart swells. This is the first time Mom is trying one of my creations. I guess I've come a long way since my flower soup.

For the first time in decades, Ramires and Molinas blend in with cheers and excited hugs. No more yelling, no more fighting. Just a group of neighbors standing together.

FRIDAY, JUNE 24

The next day, Mom and I stand in front of Salt, while Pedro, Seu Romário, and Dona Eulalia stand in front of Sugar.

We're back to eyeing each other from our respective sidewalks, our street dotted with bonfires to celebrate St. John's Day tonight. I wink at Pedro. And he smiles back.

Silently, Mom and Dona Eulalia meet in the middle of the street. They pull out the recipes that once made the legendary Salt and Sugar cake and extend them to each other like an official peace offering.

They place the recipes in a glass box, piecing them back together. Reuniting our bakeries' hearts. Reuniting our families. Like Great-grandma Elisa and Dona Elizabete Molina once dreamed.

The dream we dream together now.

EPILOGUE

SIX MONTHS LATER...

"Hey, Lari, Pedro!" Dona Eulalia calls from inside Salt. "It's time!" She begins ushering the crowd of Sugar bakers into Salt's kitchen.

Ever since Chefs Rosa, Giselle, Augusto, and Lorêncio offered the contract, the Gastronomic Society has started a massive publicity campaign to help community bakeries, too. Salt and Sugar now join together to keep up with the catering orders coming in from all around the metropolitan area.

"We should go," I mumble into Pedro's shoulder.

"Just a little longer," he says, squeezing me tight against his chest.

"Do I have to beg you fancy chefs?" Dona Eulalia shouts over the hustle and bustle of customers. We're not members of the Gastronomic Society—*yet*—but it doesn't stop Dona Eulalia from teasing us. We're scheduled to take the entrance exams next month.

"Pedro!" Seu Romário's voice booms in the back, and we

turn around to step into Salt, just as Isabel comes out with a cake to deliver to a customer.

Pedro pulls me back at the last second, helping me dodge the collision. "Some things never change," he says, smiling.

The Salt and Sugar bakers mill about Grandma's wooden counter. Dona Eulalia, Seu Romário, and Dona Selma stand in the back, along with PC, Cintia, and Victor. It's the first time Pedro and I are teaching a cooking class and we need all our loved ones here. I'm glad they came to support us, even though they've been super busy lately.

PC is a chef himself now, after he found his grandmother's recipes and rekindled her old baking business. He's already been invited to sell his pastries at an official booth during Caruaru's big St. John's festivities next year!

Cintia is the reigning regional mathematics champion! She was so nervous when she went to compete two weeks ago, but we were all there to support her. She's been on the cover of our newspapers ever since, and she's busy preparing for the state competition next.

Victor has started writing a food blog and he's filming segments for his new YouTube channel. He's gathering quite a following after he posted his first videos, where he sits down at family-owned businesses and talks about his favorite dishes.

There's just one person missing.

Mom enters the room in a hurry. "I got my laptop," she says, ready to type her notes.

Mom's been helping me transition into full-time baking. Once a helicopter parent, always a helicopter parent. She's constantly telling me to focus on studying for the Gastronomic Society's entrance tests, while I help her with her vestibular prepping.

Mom's going to apply for Federal University's fashion design program next year. She'll be the first Ramires to go to college! She's taking adult classes that Pimentel teaches, and now it's *my* turn to make sure Mom's paying attention in class.

Under our families' and friends' supportive gaze, Pedro and I start our lesson by listing all the ingredients in the Romário and Julieta cake. It's been a big hit, with demand increasing, and now that we finally get to hire more bakers, we figured it would be a great opportunity to gather everyone and put a class together, so the new staff can learn to recite the recipe in their sleep.

Deals Deals cars still go up and down the Olinda streets, watching, lurking, but they know this time they can't swallow us alive. Not while we're together.

Mom begins typing carefully, whispering back and forth with Dona Eulalia. Seu Romário sits on a stool by the counter, his eyes focused on the ingredients. Our bakers peer over each other. And I know… I *know* Grandma is here with us, too.

It's not like everything has been solved between all of us, like a lifted curse in a storybook. And I know we still have a lot to learn from each other and a lot to forgive. But standing side by side in the kitchen, *together*, seems like a new chapter in our families' shared story, one full of hope.

I open the oven and a whiff of warm air escapes like a sigh. Salt is coming alive.

The End.
Or is it…?

★ ★ ★ ★ ★

ACKNOWLEDGMENTS

Becoming a writer has been my dream ever since I was a kid, and I'm grateful for everyone who helped me through every step. *Salt and Sugar* definitely is the result of a group effort— a dream dreamed together with so many people in my life— and I'd like to take a moment to thank everyone.

Firstly, I'd like to thank Márcia Carvalho. My mom was the best friend a daughter could wish for. She surrounded me with books and fought for my education despite all the adversities. I wrote *Salt and Sugar* in the years following her passing as a way to heal and reconnect with my childhood memories and I know she'd have been so proud of it. I love you, Mom. Saudades para sempre.

I want to thank my grandparents, Juliana and Arnaldo Carvalho, who raised me like I was one of their own children. They protected me and loved me, offering me the safest home where I could play, learn, and explore my first inklings of dreams. I want to thank my uncle Eduardo Carvalho, too, who was like a father to me and the best storyteller. I wouldn't be a writer today if it weren't for them. Muitas saudades. Rest in peace.

A special thank-you to Michael Bethencourt. Love of my life. My best friend. My husband. My life partner. Thank you for loving me and standing by my side. This book wouldn't be here if it weren't for your constant love and for dreaming this dream together with me. Thank you for never letting me give it up. I love you.

Many thanks to my first-grade teachers, who included my very first story in a Portuguese test. It was about a bug named Silvia, and it got me in trouble with a kid also named Silvia, who swore revenge because she thought I'd named the bug after her. It was a little startling, but it also made me realize I really wanted to be a writer when I grew up. By the way, Silvia, if you're out there reading this, I swear it wasn't on purpose!

Thank you to all the teachers and academic advisers in my life, everyone who believed in me and in my dream and told my mom I should be a writer. Thank you to my high school teachers at Colégio Militar do Recife, and everyone involved in the Youth Ambassadors Program, which opened so many doors that ultimately changed my life forever in the best way possible.

A special thank-you to Rachel Russell for cheering me on since our early querying days. Thank you for your thoughtful advice on the first draft of *Salt and Sugar*. But, above all, thank you for being my friend and for the daily jokes you sent me for a whole month to cheer me up. *Salt and Sugar* wouldn't be here without your support.

Thank you one thousand times to my incredible agent, Thao Le, for believing in me. I mean it. You championed *Salt and Sugar* and loved the story as much as I did and I'll always be grateful. And thank you to everyone at Sandra Dijkstra Literary Agency and all my agent siblings for all the support.

I have so much love and gratitude for everyone who put together LatinxPitch. This event was like a breath of fresh air during one of the most difficult moments in my life and helped me make incredible connections that led to *Salt and Sugar* going to auction. You're one of the reasons why my dream came true.

Rebecca Kuss, thank you for being my acquiring editor. Thank you for connecting with my story and for believing in it. We didn't get a chance to finish this publishing journey together, but I'm grateful for all the support. Your connection to my story as a reader means a lot to me.

Thank you, thank you, thank you to Claire Stetzer, my editor, for guiding me and helping me shape *Salt and Sugar* into the book that it is today. I'm so grateful for everything. Thank you to Bess Braswell and everyone at Inkyard Press and HarperCollins for believing in my story and making my dream come true. Many thanks to Gigi Lau, the designer behind the cover art, and Andressa Meissner, the illustrator. Thank you for creating such a magical cover. I can't stop staring at it!

I'm sorry if I forgot someone, but just know that I'm so thankful. This felt like such an impossible dream when I was a kid… I still can't believe I get to write about characters who were inspired by my childhood, navigating life and dreaming in the cities of my heart. Um cheiro, Olinda and Recife.

And last but not least, I'd like to thank *you* for reading *Salt and Sugar*. This has been such an incredible journey and I'm so grateful that I got a chance to share this Brazilian story with you.